Books by Amanda Scott

DANGEROUS LADY
HIGHLAND TREASURE
HIGHLAND SECRETS
HIGHLAND FLING
DANGEROUS ANGELS
DANGEROUS GAMES
THE BAWDY BRIDE
DANGEROUS ILLUSIONS

Published by Zebra Books

HIGHLAND SPIRITS

Amanda Scott

Zebra Books
Kensington Publishing Corp.

http://www.zebrabooks.com

ZEBRA BOOKS are published by

Kensington Publishing Corp.
850 Third Avenue
New York, NY 10022

Zebra and the Z logo Reg. U.S. Pat. & TM Off.

First Printing: October, 1999
10 9 8 7 6 5 4 3

Printed in the United States of America

Dedicated to

June F., Sharon K., Mensch, Angela J., Ginger & Dayna,
and the rest of the support staff.

Thank you all, very much.

CHAPTER ONE

The Scottish Highlands
March 25, 1765

Penelope MacCrichton sat still, scarcely daring to breathe, as she watched the tall, broad-shouldered figure approach through the dense, mist-laden woods. A giant charcoal-gray deerhound kept pace like a floating shadow of Satan beside him.

The figure was that of a young man, large, handsome, and powerfully built, armed with a dirk and wearing a gray-and-muted-green-plaid kilt. Long, raven's-wing black hair flowed to his shoulders, waving lightly with his movements. His bare feet were thick with mud, and his fierce scowl made him look puzzled and angry, but he did not frighten Penelope. She had seen the figure and his dog before; not many times, but often enough to make them both familiar to her.

Neither man nor dog paid heed to the thick-growing

trees or dense shrubbery; however, as she knew from long experience, such barriers presented no more obstacle to this pair than they would to any other ghosts.

The man's mouth looked large and cruel. His eyes were narrowed and flintlike, as if in anger or distress; but as always, both the figure and the huge dog beside him seemed unaware of her presence, and neither made a sound as they passed. That the ground beneath their feet was damp from melted snow, and covered with the thick carpet of leaf mold that had accumulated over centuries might account for the silence of their footsteps. Nonetheless, branches reaching out from every direction would have rustled as they brushed against most passersby. Thus the silence of the two was particularly eerie and unnatural.

The sudden, rippling *tirrirri-ripp* of a snow bunting diverted Penelope's attention. Glancing toward the sound, she saw the little black-and-white bird hopping about on the ground nearby, searching for insects and seeds. When she looked back, the manly figure and that of the giant deerhound had vanished.

Penelope did not try to follow them, knowing that such an attempt would prove useless, and knowing, too, that the pair would have vanished even had she been looking right at them. They were not of this earth, that pair. Nevertheless, she felt a glow of satisfaction as she rose from the fallen log where she had been sitting and brushed off her skirt. She had walked this way on purpose, hoping to see them, like paying a call on old friends.

It had been months since the last time, before winter had set in and cast its lingering blanket of white over the Highlands. Spring had been in the air for nearly a fortnight now, but it was a wet spring, requiring the children to stay indoors more than they had liked, which meant that Penelope had had little time to call her own. Mary, Countess of Balcardane, was kind though, for her own dependent childhood had taught her to understand as few others of the nobility did the burden that gratitude laid upon the grateful. She was careful never to take unfair advantage of Penelope's delight in the three children of Balcardane.

Thus, when the first true break in the weather had occurred near Lady Day, and the earl decided to journey from Balcardane to Dunraven Castle, on the southeast shore of Loch Creran, to collect his rents, Mary had prevailed on him to take her, their children, and his two foster children along. She had done more than that, though, for when the next morning had dawned with clear, sunny skies smiling down on the mist-shrouded loch, she had told Penelope to take the day unto herself.

"I'll mind the bairns, love," she had said. "You do as you like. Duncan has taken Chuff and two of the men across the loch to Shian Towers to be sure that all is well there, so I shall ask Cook to prepare a picnic for the children and me. We'll walk up to the top of the hill behind the castle, where it should stay sunny and warm all day. Later, if you decide to seek company, you can find us there."

Enjoying her solitude, Penelope had walked to the Narrows at the northeast end of the loch, and crossed to the western shore, to wander through the woods above Shian in search of her ghost. Now, mission accomplished, she turned with a light heart back to Dunraven, noting changes in the landscape that had escaped her notice before.

Already the leaves of primroses and wood sorrel were pushing up through the newest layer of the thick leaf mold carpet, searching for air and sunshine. Spurge, with its large leathery leaves, bronzed and purple, showed new curved shoots, so she knew that in a month the woods would be full of yellow spurge saucers with their strangely shaped little flowers inside.

Fresh nettles and dock leaves that the snow had squashed

flat to the earth stretched upward again, and violets that had borne their old leaves through the winter were unfolding new ones. Looking into their hearts, she could see the new flowers budding. Patches of sunlight revealed lesser celandine coming into leaf, and nearer the burn, greater celandine also, its stalks already charged with the deep yellow juice that Mary would collect for her eye wash. Its roots were good for other remedies, too, Penelope knew.

Emerging from the woods near the Narrows, she enjoyed a view straight down the long arm of the loch. As she knew from a map of the Highlands on the wall in the earl's bookroom at Balcardane, Loch Creran had the shape of a large check mark with its long arm running about six miles northeast to southwest and its short arm running about two miles southeast to northwest. The long arm was pinched about a third of the way down, at that point known logically enough as the Narrows, where it was possible for a careful pedestrian to cross from bank to bank.

The loch's source was a snow-fed burn that flowed swiftly down through Glen Creran, and at its outlet its waters spilled past the little island of Eriska into the Lynn of Lorne, near its confluence with Loch Linnhe. Shian Towers, her brother's estate, sat on the point of land that formed the angle of the check and included everything north of the castle to the Strath of Appin. Across the loch lay the vast lands of Dunraven, once a great fortress guarding Campbell lands from Appin Country marauders, now merely one of Balcardane's many holdings. The steeply sloping hillside on the Dunraven side was green with heather and bracken.

Sunlight dappled the rippling waters of the loch and bathed the earth with its healthy warmth. All around her, in the woods and out in the open, birds sang joyfully. The twittering of the last few weeks had turned to cheerful songs, for they had finished their squabbles over the best nesting sites and ownership of building materials, and were now busy hatching eggs or feeding nestlings.

As Penelope crossed to the sandy cart track that ran to the crest of the hill from the path by the river, separating oaks, beech, holly, and birch from the pine woods that spread over into the next glen, she heard a familiar voice call her name.

Turning back, she saw her brother's familiar figure loping toward her from the grassy slope that separated Shian Towers from its vast acres of woodland. Beyond him, the castle's crenellated walls loomed on the horizon, and below the castle she could see three men in a sailboat putting out into the loch from the dock near the water gate.

"I thought you might have come over today," Charles, Lord MacCrichton, shouted as he crossed the burn in two long leaps from boulder to boulder. "I told Himself I'd walk back so I could bear you company if you had. Did you run away from the brats, lass?"

She smiled, waiting for him to come nearer before she said, "They are not brats, Chuff, and you are a villain to call them so."

His eyes, singularly light in color with heavy dark lashes, crinkled at the corners when he chuckled. Reaching out to pull one of her thick golden braids, he said, "You look like a bairn yourself, lassie, with your hair all twisted in plaits."

She shrugged. "I had them pinned up in ladylike coils before, but some of the pins fell out when I ran down the hillside, so I pulled out the rest."

"And lost them all, I'll wager," Chuff said with a grin.

"Well, some, but the others I put in my pocket," she said, patting that part of her skirt beneath which the pocket lived.

His hair was tied simply at the nape of his neck with a

narrow black ribbon; for, like Black Duncan Campbell, fifth Earl of Balcardane, Chuff disdained the wigs and periwigs of more fashion-conscious men. Although in childhood his hair had been nearly as blond as Penelope's, it had darkened over the years to a soft golden brown. Early responsibilities had aged him prematurely, so that he looked older than his twenty years, but he was, in his sister's opinion and that of a number of the other young women in Appin Country, a strikingly handsome young man.

He wore a rough coat and breeches, but they were well cut, and although mud coated his boots, his linen was clean and snowy white. He did not wear a hat. If, upon leaving Dunraven, he had taken one with him, or gloves, he had set them down somewhere at Shian and forgotten about them.

Penelope smiled at him again and linked her arm companionably with his.

He smiled back, but as they walked, the smile faded and a frown took its place. "There's smoke again yonder," he said. "They'll be burning more trees at the Taynuilt bloomery, damn their unnatural hides."

Penelope shook her head at the great plumes of gray smoke rising above the hills to the south. "I'm glad Himself won't let them burn our woods," she said.

"We're fortunate, lass. Them that need to bring in sheep to survive the English destruction of the clans must clear land for grazing, and when cut wood brings money as well, it's more temptation than most men can resist. 'Tis a crime, nonetheless, to burn every forest within range just to melt a bit of metal."

"Himself says they do it only in Scotland," Penelope reminded him. "The English have laws against using their wood to smelt iron."

"We have laws to protect our forests, too," Chuff said,

"but no one enforces those laws here like they do the English ones. We've got bloomeries sprouting up all over Scotland, they say, maybe a hundred or more, and it takes five tons of timber to smelt just one ton of pig iron. Still, there's a huge demand for the iron nowadays, so I'll wager they'll keep doing it till the wood runs out."

"I wonder if that's why he looked so angry," Penelope said musingly.

"Why who looked angry?"

She threw him a saucy look. "You'll only be calling me daft again if I tell you, so just you never mind who."

He tried to look stern as he shook his head at her, but his eyes twinkled. He said, "You're saying you saw your ghost again, are you?"

"Do you doubt me, sir?"

"I don't doubt that you believe in him, Pinkie," he said, calling her, as he usually did, by her childhood nickname. "I just don't believe in ghosts, myself."

"It seems odd that you've never seen him, since the land he haunts belongs to you," she said thoughtfully.

"Not all the land," he protested.

"I've only ever seen him on Shian land, Chuff."

"Never at Balcardane or Dunraven?"

"Never. Only in the woods above Shian and twice . . . twice inside."

"When?" he demanded. "You never told me you'd seen him inside." He sounded indignant, which was understandable, since Shian Towers belonged to him.

"I never told anyone. You're the only one to whom I've mentioned him at all, and you said I was daft and teased me about him when I did tell you."

"I never teased you that much, Pinkie, did I?"

His voice sounded troubled, so she hastened to reassure him. "Not so much," she agreed, thinking that, much or not, it had been enough to silence her.

"I remember the first time you told me about him," Chuff said. "It was when we all came to Dunraven the summer after the old earl and our uncle died. You didn't say you'd seen your ghost before that, but you must have if you saw him inside. You weren't inside again for years afterward, and I don't think you've stayed there overnight since the day we left, as children."

"Aye, I did see him before ever we went away to live with Mary and Himself." She hesitated, but he was looking down at her with a frown and she knew he would not let her stop there. "Do you remember, Chuff, when the laird—our uncle—sent me to work in the kitchens soon after we arrived at Shian?"

"Aye."

He spoke curtly, but she knew his anger was for things that lay in the past. Quietly, she said, "There was a man who worked there. Looking back, I think he must have been only a scullion, but of course, everyone in the castle then was more important than I was, and much bigger. I was not yet seven."

"And scrawny," he said. "You were right scrawny then, lass."

"Well, so were you. That man delighted in teasing me. He struck me once, and he pulled my hair, but even worse, he liked to pet me like a dog or cat. It made my flesh creep when he would touch me. On a day not long before we left he was particularly horrid, and I had begun crying. Don't look so fierce," she added. "He's probably dead by now. Many of them died when the laird did, after all."

"Go on about your ghost, lass."

"Well, it was then. The horrid man had caught hold of me, and I was trying to get free. He shook me, then suddenly he cried out and let me go so abruptly that I fell. When I looked up *he* was there."

"He?"

"My ghost. He stood between us, and the man who had been tormenting me just stood there glaring. At first I thought my ghost was real, and that the man was glaring at him, but he wasn't. The horrid man took a step toward me, then stopped and threw his arms around himself in the way one does when one is very cold. He began shivering something fierce. Only it was not cold, Chuff, because we were near the kitchen fire. He told the cook he was going to fetch wood, and he never came near me again. Of course, we went away with Mary soon after, but still . . ."

When she paused, he nodded. "Why didn't you tell me this before?"

"I would have, I suppose, if you had believed me when I told you about seeing him in the woods that time, but when you didn't, I guess I decided you didn't want to know any of the details about him. You were jealous, I expect."

He snorted.

"No, really, Chuff. You were only nine then, remember, and you were so protective of me that I am not sure you would have welcomed any other protector."

"Hoots, lass, it's natural for a brother to look after his sister. Mrs. Conochie who cooks at Shian now, has got two bairns, and although there's no one for them to fear here, her Tam watches over wee Flora like I watched over you. For all that, though, I can tell you I welcomed Himself when he came, and our Mary."

"Yes, but they were different. They protected both of us, and your inheritance. They were real, Chuff, and willing to take the place of the parents we had never known. Before you came to trust them, though, you still looked after me," she added gently. "You did so until Himself sent you off to school."

"Aye, and I didn't much want to go then, either," he admitted, giving her arm a squeeze. "You looked so sad the day I left. I'll never forget that, lassie. If I had known how you pined for me——"

"I'm glad they didn't tell you," she said quickly. "Charles, Lord MacCrichton, should be an educated man. They were right to send you to Edinburgh, and it's right that you should go to Oxford now."

"Anything more that I need to know I could learn from Himself," Chuff said.

"He says you cannot, that one needs to know too much nowadays, that things are changing so rapidly that one man on his own cannot keep up with the changes."

"Then I could study at Edinburgh," he said. "I'd not need to be so far from home, Pinkie. I miss you, too, you know, when I'm away."

"I do know," she said, "but Himself says we must learn more about England and the English, and at least he's letting me go to London, too, Chuff."

"Do you *want* to go?"

"Well, I don't want to leave the Highlands, but I do want to see where you'll be, since he will take me," she said. "He and Mary both say that England is not the scary place it's always been in my mind, and that I ought to see as much for myself. Most of all, though, it means not having to say good-bye to you so soon. Before you have to go to Oxford we'll have at least six weeks together in London."

"To get a little town bronze," Chuff said, grinning, as he repeated the phrase they had heard the earl use more than once. "You'll like dressing up, Pinkie."

"Aye, I will that," she agreed, "but not as much as Lady Agnes will."

Chuff chuckled. "Lady Agnes has always wanted to go to London, has she not, but I wonder how much she'll like it there if people insist on calling her the Dowager Countess of Balcardane, instead of Lady Agnes Campbell."

"She's such a dear that I daresay they will call her whatever she tells them to call her, especially since she will keep right on explaining to them why they must do so until they feel as if their eyes have begun spinning in their heads," Pinkie said, thinking fondly of the earl's chatty mother, who had accepted two ragged children into her household as easily as if they had been her own grandchildren.

"She'll fair talk the hair off their heads; that's true enough," Chuff said with the twinkle that generally lit his eyes when he spoke of Lady Agnes.

"She's just as much Lady Agnes as she is the dowager countess, anyway," Pinkie pointed out. "And she's been Lady Agnes since she was born, after all, not just since she married, because her papa was an earl just like Himself's papa was. I had to learn all about that sort of thing, you know," she added. "It wouldn't do for me to make mistakes in company, after all. Things like that are important for ladies to know, Mary says, although she don't seem to care much about them herself."

Instead of making the light response she expected, Chuff remained silent for so long that she looked up at him to see why. He was frowning again, but he was not gazing at the smoke this time. He was just staring into space.

"What's wrong, Chuff?"

A muscle jumped in his lower cheek, and for a moment she thought he would refuse to tell her. Then he looked at her and seemed to make up his mind. He stopped walking and turned to face her directly, taking both of her hands in his and holding them tightly.

Pinkie felt a little shiver race up her spine. Whatever he was going to tell her would not be pleasant. "What is it, Chuff? Why do you look so fierce?"

"Have they spoken to you about London, lass?"

Surprised, she said, "Of course they have. Lady Agnes talks only of gowns and fashions, of course, but Himself and Mary have talked of practically nothing but London and Oxford for weeks. You know that."

His expression did not change. "I know we've talked about how it will take weeks to get there from the Highlands, and how we will travel, and where we will stay along the road and when we arrive. We've talked about fabrics, tailors, and dressmakers. We've talked about coaches, wagons, inns, baggage, servants, whom and what we'll take with us, how many horses, dogs, and so forth. What we have not talked about, Pinkie lass, is the reception we are likely to receive there."

"Goodness, Chuff, you sound like you do not expect to enjoy it at all. I thought you had decided it would do you good to go."

"It will do me good," he said, his tone still grim. "Whatever I said before, I do know that I will benefit from a broader education. I'm not the one I am concerned about."

"You're worried about me?"

"I am. Clearly, no one has spoken to you about one very important matter. He only just warned me, or I'd have told you myself earlier. We did not attend many parties together last spring when you visited me in Edinburgh."

Bewildered by the apparent non sequitur, she said, "You were still in school. When you could spend time with us, we did other things, things that were fun. I found that I did not much care for parties, anyway."

"Aye, I remember. I remember that when I asked you why you didn't like them, you told me you thought them tedious."

There was an accusatory note in his voice this time, and she found herself answering defensively, "But that's perfectly true. They *were* tedious. I suppose if I had been one of the more popular girls, I might have liked them better, but I wasn't, Chuff. I'm still shy with most people, you know. I always have been shy. And, in Edinburgh, shy girls don't seem to attract many handsome young men who want to dance with them."

She saw hesitation in his expression, but then he straightened, squaring his shoulders in the same way she had seen him square them after he had misbehaved, and knew that he faced a scolding or punishment. "I believed that then," he said gently, "just as you still believe it, lass. But Duncan told me it was more than that."

Chuff never called Himself Duncan when it was just the two of them. Between themselves they still referred to him the same way they had when Black Duncan Campbell first came into their lives. He had seemed utterly godlike to the two children then, and they had mistaken him for lord of all he surveyed. They had soon learned that he was as human as anyone else, and they had come to love him like a father, but that had not diminished their awe of him. That Chuff called him Duncan now reminded Pinkie that they were both nearly adults, although she was still eighteen and Chuff would not legally come of age until June.

"What more could there be?" she asked.

"Did they say nothing to you about what to expect in London?"

She thought for a moment. "He told me he would give me a dress allowance so that I can order dresses made in the latest fashions, and he said that I should not be dismayed if some of the English nobility hold their noses in the air when they meet members of the Scottish nobility. He said our connections to the Duke of Argyll and the Earl of Rothwell will prevent anyone's being truly rude to us."

"Is that all he said?"

"Aye. All that I can remember, at all events. Mary schooled me more on the sort of manners that will obtain in London society, for she has learned all about them from her cousin Maggie Rothwell. And Mary said we had best not mention her gift of second sight, because the English take a dim view of such things and tend to believe that the Sight does not exist.'' She felt a sudden bubble of laughter and squelched it, saying in a carefully even tone, ''Are you afraid that I might mention my ghost, Chuff? Indeed, I can easily promise you that I will not.''

Instead of laughing, as she expected, he just shook his head. His demeanor remained solemn. ''Pinkie, if they haven't said anything, doubtless they will say that I ought not to speak of it either, but I cannot believe silence in such matters is wise. The problem does not affect me as much as it will you, because whatever their English scruples may be, I am still *Lord* MacCrichton. Furthermore, I am wealthy, a plain fact that will outweigh any number of sins, I'm afraid.''

''What sins, Chuff? I've done nothing to be ashamed of, I promise you.''

''I know you haven't, lass, but the people who ignored you in Edinburgh did not do so because you are shy. You've got over much of that, anyway, so long as you are with people who are kind to you. But it will be worse in England if they find out, and I cannot believe it is right not to warn you to take care.''

''If they find out what?''

''About our parents, Pinkie.''

''What about them? Our father was the younger son of the seventh Lord MacCrichton. Do you mean because he died serving Bonnie Prince Charlie?''

''I imagine that will count against us with some English folks, but that's not the worst of it,'' Chuff said. ''Don't you remember what they called him, lass?''

Pinkie shook her head. ''No one talks much to me about him,'' she said.

Chuff sighed. "That's because they are afraid of Black Duncan," he said. "No one hereabouts dared taunt us about either of our parents, but don't forget that folks have long memories, lassie. If it should become known in London that you are the daughter of Daft Geordie MacCrichton and his woman, Red Mag—"

"They called him *Daft* Geordie? How unkind, and how absurd to fret about it now, since it was due to his being our father that you inherited Shian Towers and the Mac-Crichton title and fortune. Moreover, they were married, Chuff. We've got a copy of their marriage lines in the muniments room at Balcardane."

"Aye, we do that," he agreed.

When he said nothing more, she thought about what he had said already. "I mustn't tell people about all that. That's what you mean, isn't it?"

"That's part of it," he agreed. "But that's not all, lass. If people should find out, they won't like it that your father was called daft, and more than that, they won't like it that your mother was a dreadfully common woman."

"They're your parents, too," she muttered.

"Aye, and I never said it was fair," he said. "I might find a lass whose family would turn me down flat out of fear that our children might be a bit off, like our father; however, it's much more likely that my fortune will more than make up for any other deficiency. It's my own line that's tainted, after all. No one would blame my wife or her ancestors for any backward offspring."

"What a horrid thing to say!"

"I'm not saying it. It's what others will be thinking, though."

"Is that what they'll think about me, that I'm tainted? Just because I don't have money?"

Evenly, Chuff said, "Between us, Duncan and I will see

to it that your dowry is a lucrative one, lassie, but there are many who will think no amount can make up for the possibility of your introducing lunacy to a proud, untainted noble line."

"Then I won't marry a nobleman," Pinkie said. "In fact, I don't think I want to marry at all. I have never met anyone who was half the man that you are, or Himself, or half the man my ghost is, for that matter."

Chuff smiled and shook his head, giving her hands a light squeeze before he released one and drew the other through the crook of his arm. "You'll marry, Pinkie lass. You're far too bonnie to remain single. I just didn't want you going to London unarmed, so to speak. The last thing you want is to fall in love with someone who will cast you off because he suddenly learns the truth and thinks your parents make you unsuitable to marry him."

"I'd never fall in love with such an arrogant man," she said stoutly.

"I don't think love is so predictable," he told her.

"Piffle, I know exactly what sort of man I could love, and that sort isn't it, definitely."

"You don't even know any eligible men," Chuff said with a chuckle. "The only male I've heard you talk about besides Duncan or myself and a few kinsmen is that ghost of yours, and you don't have any way of knowing what sort of man he was, or even if he ever existed outside your imagination."

"I do, too, know," she said fiercely. "I know exactly what he's like. He has all the virtues I admire and none of the faults I detest."

"And he rides a white horse, too, I'll wager, and rescues fair maidens from fire-breathing dragons! Well, it doesn't matter if he does do all that. You can't fall in love with a ghost, Pinkie, and no mere man could ever be that perfect."

"Don't be absurd, Chuff. I haven't fallen in love with a ghost, and he doesn't ride a white horse. Come to think of it, though, he does own a magnificent deerhound that walks like a shadow at his side."

He looked at her in surprise. "A deerhound?"

"Aye, and so my ghost, dear brother, is a Highlander, and at least an earl or the chief of his clan, because no one of lesser rank is allowed to own deerhounds."

Chuff's eyes were twinkling again. "Just so you're truly not in love with this paragon, lass."

"Well, I'm not," she said firmly, "and I know that men are not perfect, sir. When I said he had all of the virtues I seek and none of the faults I detest, I meant only that and no more. I shall be able to overlook what faults he has if I love him. Just as I overlook yours," she added sweetly.

He chuckled. "We'd best be getting back now, lass. Himself and the men have reached the Dunraven dock, so he will be looking for me soon, and I see Mary and the bairns on the hillside, waving." Chuff waved back.

Pinkie waved, too. Her lovely holiday was over, but she enjoyed the children and looked forward to hearing about their day. They would be going to London, too, which was why Roddy stood there on the hillside, waving, with his mother and younger sisters, instead of being away at school.

His father had said he was old enough, at ten, to go to Edinburgh, but Mary had said he would learn more by traveling to London than by pining away at school, wishing he were with them. Himself had not approved, but although no one else could change his mind once he'd made it up, Mary could, and so Roddy was going, and his father would hire a tutor when they got there. Pinkie thought Roddy was more excited about going than anyone else was. As for herself, she resolved to savor each day she had left in the Highlands, because if Chuff was right to worry, then London might prove to be even worse than she expected.

CHAPTER TWO

Mingary Castle
The West Highland Coast
A Fortnight Later

"Even worse than I thought," the Earl of Kintyre muttered to himself as he stared glumly at the last page of the accounts his steward had set before him earlier that chilly spring afternoon.

At the sound of his voice, the large dark gray dog that lay curled near the tall, paneled doors separating the bookroom from the great hall opened its liquid, dark brown eyes and lifted its furry head. Its warm, steady gaze looked sympathetic enough to draw a smile from its master.

"Staring at these numbers doesn't make them look any better, Cailean," the earl said. "I had hoped we might buy sheep, even though introducing collies to your domain might strain your family's dignity a wee bit. Unfortunately, I'd have to cut down the forests to accommodate the sheep's grazing needs, and that would play right into Campbell's hands. I cannot bring myself to do it. Not yet, at all events.''

With a sigh, he picked up a letter near his hand on the desk. He had already read the thing twice since the runner had brought it. A third reading was not likely to alter the words or the arrogant scrawl in which they were written. Reading it was like probing a sore tooth. It hurt, but one kept doing it anyway.

The moment he moved, the dog's tail began thumping against the wood floor, and the earl allowed himself a moment to gaze in simple pleasure at the elegant creature. Then the tail fell silent, and Cailean's ears lifted.

Small for the dog's great size, they sat high on its broad, flat, tapering skull. In repose, they folded back like a greyhound's, but now they cocked forward alertly, their drooping tips silvery where light from a nearby window touched them. The main part of each ear was glossy black, darker than the rest of the dog—except for the tip of its nose— and felt as soft as a mouse's coat when stroked.

The earl thought at first that Cailean was responding to his movements and voice, but then the dog turned its head toward the door, and he heard what it had heard much sooner, a rapid clicking of heels on the stone floor of the great hall. A moment later, the door swung back on its hinges, and his sister entered the room.

Even to her brother's critical eye, Lady Bridget Mingary, at sixteen, was beautiful. Her long black curls, unconfined by any cap, looked as soft and as shiny as the large blue satin bow into which she had confined a bunch of them at the back of her head.

Her round face and large, almost circular, dark blue eyes gave her a baby-faced look. Her tip-tilted nose was small, neat, and adorable; and her full, pouty lips and round cheeks owed their deep rosy color to nature rather than to rouge. Her chin, too, was softly rounded, and her smile, when she chose to display it, was wide and revealed small, even, sparkling white teeth.

Bridget's body was all gentle curves from her full, plump bosom to her tiny waist and flaring hips. Her hands and the neatly shod feet peeping beneath the hem of her gown as she walked were small and dainty, her fingernails neatly rounded at the ends and delicately pink. Her skin was rosy and smooth, without a blemish. She would undoubtedly grow plumper with age and look more like Michael remembered their mother looking, but at present, she was undeniably lovely. Unless, of course, one considered her temperament.

As she strode into the room, the dog rose with graceful dignity tinged by wariness to watch her.

Lady Bridget said sharply, "Stay, Cailean! Don't touch my gown. Michael, do you like this dress? You'd better. It is the only silk one I own."

He repressed a surge of irritation, knowing full well that she did not care what he thought of the green-and-white-striped gown she wore, although its overdress, opening as it did in a vee down the low, square-necked bodice and falling away at her impossibly narrow waist to expose an underdress of sunshine-yellow satin, was extremely becoming. Exerting himself to sound more patient than he felt, he said, "You cannot have a new dress, Bridget. I'm sorry, but I thought I explained my reasons clearly the last time you asked me."

"Michael, you've simply got to be reasonable. I've written to Aunt Marsali, as you know, for you gave my letter to Mr. Cameron yourself before he left to visit his brother in Edinburgh. In any event, you did not say that I must not write to her."

"Why on earth would I forbid you to write to our aunt?"

"Well, you didn't, that's all, and you must have known

that I would be asking her to take me to parties this spring, for she promised that she would do so when I grew old enough, and I have decided that I am, so I simply must go to Edinburgh this year."

"Bridget, we have had this conversation too many times. Even if I agreed that you are old enough, which I do not, I cannot afford to send you to Edinburgh."

Her lovely eyes welled with tears. "But how will I ever get married if I never meet anyone? You never think about me, Michael. You think only about your stupid dogs and this horrid, drafty, decrepit old castle, and never, never about me!"

Her voice had risen alarmingly, and he spoke quietly in an effort to calm her. "I do think about you all the time," he said, "but it is my duty as chief of our clan to think about all our people, and about Mingary."

She stamped one small foot. "But what about *me?*"

He remembered the letter. "I received another offer for your hand."

Her neatly arched eyebrows snapped together in a scowl. "Another one? Dare I ask if this one, like all the others, comes from Sir Renfrew Campbell?"

"It does," he said evenly.

"I am surprised that you do not simply order me to marry him," she snapped. "You would then be rid of me, at all events."

Goaded, he said, "He wants my forests still, for his damned bloomery."

Her chin rose. "You should not use such language in my presence, sir."

Her sudden hauteur nearly made him smile. He said, "You are quite right. I should not. I beg your pardon."

She grimaced, tossing her head. Then, looking at him more narrowly, her voice laced with suspicion, she said,

"You are not begging my pardon because you mean to make me marry that horrid creature, are you?"

He sighed. "No, Bridget, I will not make you marry him."

"Good, because he is horrid and cruel, not to mention old enough to be our father. I daresay that, if the truth were known, he murdered his first wife."

"He did no such thing, and I hope you have not spouted such gibberish to all and sundry," Michael said curtly.

She shrugged.

"Look here, Bridget, you know that I owe Campbell a good deal of money, do you not?"

"It is not your debt," she said, tossing her head again. "Everyone knows that it was Papa who borrowed that money from him. I do not see why you should have to pay him a penny. When Papa died, by rights the debt should have died with him."

"You know that is not how such things work. I inherited our father's debts just as surely as I inherited Mingary. It is my lawful duty to repay Campbell in full." He did not add that he had no notion of how he was going to do so.

"Then pay it," she snapped. "I am sure it is no concern of mine, Michael, and I find it quite tediously boring always to be hearing how poor we are. You have said that Sir Renfrew wants the forests. Why do you not just sell them to him?"

"Because I do not want him to burn them if there is any way to save them," he said. "Already quite half of the Highland forests are gone, and in any case, he is willing to forgive only half of the debt in return for them."

"Then *tell* him he must forgive the *whole* debt," she said, flinging her arms wide. "Really, Michael, that seems quite ridiculously simple to me. Indeed, if you were at all wise about such things, you would tell him that he can have only half the forestlands as payment for the whole debt, and then make him pay good Scots silver for the rest of what he wants. If you did that, sir, I could go to Edinburgh for weeks and weeks and wear lots of pretty dresses.''

"Bridget, even you must see that I cannot force him to accept my valuation of the forests or the land. I have only until the third anniversary of our father's death to repay the debt, and I cannot demand terms of him that he is unwilling to grant.''

"The third anniversary!" Her eyes grew wide. "But it will be three years on the first of June, Michael. That's less than two months away.''

"Yes, I know. So you see—''

"You will just have to sell the dogs," she said flatly.

"Even if I could do that—''

"But why can't you? You are forever telling me how extremely valuable they are, that at one time a single leash of deerhounds was the fine whereby a noble lord condemned to death might purchase his reprieve! You just don't want to sell them, Michael. You care more for your dogs than you do for me!''

Coldly, Michael said, "If I do, it is because they are better behaved." He was sorry for the words, however, the instant they left his mouth.

Bridget's generous bosom swelled with indignation. "How dare you say such a horrid thing!"

"I should not have said it, but it is very often true, Bridget, and if you want to find a gentleman willing to marry you one day, you must learn to think occasionally of someone other than yourself.''

"I do think of others! At least, I would if I ever saw anyone else to think about. But thanks to you, I never do. I am stuck here in this horrid pile of rocks for months on end, without a single, solitary person to talk to, Michael.''

"You exaggerate, my dear. There are any number of people here to talk to.''

"Oh, servants," she said with a dismissive wave of her hand.

"Not just servants," he said, keeping his temper with difficulty. "We are surrounded by kinsmen and—"

"But not real people," she said. "Not people of our own class, Michael, and if you think for one minute that having rejected Sir Renfrew Campbell I am going to marry one of our tenants, when you are forever telling me that they cannot even pay to rent the lands they work, like other people's tenants do nowadays—"

"I do not mean for you to marry any of them," he said. "When the time does come for you to marry, there is no reason that you should not marry well."

"Well, I don't see why I shouldn't if you would just buy me some proper clothing and let me go to Edinburgh," she said, reverting to her original objective. "This is the best dress I own, sir, and just look at it!"

"I cannot send you to Edinburgh now. Perhaps someday, but—"

"You could if you'd sell one of your stupid dogs."

Michael sighed. "I keep telling you that I cannot get enough money to repay the debt by selling the dogs. I have explained the law of exclusive proprietorship to you, have I not?"

She glared at him. "That is the stupid law which says that no one of lower rank than an earl or a clan chief may own a deerhound, is it not?"

"Yes. So you see—"

"I quite see that it is a stupid law, and I do not see why anyone should have to obey laws that are stupid. Surely, someone would buy one and not tell."

"Some of us are working to change the law, but I do not intend to break it, and that is not the point just now, in any case. Presently, I know of only one man who wants to buy a dog from me. Unfortunately, the one he wants is

Cailean, and I am not willing to sell him merely to frank your expenses in Edinburgh."

"But—"

"No, Bridget. I don't deny that among the many ways I have considered to repay the debt, I've included the possibility of arranging a marriage for you, but—"

"I will not marry that horrid man."

"Despite your obvious assumption that I have seriously considered such a course, my dear, you are still much too young to marry anyone."

"That is preposterous, Michael. Our mother was no older than I am when Papa married her."

"That is quite true," he said, regarding her thoughtfully. There was a notion that had occurred to him, more than once, but before now he had dismissed it out of hand, believing that she was too young for marriage.

"I know what you should do," she exclaimed. "You should marry an heiress yourself, Michael! That would solve all our problems, would it not?"

"It would," he agreed. "Unfortunately, I do not know of any heiress whose family would welcome a penniless earl with lands mortgaged to the last dirt clod, who will lose all he owns if she does not instantly pay his debts for him."

"Nonsense, there must be at least one who would marry you for your title alone," Bridget said. "I don't say she would be well born, necessarily, but that need not count with you, after all. There are tradesmen's daughters, surely—"

His voice cold again, Michael said, "Even if I could find such a person before Campbell takes all I own, I would not bring her into this family. I owe more to our ancient line than to taint it with unsuitable blood, Bridget. You refuse to count even our kinsmen as persons to whom you will condescend to speak. How would it be if you could not bring yourself to speak to my wife?"

"Well, it would be very hard," she agreed, "but if she were rich you would have plenty of money to send me to Edinburgh, and I could just stay with Aunt Marsali until I find a proper husband. So you see, Michael—"

"What I see is that you are making it easier for me to consider a possibility I had until now dismissed as unconscionable," he said grimly. "However, if you truly think yourself old enough to marry, I will look into that possibility. Indeed, I'll tell you to your head, Bridget, that right now, if I thought sending you to Edinburgh would result in a timely and advantageous marriage for you, I'd do it."

"Oh, Michael, it would! You'll see. Oh, pray send me!"

"Unfortunately," he said dryly, "I doubt that a single visit of several weeks would be sufficient for you to snare a husband on your own, if, indeed, you can ever manage to do so. Nevertheless, with so little time left before June first, arranging an advantageous marriage for you may be the only option remaining to me. Indeed, had I thought you old enough . . . Ah, but I have already neglected the matter too long."

"Not Sir Renfrew!"

"No, I am not so cruel, lass, nor would Scottish law allow me to arrange any marriage to which you objected. But if you are willing . . . I had thought the cause lost, you see," he added quietly. "But it is quite true that arranging a marriage for you could well prove the one route by which I can still win free. It occurred to me some time ago that there is a family that might be willing to ally itself with ours."

"What family? Who?"

"First, you must understand that the most important goal of such a marriage must be to pay off the debt to Sir

Renfrew Campbell, and to do so in such a way that would prevent him from making further trouble for us."

"He is very powerful," Bridget said. "All the Campbells are powerful."

"Yes," he agreed. "They became so by siding with the English during the Risings, before you were born."

"You were only a boy then, yourself," she pointed out defensively.

"Yes, and our clan was not one that fought for the prince," he said. "But neither did we fight against him or provide support of any kind to the English. Our isolation here helped us then. As to the Campbells, they were powerful before the Risings, and became more powerful afterward. That is why our wisest move now would be to ally ourselves with them if we can."

"But you said—"

"I said I would not force you to marry Sir Renfrew. I don't even propose to marry you to a Campbell, merely to ally ourselves with one of the most powerful of them all, a close connection of the Duke of Argyll."

"But if he is not a Campbell, then how—"

"His guardian is the Earl of Balcardane," Michael said, "but the lad, as it happens, is a distant kinsman of our own. He is the young MacCrichton."

"Is he handsome?"

"I don't know," he said. "I have never met him, but he is only four years older than you are, so I daresay you will deal well enough with him. If you really are willing, I could go to Balcardane Castle at once to put the matter to the earl. As you say, my title must be worth something. Moreover, I can offer to settle a third of my land on you, and to bequeath you the rest if I should die without issue."

Her eyes widened. "All the land? To me? Can you do that?"

"Yes, because I agreed to break the entail when our

father mortgaged everything with Sir Renfrew. The likelihood of your inheriting the estate is quite small, though, you know.''

"But even if they agreed to a marriage and repaid your debt, you would still be poor, and you would own a third less land than what you own now," she pointed out, adding complacently, "so very likely you will never marry. How soon can we go to Balcardane Castle?"

"You are not going," he said.

"Don't be absurd. Of course, I must go."

"You will do as I bid, Bridget. You will stay here."

"But who will stay with me?"

"I'll be gone only a day or two. If this weather holds, I can ride through Glen Tarbert to Loch Linnhe in the morning, take a boat across to Kentallen, and hire a horse at the inn. I should reach Loch Leven and Balcardane by midafternoon."

"Well, I'm still going with you. You cannot leave me with only servants to look after me, Michael. What if something happens to you? What then?"

"Nothing is going to happen to me. You will stay here."

"But I want—"

"By God, you will do as I tell you for once," he roared, smacking the desktop with his hands as he rose to his feet. "I've got half a mind to let Sir Renfrew have you, after all. Seek your room now, and do not let me see your face again before I leave in the morning."

She hesitated, as if she meant to argue; then, muttering furiously to herself, she turned on her heel and stormed from the room, slamming the door behind her.

Michael looked at the dog, which had curled up on the hearthstones again. "Sometimes I wish I were a more violent man, Cailean," he said quietly.

The dog's tail thumped the floor, as if in agreement.

Fortunately for the earl's continued calm, his sister did

not show her face again before he and Cailean left Mingary
for Appin Country the following morning. The sun was
shining brightly; the breeze blew from the southwest and
was strong enough to send his hired sailboat skimming
across Loch Linnhe in good time. The landlord at Kentallen Inn was able to provide him with a good-looking black
gelding at small cost, but that was the end of his good
fortune for the day.

He saw Balcardane Castle's famous square tower some
time before he got near enough to see the whole castle,
and his pulse quickened at the sight of it. He knew enough
about the MacCrichton's parentage to think the lad or his
guardian might welcome the simplicity of an arranged
marriage, and that thought sustained his optimism until
sight of the massive castle planted solidly on the hillside
above the rippling waters of Loch Leven reminded him in
no uncertain terms of the power of its master. He realized
that that power could mitigate the qualms that any noble
father might have about allying a daughter with the questionable MacCrichton line.

Michael was glad he had brought along a miniature of
his sister. Her beauty must count as a considerable asset,
and any guilt he felt at not bringing her in person, he
suppressed. His mission was difficult enough, for he knew
that his pride might hinder his good intentions. One hint
of Bridget's temper, though, and all would fail.

His heart was pounding by the time he reached the tall
double gate. One side opened enough to allow a lackey
to emerge even as he drew rein.

"What will ye, sir?" the man asked, touching his cap
politely.

"Pray, inform your master that the Earl of Kintyre seeks
an audience with him on a matter of some import,"
Michael said.

Seeing the lackey's eyes widen, he realized that coming

alone had been counterproductive, and wished he had been able to provide himself with a proper tale. On the other hand, he would then have had to hire horses for the others, as well, and he could not afford that. He held the lackey's gaze with his own.

The man said ruefully, " 'Tis a pity, me lord, but the master's awa'. Ye're welcome to Balcardane's hospitality, but I canna give yer message to his lordship."

"When will he return?"

The lackey seemed to measure him for a long moment. Then he gestured toward the inner courtyard. "Will ye enter, me lord? I'll fetch our captain straightaway."

Understanding that the man was reluctant to give information about his master's plans to a stranger, Michael nodded and urged his mount through the open gateway.

Shutting the gate behind him, and dropping the iron bar into place, the lackey waited politely for Michael to dismount and precede him across the vast stone courtyard toward the stables.

Glancing around, Michael decided that an enemy hoping to take Balcardane during its master's absence would be sorry to have made the attempt. Men at arms stood everywhere. Swords clashed in one corner of the yard, where a group sat watching two men practice their skill. He counted at least twenty others in plain sight on the walls and in the courtyard, which told him there were undoubtedly at least three times that many on the premises. The ones he saw were well equipped and looked well fed. The earl was clearly a man of extreme wealth and power.

"Good afternoon, my lord," a large, muscular man said, approaching him. "I am Bannatyne, his lordship's captain of guards. The lad tells me ye're wishful to see his lordship."

"Aye," Michael said. "I come from Mingary, on the

peninsula of Ardnamurchan. I can return another day, if
necessary, but if his lordship means to return shortly, perhaps it would serve me better to stay here.''

"I cannot say when he will return," Bannatyne said,
watching him narrowly.

"I understand your reluctance," Michael said. "I should
be wroth with any man of mine who revealed my whereabouts or intentions to a stranger. The matter I wish to
put to his lordship is one of some import, however. It
concerns young MacCrichton, as well. Is it possible that
they have traveled to his estates?"

"The family departed for London some days ago," Bannatyne said, evidently making up his mind to trust him
with that much information. "For the Season."

"Devil a bit," Michael said, his mind beginning to race.
The most likely reason for Balcardane to take the young
MacCrichton to London was to introduce him to society,
and the most likely reason for that was to arrange his
marriage. There was no time to be lost. "Thank you. I
shan't trouble you for hospitality. If I hurry, I can still make
it back across Loch Linnhe before dark."

It was late when Michael returned, so he did not see his
sister till the following morning. When she hurried into
his bookroom after breakfast, he looked up from the work
on his desk to greet her with a wry smile.

"Good morning, Bridget."

"I did not think you would be back so soon, Michael.
What did they say?"

"They said nothing at all," he replied. "They have gone
to London."

Her face fell ludicrously. "Oh, no! How horrid! Now,
what shall I do?"

"Did you want me to succeed, then? I should not have guessed it."

"Well, to speak truly, I don't know what I want, but it seems a shame that we shall never know if I might have married Lord MacCrichton. He is rich, is he not?"

"Aye, although I do not yet know the full extent of his fortune," Michael said. "As to our never knowing if he will have you, I cannot predict that either."

"I don't understand you. Why are you looking so oddly at me?"

"Well, I was just wondering if you still want to visit Edinburgh."

"If I—Merciful heaven, sir, do not tease me! You know I wish it above all things. Do you mean to take me, after all? Oh, Michael, say that you do!"

"I am inquiring presently into numerous possibilities," he said. "I've written a letter to Aunt Marsali that I will send with a runner to Fort William for the first post to Edinburgh, and if you will grant me a few minutes' more peace, I mean to finish this letter to go with the same runner."

"But you said that you have no money!"

"I am going to sell Glenmore a dog," Michael said evenly.

"The Earl of Glenmore? But you said he would take only—"

"—only Cailean, that's right." Michael glanced at the great dog, which lifted its ears and began thumping its tail at hearing its name. Ignoring the sick feeling in his midsection, he said, "The sum he has offered won't repay the debt to Sir Renfrew, but I believe it will be enough to take the three of us to London in style."

"London!" Bridget stared at him in astonishment. Then, as if fearing to put the matter to a test, she turned and left the room without another word.

CHAPTER THREE

Glen Moidart
Near Ardmolich
Later That Same Morning

When the bell rang to announce that his men were ready to tap the iron, Sir Renfrew Campbell looked around his newest bloomery with satisfaction. The iron ore from England had made it safely from his wharf at Abernish to the smelter in the lush forest that had once belonged to the MacDonnells and which was now part of his own vast, sprawling estate. Sir Renfrew was one of the largest land-holders in the Western Highlands. Much of his property—from its northern boundary on the original MacDonnell estate near Arisaig, which he had inherited from his mother, to the east as far as Glen Finnan and to the south as far as Glen Tarbert—was heavily timbered. A grateful government had awarded the estates to him for his Campbell loyalty after the failed Rising twenty years before.

When he looked at his trees, Sir Renfrew did not see lush green oaks, beeches, and Caledonian pines. He saw good English gold, and he was no fool. Much as he owned, he knew that he needed more. He was burning five tons of timber for each ton of iron he produced, and at such a rate a bloomery denuded its forests more rapidly than anyone had expected, and then had to be moved.

The bell rang and rang to announce the tapping, and children who had been gathering dead wood for fuel from the forest floor ran from every direction to see the grand sight of molten metal pouring like the devil's own blood from the furnace mouth. One small one, holding her skirt to her chin and flying barefoot over the pine needles, rocks, and cones in her path, tripped over a root and sprawled right at Sir Renfrew's feet. Tangled in her skirt, she fell again when she tried to get up, and began to wail in frustration.

Bending over, he picked her up, set her on her feet, and dusted her off. "Cease yer bleating, lassie," he said kindly. "Ye willna die of a wee fall, ye ken."

"I want tae see the deevil's fires," she sobbed.

"Aye, sure, and so ye will. Yonder they spew from the furnace, and they'll be pouring forth the whole livelong day, so ye canna miss seeing them. Here," he added, reaching into his pocket for a halfpenny when she looked at him with her lower lip extended and tears spilling down her pale cheeks. "Here's a wee copper bit to make ye smile again."

Blue eyes widening, the child took the halfpenny and clutched it in her grimy fist. Beginning to turn away, she remembered her manners and bobbed an awkward curtsy before dashing off to see the tapping.

He watched her go, then turned when he heard his furnace manager's voice call out behind him.

"It looks to be going well, MacIver," Sir Renfrew said with a nod. "Ha' ye the figures yet from the last run?"

"Aye, sir. Took just over a hundred pounds o' wood, that 'un, but this'll tak' more. We've no so much o' the hardwoods left till we can cut more, and whilst the pine burns hot, it burns gey quick as well." He handed Sir Renfrew a sheaf of papers. "Mr. MacPhun said tae give ye this, sir. 'Tis the list o' them what still owes the furnace stores for flour and meal and whatnot."

Sir Renfrew scanned the list. "Did he tell ye who owes the most?"

"Aye, Gabhan MacGilp."

"He owns a cow, does he not?"

"Aye, a fine one, and a wee pony as well."

"Tell MacPhun to go and put my brand on the cow. Tell him MacGilp can buy her back when he pays his shot for his supplies. That will bring the others in quick enough, I vow."

"Most ha' no siller tae pay," the man said uneasily.

"They'll find a way. Tell them they can work extra hours in the gravel pits or loading gravel and tobacco if they want to earn more, or they can sign on with one of my ships."

"Aye, I'll tell them, but most work eighteen t' twenty hours the day, as it is, and the ones wha' fancy a life at sea ha' gone wi' the boats already."

Sir Renfrew, being of no mind to listen to paltry excuses, turned away without reply. Then, bethinking himself of another matter, he turned back and called to the man, "Has MacKellar returned yet from Mingary?"

"Aye, sir. I saw him ride up tae Dunbeither House earlier when I were up on the ridge top. Likely he stayed the night wi' his granny at Shielfoot. He'll likely be along straightaway."

Sir Renfrew nodded and dismissed the man, then turned

and walked up to the furnace. Built from bricks he had imported all the way from Wales, it was huge, two stories high. Such height was necessary because the charcoal and iron ore were poured into the closed furnace from above. Then, from below, a set of bellows blew the furnace to the great heat required to melt iron from the ore. A huge iron wheel, turned by water running along a lade from the River Moidart, powered the bellows.

Although that particular bloomery had been in operation little more than a month, the clinker dump—the pile of slag from the reduction process—was vast. He walked past it to the sheds behind it, where the ore and charcoal were stored. A short distance beyond that, men were building a second kiln to produce the charcoal from the cut wood.

Charcoal burned hotter than fresh-cut wood, which meant more sustained heat from even the softest timber, but a solitary kiln could not produce it quickly enough, so presently they were burning only small amounts of charcoal compared to the tons of wood they burned. With two kilns, he would be able to produce more of his own bricks, too, which would eliminate the necessity of purchasing any more in Wales. Scotland produced few bricks, so at the rate the bloomeries were sprouting, there would be a good market for the ones he did not need himself right here, just as there was a market in England for his gravel and the tobacco he shipped duty-free. Sir Renfrew was an entrepreneur with an eye to the main chance.

He was mentally measuring the pile of charcoal in the shed when MacKellar found him. "I've brought yer reply from Mingary, sir," the man said, touching his cap and holding out the folded missive.

Breaking the wax seal that bore Kintyre's signet, Sir Renfrew read the earl's bold, black scrawl swiftly and with increasing annoyance, then looked up to find his henchman eyeing him warily. "Hold yer whisst, man," Sir Renfrew said. "I've never yet killed a messenger for bringing me bad news."

"It's bad then, sir," MacKellar said, adding with a frankness that Sir Renfrew would put up with only from one who had served him long and faithfully, "I feared it. The earl's a proud man, they say. Still, he offered me hospitality, so I couldna be certain of his mind."

"He's a Highlander, MacKellar. He'd not deny ye hospitality, even if he were one that still acts as if the incident at Glencoe happened yesterday instead of nigh onto seventy-five years ago."

"I'm kin wi' the Campbells," MacKellar said, "so I'd no blame him if he refused me. My family had naught tae do with it, mind, but it was a Campbell who began it by claiming hospitality and then betraying his hosts when he led the soldiers in to murder them in their beds."

Grimacing, Sir Renfrew said, "Ye're but one man, MacKellar, and if ye think that even an army could attack Mingary in the middle of the night without warning, ye paid little heed to the place."

"Nay, then, it couldna. I saw no men-at-arms on the walls, but the castle sits on a promontory high above sea and forest, and his dogs would give warning, sure enough. I never saw the like o' them, I can tell ye. As big as ponies, some are."

"Aye, so I'm told." Sir Renfrew stared at the missive in his hand. "We must do something to bring Kintyre to his senses, though. I ha' made him a generous offer, and this reply offends me. I must show him it's not wise to do that."

"Will ye write him again, then?"

"Nay, I willna repeat myself, MacKellar. Did ye see Lady Bridget?"

"Aye, sir, I did, for she was in the courtyard with her

maid when I arrived, and I'm thinking she's as bonnie as ever they say she is."

"Then I shall wed her."

"Um . . . begging yer pardon, sir, but I did hear . . ." MacKellar fell silent.

"Speak up, man. What did ye hear?"

"Well, they do say that Lady Bridget has a temper, sir, that she is not kind."

Sir Renfrew dismissed the criticism with an impatient gesture. "What about it? D'ye think I canna tame the lass and bend her to my will?"

MacKellar smiled. "Nay then, sir. The lass will learn what's good for her soon enough."

Sir Renfrew chuckled. "I wouldna mind if it takes a bit o' time. I enjoy a challenge, MacKellar. I'll most likely enjoy it more than the wee lassie will."

His smile fading, MacKellar said, "Aye, sir, ye will that."

CHAPTER FOUR

London

Thanks to the state of the roads throughout Scotland and northern England after weeks of intermittent rain, the party from Balcardane took nearly three weeks to reach London. A retinue of servants riding saddle horses accompanied three heavy traveling carriages bearing Balcardane's coat of arms elegantly painted on their doors. Pinkie occupied the lead carriage with the countess and Lady Agnes, along with Chuff and the earl on those occasions when the men chose not to ride their horses. The children followed in the second carriage with their nurse and a nursemaid; while the ladies' personal maids and the men's valets followed in the third with Fergus Owen, who would serve in London as the earl's house steward.

In addition to the three coachmen, others who accompanied the party included four grooms, three footmen, and several men-at-arms to protect them from the highwaymen

and footpads for which English, and even Scottish, roads
were infamous. Their baggage traveled ahead by wagon,
accompanied by more armed outriders. The servants wore
Balcardane's green-and-gold livery, and the men-at-arms
wore his colors and carried his banner. All in all, Pinkie
decided, they must present as grand a sight as any royal
procession.

The earl and Chuff rode as frequently as they could,
one or the other occasionally taking young Roddy up with
him as a special treat.

The earl had traveled to London twice before, but that
afternoon everyone else got a first glimpse of the vast city
from the top of Highgate Hill, after the lead carriage had
passed through an ancient low-arched brick gateway so
narrow that but for their coachmen's skill one or another
of the carriages must have scraped its sides. Because there
were buildings in the way, their view was not as panoramic
as it might otherwise have been. Nevertheless, they saw a
sprawling metropolis much larger than Pinkie had dared
to imagine, and they could see the River Thames to the
south, like a silver ribbon binding the city in place.

Long before the party clattered onto London's cobbled
streets, people had turned out to watch their passing, and
the closer they drew to the metropolis, the larger the
crowds seemed to be. This was especially true in the village
of Islington, which, with all the activity surrounding its
passenger and mail coaches, was as bustling a place as any
Pinkie had yet seen. The road to that point was not paved,
and the horses' hooves and wheels of passing coaches flung
muck all about, so that the ladies had long since put up
the glass, and even when they reached the city's cobblestones, they felt no immediate inclination to let it down
again.

At first, Pinkie thought that the crowded streets in London were the result of curiosity similar to what they had

met before. Then she realized that although many did turn heads to watch them pass, just as many paid them no heed. The packed footways were marked off from the roadway by posts clearly intended to mark a boundary for pedestrians, but doorsteps to shops and houses jutted into the footway, making it necessary for the pedestrians to step frequently into the road. And there the rapidly moving vehicles seemed utterly to ignore them.

Pinkie thought the city resembled nothing so much as a giant, noisy anthill. Carts, wagons, coaches, and pedestrians bustled everywhere along the wide road and the narrower ones intersecting with it, into courts and yards and alleys that twisted away through narrowing and widening lanes into rectangular pockets that seemed to have no outlets. She saw buildings that rose to heights of four, five, and even six stories; and, in some places, stone or brick walls lined the road. From time to time she would see a truly fine structure, such as a church or a hospital, and twice she saw sedan chairs with a gentleman inside swaying along between two, or sometimes four, chairmen.

Tradesmen's signs hung over the shops, swaying in the breeze that wafted up from the river. One hung tipsily from a single chain, its other having come loose, and threatened to clout the head of any unwary pedestrian who walked beneath it.

Even with the windows up, the din was ear-shattering. The dowager countess, though generally talkative, had remained unnaturally silent since Highgate Hill, too busy watching the passing scene to talk, other than to point out certain amazing sites when she saw them, of course. In the busy street, however, the noise precluded any rational conversation.

Above the racket of iron wheels and horseshoes on the cobblestones, sounded a constant clanging and ringing of bells—not only church bells but handbells. Dustmen,

sweeps, knife grinders, and postmen all carried bells of
one sort or another. Adding to the din was a cacophony
of cries from the costermongers and other assorted vendors who littered the pavement, all of whom tended to
dart from the footways out to the vehicles—or even to
dash in front of them—crying their wares without ever
seeming to stop for breath.

Their voices rang in chorus with the bells, making it
difficult to know just what each one was saying: "Brick
dust! Buy my cod! Knives to grind . . . dainty live cod! New-
laid eggs . . . last dying confessions . . . sixpence a groat
. . . Scissors to grind! . . . of all the malefactors . . . Cat's
meat . . . chairs to mend . . . fresh cat's meat! . . . executed
at Tyburn last week! Buy my roasted pig! Crab, crab!
Oysters, buy my oysters! Will ye crab? Artichokes! Swe-e-e-
e-eep, fresh artichokes!"

Before long, the pace slowed considerably, and soon all
three coaches were creeping along in a jam of street traffic.
Pinkie had given up trying to make sense of it all by then,
and just gazed out the window, fascinated, resisting the
urge to cover her ears. She would have liked to hold her
nose though, had she not feared to offend passersby, for
the stench of raw sewage running along a kennel down
the middle of the road was nearly as overpowering to her
senses as the din.

As they negotiated the turn into Oxford Street, she could
see the other two coaches just behind. The window of the
second one was down, and Roddy hung out precariously,
prevented only by his nurse's firm grip on his jacket from
falling into the road. His delight was clear in his wide eyes
and open mouth, and Pinkie envied him his ability to
ignore the noise and the press of unwashed humanity.

After a time, the coach turned again, into Park Street,
and the din abated at last. Bells still rang, but they seemed
more distant and less deafening; and when Mary suggested

letting down the windows again so they could see better, neither Pinkie nor Lady Agnes objected.

Sedan chairs appeared frequently now, a number of them holding fashionable ladies instead of gentlemen. Vendors still cried their wares, and once a woman thrust a bunch of lavender in through a window, but she released it and backed away with a bobbed curtsy when the earl tossed her a sixpence. Pinkie picked up the little nosegay and inhaled its agreeable scent with delight.

The street was much cleaner, the pedestrians fewer and generally better dressed. For a short distance, she saw shops with bowfront windows and glass doors, through which she saw intriguing articles of elegance and fashion. The shop fronts bore numbers now instead of signs swaying perilously over the walkways, and the stones of the street were flat, rather than rounded.

The houses here were built of stone, and new gutters lined each side of the street instead of a kennel down in the center. There were raised footways, and doorsteps no longer jutted into them. The greatest discomfort for the passengers now occurred when the coaches bumped over the raised causeways that served as pedestrian crossings at the intersections through which they passed.

It was dusk by the time the coaches drew to a halt before a large pedimented house on South Street near Tyburn Lane. Built of brown brick with carved stonework and midlevel windows dressed with pediments and balustrades, the house was elegant. A pair of stone columns supported the broken pediment over the entrance, which contained an elaborate cartouche displaying a coat of arms. The house faced north and was five bays wide. Wrought-iron railings flanked seven stone steps leading to the entrance and set off the areaway steps from the flagway.

The countess regarded the house critically for a long moment without moving, then smiled through the open coach window at her husband, who had dismounted and handed his reins to a lackey.

"Like the looks of it, do you?" he said, strolling up to speak to her.

"Rothwell and Cousin Maggie chose well, sir," she said.

Lady Agnes nodded fervently, leaning forward to say, "I do not mind telling you, Duncan, I had begun to believe I would never be able to think in this city. To imagine, I have dreamed for years of coming to London, and my first impression, with all that clatter and shriek, was that I should never dream again, of anything. But this street is quite peaceful, is it not, and that lane yonder does not seem to bear a great deal of traffic either. Indeed, with all those trees hanging over that brick wall on the other side, it looks more a country lane than anything in a great city."

"That street is Tyburn Lane, ma'am," the earl said, "and that brick wall is the boundary of Hyde Park. You may drive there if you take outriders with you. The park has a reputation for harboring footpads and their ilk, but otherwise it is said to be quite pleasant." To Chuff, who had also relinquished his horse to a lackey, he said, "I believe Rothwell said that we can hunt in the park, too, lad, if we like."

Chuff nodded, smiling at Pinkie. She could not tell what his first impression of London was, or even if he had yet decided what he thought. Chuff generally kept his thoughts to himself unless he felt obliged to reveal them.

Lady Agnes said, "I do think that one could be quite happy here, once one becomes accustomed—and meets people, of course. We must begin at once to prepare for that happy event, must we not? Surely members of the beau monde will begin to pay calls as soon as it becomes known that we are in residence here."

"Aye, they will," the earl said, opening the door and

assisting his wife to the flagway. As she shook out her skirts, trying to smooth the worst of the wrinkles, he performed the same office for his mother while Chuff assisted Pinkie.

One of the footmen had run up to pound on the front door. Observing him with visible surprise, Lady Agnes said, "Do they not have proper brass knockers here in London, like they do in Edinburgh?"

The earl chuckled. "They do when the residents are at home, ma'am, but not when they are out of town. Our knocker will go up straightaway, I promise you."

The door opened, and a slender middle-aged man in biscuit-colored breeches, a neat dark coat, and a powdered bag wig looked out and smiled when he saw them.

"Welcome, my lord, welcome," he said. "Your baggage wagons arrived only an hour ago, but Lord Rothwell warned us to expect your arrival daily after the first of the month, so everything is quite in readiness for you. I am Peasley, sir, George Peasley. I have served at Rothwell London House in the capacity of underbutler for some years now, and his lordship was kind enough to suggest that I might serve as your butler here at Faircourt House. My wife, Bess, has been acting as our housekeeper—pending your arrival and approval, of course."

"Aye, I know," the earl said. "Rothwell suggested the arrangement when he wrote to tell me that he had hired Faircourt House on my behalf from the marquess. I'm sure that you and Mrs. Peasley will serve us well. He promised to provide me with a running footman, too, since none of my lads knows London at all."

"Indeed, sir, you will find our Jeremy entirely satisfactory. Quite dependable, and I should know, sir, for he is my nephew and knows the city as well as I do."

While he talked, Mr. Peasley had made gestures toward someone inside the house, and several men hastened into the street now to unload such baggage as the coaches carried, and to direct the outriders and men-at-arms around to the mews. Within minutes, the personal servants and the nursemaids and their charges had been whisked upstairs, and Balcardane and his party had passed through a grand marble entrance hall, up a wide marble stairway, into a splendid yellow-and-white saloon. The room boasted boldly modeled plaster decoration, coffered ceilings, modillioned cornices, pedimented doorcases, a floral carpet, and ornamented furnishings. A neatly dressed maid under Mr. Peasley's direction began to serve refreshments as soon as the three ladies and the gentlemen were seated.

Pinkie had all she could do to conceal her awe. She had seen a number of noble homes in Edinburgh, and she had lived for the past decade in one or another of two sprawling Scottish castles, but she had never seen the equal of Faircourt House. From outside, the house had seemed elegant, to be sure, but it had been no more than well-arranged bricks, stonework, and iron. The marble entry with its tall columns, black and white marble floor, and swooping stairway had taken her breath away. The saloon, with its elegant furnishings, delicately gilded in what she would soon learn was "the French taste," made her wish Mr. Peasley had shown them first to their bedchambers. She was certain that dust from the road still clung to her skirts and was even now depositing itself on the lovely blue damask upholstery.

After a sip from her cup, Lady Agnes exclaimed, "What very fine tea this is!"

Peasley said, "Lady Rothwell sent it, your ladyship. She expressed the hope that it would prove to your liking. The house contains a proper tea-drinking room, of course, but after your long journey, Mrs. Peasley and I thought you would prefer to relax in here for a time. Oh, but that reminds me, my lord," he added, clapping a hand to his breast, then reaching inside his coat. "His lordship sent this message for you. I put it where I should not forget it, and here I've nearly gone and done so."

The earl, who was taking a mug of ale from a tray the maid held out to him, accepted the letter with his free hand. He was looking for a place to set down the mug when one of his own footmen entered, observed his need, and quickly drew forth a side table for his use.

"Thanks, lad," he said, setting down the mug, then breaking the seal on the letter. With a shrewd look at the footman, he added, "You got yourself sorted out right quickly, did you not?"

"Aye, my lord." The young man glanced at the maid and the butler. "Fergus Owen thought ye'd be wishful to ha' some of yer ain folk about, not meaning any disrespect to ye, Mr. Peasley."

The earl said, "This is Dugald, Peasley. He is generally a dependable lad."

"Indeed, my lord, he looks it," Peasley said, regarding the tall, well-built young footman with approval.

Pinkie sipped her tea, resisting the impulse to get up and wander about the saloon. She would have liked to look more closely at the gilded pier glasses and mirrors, and the paintings on the walls, or just to look out the window to see what she could see. She noted that Lady Agnes was as fascinated as she was, and was not troubling herself to conceal the fact.

The dowager was a plump little woman in her late fifties with soft features and pale blue eyes. Her once mouse-brown hair had turned splendidly white with age, which she thought a great blessing, since she required no powdering to be in the mode. Her delight in her first trip to London was nearly palpable.

Catching Pinkie's gaze, Lady Agnes said brightly, "This is a splendid room, is it not? I dare swear that I have never seen its equal. The marquess must have spent a vast amount of money buying all this gold furniture, don't you agree?''

Pinkie nearly did agree, but when she saw Mary hide a smile, she said only, "It is quite a lovely room, ma'am, to be sure."

The earl said, "That will be all for now, Peasley, thank you. Be so good as to send Fergus Owen to me when you find him. He is my house steward, and you will take your orders from him. I expect we shall need a few more servants, and I know he will welcome your advice on the subject."

"Certainly, my lord, and thank you, sir." Gesturing to the maidservant to follow him, the butler left the room.

"You may go, too, Dugald," Duncan said to the footman. "You would be wise to take yourself belowstairs and learn quickly how things are done here. Many of their ways will doubtless be different from what they are at home."

"Aye, sir, but what if ye need me? How will I know?"

"I am sure that someone will come if I pull that bell," Duncan said, gesturing toward the bellpull by the fireplace. "I can send for you if I want you. You'll be taking your orders from Peasley, you know, as well as from Fergus Owen."

"Aye, Mr. Peasley seems fair enow."

"You will have to wear powder here, Duncan," Lady Agnes said abruptly when the lad had gone. "I daresay our menservants should wear it as well, just as Peasley does. Fergus won't care much for that, I expect."

"He'll dislike it less than I will," the earl said, scanning the letter in his hand. He looked at his wife with a smile. "Maggie wants us to dine with them tomorrow."

"How could she know that we would arrive today?" Mary asked, surprised.

"She didn't," he replied. "Her letter says we are to come to dinner at four o'clock the day after we arrive, even if it's a Sunday. We'll test our new running footman by sending him to Rothwell House with our acceptance and our thanks."

"I should think we would have heard from Argyll, as well," Lady Agnes said petulantly. "Perhaps, however, the duke is put out because you accepted Rothwell's assistance instead of his in finding this house. I do not say that Rothwell has chosen ill, for he did not. This is quite adequate for our needs, but still, his grace may be displeased that you failed to seek his advice, Duncan, and that would never do."

"Nay, then, ma'am, it would not," Duncan agreed, "but I would never have been so daft as to ask him to serve as my house-finder. The duke is past the age mark now, and would not thank me for setting him such a tedious task, particularly when Rory had offered to see to it. Argyll likes him better than me, after all."

"Perhaps, although I do not think his grace has ever really recovered from the shock of Rory's—that is, to Rothwell's—marriage. And as to being obliged to him, I am persuaded that Argyll's son, John, would have served you quite as happily."

"Colonel Campbell has other matters on his mind, ma'am, for his regimental duties keep him fully occupied," Duncan murmured, his attention shifting to the letter in his hand again. "Maggie reminds us that she means to present Pinkie to the queen at a drawing room," he said a moment later, drawing their attention again. He glanced up, adding with a wry smile, "Apparently, she and Rothwell mean to give a ball in her honor, as well, on Saturday, the eleventh of June; and you will be pleased to learn, ma'am, that they have invited the colonel and his lovely wife to attend."

Mary said with a chuckle, "Just how do you know she is lovely, sir?"

He said sternly, "Do you doubt my faithfulness, madam?"

"No, sir, merely your clairvoyance."

With a wry smile, he said, "I have seen her, although she was married to the Duke of Hamilton at the time. She and her sisters are all quite famous for their beauty, my love, although in my humble opinion, theirs fair pales beside your own."

"Flatterer." But the countess blushed rosily and looked pleased.

Lady Agnes, who had done her best from the isolation of the Highlands—with the willing assistance of a host of correspondents—to keep up with the gossip of the beau monde, said thoughtfully, "I'd quite forgotten that Elizabeth was so famous for her beauty. It's been some time since those days, of course, and she's been married to John Campbell for nigh onto six years now, but I daresay she still retains her captivating manners. She was one of the Gunning sisters, you see," she added, clearly for Pinkie's benefit, since no one else was paying her much heed. "Lud, but they *were* famous, years ago. Elizabeth became Duchess of Hamilton, and then Hamilton died and she married John Campbell. Now, if he succeeds his father, which he must do if Argyll does not outlive him—and sometimes one does think that Argyll means to live forever—But if John Campbell does succeed, she will have married two dukes, won't she? I wonder if anyone else has ever done that."

The earl and his countess, speaking quietly to each other, seemed still to be paying no heed to Lady Agnes, and Chuff had left his seat to gaze out one of two tall windows that Pinkie thought must overlook Hyde Park. Thus, she felt obliged to reply. "I'm sure I do not know if anyone has, ma'am. It is surely a great thing to have married *one* duke. Two seems a bit greedy, to my mind."

"Aye, that's true enough," Lady Agnes agreed, "and

what's more, she's Irish. Her mother, Bridget Gunning, was no more than the housekeeper at Somerset House, after all, but about fifteen years ago Elizabeth and her sisters were the rage of London. They were said to be of such surpassing beauty as to drive sane men to madness. Her older sister married the Earl of Coventry. There is a younger one, too, although I do not believe she has chosen a husband yet.''

"Goodness me," Pinkie said, "they sound like three Cinderellas."

"Too good to be true, you mean," Chuff said from the window, proving that he had not been entirely deaf to Lady Agnes's chatter.

"Aye, lad, and so it would be," Duncan said, "if they had not suffered tragedy as well. I beg you, ma'am, not to prattle of John Campbell's affairs in company. Remember that he and his lady lost their only son less than a year ago.''

"Aye, that's true, and a tragic loss it was, too," the dowager said.

Before she could launch herself into what Pinkie was certain would be a recitation of every detail of the child's final hours, Mary said hastily, "If you have finished your tea, Pinkie love, perhaps we should ring for someone to show us to our bedchambers. I want to change my dress and look over the rest of the house."

The door to the gallery opened as she was speaking, and the Master of Dunraven entered with his usual haste and lack of ceremony. His dark hair was tousled, his shirt had come untucked from his breeches, and he had a smear of something on his right cheek that looked suspiciously like strawberry jam.

Mary exclaimed, "Roddy, where have you left your manners, my love?"

"Well, I ha' been searching for you everywhere, and yon

blathering fool, Peasley, said you didna want to see me, but I kent you would, so I came. Please, sir," he added, looking up with a beseeching air at his scowling father, "I want to go into the garden. The lass who brought up our supper said it is a fine garden, and if I do not go out at once, it will soon be too dark to see anything."

Sternly, Duncan said, "Does Lucy know where you are?"

"Nay then, but she willna care," was his heir's unabashed reply. "She's busy helping Anna get the bairns off to bed."

Mary got up at once. "I must go up to them, then. Thank you, Roddy, for reminding me. You have been a very good laddie today, and I am quite pleased with you." Shooting a speaking look at her still frowning husband, she added, "Pinkie, if Mama Agnes will excuse us both, perhaps you should come upstairs with me. We must make a list of questions to ask Maggie tomorrow."

"I'll go, too," Lady Agnes said, glancing warily at her son and grandson. "We must ask Maggie to tell us where to find George Hitchcock's silk warehouse. I have it on excellent authority that he sells the very best silks in all London—somewhere near St. Paul's Cathedral, I believe."

Duncan still had not spoken, and for once his son was showing the good sense to keep silent. Pinkie glanced at Chuff as she got up to follow Mary and the dowager, and she saw that he, too, was watching father and son.

Chuff smiled reassuringly at her, and as she left the room with the other ladies, she heard him say calmly, "I mean to walk in the garden myself, sir, just to stretch my legs after being in the saddle all day. If you like, I'll keep an eye on the scamp whilst he explores a bit. 'Tis likely he'll sleep better for the exercise after all the hours he's spent this past week cooped up in the coach with his sisters."

"Aye," Duncan said evenly. "He'd better sleep well, for he is going to have a tutor just as soon as I can hire one—

a good, strict man who will thrash him soundly when he gets up to mischief or fails to learn his lessons."

"I dinna mind if he's strict," Roddy said cheerfully, "just so long as he knows all the best places to see in London. This is a fine city, is it not, sir? May I please go out with Chuff now?"

"Aye, rascal, you may, but do not let me hear about any misconduct or it will be the worse for you. Do you hear me?"

As the boy assured his father that he did, Pinkie shut the door, grateful to Chuff for intervening, and wondering what imp of Satan got into Roddy that he dared talk to Himself so. Neither she nor Chuff would have dared say such things to him when they were Roddy's age. The lad didn't always get away with it, of course. He had been lucky today.

On the gallery near the stairway, a stout woman in a striped buff-and-brown taffeta gown and petticoat over a wide oval hoop awaited them. Had the chatelaine of keys dangling from her waist not proclaimed her status, Pinkie would not have known her for the housekeeper. Her demeanor was as dignified as her attire was elegant. Her coiffure was simple but well powdered, and one could easily have mistaken her for a lady of consequence.

"Your ladyships," she said, acknowledging Mary's rank and that of the dowager with a gracious curtsy, "pray, allow me to show you to your bedchambers now. I have taken the liberty of ordering hot water for you, and for you, too, of course, Miss MacCrichton," she added with a polite nod. "If you will all follow me, the stairs continue from this hall, just along here."

As she spoke, she gestured toward a door on the opposite side of the grand stairway from where they stood. The gallery was semicircular, and at its center a corridor led away from the head of the grand stairway to other rooms.

The door to the stair hall matched the one through which they had entered the saloon.

"Thank you, Mrs. Peasley," Mary said. "We appreciate your thoughtfulness."

"It is my pleasure to serve you, my lady. This way." She walked into the stair hall, moving with the ponderous grace of a ship at sail.

Small gilt chandeliers suspended from the ceiling at each half-landing lighted their way to the next floor.

When they entered the countess's bedchamber, Mrs. Peasley said, "His lordship's rooms are there just beyond yours to the west, my lady, overlooking the back garden and the park. Your dressing room adjoins his. That doorway on the other side leads to your sitting room, and I have put Miss MacCrichton in the room next to that. The dowager Lady Balcardane will have the set of rooms next to hers at the end, and Lord MacCrichton will have the bedchamber across from hers, which faces South Street. I trust these arrangements will suit you."

"They will suit us very well, Mrs. Peasley," Mary said. "Thank you."

Before leaving them, the housekeeper said, "With regard to meals, my lady, it has been our practice at Rothwell House to serve breakfast at ten and dinner at four, with a light supper to follow at nine-thirty or at the mistress's convenience. Will those times suffice for you, or do you wish to alter them?"

Exchanging a look with Pinkie, Mary said, "It has been our custom to breakfast much earlier than ten, Mrs. Peasley, so perhaps you had better expect at least some of us to do so here, as well, although I daresay we shall quickly adapt to London ways. Tonight, however, I believe we will all want our supper at eight o'clock. I, for one, intend to retire early, although the gentlemen may desire to go out afterward. In any event, they will be hungry soon. It has been a long day."

"I will see that everything is as you wish, ma'am, and may I say that we are all delighted to welcome you and your family to London."

"Thank you, Mrs. Peasley. Pinkie—and you, too, Mama Agnes—as soon as you have washed and changed your dresses, please come to my sitting room. We must make some decisions, you know. There is a great deal for us to do."

In the bedchamber the housekeeper had allotted to her, Pinkie found Ailis, her maidservant of many years, waiting for her. The room, if not as ornately decorated as the others she had seen, was spacious and quite acceptable. As she performed her ablutions and allowed Ailis to help her change from her traveling dress to a dimity frock in her favorite shade of pale green over a hoop not nearly so wide as the housekeeper's, she decided that London might be a pleasant place, after all. She certainly looked forward to dinner at Rothwell House.

The only cloud casting a shadow over her pleasure was the memory of what Chuff had said to her the day they had walked together from Shian to Dunraven. She could not help but wonder if knowledge of her parentage—of Daft Geordie and Red Mag—would affect Lord and Lady Rothwell's behavior toward her. Then, recalling that Maggie intended to present her to the queen, and that the Rothwells meant to give a ball in her honor, she grew cheerful again. Surely they must know her history, and if they did not fret about it, who else in London would dare?

CHAPTER FIVE

Castle Mingary

The woods were lush, green, and alive with chirping birds and other, shyer creatures that moved like shadows through them. The air around him felt warm, and although the woods were dense and filled with shadows, sunlight streamed through every opening in the canopy overhead, glinting on branches, needles, and leaves. Where rays touched flowers on the forest floor, they brightened their colors, making them look like jewels dropped by some previous visitor.

He felt a sense of hope and expectation, and a stirring in his loins that increased as he progressed, as if it fed both from his expectation and his pleasure in the beautiful woods. He was nearing his destination. He could feel it in every fiber of his body. Weary though he was from his long journey, his step lightened, and when he glanced down, the big dog moving gracefully beside him looked up and wagged its tail. He stroked its head and lengthened his stride.

Emerging from the woods into bright sunlight from a cloudless sky, he saw the castle below at the foot of a heather-clad hill, a castle as unlike his own sprawling pile as a castle could be. The curving, crenellated curtain wall enclosed a five-spired tower house on a point of land that jutted into a sparkling blue loch.

Instinctively—for he had no conscious awareness of the castle's name or even where he was, exactly—he knew that it was the place he sought.

Anticipation changed to urgency, and he began to run. With every step, his urgency increased. He was flying now, moving so swiftly that he had no sense of his feet touching the ground, yet the castle seemed no nearer. If anything, it seemed to grow smaller, more distant. The faster he ran, the smaller it grew, as if a mouth to another world had opened and was swallowing it whole. Urgency turned to terror. He tried to shout, to tell it to stop, to wait for him— please, please, to wait—but no sound came from his throat.

The sky darkened. Wind blew. Thunder clapped without lightning, rolling and surrounding him, like a vast chamberful of drums. His knees grew weak, and his legs no longer responded automatically to his wishes. Every step required more effort than he could spare, as if he slogged through a thickening quagmire. Despair overwhelmed him when black darkness enveloped the castle, and Michael awoke, sitting up in bed, his heart pounding, his mouth dry.

A cold, wet nose pressed against his hand, startling him. Coming slowly to his wits, he silently stroked Cailean's furry head, realizing that once again the huge dog had managed to sneak into his bed during the night. Despair subsided, but a sense of loss swept achingly through him and made it impossible to speak.

He felt clammy with sweat, although the air felt chilly. At least he was no longer slogging through whatever muck it was that had kept clutching his feet. Nor was the room around him as black as the horror of his dream.

Early dawn light outlined the curtains over the two arched windows, and he could make out the shapes of the furniture in his bedchamber. He guessed it must be nearly six o'clock, time to get up, but he gave himself a few more minutes to let his heartbeat return to normal while remnants of the dream faded from his memory.

The dream was not new. He had dreamed it many times—not, however, in quite the same way, because except for the castle and its Highland setting, the details varied from dream to dream. Sometimes he was inside; more often he was outside looking down on the castle from the hill. Although frequently, as in the most recent example, he felt as if he were approaching it for the first time, other times it was as if he lived there. Even then, however, he was aware that the castle did not belong to him. "His" castle was always somewhere else. Indeed, he was as certain as he could be that "his" castle remained Mingary, although in the dreams he never had any sense of being the Earl of Kintyre.

The dream had recurred so many times since his childhood that he suspected it sprang from a family legend about an ancient heir who had disappeared on a journey. Shortly before the dream's first occurrence, a well-meaning uncle had related the tale to him as a bedtime story, and the dream had recurred two to three times a year since. Consequently, Michael knew the castle and its lands intimately.

What altered most were the physical feelings the dream engendered. Generally, it would begin with warmth, either from the sun or—if he was inside—from a hearth fire. It nearly always began with a sense of anticipation, as if he were looking for something special and expected to find it. What it was he did not know, although frequently, like today, it seemed to be a woman. The ancient heir had supposedly gone off to seek his fortune, a mission that Michael had always thought foolish, since the chap had expected to inherit Mingary and all its lands. The estate had been worth a fortune in those long-ago days before the English had imposed their rule on the Highlands and destroyed the old clan system.

Whatever it was that he sought in the dream, he never seemed to find it. Frequently, the dream began pleasantly and ended in fear or distress. Other times he would wander around the walls of the castle, or through the woods, without incident. In the latter dreams, his sense of anticipation was slight, but likewise the ending did not cast him into black despair. Sometimes, he met people in the dreams, children or folks he recognized as peasants or others who seemed to be his peers. One thing was consistent: The stronger his sense of pleasurable expectation felt at the beginning, the stronger was the sense of doom that struck at the end.

Inhaling deeply to clear the last shadows of the dream from his mind, he got up, hooked back the curtain from one window, and rang for his man to bring him hot water. He had much to do if he and Bridget were to be away the next morning.

Despite his desire for haste, it had taken nearly a fortnight to receive the desired replies to his two letters, but the second had arrived the day before, and he wanted no more delay. Time was short. Even if they encountered no major obstacles, it could well be May first before they reached London.

Twenty minutes later, washed, shaved, and dressed for the day, he went downstairs to break his fast, the great deerhound following faithfully at his heels.

While Michael ate his porridge, he read over the list he had made, crossing off items he had dealt with the day before, and noting what remained to be done before they could leave for Edinburgh. When he had finished eating, he sent a message to his bailiff, asking that worthy to present himself later in the morning, then retired to his bookroom to write letters to two friends, which he could post from the Scottish capital. The dog followed, curling up in its favorite spot before the fireplace.

He was sprinkling silver sand over the second letter when the door from the hall opened and his sister entered the room.

Looking up in surprise, he said, "You are up early."

"I awoke and could not go back to sleep," she said, "so I dressed and came down to get something to eat. Are we really leaving tomorrow, Michael? At last?"

"We are," he said. "Our aunt is doubtless awaiting our arrival in Edinburgh with great impatience."

"Yes, I suppose she is," Bridget said. "I'm feeling a trifle impatient myself."

Amused by the understatement, Michael resisted pointing out that she had nearly driven everyone at Mingary to distraction with her demands and frequent questions. She had packed and unpacked her boxes so many times that he feared they might not survive the journey. Not a day passed that she did not spend an hour or two making lists of the items she wanted to purchase in Edinburgh, and those that must wait until they reached London. In vain had he tried to persuade her that he could not afford to purchase even half of what she wanted.

He said, "Has your Nan accustomed herself to the notion of leaving her family for such a lengthy time?"

"Aye, I had only to promise her a new hair ribbon when we reach London. I shan't have time to have a new gown made before we leave Edinburgh, shall I?"

Astonished, he said, "For your maid?"

"No, silly, for me, of course. I've told you ever so many times that I must have new gowns if I am to go to parties and balls in London, and if I have to wait for them to be made up after we arrive, there will scarcely be any time left."

"I know you need gowns," he said, "but the money Cailean will bring won't stretch to more than two or three, you know." Mentioning the dog stirred the sick feeling again, and when Cailean thumped his tail, it was all Michael could do to look at him. They would deliver the dog to its new owner on the way to Edinburgh.

Bridget regained his attention by stamping her foot and saying angrily, "I do not want to hear any more about money, Michael. Not only is it unnecessary, but it's stupid and foolish, as well, to keep talking about it. You can hardly expect this Lord MacCrichton of yours to show interest in a girl dressed in rags. Moreover, you know perfectly well that the cost of the London house will not fall upon you, since we shall be living with Aunt Marsali's Cousin Bella, and that Aunt Marsali has said she will be happy to help dress me."

"I do not like taking her charity," Michael said stiffly.

"Well, you cannot afford that sort of stupid pride if you want this venture to prosper," she snapped. "You are putting a great deal of trust in his lordship, and far too much in me. If I do not like him . . ."

When she paused meaningfully, glaring at him, he said with as much patience as he could muster, "All I ask, Bridget, is that you behave like a well-bred Highland lady should. You do not want to shame the name of Mingary."

"As if I would do any such thing. I know very well what is due to my great name, sir, and it is *not* to be dressed in rags."

"Your gowns look quite suitable to me," he said, knowing the minute the words had left his tongue that he had merely offered tinder to a spark.

She fired up at once. "You do not know anything about feminine attire, Michael. You rarely go into company, and even on those few occasions during the year that we manage to dine away from Mingary, you do not heed what other women wear, or notice how painful it is for me to let quite inferior females see me looking like a tattie-bogle, wearing the same ancient gown over and over again."

"Most of those females are likewise wearing gowns they have worn before," he pointed out. "Few of our neighbors can afford much more than we can."

"Exactly so, but I am *Lady* Bridget Mingary. It is much worse for me than it is for plain Rose Martin or Sadie Sanderson."

"I know that you find it so, my dear," Michael said in what he hoped was a soothing tone. Judging by the fire in her eyes, however, it was not soothing enough. A voice in his head warned him that he had no hope of persuading her to heed his concerns. Nonetheless, he made one more effort. "Although it may prove difficult for you at times to forgo some of the pleasures you crave, you will not want to be too much beholden to Aunt Marsali."

"She *wants* to help," Bridget insisted, her voice rising sufficiently to warn Michael that unless he wanted to endure one of her tantrums, or be forced to play the tyrant again, he would do better to placate her.

"Please, lass, we cannot discuss this if you fly into the boughs. I know that our aunt has offered many times to help you take your proper place in the world, but even she cannot know how much a Season in London will cost. She is not King Midas, you know. Her desire to help will not turn the leaves of the trees into gold. You must not press her to spend more than she can afford."

"Do you think she has no mind of her own, Michael?"

"I don't think any such thing. I merely—"

"Then, pray, did you read her letter, the one she sent in response to yours?"

"You know I did. I read it before I gave it to you to read."

"Well, you cannot have paid it much heed, or you would recall that she said I would want to be well gowned, and that she would be delighted to see to the matter if you would but allow her to do so."

"I do recall what she wrote; however—"

"Oh, do be sensible! Even at the long price Glenmore is paying for Cailean, once you have paid for our journey, and set aside enough to pay for our month in London, I daresay you will have less than half of it left. Moreover, you will also need new clothing, you know, unless you mean to embarrass us all dreadfully."

"Begging your pardon, m'lord."

The servant's voice startled them both. Neither had noticed his entry.

Though he was grateful for the interruption, Michael replied more sharply than he had intended. "What is it, Connal?"

"Sir Renfrew Campbell is below, your lordship."

"Mercy," Bridget exclaimed, clapping her hands to her cheeks. "Don't see him, Michael! Send him away!"

"Don't be foolish," Michael said. Then, to the servant, "Bring him up. No, wait. Does he request hospitality?"

"Nay, m'lord. He said he and his man stayed the night at Kilmory Inn, and he craves only a few moments of your time."

"Very well," Michael replied, realizing that Campbell must have sailed from Loch Moidart to Kilmory on Ardnamurchan's north coast, and hired horses there. The journey from Loch Moidart to Mingary by road—if the meandering rough dirt track could be called a road—was nearly twenty-five miles and could take as much as two days. By sea it was only eleven miles and, with a favorable wind, could be accomplished in about an hour.

"Give Lady Bridget five minutes to disappear, then bring him up," Michael said, adding when the servant had gone, "I wonder what the devil he wants."

"You know what he wants," Bridget exclaimed. "He wants me!"

"Aye, well, I've already said he cannot have you. Now, if you do not want to see him, take yourself off to your bedchamber until he's gone."

For once she did not argue but hurried away. A few minutes later the servant showed Sir Renfrew Campbell into the room.

Gesturing toward a chair, Michael said, "Will you take a mug of ale, sir?"

"I will," Campbell said, drawing the chair up near Michael's desk and sitting down. " 'Tis a dry day and all, it is."

When the servant went to fetch ale, Michael said, "How may I serve you?"

"I'll tell ye, lad. The plain fact is that I canna understand your reluctance to pay your debt off without all this dallying about over the matter."

"I mean to pay the debt in full," Michael said. "There is still time, I believe."

"Aye, sure, perhaps. Still, 'tis a fact and all that your father would have accepted the arrangement I've so generously offered to ye."

"I cannot speak for my father, sir. Thank you, Connal," he added when the servant returned with their ale in mugs on a tray. Setting his on the desk, Michael waited only until the servant had gone again before he said, "You've made a long journey for naught, sir. I will give you neither my sister nor my timber."

Campbell drank deeply from his mug. Then, setting it down, he said bluntly, "Ye're making a mistake, lad, but I'm a generous man. I said I would tak' the lass and your timberlands in lieu o' half the debt. What if I were to tak' the same and write off three-quarters instead? No man can say that is not a fair offer."

Since he would have to forfeit all but the castle if he could not pay the debt by the first of June, Michael knew the offer was fair. Nonetheless, he said, "I cannot do it, sir. Even if my sister were old enough, she does not want to marry you. Nor do I want my forests cut down and burned to provide the English with more iron."

"Ye'd let a wee lass flout your wishes? Ye're a fool then, Kintyre." Sir Renfrew got to his feet, his expression grim. "I willna heat cold cabbage, lad, so ye'll rue the day ye didna tak' such a fine and charitable offer."

"I might," Michael admitted.

"Aye, well, dinna think that when ye canna raise the gelt, ye can come to me wi' your hat in your hand. Until the first day o' June, I'll tak' the lass and forests for half what ye owe, but after that I'll tak' it all. Not only will I never offer again what I've offered today, but forbye, ye'll find it doesna pay to thwart me, laddie."

Michael would have liked to point out that his superior rank demanded more respect, but with little substance to back the demand, he decided to overlook the man's manners. In truth, Campbell gave him the shivers, and the sooner he saw the back of him the better he would like it. Consequently, he replied as politely as he could and rang for Connal to show his guest out again. He did not accompany him to the stables, or urge him to linger long enough to dine.

* * *

Sir Renfrew had not expected an invitation. Indeed, not trusting his host any more than he knew his host could trust him, he had left his own man to mind the horses, with orders not to let them out of his sight.

When he reached the courtyard, he found MacKellar waiting, and as the two rode out through the main gate, Sir Renfrew said, "Did ye see the lass again?"

"Nay, laird, but I did learn that they be leaving at the skreich of day, bound for Auld Reekie."

"Edinburgh, eh. Now, I wonder what's possessed the lad to take her there."

"I dinna ken, laird, but he's no keeping her there. They be bound for London town, his men say, and from what I'm told, they mean tae stay a month or more."

Sir Renfrew received the news with annoyance at first, but when his nimble brain had considered the prospects, annoyance changed to grim satisfaction. "I'm thinking," he said a half hour later, "that this turn of events may prove advantageous to a man o' my clever notions."

"Will it then, laird?"

"Aye. I'm thinking I've got a ship bound for Bristol in a sennight. I've no been nigh London these five years and more, and forbye, I'm thinking 'tis time I returned to see how the city has changed. Let's ride, man. There will likely come a mist later, and I dinna want to spend the night at Kilmory."

No mist marred Michael's plan to leave Mingary early the following morning before the birds had begun to sing. The starry sky had a clear hardness after a night of frost, and a keen, stiff breeze from the northwest sped their boat through the Sound of Mull. They reached the harbor of Oban on the west coast of Lorne as the sun was rising, less than three hours after leaving the castle.

Snow still capped the higher peaks beyond the village, but spring had arrived on the shore, where primroses and violets bloomed in abundance.

Michael stepped ashore with a sigh, wishing it had been possible to sail all the way to Glasgow, from whence it was but forty miles to the capital, much of it by post road and all of it fit for a coach. With a healthy breeze like the one that had sped them to Oban, they could easily have reached Glasgow in a single long day by making use of the narrow neck of land that separated the head of West Loch Tarbert from Loch Fyne on the River Clyde.

Since the time of Robert the Bruce, it had been common practice to have men pull one's ship across that bit of land—less than a mile wide—rather than sailing around the peninsula below it, thus saving more than a hundred miles in distance. But sailing to Glasgow would mean entrusting someone else to deliver Cailean to Glenmore, whose estate lay near Dalmally. Whoever delivered the dog would have to collect the money Glenmore had agreed to pay, too, and deliver it to Michael in Edinburgh. It was more practical and safer to deliver the deerhound on their way.

Hiring horses for the five of them—Bridget and her maid, Michael and his man, and Connal to tend the horses—they set forth from Oban an hour later. They spent the first night at Dalmally, where Michael sadly bade the deerhound farewell, and the second night with kinfolk at Lochearnhead.

The weather held, and they easily made Stirling on the third day. Leaving Connal there with orders to return the horses to Oban, Michael hired a coach and four the following morning to take them the rest of the way. They made good time on the post road and entered the capital that afternoon, arriving at Lady Marsali's town house in Castle Street shortly before four o'clock.

Bridget eyed the exterior of the gray stone house doubtfully. "It is very plain, is it not, Michael? I thought it would be much grander."

"Just wait," he said, helping her alight from the coach.

Chalmers hurried up the short flight of stone steps to apply the knocker, and soon thereafter the door opened to reveal a tubby little man in yellow breeches, a black frock coat, and a powdered tie-wig.

"Come in, my lord," the man said. "Her ladyship is expecting you."

"Good day to you, Andrew," Michael said, smiling. "I trust she has not fretted herself into a lather with impatience."

"Now then, sir, ye ken full well that her ladyship never frets. Would this bonny lassie be the Lady Bridget, then?"

"Aye, she would," Michael said as he linked his arm with Bridget's to escort her up the steps. "This is Andrew, my dear. When I was in school here, he took excellent care of me. Where will we find her ladyship, Andrew?"

"Upstairs, sir, in her drawing room. I might just add that she generally dines at half past three now, sir, but she has put dinner back today, pending your arrival."

"Devil a bit, she must be starving."

"Aye, sir. Shall I show ye to yer rooms to rid yourselves o' the road dust, or straight along to her?"

"To her, I think," Michael said. "We can change for dinner after we've made our salutations. You may show our servants where to put our things, however."

"Aye, sir, I've a lad on the way to attend to that. Come along now."

Bridget had been unusually silent, and Michael, knowing that the plain little entry hall with its pale green painted walls, bare flagstone floor, and three straight-backed chairs had done little to impress her, gestured for her to follow

Andrew into the equally ordinary stair hall and up the stairs.

Andrew moved straight ahead to open a pair of white double doors with shiny brass fittings. Pushing them wide, he stepped into the shadowy room beyond and said, "His lordship and Lady Bridget have arrived, my lady."

Bridget glanced at Michael, but he only smiled at her and gestured for her to precede him. As she did, Andrew opened one set of curtains, allowing the late afternoon sun to spill into the room. Bridget gasped.

The drawing room walls, hung with silk and cotton damask in two shades of gold, matched colors in the gold and rose-colored Savonnerie carpet. Deep rose pink curtains matched the upholstery on the gilded cane-backed chairs. Ornately carved walnut console tables and side tables held Sevres bowls of fresh spring flowers and other beautiful porcelain pieces. A pair of gilt-framed oval mirrors graced the walls between the three windows, and over a pedestal table at one side of the doorway hung a matching gilt-framed clock. Suspended from the center of the ceiling, a delicate cut-glass chandelier glittered where rays of sunshine touched it.

A sleepy voice said, "So you are here at last, are you?"

Michael, having become acquainted with the room some years before, while he was a student at the university, had spied the sole occupant of the room the moment he entered, but he saw his sister start at the sound of Lady Marsali's voice. As she turned to face her ladyship, Bridget's eyes widened.

Michael hid a smile, saying, "I hope we did not waken you, Aunt."

"Oh, no," she said, still reclining—as she had been when they entered—against cushions piled at one end of a giltwood-framed sofa that was upholstered in the same deep rose-colored damask as the chairs. Her little feet were propped on another cushion, and the only concession she had made thus far to their entrance was to lift the lacy white handkerchief that had covered her face to peer at them. Wearily she said, "Is it really necessary to open *all* the curtains, Andrew?"

"Aye, ma'am, it is," he said with a fond smile. "Ye'll be wanting to ask after their journey, I'm thinking, before they must change their dress for dinner."

"I suppose you are right," Lady Marsali said with a sigh.

Michael said, "Do you need assistance to sit up, Aunt?"

"I do not. You keep a civil tongue in your head, and, pray, do not feel obliged to recite every detail of your journey. I daresay that, when all is said and done, it was as tedious as any other journey."

"Don't you like to travel, ma'am?" Bridget said. "I liked it enormously. First we sailed to Oban, which I have done twice before, but then we hired horses and rode to Dalmally, where we enjoyed Lord Glenmore's hospitality overnight, and then to Lochearnhead, where we stayed with some cousins of Papa's."

"They are my cousins, too, dear," Lady Marsali said, sitting up at last and without visible effort. A comfortably padded little woman, she wore a simple pale pink, sack-backed afternoon gown and matching pink slippers. A lacy cap perched atop her hair, which was arranged in fashionable twists and curls from which wisps had escaped during her nap. "It was I who suggested that you spend a night there, when Michael wrote that you would pass through Lochearnhead. As to my opinion of travel, I find it quite wearing. Nothing but ruts and bumps and dust, and more dust. I don't know why I do it."

"But don't you *want* to go to London, ma'am?" Bridget's voice began to rise. "You won't change your mind, will you? That would be dreadful!"

"Don't fret, child," Lady Marsali said. "I may not like

to travel, but I shall like *being* in London very much. My cousin informs me that her house is tolerable, and I daresay we shall all enjoy ourselves enormously once we have arrived."

"I do wish there were not such need for hurry," Bridget said. "I would have liked to have at least one or two gowns made up before we leave Edinburgh."

Lady Marsali smiled. "My woman has taken care of that, child. We find it quite easy here in Edinburgh to receive the latest patterns from London and Paris, you know, and Louise is a skilled seamstress. You will recall that you sent me your measurements some time ago, and she used them to make several gowns for you. You need only allow her to fit them properly, and the thing is done." She glanced at Michael. "I cannot think your mission will prosper, however, my dear."

"We can but try, ma'am," he said.

"Aye, well, that's so, and even if things do not go as you hope, perhaps you will manage to win through in some other way."

"Perhaps," he agreed, "but we can afford to stay no longer than a month."

"We'll see about that," she said. "I don't fancy getting there only to have to turn round again and come home. Most unsettling that would be. I should prefer to stay at least until the middle of June. How long will this journey take us, by the bye? I have heard of mail coaches traveling the distance in only four days, but I cannot think that sounds at all comfortable for ordinary mortals."

"No, ma'am, for I am persuaded that they must drive through the night, which I know you would not like at all. The distance is nearly four hundred miles, but I think we can do it in a week without too much discomfort."

"Well, that remains to be seen, does it not? I asked Andrew to begin saving the newspapers for you the moment I learned you were coming to town. He will have put them in your bedchamber."

Accepting this less than subtle hint, he said, "Thank you, ma'am. If you will excuse us now, we'll change for dinner. I presume they will be serving it shortly."

"Lud, yes," her ladyship said with more energy than she had yet shown. "I am told that the dinner hour these days in London can be as late as five o'clock, so I have been trying to adjust myself, but it is not a pleasant business. Perhaps my cousin will not insist that we dine so late as that."

"I don't care how late we dine, ma'am," Bridget said. "Now that I know I shall be well dressed, I quite look forward to London."

CHAPTER SIX

Pinkie passed her first week in London in such a whirl of activity that she never seemed to know if she was on her head or on her heels. The city was unlike anything she had experienced before—overwhelming, exhausting, and fascinating. Mary and Lady Agnes seemed determined to turn her out in grand style, and she spent hours with silk mercers, mantua makers, milliners, shoemakers, and even a dancing master. She did not mind the latter, however, since the time she spent with him she also spent with Chuff. He, too, was busy acquiring new clothes, new friends, and new amusements.

Both of them knew how to dance, of course, but there were any number of new steps—even new dances—for them to learn if they were to enjoy their Season in the metropolis. According to their mentors, terpsichorean accomplishment was especially important if they were to gain entrance to a new, extremely fashionable set of assembly rooms that recently had opened in King Street, St.

James's. They had no sooner learned of its existence, during their initial visit to Rothwell London House, than Lady Agnes decided that both Pinkie and Chuff must attend the first subscription ball to be held there.

Rothwell London House had proved even grander than Faircourt House when the family went to dine the afternoon following their arrival in town. The dinner also proved grander than expected, because, not knowing exactly when they would reach London, Lady Rothwell had previously arranged a party for that date. She simply included them, though, saying it would be good for them to meet others.

Rothwell House overlooked the Thames, and no sooner had Balcardane's party entered the drawing room and been announced to their host and hostess than the latter suggested they take a turn on the terrace.

Lady Rothwell was kin to Mary, and his lordship was cousin to Duncan, and thus another member of the Duke of Argyll's powerful Campbell clan. At times in the past, the women's clans had been Campbell enemies, but like others who had taken opposing sides during the two failed Scottish risings, they had made peace in the years that followed. In the Rothwells' case, Pinkie knew that peace had come at a price, because after the Scots' defeat at Culloden, the English government had awarded to Rothwell estates belonging to the Chief of the MacDrumins. Rothwell's falling in love with MacDrumin's daughter had turned calamity to victory, however, and the estates, still managed by her father, had grown exceedingly profitable. Pinkie had met both Rothwell and Maggie several times before, in the Highlands.

"The river is looking its best today," Maggie said, linking arms with Mary. "I vow, 'tis the prettiest prospect in London, so do come and see it whilst you tell me about your journey. Charles," she added, smiling at Chuff, "bring

your sister and Lady Agnes out, too. I know that Rothwell
and Balcardane will be talking politics and tobacco until
our other guests arrive, so unless those subjects fascinate
you . . ."

When she paused expectantly, Chuff returned her smile,
saying, "I shall certainly prefer the river, ma'am."

Leaving him to escort Lady Agnes, Pinkie followed Maggie and Mary through a set of French doors onto the
flagged terrace that ran along the front of the house.
Except for the limited view she had had through the draw-
ing-room windows upon entering that room, she had
scarcely caught so much as a glimpse of the Thames since
entering the city, so the panoramic view astonished and
delighted her.

She went to stand by the iron railing that separated the
terrace from the water some ten feet below her, lapping
at the stone wall. A landing and water stairs led up to
Rothwell House at the south end, where they served the
house next door as well.

Rowboats, wherries, and sailboats dotted the waterway.
The opposite riverbank contained only a few warehouses.
Beyond them lay fields and woodland. In the distance to
the north, where the river curved to the right, she could
see the dome of St. Paul's Cathedral rising above the
sprawling city.

"Pinkie dear, come here," Mary said, interrupting her
reverie. "We have been talking about fashions, and Maggie
means to send her mantua maker—that is, her modiste—
to us on Friday, so tomorrow we must shop for fabrics."

"Yes, indeed," Lady Agnes said, turning from the river
view and deserting Chuff to join them. "I want to visit a
good silk mercer. Someone recommended George Hitchcock's silk warehouse, which is somewhere near St. Paul's,
I believe."

"Yes," Maggie said. "His merchandise is excellent."

"I know that fashions change more quickly here in London than they do in Edinburgh, let alone in the Highlands," Lady Agnes went on in a rush, "and we do want to be utterly à la mode. After years and years of hearing Balcardane—Duncan's father, of course, not Duncan—telling me that new gowns were too dear even to think of buying any, I mean to enjoy myself, I promise you. Balcardane, rest his soul, was a good husband but a dreadful nipfarthing—and you needn't look at me in that way, Mary, because everyone knows he was. He had a great reputation for it, and was quite proud of that. In any event, I daresay that since fashions change here as quickly as they do, silk may have gone out of style and been replaced by something else. Our seamstress in Edinburgh—for call her a modiste, I will not—assured us that the gowns she fashioned for us are the latest style, but I can see by looking at yours, Maggie, my dear, that they are no such thing."

She paused to draw breath, and Maggie said with a smile, "I assure you, ma'am, that dress you are wearing is lovely. Anyone who sees it will know it cost a great deal and was fashioned by a highly qualified seamstress. My dress is just Frenchified, that's all. It's become the rage to do everything as the French do, you see, which makes no sense at all. I resisted at first, because I frequently have been disappointed in the French. They let our prince down dreadfully, did they not?"

Pinkie heard Mary inhale sharply, at which Maggie burst into a peal of laughter. "Oh, dear, how fortunate that Rothwell did not hear me! He would be so vexed, although after so many years of marriage he knows that I am frequently put to the blush by my unruly tongue. At least the danger is not so great as it once was, but, my dear ma'am, I do beg your pardon if I have offended you."

Lady Agnes looked bewildered. "Well, I'd willingly pardon you, my dear, if I had the least notion of how your words might have offended me."

Maggie exchanged a roguish look with Mary. Pinkie, as confused as Lady Agnes was, glanced at Chuff, but he stood gazing at the river scene and seemed not to have overheard. After a short silence, Mary said to Lady Agnes, "Maggie has remembered that you are a Campbell, ma'am, just as Rothwell is. You must recall that she is a MacDrumin. Her loyalty was to—"

"That upstart prince?" Lady Agnes raised her eyebrows. "Lud, my dear, was it indeed? I never paid much heed to all that nonsense, you know, although my late husband was in the thick of it, of course; but he never told me what he was doing from one moment to the next, you see, or why he was doing it. I always thought the prince a rather foolish young man, myself, to stir up all that trouble and fuss, but I will not say so if you supported his cause."

"He was foolish," Maggie agreed with a sigh, "but we will not talk politics when we have far more interesting topics to discuss." Raising her voice slightly, she said, "Charles, lad, do not keep such a distance, but come and join us. I trust that you want to meet all the eligible young women in London, just as your sister will want to meet all the eligible young men."

Chuff had turned when she called his name, but at these words he looked nonplussed, and Pinkie was certain that her own face must reflect his discomfiture. He did not have time to reply, however, for a footman stepped out then to announce that Lady Rothwell's other guests were beginning to arrive.

They went back into the house, and before the company sat down at a long table in the elegant dining room, Pinkie had met Colonel John Campbell and his wife, and decided the world had not lied about the latter's beauty. She also met Sir Horace Walpole, a slender, pale-complexioned gentleman with twinkling, intelligent eyes, who wore his brown hair unpowdered, combed straight back, and tied in a queue. She did not know if that fashion was à la mode for gentlemen, but the others all wore powdered tie wigs, so she thought it was not. Nonetheless, she saw that Duncan and Chuff both regarded Sir Horace with envious expressions, and thought they would at least attempt to adopt his style, fashionable or not.

There were a number of other guests, including several younger ladies and gentlemen—clearly invited to meet Pinkie and Chuff—including Lady Ophelia Balterley, a stout, outspoken woman with an elaborately coifed wig and a gown boasting panniers so wide that she had to take care passing through the doorways.

Lady Ophelia took a dim view of the married state and did not hesitate to say so, salting her opinions with amusing references from books that most ladies never read. Since Sir Horace was also an accomplished conversationalist—not to mention the recently admitted author of a hugely popular "Gothick" novel called *The Castle of Otranto*—Pinkie found the dinner highly entertaining.

Mary had warned her—and Lady Agnes, too—that some London hostesses desired any conversation at their dinner tables to take place only between persons sitting next to each other. It quickly became clear, however, that Maggie Rothwell was not one of those hostesses. Conversation from the outset was general and lively.

The subject of the new assembly rooms raised its head while the servants were presenting the second course, when the beautiful Elizabeth Campbell asked Maggie if she intended to purchase a subscription to the first series of balls.

"The cost is but ten guineas," she said in her soft, lilting Irish voice, "for which we will enjoy a ball and supper once a week till the end of the Season."

"Aye, I had thought of going," Maggie said, "but I was not certain if . . ." She paused tactfully, glancing at Mary and Pinkie, who sat opposite each other halfway along the table.

Sir Horace, next to Mary, was not so tactful. "The distribution of tickets," he said in a deceptively gentle voice to no one in particular, "lies in the hands of a committee of lady-patronesses, whose power is utterly absolute, so you may imagine how carefully they choose their company. The men's tickets, however," he added with a chuckle, "are not transferable. If the ladies do not like us, they have no opportunity of changing us, but must see the same persons forever."

"You are too harsh, Sir Horace," Elizabeth said, smiling. "I can easily obtain tickets for you, Maggie, and for your delightful guests as well, if they like. The first ball is set for the fifteenth of June, the day after the queen's drawing room."

Maggie exchanged a look with Mary, then said, "We shall be happy to purchase tickets, Elizabeth. Mr. Almack's rooms do seem to be growing popular."

To Mary, Sir Horace said, "The rooms opened near the end of February, you know, Lady Balcardane—three of them, and very magnificent now, but the place was nearly empty that night. Half the town had fallen ill with colds, and many were afraid to go, as the house was scarcely built yet. Almack advertised that he had built it with hot bricks and boiling water. Just think how odd if that notice, instead of terrifying everybody, had drawn them all thither."

"It sounds quite horrid," Lady Agnes said with a shiver.

"Indeed, ma'am," Sir Horace agreed. "They tell me the ceilings were dripping with wet, but the Duke of Cumberland was there. There is a vast flight of steps, and I'm told he was forced to rest two or three times. Only think how silly he would have felt had he died of a chill and, when

St. Peter asked him what he'd died of, had to reply, 'Why, I caught my death on a damp staircase at a new clubroom.' "

Everyone at the table laughed, and thus encouraged, Sir Horace went on, "Without meaning offense to anyone present, no one expected a lowborn Scot whose previous enterprises, profitable though they were, did *not* impress the fair sex, to succeed in impressing them with these new rooms of his."

Lady Ophelia said, "I believe I enjoy dancing as much as anyone, but I fear that many persons view these new assembly rooms as no more than a marriage market—a place to show off their young women in hopes of marrying them to the highest bidder—and I cannot approve of that. Much as our men would like us to believe otherwise, the married state does not benefit a woman but enslaves her. For a woman to be entirely dependent upon a man is quite unnatural."

"Most women do have minds of their own, do they not?" Maggie said with a smile before deftly turning the subject to Mr. David Garrick's recent performance as Hamlet at the Theatre Royal in Drury Lane.

Pinkie, although fascinated by Lady Ophelia and interested to hear anything else she might say, was nonetheless grateful for the change of subject. She knew that one reason Mary and Duncan had brought her to London was to introduce her to eligible gentlemen in the fond hope that she might find one suitable to marry. However, it was daunting to know that each man—and doubtless his family, as well—would want to judge whether she was worthy of him.

Gazing across the table, she wondered if the lovely Elizabeth Campbell would so quickly have offered them tickets to the new rooms had she known of Daft Geordie and Red Mag. Recalling that Lady Agnes had said Elizabeth's mother was just someone's housekeeper, she decided that perhaps her own antecedents would not matter as much as Chuff had feared they would. In any event, she was as certain as she could be that she would not find any man in London to suit her. As for Chuff, although he was two years her senior, he was still too young to think of marriage.

Michael had been in London less than an hour before he was ready to return to the Highlands, or to throttle his sister. Not only had their journey been a trial—with five adults crowded into his aunt's coach—but the house in George Street, Westminster, was not what Bridget had expected a London house to be. In fairness, it was not what Lady Marsali had expected either. Her hitherto high opinion of her cousin, Mrs. Thatcher, had altered considerably upon their arrival.

They had made good time, reaching London the afternoon of the last day of April. When at last their coach drew up before the house, both ladies, and their maids, leaned forward to peer curiously at it through the coach window.

Bridget said with a frown, "It is quite narrow, is it not?"

"Aye, it is," Lady Marsali agreed, "but surely it goes farther front to back than it does side to side."

"Goodness me, I should hope it does," Bridget exclaimed.

Michael, realizing at once that no manservant was going to emerge from the house, opened the coach door and kicked down the step. Getting out, he looked up and down the quiet street. The houses on both sides looked alike. Built of brown brick with simple stone bands and cornices, and wrought-iron railings to separate their belowground areaways from the raised flagway, their only individual traits were their entrances and their widths. The one before which their coach had stopped was tall—five stories—but only three bays wide, boasting one narrow window on each side of a simple entry, and three windows each on the upper floors.

When his man jumped down from the seat next to the coachman, Michael said, "See if anyone is at home, Chalmers. I'll assist the women."

"Michael, this is horrid," Bridget said from the coach as he helped Lady Marsali to the flagway. "This cannot be the fashionable part of town."

"I must say," Lady Marsali said with a sigh, "it is not what I expected, either, but I am sure it will look much better inside. All of these houses along here appear to be much of a muchness, after all."

"But not of a fashionable muchness, ma'am," Bridget said bitterly, following her from the coach.

A maid in a simple blue dress, white apron, and mobcap opened the door of the house at last and bobbed a curtsy when Chalmers revealed his master's identity.

"Come straightaway in, m'lord," the maid said. "Me mistress be expecting you, and I am to take you right up to her."

The entry hall did nothing to raise Bridget's spirits. It was small, drab, and carpetless; and the stairs at the back left side of it were plain dark wood and rather too narrow for modern hoops. A single closed door on the right apparently led to a room of one sort or other, and another door at the back next to the stairs suggested that another room might lie behind it. The hall contained only a single side table next to the door on the right, beneath a plain wood-framed looking glass.

"This way," the maid said politely, leading them up the stairs, her shoes thumping on the wooden steps.

"Just one moment," Michael said. "What about our people and the coach?"

The maid said in surprise, "They won't drive away, will they, sir?"

"Nay, of course they will not, but neither do they know where to put up the coach and horses, or whereabouts to settle themselves."

"Well, after I've taken you to mistress, I'll send the kitchen boy to lead your coachman round to the coach house, won't I? I'll also show your servants where to put your things, and where they are to sleep. How many have you got, then, sir?"

"Three, plus the coachman," Michael said.

Bridget said in astonishment, "You won't expect *our* people to carry up all our things, I hope. Nan and Aunt Marsali's Louise are not at all accustomed to such tasks. Surely you must have menservants to carry in the luggage, at least."

"We keep but the one kitchen boy," the maid said. "This is not a household of men, miss. As to your coachman, my lord, he must sleep in the coach house."

"I am *Lady* Bridget," Bridget said haughtily.

Bobbing another hasty curtsy, the maid said equably, "Yes, m'lady. I won't be forgettin' again. Now, come along, do." With that, she spun around on the ball of one foot and clattered up the stairs, leaving them to follow her as they would.

Before doing so, Michael looked at Chalmers, who said, "Aye, then, I'll see tae the luggage and tae the beasts, m'lord. Rankin will help," he added, referring to Lady Marsali's coachman.

Michael nodded, then followed the others.

The stairway made a right-angle turn before reaching the next floor, where the landing faced an open doorway with another to the right. The maid stood in the latter doorway, clearly waiting till all three of her charges had assembled.

As she stepped aside, she said over her shoulder to some-one in the room beyond, "Here they be now, ma'am."

Michael gestured for Lady Marsali to go in first. He and Bridget followed.

The room filled the entire width of the house and over-looked George Street. Blue curtains hung at the three windows, and a blue, yellow, and pink floral carpet covered the floor. A fireplace with a plain white marble mantel and a brick hearth filled the end wall to the left as they entered, and a shallow alcove to the left of it held shelves full of books and knickknacks. Other furnishings included side chairs, a game table, a spinet, and side tables bearing clusters of memorabilia. Their hostess, a thin little silver-haired woman in a dark green wool afternoon gown, sat on the edge of a claw-footed blue sofa against the wall to their right as they entered.

"Do come in and sit down, my dears," she said without rising. "Sal shall bring you tea if you like."

"Bella, this is my niece, Bridget," Lady Marsali said, "and this, of course, is Kintyre. My dears, this is my cousin Arabella Thatcher."

"How handsome he is," Mrs. Thatcher said, more as if Lady Marsali had shown her a picture of Michael instead of the real thing. "He will set all the ladies in a twitter. But sit down, all of you, do. You are making me giddy. I have been so impatient for your arrival that I have quite worn myself out."

Bridget glanced at Michael.

He saw none of his amusement in her expression, how-ever. She looked irritated, and he knew that she resented Mrs. Thatcher's having singled him out for comment with-out mentioning her. Accustomed as she was to being the focal point of any group she graced with her presence, his sister had taken offense.

Lady Marsali, oblivious of Bridget's sentiments, instantly

drew one of the chairs near the sofa, sat down, and said in a tone of deep relief, "I cannot tell you, Bella, what a comfort it is to sit down on something that does not rock and jostle one's bones to bits."

"Indeed, this is a pleasant room," Mrs. Thatcher said complacently. "Sal will bring our tea shortly, I daresay. Perhaps you could stir up that fire some, Kintyre."

"Do you have no other servants, ma'am?" Bridget asked. "His lordship ought not to be doing such menial tasks."

Michael, dealing with the fire, concealed a wry smile. These past few years at Mingary he had dealt with far more menial tasks than fire-stirring, but if Bridget wanted to play the grand Scottish lady, he would not put a spoke in her wheel.

Mrs. Thatcher said, "I live quite alone, my dear. Why should I pay a houseful of servants to do nothing much at all?"

"Not a houseful, perhaps, but surely a manservant or two would lend you more consequence, ma'am."

Mrs. Thatcher laughed. "I do not require more consequence, and I can assure you that in a house the size of this one, menservants would bring me more scandal than distinction. Where on earth would I put them? There are but four small bedchambers in the attic, and but two rooms each on the other floors."

Lady Marsali said, "I did think your house would be larger, Bella."

"Then you know little about London houses," Mrs. Thatcher said calmly. "With the exception of the palaces of the great aristocrats and the rookeries of the very poor, nearly everyone in London, from earls to artisans, lives in this sort of a house. The object, as I see it, has been to stuff as many houses as possible onto as little land as possible, so the houses all grow upward instead of sprawling out and about like they do in the country."

"But we passed bigger ones," Bridget protested. "Even in this street, several houses are wider than this one if not taller."

"Oh, yes, but that only means the front and back rooms on each floor are wider, my dear, not that there are more rooms in those houses. Most London houses have but two rooms to a floor—except for the great old ones near the river, of course, and some of the grand ones in Mayfair."

"But how can we possibly hold a ball here, or even a small party?"

"Bless my soul, child, why should we do any such thing?"

In visible dismay, Bridget looked from her brother to her aunt before she said, "Why, for me, of course. Is that not what most people do when they present someone to society?"

Mrs. Thatcher raised her eyebrows. "I suppose some people do hold balls in their own houses, but that would not suit me at all. Only think of the enormous expense—and the work! It mustn't be thought of."

"Well, we must think of *some*thing. Tell her, Michael!"

Quietly, Michael said, "Nay then, lass, hold your whisst, lest Mrs. Thatcher find you wanting in manners. I should not think of telling her anything of the sort, in any event. This is her house, after all, and she is generous to share it with us."

"But—"

Lady Marsali cut in swiftly, "Hush, Bridget. Kintyre is right, you know. Moreover, I explained our needs to Cousin Bella when first I wrote to her, and when she replied, she assured me that nothing could be easier than introducing you to numerous persons in the first circles. Suppose you sit down and let her explain."

Regarding Mrs. Thatcher doubtfully, Bridget obeyed without bothering to draw the chair she had selected away from the wall.

"There's a good lassie," Lady Marsali said soothingly. "Now, then, Bella, tell us how we are to go on in London, if you please."

"Pshaw, my dear, there is nothing to it. One simply examines one's invitations with an eye to accomplishing one's goals, and sends one's acceptances accordingly. Whom do you wish to meet?"

"Everyone," Bridget exclaimed at the same moment that Lady Marsali said with a slight chuckle, "Do you receive so many invitations as all that, Cousin?"

"Yes, I do," Mrs. Thatcher said simply, choosing to answer the latter question first. Then she said to Bridget, "I know everyone, of course, but I daresay you ought to be rather more selective, child, for there are many who would do your credit no good. I shall present you to the queen, of course, and I have already arranged for tickets to attend subscription balls at the new assembly rooms."

In an awed tone, Bridget said, "Do you really know everyone in London?"

"Bless my soul, what a notion! I should not want to know the riffraff, my dear, but I believe I am acquainted with everyone of consequence. My mother, you see, was sister to a marquess. I was her fourth daughter, however, and even with connections to a marquess, one rarely has fortune enough to endow four daughters. It was quite providential that Mr. Thatcher did not care a fig about my lack of a dowry, and even more providential that he was a man of wealth himself."

Bridget frowned. "Is a large dowry essential, then?"

"It is of great import, certainly. Other things matter, as well, of course, but without a dowry, a girl is defeated from the outset. You do have one, do you not?"

"She does," Michael said before Bridget could speak. "I wonder, ma'am, what you can tell us about the Earl of Balcardane?"

"Balcardane?"

"Aye, I was told that he had come to London. Do you know him, ma'am?"

Mrs. Thatcher's brow knitted for a moment. Then she said, "I cannot claim a personal acquaintance. He is years younger than I am, and I never met his father, for he rarely came to London and I've not set foot in Edinburgh since I was a gel."

"I thought you said you knew everyone," Bridget said.

"Everyone of consequence," Mrs. Thatcher said. "Balcardane is cousin to Rothwell, you see, and I do know Rothwell—and his countess, too. Indeed, I was invited to dine at Rothwell House just a week ago, but due to another engagement, I had to send my regrets. Horace Walpole told me it was an exceedingly fine dinner, too," she added with a sigh. "Indeed, now that I think of Horace, I believe he also told me that Balcardane was there. Is he a friend of yours?" she asked Michael.

"No, ma'am, but I intend to seek him out at the first opportunity. Indeed, I do not think I shall await an opportunity. I need only to learn where he resides."

"Now, that I can tell you, because he has hired Faircourt House, which is quite near Hyde Park. Its property backs up against Chesterfield House, which will make it quite easy for you to find."

"Excellent," Michael said. "Then I shall visit him first thing tomorrow."

"Perhaps you should wait until after eleven o'clock," Mrs. Thatcher suggested. "Most gentlemen do not welcome callers earlier than that, but fortunately—since I believe you still require proper clothing to put you in the mode—it is quite à la mode now to pay calls in buckskins and a plain frock coat. You can even wear your own hair, sir, although to visit an earl on such a venture, I recommend that you powder it, at least."

* * *

Accordingly, dressed in much his usual fashion but with powdered hair, Michael presented himself at Faircourt House the following morning on the stroke of eleven. One look at the house—along with his memory of what Mrs. Thatcher had said about London houses—gave him to suspect that he ought first to have sent a message, requesting an audience. As he hesitated, the front door opened, and an energetic-looking young man emerged, stopping on the step when he saw Michael.

"Good morning, sir," the youth said.

"Good morning," Michael replied. "Is it possible that Balcardane is at home this morning, and would agree to welcome a caller?"

"Aye, he's in the bookroom. Peasley's lurking about somewhere in the nether regions though. Shall I take you in, myself, sir? I am MacCrichton. I live here, too."

"Kintyre," Michael said, shaking the offered hand and thinking he had chosen well for his sister. Young MacCrichton was a well-set-up gentleman, one he thought Bridget might even deem handsome. "I'd be obliged to you, lad," he said.

Moments later, he was facing the Earl of Balcardane, and his confidence had diminished. The earl was of another sort entirely, and Michael remembered that many men still referred to Balcardane as Black Duncan Campbell. From the stern look he encountered when young MacCrichton presented him, he decided the name likely had more to do with temper than with Balcardane's black hair.

Pulling himself together, he said quietly, "I've come to you on a personal matter of business, my lord."

"Leave us, Chuff," Balcardane said.

"Your servant, sir," MacCrichton said with a slight bow to Michael as he took himself off.

Balcardane said, "Have we met before?"

"No, sir," Michael said. "Indeed, you may think me presumptuous or mad, for at times I think I must be. Were it not for circumstances that make it necessary to approach you boldly—"

"I will accept that such circumstances exist," Balcardane interjected bluntly. "What do you want of me?"

"I would like your agreement to arrange a marriage between MacCrichton and my sister, sir. Lest you think her unworthy, let me assure you that—"

"I will allow that she is worthy," Balcardane said. "However, MacCrichton is not of age yet. I doubt that he has even begun to think of marriage."

Michael chose his next words with care. "When he does think of it, sir, he might wish to ally himself to an honorable, ancient title. He might also desire to increase his land holdings. My sister is entitled to a third of my land as her dowry. I would see her marry well, and very soon."

Balcardane had not invited him to sit, and the expression that crossed his face now reminded Michael of his least favorite schoolmaster. "Why so very soon?" Balcardane asked.

"When my father died three years ago, he left a debt that he had been unable to pay. He offered our estates as surety, though they are worth much more than the debt. If I cannot repay the debt, his lender will seize my land."

"You would prefer to sell your sister?"

Michael felt heat rush to his face. "I do not sell her, sir, but desperate times require desperate measures. You will agree that the situation in the Highlands these twenty years past has led many to do what they otherwise would not do."

"Agreed. How would her marriage to MacCrichton help you?"

"The debt is owed to a Campbell," Michael said, realizing that frankness would serve him best. "I had hoped that we could work out the marriage settlement so that he would get his payment and I could save our land."

"Who is he, exactly?"

"Sir Renfrew Campbell, sir. His mother was a MacDonnell, and after the Forty-five, the Crown awarded him her family's estates and forest lands. He is burning them to fuel his ironworks, sir, denuding the land for profit. I do not want that to happen at Mingary if I can do anything to stop it."

"I can understand that," Balcardane said, his harsh features softening at last. "I face much the same problem. The bloomeries offer such sums for wood that my tenants, if they dared, would doubtless sell them my forests."

Michael remained silent. The notion that Black Duncan's tenants would dare do any such thing was patently absurd.

"Very well, lad," Balcardane said after a momentary silence. "I will not throw you out on your ear. However, MacCrichton will marry when and where he chooses. The best I can offer you is that I will not forbid him to marry your sister."

It was far from what Michael had hoped, but he knew that it was fair. Moreover, he told himself as he took leave of the earl, he did not think MacCrichton—now that he had seen him—would prove invulnerable to Bridget's charms. Thus, if he could just persuade his headstrong sister to keep her temper in check—

His reverie shattered when the footman escorting him through the hall opened the front door and four large, liveried men entered, bearing an elegantly appointed chair. The front pair, forced straight on by the pair at the rear, nearly collided with him before he gathered wit enough to step out of their way.

"Pray, forgive us," the chair's inhabitant exclaimed as they set it down. She pushed open the chair door herself right in front of him before any of her bearers could open it for her, and extended one small hand for Michael's assistance.

"Aye, sure," he said, unable to think of anything more intelligent to say as he grasped her hand in one of his much larger ones. Even through his glove and hers he could feel the warmth of that little hand. It sent an odd, tingling tremor right up his arm, while another tremor struck him nearer the core of his body. He could not imagine that there was anything for which to forgive her.

As she emerged, honey-gold curls tumbled around her pixielike face, and a pair of large blue eyes regarded him with candor. The wide skirt billowing from her tiny waist as its hoop extended made her look even smaller, and more delicate.

"I was just leaving," he said, wondering what demon possessed his tongue that he could think of no more graceful words, or more polite ones, to say to her.

"Pray, sir, do not let me keep you," she said, stepping nimbly out of his path. "Dugald, when you have seen this gentleman out, I want to speak to you."

"Yes, Miss Penelope."

As the chairmen picked up the chair and disappeared with it into the nether regions, Michael strode from the house, avoiding the footman's gimlet eye, and feeling more like an awkward, infatuated schoolboy than a belted earl of Scotland.

CHAPTER SEVEN

Determined not to reveal unbecoming curiosity about Duncan's visitor, Pinkie went into a small parlor off the hall to wait while Dugald showed him out. The visitor was a distractingly handsome man, she thought, and she felt strangely attracted to him despite his rudeness. He certainly lacked the polished airs and graces that came so naturally to most of the gentlemen she had met in Edinburgh the previous year, and in London since her arrival.

Dugald's return put the visitor out of her mind.

Urgently she said, "Dugald, do you know if Master Roddy has permission to be out and about on his own this morning?"

"Nay, miss, he doesna have any such thing. The mistress tellt him tae stay wi' the bairns till his new tutor arrives this afternoon."

"Well, I am nearly certain that as my chair turned into South Street I saw him dart round the corner. Doreen ran to see if she could catch up with him, but I am afraid she will be too late. Is my brother at home?''

"Nay, miss, Lord MacCrichton went out nigh on to twenty minutes ago, whilst Himself were speaking wi' yon gentleman that just left.''

"Who is that gentleman, by the bye?''

"Called himself Kintyre, miss.''

Dearly though she would have liked to inquire about Kintyre's business with Duncan, she knew better. Dugald would not tell her even if he knew, and the likelihood was that he did not. At the moment, however, she had a greater worry.

"We must find Master Roddy, Dugald; and, if my brother has gone out, I expect I must do it myself. Perhaps if I go after Doreen and the two of us walk over and have a look in the park—''

"Nay, ye mustna do that! Himself forbade any female in the house to go into yon park without a proper male escort. He said there be footpads and such, miss, and it's no safe for a lady. I could go, however," he added quietly.

"Then go quickly, because if it is not safe for us, it is no safer for a child. I'll run up and make certain that he is not in the house, but I am nearly as sure as I can be that I saw him. If I do find him upstairs, though, I'll send a lad after you, so if you do not find him quickly, turn back, and we will decide what next to do.''

"Aye, but happen we should tell Himself straightaway, miss.''

"No!'' Pinkie quickly controlled her dismay, adding more evenly, "There is no cause to tell anyone else until we are quite sure it was Roddy I saw; but if you do find him, bring him back even if you have to carry him.''

"Aye, miss, he willna get the better of me. I ken that laddie well, I do.''

"Thank you,'' Pinkie said.

Hurrying upstairs, she learned, just as she had feared, that Roddy was not in the nursery with the little girls. Nor was the countess at home to advise her, for Mary and Lady Agnes had gone out earlier to pay calls. Pinkie had elected instead to go to nearby Shepherd's Market with her maid to buy ribbons and lace from a milliner's shop there, to replace the trim on a gown she had worn the previous year in Edinburgh. Maggie Rothwell's mantua maker, praising the gown, had assured her that with some new trimmings it would be absolutely à la mode.

In the nursery, Pinkie asked Lucy, the nursery maid, how long it had been since she had last seen Roddy.

"Not long, miss. The wee laddie told Nurse not a quarter-hour since that he were going out to play in the garden."

Hurrying back downstairs, Pinkie met Doreen on the landing. Anxiously, she said, "Did you find him?"

"Nay, miss, I saw nary a sign o' the scamp, though I might ha' seen him, had our Dugald no called me back just when I was crossing Tyburn Lane to ha' a look in yon park."

"Well, I hope Dugald finds him," Pinkie said with a sigh, "because if we have to set up a hue and cry, poor Roddy will land in the suds again."

"Aye, miss, that tutor of his canna get here too soon, I'm thinking."

Pinkie could only agree. The little boy had fallen into mischief more times than she could count since they had arrived, for Duncan had underestimated the time required to find and hire a suitable tutor. In the end, Rothwell had come to his aid again, recommending a friend's son, a young gentleman who had fallen ill early in the Easter half at Cambridge and intended to rusticate until the summer term began. Mr. Terence Coombs was to present himself that afternoon.

Dismissing her maid, Pinkie continued downstairs to the

hall, where she was relieved to see Dugald coming into the house with Roddy at his side. "There you are, you naughty rascal," she exclaimed. "What are we to do with you? Where did you find him, Dugald?"

"Yes, where, Dugald?"

All three of them jumped at the sound of Duncan's deep voice.

Dugald flushed, but Roddy squared his shoulders and looked up at his father, who had apparently just emerged from the bookroom at the east end of the hall. "Dinna scold Dugald, Papa, for it were nane of his doing. I found a wee gate at the corner o' the garden, leading to the road. I wanted to see if I could get into that park across the way, and I could, so I went in to ha' a look. Are ye vexed wi' me, then?"

"I am," Duncan said sternly. "Come to the bookroom and we will discuss it right now. Had no one given you orders to remain inside this morning?"

Roddy shook his head, surprising Pinkie, until he said, "Mam said she kent I would enjoy playing wi' the bairns, but I didna enjoy it at all, for they was squallin' something fierce, and putting Anna in a fierce mood, so I went out to the garden."

Although Duncan was still frowning when he and his small son retired to the bookroom, Pinkie thought that perhaps Roddy would talk his way out of punishment this time. Nevertheless, Duncan's patience—never great—was wearing thin. She hoped Mr. Terence Coombs would prove to be a conscientious tutor.

According to Rothwell's recommendation, the young man would be exactly right for Roddy, because he was an excellent scholar with a quiet way of speaking that would indicate an even disposition. The adults had high hopes for Coombs, but those hopes dimmed the following morning when the family gathered for breakfast, and Roddy declared his new tutor to be a "blethering, gigot-headed bubblyjock."

"You will listen to him nonetheless, sir, and you will obey him," Duncan said grimly in reply to this blunt opinion.

"I like Coombs," Chuff said when Roddy looked rebellious. "He seems a knowing lad to me. He's a second-year man at Cambridge, after all, Roddy."

"Aye," Roddy said. He looked as if he would like to say more, but after a speculative glance at his father, he subsided, and Mary quickly changed the subject.

Pinkie paid little heed to Roddy or his tutor for the rest of the week, because her own affairs kept her busy. Due to the kind offices of Maggie Rothwell and her many friends, the new residents of Faircourt House received a constant flow of invitations. Thus, each morning after breakfast in the cheerful morning room, the three ladies indulged in the pleasant task of deciding which invitations to accept and which would require a note of polite regret.

Soirees, musical evenings, routs, ridottos, drums, concerts of ancient music, and plays filled their evenings. Invitations also came for breakfasts—which, rather oddly, took place in the afternoon—and for a flattering number of other interesting entertainments. At several of these events, Pinkie saw the tall stranger who had visited Duncan. Twice, when she saw him in the company of a stunningly beautiful girl who looked no older than sixteen or so, she felt a twinge of pique. That the girl seemed nearly as interested in flirting with Chuff did not mitigate that feeling.

Nearly a week after first meeting the tall stranger, Pinkie attended a large, formal dinner party with Mary, Chuff, and Lady Agnes—the sort where one talked only to one's dinner partner and the gentleman on one's left. When the hostess announced after dinner that there were enough couples for dancing in her drawing room if someone would play for them, Pinkie volunteered.

"How kind you are, Miss MacCrichton," her hostess said gratefully. "I promise that I shall find someone else to take your place before long, so that you, too, may enjoy the dancing."

"Thank you, ma'am," Pinkie said, "but do not fret if no one else wants to play. I don't mind doing so in the least."

"You are generous to say so, my dear, but I know better. No more than half an hour, and then you must join the dancers if I have to take your place myself."

Pinkie smiled, certain that the woman, though well meaning, would soon forget in the bustle of looking after those guests who did not choose to dance.

Her hostess drifted away while Pinkie selected music for a country dance and began to play, and Pinkie soon saw her talking with Chuff, Terence Coombs, and the strikingly beautiful young girl she had seen before. Really, she thought, no one deserved to be so pretty. Bad enough were the creature's dark curly hair, huge dark blue eyes, and skin that looked as smooth and silky as cream. Worse was the way her striped lustring gown hugged her exquisite figure, swelling gently upward from her tiny waist to a soft, plump bosom, and swaying seductively below, beneath a hoop almost too wide for dancing. Had she not possessed grace enough for two, she could never have managed it so deftly.

Looking at her music, then back at the girl, Pinkie reached blindly to turn her page and caught the edge instead. The music book tilted and would have fallen over had not a large, firm hand reached out to steady it.

Glancing up in surprise, she saw that her rescuer was the fascinating man who had visited Duncan. As her gaze met his, her body tensed and she missed a note. She could feel her heart beating. Looking quickly back at the music, striving for calm, she managed to murmur her thanks.

"Aye, you're welcome," he said.

Glancing back at him, she saw that his gaze was fixed on the page. He wore a dark-blue cut-back frock coat with fashionably narrow skirts, a velvet collar, and gold-edged buttonholes. His waistcoat was beige, almost skin-colored, with a small floral pattern in pink and lavender. It was also quite short, as she knew the latest mode demanded, and in her newfound knowledge of fashion, she also recognized that he had shunned Frenchification in favor of a wholly English look.

Though she returned her attention to the music, his image remained in her mind's eye and seemed somehow familiar. His dark blue eyes, set deep beneath their shaggy brows, had knitted in concentration as he followed the music with his hand poised to turn the next page. He wore his hair powdered and tied at the nape of his neck with a black ribbon, but his expressive dark brows indicated its true color.

She was aware of him as she had never been aware of a man before. Without looking at him, she felt his presence like a crackling in the very air beside her. A particular vitality emanated from him, an attitude that said standing still was not his way, that he preferred to be up and doing. Again she experienced a sense of being drawn to him, as if he were someone known to her, someone she liked and trusted.

That thought diverted her, and she missed another note. Recovering, she played more carefully, drawing in to herself, trying to pretend he was not there. When the piece was over, he turned the page.

"You play well," he said. "Do you know this one?"

"Aye, I know it, but I do not think it lends itself so easily to dancing as the one after it does," she said. She knew that she ought to point out to him that since no one had properly introduced them yet, they ought not to be speaking, but in view of his kindness in turning her pages, such a reminder seemed churlish. She held her tongue, playing a few bars of the next piece so that the dancers could make ready. Before they all were in place, however, her hostess returned with another young woman at her side.

"Miss MacCrichton, I have just learned that Miss Carlisle twisted her ankle earlier today and would welcome an excuse to avoid the dancing. She has asked me to let her play for the dancers instead, so if you do not mind . . ."

"Not at all," Pinkie said, smiling at Miss Carlisle. "I hope your injury is not a serious one."

"No, no," Miss Carlisle replied, glancing flirtatiously at Kintyre. "The merest twinge, I promise you, but I am afraid that if I dance, I may injure it more, and if I am not otherwise employed, the gentlemen will keep asking me."

"Do you know this air?"

"Oh, yes, I can play anything at all. Is that the one you have chosen? It will do very well, I'm sure. Thank you."

Pinkie stood up and stepped away from the bench to let her sit down, which she did with a great flourish and rustling of silken skirts. Her fingers were sure as she touched the keys, and her competence soon became clear. She played the same few bars that Pinkie had played before, then glanced up, her expression altering ludicrously when she saw that the two of them were alone at the piano.

"But where did he go?"

Pinkie, too, was staring at Kintyre's back as he strode away. He had left them without a word. Clearly, Miss Carlisle had expected him to continue turning pages for her, and was annoyed that he would not. Pinkie was irritated, too. Simple manners might have suggested to Kintyre that he ask her to dance. Everyone else had partners, so there were no other young men standing idle.

Instead, however, his lordship strode across the room

to where the beautiful girl who had danced earlier with
Chuff was talking to an older man. She looked angry, but
Kintyre walked up to her as bold as brass and put his hand
on her arm. Then he turned to the man with her, and
whatever he said to him must have made the other man
angry, too, because he turned and walked out of the room.

"What the devil is Sir Renfrew Campbell doing here?"
Michael demanded, watching with lingering irritation as
the older man walked away.

"He said he came for me," Bridget retorted. "I thought
you had made it plain that I won't marry him, Michael."

"I did."

"Then what madness possessed him to sail all the way
to London—well, to Bristol, at all events—from Poll
Beither Bay, which is what he said he did?"

"Keep your voice down, lass," Michael said. "You do
not want to make a gift of our affairs to everyone in this
room."

"I won't, but is he mad, Michael? I think he must be,
do not you?"

"I expect he has business in London, lassie. If he is here
tonight, it is because he has friends in the beau monde
with entrée to the first circles. Don't bother your head
about him."

"That is easy for you to say. That madman does not want
to marry you. He told me I would be a beautiful addition
to Dunbeither House, a perfect hostess for his friends
and a mother for his children. He makes my skin creep,
Michael."

"Aye, perhaps, but he cannot force you to marry him,
Bridget."

A foppish young man approached, clearly with the intent
of asking her to dance, so Michael left them and wandered

away to look for a terrace or some other place where he could escape the noise for a while. He had been glad to see his sister dancing with MacCrichton earlier, but he could not see that she had made any great impression on the lad, for he had not sought her out again. He had, in fact, spent more time talking to the gentleman she danced with now than to any of the ladies.

Pinkie did not speak to Kintyre again that evening, but as the days and evenings passed, she saw him frequently, and each time the sense of familiarity grew, although she could not imagine where she might have seen him before. He and his sister, Lady Bridget Mingary—for she had quickly learned the beauty's identity—seemed to be present at nearly every social event that the ladies from Faircourt House attended. Kintyre nearly always escorted his sister, but although Chuff and Duncan frequently escorted the ladies of their own household, they were not nearly so consistent in this duty as Kintyre was.

The Saturday night following the dinner party, everyone who was anyone in London attended the ball that the Rothwells gave in Pinkie's honor. Rothwell even managed to present her to the Dowager Princess of Wales, who joined them for dinner along with other noteworthy guests. Lesser persons began arriving afterward.

Standing in the reception line with the Rothwells and her family, Pinkie greeted newcomers as they entered, feeling as if she were doing so in a dream. She did not feel that she really knew any of the guests, even those whom she had met since her arrival in London. Everyone had been kind to her, but she could not help wondering if they would be as kind to the daughter of Red Mag and Daft Geordie. There were moments when she wanted to speak her parents' names aloud in company, just to see what the reaction would be, but she could not do so, of course. Even if she had had the nerve, she would not betray her family so.

Chuff clearly enjoyed London's social life, and had made a number of friends, not least among which was Terence Coombs. Mr. Coombs was among the first of the after-dinner guests to arrive that evening, and Chuff received him with a grin. Later, when the orchestra began to tune its instruments for dancing, and while Pinkie waited for Rothwell to claim her hand for the first dance, she watched the two young men chatting. She wished Chuff were standing beside her, and felt brief displeasure with Mr. Coombs for keeping him from her side. At least, with Chuff, she could talk without worrying that she might say the wrong thing.

"Good evening, Miss MacCrichton."

Pinkie jumped at the sound of the familiar voice, then turned with a quick, involuntary smile of welcome. "Good evening, sir. Have you only just arrived?"

"Aye," Kintyre said. "My sister forgot her reticule and insisted that we return to fetch it."

"I believe that must be quite the longest sentence you have spoken in my presence," she said.

"Is it?"

Feeling unaccustomed heat in her cheeks, she said rue-fully, "I spoke without thinking. I have been trying to keep a guard on my tongue, and I thought I was succeeding, but now I see that it is no such thing. Pray forgive me."

"There is nothing to forgive," he said. "You merely said what you were thinking, after all, and doubtless spoke no more than the truth."

She could feel the energy radiating from him. He appeared to be composed and calm, but when she looked into his eyes, she encountered an intensity that made it hard to look away again. It was as if he were studying her, but she thought she was probably being egotistical even to think such a thing.

Abruptly he said, "Will you dance with me?"

"Now? I mean, they haven't begun playing yet, and moreover, I am engaged to dance the first minuet with Rothwell, because he is giving the ball for me, you see. Chuff—my brother, that is—is to open the dancing with Lady Rothwell. The orchestra will play minuets for the first two hours and then country dances."

"Aye, I know that, but unless you've made yourself a list and promised all your dances, there must be one that you can save for me."

Her lacing suddenly seemed unnaturally tight. "You may have the second minuet, sir, if you want it. I have made no one any promises."

"Then the others are slackers," he said. "I will see you anon, lass."

He walked away, leaving her with strangely mixed emotions. On the one hand, he had seemed so sure of her that she would have liked very much to have told him she had no dances left, but on the other, she would have been disappointed to have had to turn him down. Still, it was arrogant simply to have asked his question and walked off when he'd got his answer. A more civilized man would have stood with her and chatted politely until her partner arrived to claim her hand.

As she watched him, the sense of familiarity twitched again. Since that first day, when she had nearly knocked him down in her haste to know if she had seen Roddy going into Hyde Park, she had spent a good deal of time thinking about Kintyre. That she could know him and not remember him was patently absurd, so she had quickly decided that she did not know him.

When the notion struck her that he bore a slight resemblance to her ghost, she blamed her overactive imagination and Sir Horace Walpole, because soon after that first dinner at Rothwell House she had acquired a copy of Sir Horace's book, *The Castle of Otranto*, and she had been reading it in spare moments ever since. The absorbing tale, full of ghosts and supernatural occurrences, as it was, had doubtless stirred her imagination to see a slight resemblance between Kintyre and her ghost.

Still, she thought, he did have the same craggy features, the same deep-set dark eyes, and beneath all the powder—if his dark eyebrows did not lie—he had the same dark hair. Even so, he was not the same, for her ghost was kind and protective, while Kintyre was arrogant, even rude. If he felt compassion for anything or anyone, she had not seen it. He did keep an eye on his bewitching sister, but that did not count, for it was no more than his duty to look after her.

Rothwell's approach put an end to her musing. He was dressed in the finest French fashion, his black frock coat, white and silver waistcoat, and black velvet knee breeches all laced with gold. In one hand he carried a small filigreed enamel snuffbox. As he took Pinkie's hand to lead her onto the rapidly clearing floor, he tucked the little box into the fob pocket of his waistcoat.

"Are you enjoying your party, my dear?" he asked with a smile.

"Oh, yes, sir. Everyone has been so kind, and it is all quite grand, is it not?"

"It is, indeed," he said, smiling, "but not so grand, Maggie assures me, as your presentation on Tuesday will be, or the ball at Almack's the following night."

"It is kind of her to present me to the queen," Pinkie said.

"You will enjoy it, I expect. Court life can be most amusing."

"Aye, perhaps," she said, thinking how much nicer a day in the Highlands would be, with the sun shining brightly and scores of birds twittering from the trees.

"Do you miss Scotland a great deal?" His tone was sympathetic.

She started. "H-how did you know what I was thinking, sir?"

Rothwell smiled. "Maggie used to look just that way from time to time—her faraway look, I always called it. She would be dreaming of the Highlands."

"But her home is here in London!"

"It is now, but it was not always so, you know." The orchestra began to play music for the first minuet, and Chuff and Maggie joined them in that stately dance.

The pattern of the dance made further conversation difficult, and after the first few steps, others joined them, adding to their set and forming two others.

When the music stopped, as Pinkie and Rothwell turned toward the side of the room where she had last seen Duncan and Mary, Kintyre suddenly appeared right in front of them.

"My dance, I believe, lass."

"Aye, it is," she replied, feeling suddenly shy. Swiftly collecting her wits, she said politely to Rothwell, "Do you know Kintyre, sir?"

"Aye, we've met. His hostess is a friend of my wife's. Are you enjoying the evening, lad?"

"Aye, thank you, sir. Shall we join our set, Miss Mac-Crichton?"

He danced competently, without trying to make conversation, but again she was conscious of that repressed energy. When the music stopped, and he escorted her toward Mary and Lady Agnes, she said impulsively, "Who is your hostess, sir?"

"Her name is Arabella Thatcher. My aunt, Lady Marsali, and my sister and I are all living with her in her house for the Season."

"I think I have met Mrs. Thatcher," Pinkie said thoughtfully. "A sprightly lady who wears rather amazing wigs, is she not?"

"Aye, that's her," he said. "She has silver hair, and when first I met her, she had arranged it in a glorious mass of curls, but when she goes out, she does wear immense, imposing wigs."

Pinkie smiled. "She seems like a kindly woman."

"Aye," he said.

They had reached Mary and Lady Agnes, so Pinkie presented him to them, and as she did, she realized that he and she had still not been properly introduced to each other. He did not seem to mind—if he had noticed—and the lack did not much disturb her either. She hoped, however, that neither Mary nor Duncan would ask her who had presented Kintyre to her. They might not accept such informal behavior as willingly as she did.

He did not approach her again that evening, and she tried to put him out of her mind. Chuff had disappeared with Terence Coombs and one or two others, and she suspected that they had gone in search of the card room. She hoped they had not left the house altogether in search of more lively entertainment.

Sunday passed quietly, but Monday afternoon, while Pinkie and her maid were deciding what articles of jewelry would best complement the dress Pinkie intended to wear that evening to a rout ball at Sefton House, Lucy burst into the bedchamber without so much as a rap on the door.

"Miss Pinkie," she exclaimed, "is he here?"

"Is who here?" Pinkie demanded, but her stomach tightened, for she knew who Lucy meant even before the nursery maid replied.

"Master Roddy's gone," Lucy said. "Mr. Coombs didna come today at ten o'clock, which is his usual time; and, an hour ago, Master Roddy said he would go to the schoolroom to wait. We've just learned that Mr. Coombs still hasna come, though, so Nurse asked me to see that the laddie had not got . . . that is . . ."

"To see if he'd got into mischief," Pinkie said, supplying the words the nursery maid was so clearly reluctant to speak.

"Aye, miss, that's it."

"It does no good to wrap up the words, Lucy. Does anyone know where he might have gone, or when he left?"

"Nay, then, miss, for no one's seen him this past hour. Dugald looked in the back garden, and now he's gone across to the park, but if the laddie went there, he's for it when Himself finds out, for he did tell him he was no to go there without someone older, and there's none who might ha' gone with him."

Turning at once to her maid, Pinkie said, "Doreen, fetch my cloak and one for yourself. We must search for him. And, Lucy," she added sternly, "tell no one else about this until we return. There is no cause yet to alarm the entire household."

"But what if Mr. Coombs comes?"

"Tell him we are displeased with him for being so late."

"But what if Himself asks about Master Roddy?"

"He won't unless Mr. Coombs arrives and tells him he's missing."

"But what if—"

"Lucy, just go back to the nursery. No one is going to ask about Master Roddy, because everyone who matters will assume that he is with his tutor. If Mr. Coombs should arrive, tell him that I have gone to fetch Master Roddy and to await us in the schoolroom. That way no one will fly into the boughs—at least, not until Doreen and I return. If we cannot find him, then we can all begin to worry. I daresay he has only gone for a walk round the neighborhood. He is not stupid, and he knows perfectly well how much trouble he will be in, so he will not do anything too foolhardy—I hope." She added the last two words in an undertone, but Lucy and Doreen heard her, because both nodded fervent agreement.

Leaving the house, Pinkie and Doreen walked briskly down Tyburn Lane to Dean Street, and on past Caldwell's Assembly Rooms, where two years before—or so several people had told Pinkie—the seven-year-old prodigy, Wolfgang Mozart, had performed a concert accompanied by his four-year-old sister. Pinkie and Doreen saw no sign of the un-prodigal Master Roderick, however, and so they continued into South Audley Street till they came to its end.

Crossing Curzon Street, they entered the area known as Shepherd's Market, where long had been held the annual May Fair that gave the area its name. Few coaches ventured into the area, but there were many horses with riders, even more chairs, and a vast number of bustling pedestrians. As Pinkie and Doreen passed the old two-story market house, Pinkie spied their quarry at last.

"There he is!" Without a thought for propriety, she shouted, "Roddy!"

The boy glanced over his shoulder and grimaced with annoyance.

Pinkie put her hands on her hips and glared back at him as best she could through the teeming crowd.

With a resigned shrug, Roddy turned toward them.

Just then a horseman reined his mount near the boy, leaned from the saddle, and grabbed his coat, heaving him from the pavement.

Pinkie screamed.

CHAPTER EIGHT

"Stop him!" Pinkie shrieked. "Oh, pray, stop that man!"

Although she knew that she could never reach Roddy in time, she dashed forward, pushing people out of her way and continuing to shout, hoping that someone would heed her cries. It looked certain, however, that she would be too late. The rider was far ahead, and too many people stood in her way.

Heads turned when she shouted, of course, but no one took a step toward the rider still trying to hoist the boy up and over his saddle.

Roddy was doing his part to free himself, squirming and struggling, all the while yelling, "Let go, you villain, let go!" Indeed, the lad seemed to have wriggled half out of his tight-fitting jacket when the horseman, realizing that he was about to lose him, reached down with his free hand and grabbed one flailing arm.

At that moment, seeming to materialize out of the air, a huge dark gray dog streaked through the crowd, its angry snarl terrorizing all nearby into scrambling out of its way. The horseman looked up, startled by the snarl. He still clutched the back of Roddy's jacket with one hand and an arm with the other. With a look of horror, he tried to kick his horse to action, but the animal also seemed awestruck and pawed the ground instead, teeth bared and eyes growing round and wild.

The dog, looking at least half as large as the horse, leapt then with another snarl, whereupon the would-be kidnapper released Roddy, snatched up the reins, and kicked his horse much harder, making it leap forward at last.

Roddy dropped like a stone and would have fallen hard on the pavement had not the dog twisted with amazing agility to land beside him, allowing him to grab the shaggy fur at its withers to steady himself and land standing.

Pinkie had stopped involuntarily at the first sight of the huge creature, but her surge of relief at Roddy's narrow escape evaporated when the dog twisted from the villain apparently to attack the boy instead. Crying out again, she rushed forward, raising her arms and waving them, hoping to frighten the beast away.

"Dinna fright him," Roddy called to her. "He's gey friendly. See?"

She did see, clearly, for when the lad reached to put his arms around the huge creature's neck, and hugged him, the dog's long pink tongue lapped his cheek.

The dog stood nearly a yard high at the shoulder, the top of its head only inches below Roddy's, its dark eyes wary and watchful. Its head was rather flat on top, its black muzzle long and pointed. Its ears stood erect, but their folded tips and the boy's arm draped across its shoulders softened its otherwise fierce appearance.

Reassured, Pinkie slowed to a more decorous pace.

Glancing back to look for Doreen, she saw the maid moving steadily in her wake through the crowd.

Edging around those now gathered around boy and dog—albeit at a discreet distance—Pinkie would have gone straight up to the pair had not a stout woman grabbed her by an arm and stopped her in her tracks.

"Art daft, girl? That beast will tear ye limb from limb an ye go near it!"

"Nay, then," Roddy said cheerfully. "He'll no harm her. He's friendly, I tell you. He only wanted to keep yon villain from abducting me."

Several voices in the crowd spoke at once. "Abduct you? Was that man not your father, then? Who was he? Who are you, boy?"

Hearing the latter query, Roddy straightened, saying, "I am Master of—"

"He is Master Campbell," Pinkie interjected quickly in a tone loud enough to drown out the boy's more specific reply. Quickly, she freed herself from the woman's grasp and moved to stand beside him, adding, "You must come along home now at once, Roddy, and let your new friend return to his master."

A wiry man dressed somewhat better than most of the crowd said sternly, "Ye be too young to be his mother, mistress. Be ye his nurse or his governess?"

"Neither, sir," Pinkie said. "I am his sister, though, and I will see him safely home again."

"It is his father who should see to him," the man said, drawing a rueful grimace from Roddy.

"I expect his father will agree with you, sir," Pinkie said. "Come along, laddie." She held out a hand, and with a sigh, he took it. When they turned to walk toward Faircourt House, Doreen followed, but the dog fell into step beside them.

"Oh, dear," Pinkie said, observing this. "Whatever shall we do with him?"

Roddy chuckled. "I dinna think that will be our decision to make. Do you think you can force this braw laddie to do anything he doesna choose to do?"

With another look at the huge dog, Pinkie said, "No one could."

"That's true," said Roddy. "He's a grand lad, he is."

Watching Roddy's rescuer trot along beside them, Pinkie agreed. The dog bore itself with distinctly regal elegance.

"I think he's a deerhound," she said, suppressing a tingling sensation as she added, "I . . . I have seen one or two before. Did you see where he came from?"

"Nay, then, how could I? I was gey busy just then, if you will recall."

"So you were," she agreed. "What were you doing in Shepherd's Market?"

"Looking for Mrs. Salmon's Waxworks," the boy said. "Terence said one can see a replication of Charles the First being executed there, and also a lady lying on a bed of state with her three hundred and sixty-five children, all born at one birth. I think that last bit was just more of his blathering, though, and what's more, a man I asked said the waxworks are ever so far from here—in Fleet Street, he said."

"You should not call him Terence," Pinkie said. "He is Mr. Coombs."

"He's no but a fool bletherskate," Roddy said scornfully. "He didna even come the day. I think he and Chuff went over Westminster way to watch the cockfights there. I asked them to take me, but they said I was too young."

"Bless me, don't speak of such a thing to anyone else," Pinkie exclaimed. "Neither of them would do that, and certainly not when Mr. Coombs is supposed to be tending to your lessons. Something must have occurred to detain him, that's all, and in any event, you had no business to leave the house."

"Well, dinna scold me for it," Roddy said sourly. "I expect I'll hear enow without your tuppence added."

His expectation proved accurate, for when they entered the front hall of Faircourt House ahead of their two companions, Duncan was waiting for them in the doorway of his bookroom.

"Where the devil have you been?" he demanded, halting them on the threshold before they were properly inside.

Eyeing him with less confidence than usual, Roddy said, "Shepherd's Market, Papa. I was looking for—"

"What were you thinking, lass," Duncan snapped, taking a step toward them, "to walk in such a place as that without your chairmen or Dugald to protect you?"

Caught off guard at finding his anger directed at her, Pinkie swallowed hard, realizing he would not accept what Roddy had done as justification for her actions if he thought she had behaved improperly, or had put herself or the boy in danger.

She was still trying to think how best to answer when the boy said, "She was looking for me, Papa—she and Doreen both."

Duncan looked beyond them then to where Doreen still stood outside on the step. "Ah, I see," he said, but nothing in his tone gave his listeners reason to think the information had soothed his temper so much as a jot. "You go and wait for me in the bookroom, Roderick. Don't say another word," he added when Roddy drew an audible breath. "This time I will do the talking—all of it—although after I've said all I mean to say, your voice will doubtless be heard throughout the house."

Glumly, Roddy turned away, but a diversion occurred before he had taken a step. Hidden from Duncan until then by Pinkie's wide skirt and the open door, the huge dog stepped forward, inserting itself between its young charge and the man who had dared to threaten him.

"What the devil is that?" Duncan exclaimed, adding in a roar, "Dugald, Peasley, bring some men out here, and get rid of this beast! You there, Doreen, get inside and shut that damned door."

"Wait, sir, he's harmless," Pinkie said hastily as her maid slipped into the hall beside her and closed the door. "At least . . ." She hesitated. Then, gathering her courage in the face of the darkening frown on Duncan's face, she said to Roddy, "I do think we must tell him everything that happened."

Duncan's eyebrows shot upward. "Everything, eh? Very well, you tell me, Pinkie. You, sir, can go into the bookroom as I commanded you to do. Neither that monster nor anything you might say to me will save your skin today."

"Yes, sir," Roddy said with a sigh of resignation. However, when he tried to step forward, the dog moved, too, preventing him from going toward Duncan.

"Bless my soul," exclaimed Mr. Peasley, entering by way of the green baize door at the back of the hall. "Whoever brought that beast in here?"

"He brought himself," Duncan said grimly. "You'll need some stout lads, Peasley, to put him out again."

"No, Papa, you must not put him out. He will do as I bid him, I think."

"Will he, indeed?"

"Aye, he will," Roddy said. Gently laying one hand on the dog's great head, he said confidently, "Lie down, sir."

To everyone's astonishment but the boy's, the dog obeyed.

"The devil," Duncan muttered.

"Bless my soul," exclaimed Mr. Peasley. "But what shall we do with him now, my lord?"

"Please, sir," Pinkie said to Duncan, "I believe he saved Roddy's life."

"*What?*"

"Aye, Papa," Roddy said. "When I was in the Shepherd's Market—"

"I'll hear it from Pinkie," Duncan said sternly. "If you can control that beast so easily, take him out to the mews and command him to take his orders from whichever of the stable lads will agree to look after him. Then bring yourself back to my bookroom without him. Our business together remains to be seen to."

"Yes, sir," Roddy said with another sigh. Touching the dog's head again, he said, "To heel, me laddie. We'll find you some dinner."

When they had gone, Duncan looked expectantly at Pinkie, and she explained what had happened.

"Where the devil was young Coombs whilst all this was taking place?"

"I do not know, sir," she said. "He did not come to the house today."

"I'll deal with him shortly, too. Did you recognize the horseman, lass?"

"No, sir. He was no one I had seen before. I do not believe he can have been following Roddy, so perhaps he merely saw a chance to snatch up a well-dressed child and make off with him."

"You may be right. In any event, I suppose I must be grateful to that monster. Perhaps I should even offer him a home out of gratitude, but how anyone can afford to feed him, I do not know."

Interpreting the comment as a mild jest, Pinkie smiled, but Duncan was not through with her.

"The moment you knew he was missing, you should have told me," he said evenly. "You had no business running off on your own to find him, lass. This is not home, where it is safe enough now for you to wander at will. This is London, and you might as easily have been a target for that villain as the lad was. Do not put yourself in such danger again, or you, too, will know my wrath."

"I won't, sir," Pinkie said meekly.

He nodded dismissal and returned to his bookroom. Not wanting to be anywhere nearby when Roddy joined him there, Pinkie gestured to Doreen and hurried upstairs to prepare for Lady Sefton's rout ball.

How word of the strange rescue swept so quickly through the beau monde, Pinkie would never know, but she and the others from Faircourt House had been at the rout ball no more than twenty minutes before people began to speak of it to her. Since she had said not a word about it to anyone at home except Duncan, among the first to demand explanations had been the countess and dowager.

When Pinkie had explained, Mary said in distress, "It is my fault. I have been so busy with mantua makers and milliners during the day and parties at night that I've scarcely had time for the poor laddie, and Duncan is too busy with his tobacco lords and such like things to pay heed to him as he does at home."

Duncan, rejoining them in time to overhear her, said, "Don't blame yourself or me for the lad's mischief, love. He is old enough to know the difference between right and wrong, and to obey orders when he receives them."

Eyeing him with displeasure, Mary said, "What did you do to him, sir?"

He drew her away to speak privately to her, whereupon Lady Agnes said tartly, "I daresay he thrashed the poor lad. He's a stern man, is Duncan, like his father before him, but Roddy should never have gone into the streets alone. How that tutor of his allowed it, I do not know, nor do I know why your brother does not keep a closer eye on Roddy. How Chuff manages to occupy his time to such an extent that we rarely lay eyes on him from dawn to dusk, I do not know.''

Pinkie did not know either, and she had begun to worry. Not until half an hour later, when she saw him pass through the reception line and enter the ballroom while she was dancing a reel, did she relax. He was with Terence Coombs, however; so, much as she would have liked to scold him, she could not do so. In any case, she was too astonished by his appearance to think about anything else.

At Faircourt House, Mr. Coombs always appeared tidily dressed, without any display of fashionable quirks beyond wearing a powdered periwig. She had noticed that he dressed more fashionably, even foppishly, for evening functions, but Chuff had scorned to follow his example. Both Duncan and Chuff had flatly refused to shave their heads to accommodate fashionable wigs. They simply powdered their hair when necessary, to appear in company, and both had expressed relief upon learning that many younger men had begun defying the stricter dictates of masculine fashion. Many no longer wore wigs at all, except on the most formal occasions.

The moment Pinkie clapped eyes on her brother that night, however, she realized that his opinion of wigs must have altered considerably, for both he and Coombs sported impressive examples of the *perruquier*'s art. Curled and powdered, the elaborate creations made them both look ludicrously top-heavy.

Her partner, a splendidly garbed gentleman whose name she could not recall, murmured, ''Who is that pretty beau with Terry Coombs, I wonder?''

The thought of Chuff, who was nearly as tall as Duncan, as a pretty beau made her giggle, but the description struck her as apt, and she could not help staring. When the music stopped and Chuff and Coombs approached, she abandoned her partner, then found herself at a loss for words.

Preening like any fop, Chuff twirled the quizzing glass attached by a long black velvet ribbon to a button on his waistcoat and said impishly, "Well, lass?"

"Lud, sir," she said, fluttering her fan and simpering in exactly the way she had seen many London beauties flutter and simper, " 'tis such a prodigious age since last I saw you that I had begun to think you must have died."

"Well, I haven't," he said bluntly. "Coombs and I enjoyed a splendid day together, however."

"Rigging yourself out, in fact," she said, nodding. "But I protest, sir, your dress is finer than my own, and it must be quite stiff with all that silver and gold embroidery. Your scent is prettier than mine, too," she added, sniffing delicately.

"It is what the king himself wears," Mr. Coombs informed her with a confiding air and a graceful gesture of the amber cane he carried. A decorated enamel snuffbox and a lacy white handkerchief graced his other hand.

She nearly told them both what she thought of Mr. Coombs for having deserted his charge in favor of a day with Chuff, but she decided to hold her tongue. It would serve the tutor right to face Duncan without warning, and it would not hurt Chuff to learn that his splendid day had resulted in a painful interlude for Roddy. Thus, she said no more than, "Good evening, Mr. Coombs."

Before he could reply, a disturbingly familiar voice said from behind her, "This is my dance, I believe, Miss Mac-Crichton."

Turning to face Kintyre with the firm intention of informing him that it was no such thing, she found herself raising her fan instead and flirting with him over it as she said, "Is it, indeed, my lord?" It was as if someone else had suddenly jumped into her shoes.

He frowned, reminding her uncomfortably of Duncan at his most censorious and in his worst temper, as he said, "Would you deny me, lass?"

"Pay her nonsense no heed, sir," Chuff said with a chuckle. "She is merely practicing the airs and graces she sees other London lasses affecting."

With a squeak of outrage that he would dare accuse her of something she thought more nearly akin to what he was doing, Pinkie turned to give her brother a much-deserved piece of her mind.

"Not now, lassie," Kintyre said, firmly taking her hand and placing it on his forearm. "The music has begun. If we are to find our place, we must go now."

Pressing her lips together, more to keep Chuff from hearing her snap at Kintyre than for any other reason, she allowed him to draw her away from the two younger men before she said, "You take too many liberties, sir. Not only did I not promise this dance to you, but you must know that we have never yet even been properly introduced to each other."

To her surprise, he stopped and turned to face her. "Tell me this," he said, looking directly into her eyes in such a way that a warm tingling sensation shot from her midsection to her toes. "Do you prefer the delicate attentions of painted puppies like that pair we just left?"

"Painted? Surely not, sir." Involuntarily, she looked over her shoulder, trying to see Chuff again. "You must know that one of those men is my brother. He has never worn paint in his life."

"You cannot have looked at his face," Kintyre said. "Never have I seen a droller sight than those two, nor smelled such a reek outside a perfumer's shop. If you do not find rouge and perfumed powder on your brother's toilet table, I shall own myself astonished, though what possessed him to turn himself into such a popinjay I'm at a loss to know. Now, speak truly, lass. Do you doubt me?"

Much as she would have liked to tell him he was mistaken, she could not. Nor did she have to see Chuff again to know that Kintyre was right. Just the thought of what her brother and Mr. Coombs looked like touched her sense of the ridiculous, and she could not help smiling. "Since I must speak the truth," she said, "I will own, sir, that I was so amazed at the sight of them both that I was unable to speak a word. Unfortunately, I fear from the way Mr. Coombs smiled and smirked at me that he, at least, mistook my glance for admiration."

"He preens himself for Bridget, too, but you cannot admire such a coxcomb."

"No, sir." She did not add, though she was thinking it, that if Kintyre wished to do so, he could swallow up Mr. Coombs in one gulp—wig, cane, handkerchief, snuffbox, embroidery, diamond-buckled shoes, and all. Instead, she said, "Are we going to dance?"

"Aye, we are."

The second set of country dances were lively, allowing little chance for conversation, and as he had before, Kintyre no sooner restored her to her family than he disappeared into the crowd, no more to be seen that night.

When Pinkie saw Lady Bridget dancing with Chuff, she knew Kintyre must still be on the premises somewhere, because although Mrs. Thatcher and Lady Bridget's aunt were also present, she had seen enough of Kintyre to be fairly certain that he would not have left the house without them.

A few minutes later, she saw the man who had been speaking with Lady Bridget the last time Kintyre had abruptly left her. He was a pompous-looking older man in a powdered, full-bottomed wig, wearing a bright blue frock coat over an unfashionably long waistcoat of rose-pink flowered satin, and blue breeches. He squinted beneath his bushy reddish brows, as if he ought to wear spectacles, and his lips were thick and pouty, his nose red and bulbous. Pinkie saw him approach Lady Bridget, but her ladyship gave him short shrift, turning away abruptly and moving to rejoin a group of other young persons, including Chuff and Mr. Coombs.

"Who is that gentleman yonder with the long, curly wig?" she asked Duncan when he joined them, bearing punch for Mary and Lady Agnes.

Following the direction of her gaze, he said, "I believe that's Sir Renfrew Campbell, one of the Breadalbane lot. If it's the man I think, he owns a good lot of land on the west coast, near Loch Moidart."

"Is that near Mingary?"

"Aye, not so far away. North about ten or twelve miles, I'd guess, as an eagle would measure it. Mingary is Kintyre's estate. I've seen you dancing with him, lass. Do you fancy him?"

"Bless me, no, sir," she said, appalled that he would think such a thing, yet feeling that tingle again at the thought. "He is far too full of himself to suit me. I daresay he's never thought of anyone's convenience but his own."

Duncan's mobile eyebrows shot upward. "Has he offended you?"

"Oh, no, sir." She was more appalled to think she had led him to suspect that than she had been to make him suppose that she lusted after the man.

Mary said, "We must leave soon, my lord, if we are all to look our best for Pinkie's presentation tomorrow. Do you mean to stand about like a pillar until we depart, or will you deign to dance with your excellent wife?"

He grinned at her. "Since you seem to be wilting here

for lack of any partners, madam, I suppose I must cater to your needs. Come and dance, then.''

She stuck out her tongue at him but drew it quickly in again at the sound of a nearby matron's gasp. Blushing as rosily as any maiden, Mary allowed her grinning spouse to lead her onto the floor, where dancers were forming sets for a cotillion.

Michael left the ballroom immediately after returning Miss MacCrichton to her family, pausing only long enough to be certain that Bridget was dancing and that Cousin Bella and his aunt were keeping a close eye on her. It never took him long at such large social gatherings to find an unoccupied terrace or garden where he could stroll when he grew tired of the noise and confusion. Lady Sefton's ball merited the highest commendation the beau monde bestowed upon its festivities, that of being called a "perishing crush." Nevertheless, a quick turn through the state apartments soon led him to a pair of French doors leading out to the garden.

On the terrace, beneath a bright full moon, he could breathe again. It was far too chilly to draw many others outside, so he knew he would enjoy some measure of peace. He would have liked to ask Miss MacCrichton to dance again, but he dared not. In truth, what he really wanted was to have her outside on the terrace with him, alone. Just the thought of her creamy skin, her beautiful eyes, the pleasant perfume she wore—Groaning, he forced the enticing thoughts from his mind. The last thing he needed was to be putting ideas into a young girl's head that he had no intention of fulfilling. Marriage for him was presently out of the question.

Not only would a wife—any wife—add to his burdens, but he would have little to offer her until he got his affairs in better order. Indeed, he told himself harshly, he was a fool even to think of marriage in the same breath as he thought of Miss MacCrichton. Balcardane had been singularly understanding about his hope for a match between Bridget and MacCrichton. The earl would never understand an approach to Penelope, nor stand for it, for Michael knew he could suggest no good reason for such a match. Moreover, the lady herself had given him no cause to think she would welcome advances from him. Nor should she, under the circumstances.

A few minutes with such thoughts as these for company were sufficient to send him back indoors. With annoyance, he noted that Sir Renfrew had arrived during his absence, but since, for once, the man showed no particular interest in Bridget, he was able to tolerate his presence with near equanimity.

He asked no one else to dance, and was making his way through the crush to his aunt and Mrs. Thatcher when words of a nearby conversation wafted to his ears.

The man said, "They say it was the biggest dog they had ever seen—just leapt out of the crowd to rescue Balcardane's little boy! A miracle, they say it was."

Michael paused, blatantly eavesdropping.

A woman said, "Do they know whose dog it was?"

"No one has the least idea," replied the man. "They say it looked like a giant greyhound, only black instead of gray. If it's really as big as they say, though, you'd think all London would know its master."

Frowning, Michael looked around for Balcardane, but he saw neither the earl nor any member of his party. Even young MacCrichton and his foppish friend Coombs seemed to have taken their leave. Rejoining Lady Marsali and her cousin, he drew up a chair and said, "Have you heard talk of a miracle rescue today?"

"You mean Balcardane's wee son, I expect," Lady Marsali said.. "Of course, we have heard all about it, my dear. Was that not the most wondrous thing?"

"I do not know, ma'am. I've overheard just enough to whet my curiosity."

"Oh, but it was quite amazing," Mrs. Thatcher said. "Apparently, Miss MacCrichton and her maid had gone out in search of the little boy, who had wandered away from home, and they saw him just as some ruffian on horseback tried to make off with him. Miss MacCrichton set up a screech, but it would have availed her nothing had this great dog not leapt from the crowd to save the boy."

"Just how big was this marvelous creature?"

"Goodness, we don't know," his aunt said. "I daresay his size has been exaggerated by now, for they say he stands nearly as high as a man. At all events, it is quite dreadful that someone tried to steal the child, don't you agree?"

"I do, ma'am," he said thoughtfully, "but I want to have a look at that dog."

She smiled fondly. "Well, you did warn us, my dear, that you have some business regarding dogs to attend to here in London, did you not?"

"Aye, ma'am, but not oddly behaved ones. Rather, I have arranged a number of meetings with men who might help me alter the law of exclusive possession, so that our Scottish deerhounds do not become extinct. The reason I am curious about this dog is that it sounds like it might be a deerhound."

"I thought you said there were none in London," she said, surprised. "Indeed, you said there are practically none in all of England."

"That is true," he said with a grimace. "It is also why I believe I must pay a call at Faircourt House first thing tomorrow morning."

"But you cannot," Mrs. Thatcher exclaimed. "Only

recall, sir, that tomorrow is Tuesday, the day of your dear sister's presentation. You cannot abandon her, you know, not when your aunt and I have gone to such trouble to arrange it for her."

"No, I suppose not," Michael said with a sigh. "Will the proceeding take long, do you think, Cousin?"

Complacently, Mrs. Thatcher said, "It may well occupy most of the day, but you will meet any number of influential men, you know—men who doubtless can help you in your quest for information about that very peculiar law. Moreover, I believe Maggie Rothwell means to present Miss MacCrichton at that drawing room, so perhaps you can ask her about the miracle dog."

"An excellent idea," Michael said, his spirits rising considerably.

The rest of the evening passed without incident, since even Bridget agreed that an early night would make the following day's activities more enjoyable. As Michael put out his candle and settled down to sleep, he realized he was actually looking forward to a day at St. James's Palace.

The dream visited him again, long enough to wake him, but since it consisted for once of little more than wandering in a misty wood, searching for the right path, he soon went back to sleep and slept soundly for the rest of the night.

CHAPTER NINE

"Carrots and turnips, ho!"

Awakening to the unnerving female screech from the street directly below his open window just as he had every morning since arriving in London, Michael donned a dressing gown, descended to the breakfast parlor and swallowed a hasty meal. Then he spent the next two hours with Chalmers in the tiny dressing room adjoining his bedchamber, to prepare for the drawing room at St. James's Palace.

He nearly balked at the outset. One look at the tray of implements, tools, potions, lotions, and jewels that Chalmers had set out in preparation for the ordeal made him exclaim, "Is all this really necessary?"

"Aye, sure, it is, laird," Chalmers said, secure for once in his element. "I ha' made a great study of how noblemen must dress for so grand an occasion, so ye should allow yerself to be guided by me if ye dinna wish to offend her majesty. I am told Queen Charlotte be a great stickler for the proprieties, and it will be test enough of her tolerance, I'm thinkin', that ye refuse to wear a proper wig."

"I have seen what you call proper wigs," Michael said disdainfully. "I saw two of them last night that must have stood a foot high."

"I've heard of higher ones, sir, which doubtless ye will see today for yerself. Now, let me just pluck a wee few of yer eyebrows to create a more elegant line."

"Nay, then, you scoundrel," Michael said. "My lines are elegant enough."

"One hesitates to contradict ye, sir, but they are unbecomingly shaggy."

"Have done, Chalmers. Shave me, pare my nails, and do what you will with the powder, but I'll not wear paint for anyone, or perfume my body with roses."

"Sit here, laird," Chalmers said with a sigh, indicating the shaving chair.

At last, shaven and pared, his front hair curled, twisted, and pouffed to a fare-thee-well, Michael was ready to don the voluminous powdering smock so that Chalmers could sift fine white powder over his hair.

When Michael sneezed and protested the clouds of powder, his mentor informed him impatiently that he would not want any black hair showing through the white powder, that he, Chalmers, had his own reputation to consider, and to hold his whisst the noo. With a sigh of ill grace that blew powder all over the dressing table, Michael submitted, and Chalmers bound the long, powdery tresses with a narrow ribbon bow and a black silk bag at the nape of his neck.

In due time, the valet pronounced him ready to put on his court suit. This stunning creation consisted of light brown cut-velvet breeches and coat, and a silk waistcoat bearing an elaborate design of foliage worked in gold to match the coat's embroidered front edges and cuffs.

Michael's long white stockings and neckcloth were fine white silk, and his black shoes boasted golden buckles with tiny diamonds set in them, gifts from Lady Marsali that he had been loath to accept.

The tiny diamond stickpin in his neckcloth had belonged to his father, as had the gold Kintyre signet ring he always wore on his right hand.

"A snuffbox, laird?"

"I do not take snuff," Michael said, picking up his dress sword from the table where it lay.

"Nay, then, am I not perfectly aware o' that?" Chalmers said, helping him adjust the sword belt so the weapon hung properly. " 'Tis hardly necessary for ye to take snuff, sir, only to look as if ye might. 'Tis quite the fashion, ye ken."

"Aye, and why it is I do not know, for with all the hair powder floating in the air, one can sneeze all one wants to without paying out good silver for snuff and snuffboxes. I shall carry that damned cane, because I just might want to clout someone with it, but I'll be damned if I'll wear any of that lot of jewelry you've got lined up on your tray, and you can leave the perfume where it sits, as well."

"Just a dab, laird. Ye'll no want—"

"If I wanted to reek of scent," Michael snapped, "I would rather smell of good Scottish peat or heather, so until someone devises a way for me to do that, keep your odious mixtures to yourself."

"Your hat, sir," Chalmers said, retaining his dignity as he held out the flat chapeau bras that was de rigueur for any gentleman attending a court function.

Taking it, Michael said ruefully, "If the grand folk with whom I shall rub elbows today do not mistake me for a surly barbarian, Chalmers, it will be entirely due to your efforts. I am sorry to be such a constant trial to you."

"Nay then, laird. Ye're nowt o' the sort," Chalmers muttered gruffly.

Leaving him, Michael went in search of his sister and the two older ladies, fully expecting to have to kick his heels for an hour at least. Instead, he found Mrs. Thatcher and Lady Marsali awaiting him in the drawing room, and as he entered, he heard the unmistakable sound of his sister's rapid footsteps descending the stairs.

Turning in the doorway, Michael watched her approach. "I should have carried the quizzing glass Chalmers tried to give me," he said with approval.

"You?" Bridget laughed. "I cannot even imagine it, although you look very pretty today, Michael." She paused, eyeing him with visible expectation.

He could not disappoint her. Smiling, he said, "I would have made great play with the quizzing glass, my dear, but I certainly do not require one to tell you how beautiful you look."

"Very pretty, sir." She turned, fluttering her gilded fan and showing off her court dress, a mantua draped over a petticoat, both of pale blue silk brocaded in a floral pattern with colored silks and silver thread. She wore it over French pannier hoops that swelled fashionably side to side and remained flat fore and aft. Her hair was a mop of ringlets, powdered and adorned with lappets of blond lace like streamers, a multitude of jeweled hairpins, and two short white plumes. "Did you forget your gloves?" she asked him as she folded her fan to smooth her own.

"No, ma'am. I have them tucked under my arm with the damned hat."

Bridget chuckled, clearly in an excellent humor.

Mrs. Thatcher rose to her feet when they entered the room, and said, "You both look quite splendid, so if you are ready to go, we should do so at once. The men will be growing restive outside."

She looked splendid herself in a court dress of maroon and black striped velvet trimmed with gold fringe, and a magnificent pink-powdered wig at least a foot high. The wig bore such a quantity of jewels that Michael wondered how she could hold up her head under the weight. Beside her, Lady Marsali, in a much more conservative dress of yellow ribbed silk, looked her usual elegant self. Her jewelry, he knew, would compare with that of anyone at St. James's.

"We will present a marvelous display," Bridget said with satisfaction.

Michael agreed, but he soon learned that he had underestimated the extent of their display. Outside on the pavement there awaited four elegant sedan chairs, sixteen chairmen, and four footmen. All the men wore matching maroon and black livery, white gloves, and neatly tied, powdered perukes.

"Devil a bit," Michael muttered, "we've become a damned parade."

"Cousin Bella," Bridget said, "I thought you had no menservants."

Mrs. Thatcher laughed merrily, "Bless me, child, they are not mine. I merely hired them for the occasion. I dare swear there will be no footpads lurking betwixt here and the palace, but they will lend us consequence and keep the rabble from annoying us. When my dear husband was alive, we kept our own chairmen, but now that I control my money myself, I spend it only when I want to, on occasions such as this one. Kintyre, do you take the first chair, and we shall take the others."

Michael had assumed they would travel the considerable distance from George Street to St. James's Palace by coach, but he soon learned that many people preferred the convenience of chairs, especially when it came to the courtyard at St. James's, which was smaller than anyone might expect and difficult for coaches to negotiate. The chairmen might not have thought the journey such a treat, of course, but Mrs. Thatcher consistently displayed a generous nature, so Michael assumed that they were well paid.

The nearer they drew to St. James's, the more crowded the streets became. People lined the flagways to watch, making it necessary for the chairmen to carry their burdens into the street along with the usual traffic, slowing every vehicle and horse to a snail's pace. Nonetheless, the crowd's excitement became contagious. Even Michael found himself smiling when a grinning urchin nearly toppled off the curbstone, clapping his grubby hands and waving at the passing parade of chairs.

When they emerged in the courtyard amid dozens of other chairs, Bridget beamed, looking as beautiful as ever he had seen her. Her cheeks were so rosy that he suspected she had rouged them, although nature had made such artifice unnecessary in her case. Nevertheless, she looked wonderful, and he hoped young MacCrichton would be at hand to be impressed.

Unfortunately, the excitement and sense of anticipation that buzzed through the company in the courtyard soon turned to tedium inside. Long lines filled the entryway and corridors, and by the time Michael and his party reached the throne room, he was heartily sick of the ordeal. Bridget had wilted long since, and her unceasing complaints taxed what little patience he had managed to retain.

Mrs. Thatcher and Lady Marsali seemed inured to the tedium, but neither was chatty. The din around them made up for the lack of conversation until they reached the last corridor, when footmen and other royal servants began to demand silence. By the time they reached the doorway to the throne room, the so-called drawing room had begun to feel more like a church service than a social occasion.

At first Michael had paid no heed to the passing time,

but when it began to crawl he began more and more frequently to consult his watch. From then until they reached the throne room, an hour and a quarter passed and the temperature in the palace increased noticeably. As they entered the throne room the chamberlain took their names, waited a few beats, then announced Mrs. Thatcher. She approached the throne first, with Lady Marsali following.

When Michael heard his name and Bridget's, he extended his forearm and she rested one gloved hand on it while she managed her fan and her train with the other. She had practiced the movements before a mirror, and she made them now without hesitation or misstep.

Queen Charlotte proved to be a thin, pale, dark-haired little woman with a large mouth and nose. Michael knew she was at least four years his junior, for she had married King George only four years before at the tender age of seventeen, but he thought she looked much older.

"She looks tired," Bridget murmured at his side while they waited their turn to approach the throne.

"No doubt the hours she has been sitting here would account for that, added to the effort of producing three children in the few years since her marriage," he whispered back. However accurate the comment might be, he knew it was also unfair. The king was ill, and doubtless the queen worried about him.

Lady Marsali shot both Michael and Bridget a look, and they fell silent.

Two minutes later, they had made their bows, backed away from the throne, and an usher was escorting them from the room. It was then that Michael caught sight at last of Balcardane and his family, gathered near the back of the room. They were conversing quietly with Lords Menzies and Rothwell, and their wives. Miss MacCrichton, wearing

a mantua and petticoat of pale green silk trimmed with
silver lace, looked particularly appealing, Michael thought.

When she glanced toward the throne, he managed to
catch her eye. She smiled, but no sooner had she done so
than the usher murmured, "May it please you, my lord,
we must not linger. We do not want to impede the flow,
sir."

Stifling a growl, Michael moved on.

The next moment, he found himself in another hot
corridor, standing in another line, facing another hour or
more of mind-crushing tedium.

Pinkie was sorry to see Michael and his party leave so
quickly, because she was bored nearly to tears. Duncan,
Rothwell, and Menzies—all of whom had the entrée and
therefore were amongst those august persons allowed to
remain with the queen and her courtiers—had been muttering together about tobacco, of all things, and smuggling.
Several unfortunate episodes of the latter had affected the
price of the former, a product in which they had heavily
invested. Pinkie did not understand most of what they said,
and she could not imagine a more boring topic, but their
intense discussion made it nearly impossible for others in
their parties to converse.

A low buzz of chatter was inevitable and acceptable at
any drawing room, but Maggie had warned them all that
the queen frowned upon conversation that grew so loud
as to keep her from hearing the names of those being
presented. Thus it was that, although the others in Balcardane's group addressed brief comments to one another
from time to time, they did no more.

Pinkie had been surprised that the queen had not
deigned to speak to her during her presentation. Charlotte
had nodded her head, a bob more like a maid's curtsy

than the display of regal condescension that Pinkie had expected from the queen. Maggie had explained afterward that Charlotte spoke little English.

"Moreover, she knows practically no one," Maggie added. "The poor thing has been practically shut up the whole time she has been in England. I don't know what the king fears, but she keeps to her children and her household. The women who serve her say she is kind, although Elizabeth Campbell does not approve of her affectations and what Elizabeth calls a stubborn nature. But Elizabeth is stubborn, too," Maggie added with a smile, "so doubtless they simply don't get on well."

Pinkie wished she could ask questions about the queen and the court, or that she had someone her own age to talk to, but although she had met a number of young women, she had met no one she wished to call friend. Most of them, in fact, seemed disposed to be no more than politely friendly. From time to time she wondered if they had somehow learned about Red Mag and Daft Geordie, but if they had, no one had been cruel enough to fling it in her teeth. Maggie generally presented her as Balcardane's ward, which she was, of course. She would remain so for another month, until Chuff came of age and assumed that legal responsibility.

"I wish Chuff could see all this," she murmured to Mary when the gentlemen fell silent for a few moments. "He would enjoy all the pomp and splendor, I think."

"Are you not enjoying yourself?" Mary asked with an anxious frown.

Pinkie smiled, not wanting Mary to think her ungrateful. "How could one not enjoy such an event? I just wish he were here to share it."

"Drawing rooms are for the presentation of young ladies to the queen," Mary said quietly. "Duncan or Rothwell will present Chuff to the king instead, at a levee, just as soon as his majesty enjoys good health again. Moreover,'' she added with a wry smile and a glance in her husband's direction, ''Chuff probably is content to remain quietly at home today. He said he had the headache, did he not? Doubtless he drank too much last evening, with Mr. Coombs.''

''Aye, perhaps,'' Pinkie said, falling silent again. She knew that it was not drink that had put her brother under the weather but rather the confrontation that he and Mr. Coombs had endured that morning with Duncan about their activities the previous day. She knew—and she suspected that Mary did, as well—that before they had left the Sefton party, Duncan had ordered both young men to attend him in his bookroom early the next morning, and that he had been angry with them for abandoning Roddy to his own devices, and thus inadvertently putting him in danger.

The huge dog was still enjoying residency at Faircourt House. Pinkie had visited him that morning while the gentlemen were in the bookroom; and when the family at last returned from St. James's, she waited only long enough to put off her court dress and don a more informal one before visiting him again, only to learn that Master Roddy had been out before her and had taken the dog into the house.

Astonished that apparently no uproar had resulted from this injudicious decision, she hurried back inside and ran the pair of them to earth in Roddy's bedchamber. When she entered the room, she found the boy reclining on his cot against a huge pile of pillows, reading a book. The dog lay sprawled beside him, its head resting on one of the pillows, its long-legged body covering most of the otherwise neatly made cot.

Both of them looked up at her, the dog raising its head and cocking its ears. Apparently deciding that she was friendly, it put its head back down on the pillow with a comfortable sigh and shut its eyes again.

"Roddy, lad, what are you doing with that beast in here?"

Setting aside his book, Roddy grinned impishly. "He's guardin' me," he said, giving his companion's head a pat. "In the event, ye ken, that yon villain tries to steal me again, right out o' the house."

"You," Pinkie said, "are doomed to be hanged, sir. You try that tale on your papa and see if you don't earn a hiding worse than the one you received yesterday."

"And what makes ye so sure I got a hiding, then?"

Surprised, she said, "Did you not?"

Raising his chin in a way that made him look like a miniature replica of his father, he looked her in the eye and said, "That is no affair of yours, lass."

"To be sure, it is not," she agreed, concealing her amusement. "Still, I do not think you ought to keep that dog in here."

"I'll take him back out in a wee while," Roddy assured her.

"Did your lessons go well today?"

Roddy grimaced. "Yon great bletherskate tellt me if I ever split on him again, he'd thrash me fra' here to Christmas. He wouldna take tellin' that I didna split."

"The tow gangs wi' the bucket, laddie," Pinkie said gently, employing a favorite expression of her brother's.

Roddy sighed. "That's what Chuff said. He's no happy wi' me either."

"You did not split on them if that means they think you told Himself that Mr. Coombs went off with Chuff instead of attending to you. Still, you know, it was your adventure that led to his discovering theirs."

"Aye, well, it is still a wheen o' blethers, so lang may his lum reek."

Pinkie chuckled. "Does Mr. Coombs have a chimney that smokes?"

Roddy shrugged, but his eyes glinted with sudden humor.

A single sharp rap accompanied the opening of the door, and a maid said with audible relief, "There you are, miss. I looked high and low till one of the stable lads said to look in the wee lad's bedchamber. What on earth is that great beast doing in here?"

"Master Roddy is just now going to take him back down to the stables," Pinkie said soothingly. "Are you not, my dear?"

"Aye, sure, I expect so," the boy said, making a face at her.

Ignoring it, Pinkie said to the maid, "Why were you seeking me?"

"Lord Kintyre has called, miss. He asked especially for you." The maid blushed, adding, "Her ladyship said I should ask you to come down."

"Heaven bless me," Pinkie said, looking down at herself. "I'm scarcely dressed to receive callers."

"His lordship did say as he has something of import that he wishes to ask you, miss." Blushing even more, the maid avoided her eye.

"Foolish creature, do you think he means to make me an offer? He will do no such thing, so you can take that daft look off your face. And you," she added, turning to the chuckling boy on the cot, "you take that dog to the stables, *now!*"

"Aye, sure, I will," he said, still chuckling. When she continued to look at him, he sighed and swung his feet to the floor, pushing the dog out of his way to do so. The dog looked no more interested in leaving the room than the boy did.

"Shall I go and tell the mistress that you want to change your dress before receiving his lordship, miss?"

"No, thank you," Pinkie said. "He will not want to kick his heels for half an hour, which is what it would be, or more, before Doreen would decide that I was presentable. I shall go down as I am unless her ladyship has other callers."

"No, miss, only his lordship."

"Very well, then. Is my hair tidy?"

Doreen had brushed the powder out of it after the drawing room, smoothing it back from her forehead and temples, then catching up several locks at the back with a blue satin bow, and leaving the rest to hang loose.

"Aye, miss, it looks a treat."

Pinkie thought it more likely made her look like a schoolgirl, especially in the simple blue frock she wore over a demi-hoop; but whatever Kintyre wanted from her, she doubted that he would notice or care what she wore.

On the threshold, she turned back to say, "I am not leaving you to decide when to obey me, Roddy. You come along now, and bring that dog with you."

"Dinna fash yerself; we're coming. Come along, lad."

The dog heaved itself upright, and in the moment before it stepped to the floor Pinkie feared for the cot.

Roddy draped an arm across the dog's shoulders and gestured gallantly with his other hand for Pinkie to precede them. She did so, hurrying down two flights of stairs toward the gallery. At the head of the second flight, she turned back, intending to warn Roddy to take the dog the rest of the way by the service stair, but he had already turned. One hand still rested on the dog's withers.

She smiled, but as she did, the dog stopped, lifted its head, sniffed the air, and turned toward her. Its ears perked up, and its head stretched toward her, its nose still atwitch. Then it charged.

Gasping, Pinkie leapt back, awkwardly grabbing the banister to keep from falling. Her first thought was that the beast had suddenly decided she was an enemy, but it did not even glance her way before it dashed down the stairs. Looking back at Roddy, to see the dismay she felt reflected on his face, she snatched up her skirts and ran down the second flight, hoping she could somehow prevent social disaster.

"Lord, please do not let Himself be in the drawing room," she muttered under her breath. "Better still, send that beast to the kitchen." The thought that the dog might have caught the scent of meat roasting on the spit for dinner cheered her, but seeing a long tail disappear into the drawing room speedily replaced cheer with gloom. A cry of dismay from inside lent wings to her feet.

Under other circumstances her haste would have drawn instant censure from either of the two females sitting with Kintyre. As it was, no one paid her the slightest heed. She skidded to a halt, dumbstruck by the sight that greeted her.

The great dog stood on its hind legs, forepaws pressed against Kintyre's broad chest, its long pink tongue lapping his grinning face as though it were a choice piece of beef.

The earl had not powdered his dark hair. It was brushed smoothly back, and a black ribbon confined it neatly at the nape of his neck. He wore a simple dark riding coat, buckskin breeches, and polished leather riding boots—the English "country look" that had become fashionable everyday town wear for young men. His breeches were fashionably tight, too, molding his muscular thighs and other even more unmentionable parts of his anatomy. But, for once, it was not his blatant maleness or his dress that held Pinkie in thrall.

"Oh!"

Lady Agnes, clutching her breast with one hand, the

other clapped to her mouth, lowered the latter to exclaim, "Bless my soul, but I thought Kintyre was sped! Where did that dreadful beast spring from?"

"From my bedchamber, Grandmama," Roddy said, stepping past the silent Pinkie. "I brought him into the house, but I was taking him back out to the stables just now when, all of a sudden, he leapt away down the stairs."

"He must have caught my scent from the stairway," Kintyre said. "Down, Cailean. Where are your manners, sir?"

Tail wagging, the dog obeyed.

Roddy's eyes widened. "Is he yours?"

"Aye, he is." Kintyre smiled at him. "I can see that you have taken excellent care of him. I thank you for that most sincerely."

"He saved my life," Roddy said simply. "Did he run away from your house?"

"Nay, then, not if you mean from my house here in London. I think he must have run away from his new master, though, and followed me here."

Mary said, "Did you sell him to someone in a nearby town, sir? You should send word to his master that he is here."

"Unfortunately, your ladyship, his master is in Scotland, near Dalmally."

Lady Agnes said bluntly, "He never followed you all that way, sir. 'Twould be impossible."

"One naturally hesitates to contradict you, ma'am," Kintyre said, "but such a thing is not impossible for a deerhound. Their greatest gift is their ability to follow scent on the wind. We were fortunate on our journey in that we encountered no rain, so the conditions were doubtless excellent for his purpose. Moreover, my aunt's Edinburgh house lies near the outskirts of town rather than in its center, and we passed through no other cities before reaching London. Here, of course, he had no way to discern my scent amidst all the others he met. As you doubtless have noticed yourself, London reeks. For that matter," he added with a reminiscent smile, "it is as well that I did not succumb to my man's repeated pleas to douse myself with Hungary water or some other, equally noxious but fashionable potion, or Cailean might not have recognized my scent here today."

" 'Tis fortunate that you arrived whilst he was in the house," Mary said.

Kintyre shook his head. "Fortune had little to do with that, ma'am, unless you count the fortune last evening that let me overhear a particular conversation. 'Twas mention of an enormous dog leaping out of nowhere to save the boy that drew my attention. There are few deerhounds in England, fewer if any in London, and I doubt that any other breed would evoke such a description as the one I heard. I instantly feared that Cailean had run away from the man to whom I sold him, and unfortunately, that appears to be the case."

"You should not have sold him," Roddy said sternly. "Why did you?"

"I have many times cursed myself for it," Kintyre admitted ruefully. "At the time, however, it seemed the only thing to do. The question now, however, is how I am going to get him back to Glenmore. Doubtless the man thinks I've cheated him."

" 'Twould be folly to dash back to Scotland before the Season is done, sir," Lady Agnes said. "You must not think of such a thing. Surely, Glenmore—for I collect that it is the man to whom you sold this animal—will understand that you cannot do such a thing. Send a message by courier, explaining the whole."

"I will do what I must," Kintyre said, casting a puzzled glance at the still silent Pinkie. "First, however, I shall remove him from your household. I can only express again my sincere thanks for your care of him, and hope that he did not cause you any trouble.''

"None at all," Mary said.

"He is wonderful," Roddy said. "May I come and visit him before you take him back to Scotland, sir? Or might he visit us here?''

"You may certainly visit him," Kintyre said, "if your mother approves."

"She will," Roddy said, kneeling to pet the dog.

"He is too large for a house pet," Lady Agnes said.

Mary smiled. "He has excellent manners, ma'am, and we owe him much. Cailean is as welcome here as you are yourself, sir.''

"Thank you," Kintyre said, motioning to the dog, which got gracefully to its feet. "Perhaps, in that case, you will not object if I invite Miss MacCrichton to ride in the park with me tomorrow morning.''

"No objection at all, sir," Mary said, "but you must ask her, you know.''

He faced Pinkie, who still had not spoken. Nor did she speak now. She stood like a marble statue, staring at him.

"Well, lass," he said gently, "will you ride with me?''

"Aye, my lord," she said, so quietly that she feared he could not have heard her. "Aye," she said more firmly. "I would like that very much, sir, thank you.''

"I'll call for you at nine then, if that will suit you," he said.

"Can I go, too," Roddy asked, "and will you bring Cailean?''

"If you like," Kintyre said, his gaze still locked with Pinkie's, "and if your mama does not object."

"She won't," Roddy said confidently.

This time, however, his confidence proved to be mis-placed, because Mary said quietly, "You must first ask per-

mission of your papa, my dear, and do not forget that Mr.
Coombs will be coming to you at ten.''

Roddy muttered under his breath.

Kintyre said, ''Will nine o'clock suit you, Miss Mac-
Crichton?''

With difficulty, she found sufficient voice to say, ''Certainly, sir.''

He had made his leg and departed with the dog at his
side before she could collect her wits. Even then, she could
think of nothing sensible to say to the others, let alone
think how to share her shock with them.

The sight of Kintyre without powder, dressed in simple
clothing and standing beside the great dog, had made her
see in a flash that, contrary to what she had told herself
before, he was the living embodiment of her ghost.

CHAPTER TEN

As soon as she could collect wits enough to invent an excuse to leave the drawing room, Pinkie went in search of Chuff. She found him in his bedchamber, sitting in an armchair in a dark-red silk dressing gown, contemplating the fire with his slippered feet propped on the fender. Looking up at her entrance, he smiled.

Without stopping to consider her words, she blurted, "You'll think I'm mad, Chuff, but Kintyre is my ghost."

"What?" Shifting his feet to the floor with a thud, he turned around in the chair to look at her in astonishment.

"It's the truth, I tell you. He's my ghost come to life. I saw a slight resemblance before, but I thought I had imagined it."

"You're daft, Pinkie. Kintyre's as much a man as any we've met, more of a man than most, in fact."

Pinkie sighed, trying to contain her agitation. "I know this sounds daft, Chuff, and I know full well that he's a man. Still, he's the embodiment of my ghost. I ought to have understood it all when I first saw the dog."

"You ought to have seen what?"

"That Cailean—that's what Kintyre calls him—"

"Hold on a minute," he said. "Begin at the beginning. Are you saying that the dog that's been eating its head off in our stables for the past twenty-four hours belongs to Kintyre?"

"Aye, and that I ought to have seen that it's the same dog that walks with my ghost, but I didn't—not till I saw them together. I knew he was the same breed, but my dog is always at a distance, walking beside a tall man in a kilt. Cailean has always been beside Roddy, so he looked bigger to me. Still . . ."

"That's utter nonsense," Chuff said. "I won't say you imagined your ghost, lass, but you are surely imagining things now."

Silence fell between them, and Pinkie looked at him for a long moment before she said quietly, "You still don't really believe in my ghost, do you?"

"Be sensible, Pinkie," he begged. "When you first spoke of it, you were but a bairn. You had conversations with God, too, when you were distressed. For me to think you'd invented a ghost was only logical. I believe that you believe in it, but that does not alter the fact that Kintyre is no ghost. Moreover, if you believe he is your ghost come to life and have already endowed him with all the virtues you believe your ghost to have, that *is* daft, lass.

"Aye, it would be, if that were what I had done," she said tartly. "I am sorry to have troubled you, sir. I shall leave you to your contemplation."

Turning on her heel, she got as far as putting her hand on the doorknob before he said gently, "Hold now, lassie, dinna go."

She paused, feeling her throat tighten and a burning in

her eyes. A moment later, his hand touched her shoulder and he gently turned her to face him.

"Oh, Chuff, I'm not daft; truly I'm not," she said to his chest.

"Dinna greet, lass," he said, tilting her chin up so she had to look at him.

"Chuff, he looks exactly like my ghost. I didn't see how much before, because his hair was always curled in front and powdered, but today he had it combed smooth and tied back, the way my ghost sometimes wears his. It's just as dark, too, like a raven's wing. And the dog . . . When it's beside him, it's the same dog."

Chuff opened his mouth, then closed it and gave her another hug. "Lass," he said, "maybe it's the dog you've fallen for, rather than the man."

She stiffened. "I am not falling for anyone," she said. "I was wrong about him being arrogant and rude, though, so I mean to ride in the park with him tomorrow, but that's all. It was a shock, seeing them together, nothing more."

"Aye, well, I'm glad to hear it. Terry Coombs says Kintyre is all to pieces, which is the reason that silly lass Bridget keeps flirting with me. Terry says she has to marry well, and she thinks that with my fortune I'd make her a good husband. I paid him no mind at first, because he's besotted with the chit himself, and I vow he's just trying to dissuade competition. I've told him I want none of her, but still he delights in pointing out her faults to me."

"She seems silly and spoiled, but has she really so many faults?"

"Only one that matters," Chuff said with a grin. "The foolish lass would rather talk about herself than about me."

"I don't think you should marry before you've finished at Oxford, Chuff."

"Faith, have you heard me so much as mention marrying?"

"No, but—"

"Well, you'll not, either, so dinna fash yourself."

"I'd better go, so we can both change for dinner," she said. "Mary and I are going with Maggie to see *Macbeth* afterward. I expect you'll be going out, too."

"Aye, if Himself does not forbid it. He was in a rare skin this morning."

"Did you and Mr. Coombs really attend a cockfight yesterday?"

"Who's been telling tales out of school?"

"Roddy said you told him and that he begged to go with you."

"Well, if it is where we went, it's men's business and none of yours," he said severely, "and I shall have a word with Master Roddy."

"Don't scold him, Chuff. Mr. Coombs already threatened to thrash him if he ever again speaks out of turn. Indeed, he thinks you already are at outs with him for the same cause. You need say nothing."

"Terry threatened him? Well, I shall have something to say about that," Chuff said, frowning. "It's no business of his to scold our Roddy."

"He is his tutor," she reminded him.

Chuff dismissed that detail with a gesture. "He'd best not lay a hand on the lad unless he wants to deal with me."

Shaking her head at him, Pinkie left the room and went to change for dinner and the play.

It was midnight before the ladies returned. Pinkie had enjoyed *Macbeth* but thought the evening had otherwise fallen flat. The theater had been full, and the gentlemen in the pit exceedingly merry. Even the farce that followed the play had been amusing, but she was tired, she had seen no one she cared to see, and what conversation she had engaged in had proved quite unremarkable.

Waking early the following morning, she dressed with care, making Doreen fetch numerous articles of clothing before she chose exactly which riding habit to wear. The petticoat and jacket were made of stone-gray broadcloth lined with green silk. The jacket's collar and cuffs matched its lining, and her waistcoat was likewise of matching green silk, embroidered with tiny yellow-centered white daisies.

"It be sharp cold out, miss," Doreen said as she pinned Pinkie's cocked hat in place atop her curls. Handing her her gloves and whip, she added, "I'll carry your cloak downstairs to the hall, so that Dugald will have it at hand for ye."

"Thank you," Pinkie said, taking a last look in the glass and automatically pinching more color into her cheeks. As she pinched, she thought of Lady Bridget Mingary's natural roses. Since Kintyre saw his sister every day, he would scarcely be impressed by cheeks that had an unfortunate tendency to sprout freckles rather than roses or peaches, and required pinching to show color.

She had sent orders to the stable the previous evening before departing for the theater, so all she had to do now was to eat her breakfast and wait for Kintyre.

Chuff and Duncan were alone in the breakfast parlor, and when she entered, the latter was saying grimly, "There have been too many incidents of smuggling this year. The tobacco lords stand to lose a fortune if it continues. It isn't just smuggling, either, but fraud as—Good morning, lass."

As she returned the greeting, both men got hastily to their feet.

"Don't stop talking tobacco on my account," she said.

"I do not understand much about the subject, but perhaps I can learn more by listening."

In truth, she found the subject boring, but she would infinitely prefer that they talk about tobacco than that Chuff tease her—as she knew he might—about riding with her ghost. She did not think he would betray her outright, since he knew that she had not shared her ghost with anyone else in the family, but she did not trust him to keep silent on the subject, either. Even a subtle dig would catch Duncan's attention; and after that, inevitably, the cat would be out of the bag.

Sitting down with them, she helped herself to buttered toast; and when a servant entered, she asked him for a pot of hot chocolate.

Duncan said, "Bring more toast, too. Do you want porridge, lassie?"

"No, thank you," Pinkie said, spooning a dollop of jam onto her plate and replacing the lid on the jam pot.

Chuff said, "I confess, sir, I do not understand it all myself. One thinks of smuggling as bringing goods into the country without paying duty on them, or of selling goods, like whiskey, without paying the government what it thinks is its fair share. But if I understood you, the tobacco never even enters England."

"That's right," Duncan said, "although there are cases of men landing trusses of tobacco on lonely beaches, like smuggled silks, lace, or wine from the Continent. This is more complicated, though. Tobacco lords in England—and Scotland, too—have bonded warehouses to store tobacco that comes here from the colonies on its way to foreign ports. The law, you see, commands that all exports from America pass through the mother country first so the government can collect its duty. The shipper pays it when the product enters the warehouse. Thank you," he said to the servant, who entered, bringing Pinkie's chocolate and another rack of toast.

Chuff, clearly as puzzled as Pinkie was, said, "Do you mean that the colonists have to pay duty even though the tobacco doesn't stay in Britain?"

"They don't, really," Duncan said. "Once the cargo is cleared for the foreign port, the shipper gets his money back. It's called a drawback."

"But if the tobacco barely touches the shore, why must they pay duty on it at all?" Pinkie asked, pouring her chocolate. "Why ever take it off the ship?"

"To keep track of it," Duncan explained. "You see, a shipper can also claim drawback if his ship or just his cargo is lost at sea, so it is important to note the weight of the tobacco at each port of call. The customs collector at Glasgow, for example, passes information about a given cargo on to the collector at Bristol or London, but occasionally a shipper pretends to lose his cargo before it arrives, or else he pays the duty, then falsely clears his cargo for a foreign port and claims his drawback. In both cases, he actually lands cargo in England duty-free."

"How does all that affect investors?" Pinkie asked.

"It affects the price, lass. The man who can sell his tobacco at the lowest price makes the most money. If he does not have to pay the duty, he can sell it for considerably less than the man who must."

"Does no one grow tobacco in England?"

"No one," he said. "James the First disapproved of tobacco, and restricted the landing of all tobacco to the London Custom House, prohibiting altogether the landing of tobacco seed and the planting of tobacco in England and Ireland."

"Not Scotland, though," Chuff said.

"No, we can still grow tobacco in Scotland, but when we ship it to England, we must pay the duty; and our tobacco, like that from the colonies, must pass through an English port before going to a foreign destination, although the port can be Bristol now, not just London. Indeed . . ." He paused, smiling at Pinkie, who had finished her toast and chocolate. "Does all this really interest you, lassie?"

"It does, sir, more than I thought such a subject could. However, I am to ride with Kintyre at nine, so I think I had better ask you to excuse me now. We cannot leave the horses standing too long, because Doreen said that it is cold outside."

"Aye, cold enough to make one suspect that it's winter rather than spring," Duncan said. "You take a good warm cloak."

"I will," she said. "We'd better order hot bricks for the coach tonight, too."

"Certainly, if you like," Duncan said. "Where are you off to tonight?"

Chuff grinned mischievously. "We're all off together, sir. It's Wednesday, after all, and I don't think you'd be wise to let anyone else know you forgot."

Duncan grimaced. "Tonight is that damned subscription ball, is it not? The one that my mother and Maggie have made such a stir about?"

"Aye, at the new assembly rooms. They insist that we must support Mr. Almack because he is Scottish, but I think that's what young Roddy would call a wheen o' blethers. The rooms have become quite popular, according to Terry Coombs, and they've done so entirely without our support before now."

Rising, Pinkie said, "Still you *are* going, aren't you, Chuff?"

Chuff grinned. "Oh, aye, we're all going unless I'm much mistaken."

"Aye," Duncan said soberly, "we're all going, right enough."

The inhabitants of the little house in George Street were also to attend the first subscription ball at Almack's. Having learned from his sister that MacCrichton intended to grace the assembly with his presence, Michael might have greeted the day more happily had it not been for the arrival of the early morning post with two unwelcome letters just as he sat down to break his fast.

The first came from Scotland, and he had a notion of its contents before he broke the seal. He had expected Glenmore's displeasure. He did not expect a threat of legal action. Expressing his suspicion that Michael had purposefully trained the dog to run away, the earl wrote that if he did not instantly make restitution or return the dog, Glenmore would seek action against him in the House of Lords.

The second missive was even less welcome, although it contained only a reminder from Sir Renfrew Campbell that the first of June was little more than a fortnight away. Had Michael, he inquired, considered how he intended to transfer the required sum to Sir Renfrew's account with the Bank of Scotland, in Edinburgh?

Michael had not thought about that, nor could he think of any reason at present that he should tax his brain for the answer to a question that had no answer.

At that moment, he and the subject of Glenmore's letter were alone in the breakfast parlor, for none of his female relatives had yet come downstairs. Cailean lay curled on the floor beneath the table, his head resting on one of Michael's booted feet. The familiarity of the dog's presence stirred an ache in his heart. He did not know what he was going to do, but the thought of parting again with his faithful companion was too much to bear easily.

Despite his depression, Michael arrived at Faircourt House five minutes before the time he had designated. The air was crisp and the breeze wafting up from the Thames icy enough to make his cheeks tingle. Thus, when Miss MacCrichton descended to the hall moments after his arrival, clad in a becoming gray-and-green riding habit that turned her lovely eyes from pale blue to emerald green, instead of paying her a pretty compliment, he said bluntly, "You'll freeze to death."

"I am not as fragile as that, sir," she said, raising her chin. "I grew up in the Highlands, after all. A chilly day stirs no terrors in me."

She looked even smaller than usual, her waist tiny enough to span with his two hands. However, the thought of doing that sent heat coursing through his whole body. Reluctantly pushing the thought away, he said, "There is a very cold wind."

"A breeze," she said. "I put my head out of the window upstairs, and it scarcely mussed my hair."

A gray cocked hat with a small green feather perched atop the tumble of honey-gold curls that spilled over her forehead and around her small, well-shaped ears—ears that clearly would remain exposed to the elements.

"It is quite a sharp wind," he insisted. "Do you not at least possess a warmer hat and a pair of good warm gloves?"

She held out a pair of small cream-colored kid gloves. "I did not stay to put them on, because I knew that you would not want to leave the horses standing, but my gloves are warm, sir, and I have a hooded cloak, as well. Dugald?"

The footman came forward, carrying the cloak, but Michael took it from him. It had green silk lining to match her habit, and he knew the silk would protect her from the wind. He draped it over her shoulders, waited until she had fastened the clasp and pulled on her gloves, then escorted her out to the waiting horses.

Lifting her to her saddle, he watched for a moment to be sure she had a steady seat, then mounted his horse. Turning into Tyburn Lane, they entered the park through the Grosvenor Gate and walked their horses toward the reservoir and the tan and gravel roadway known as Rotten Row.

Morning rides in Hyde Park had become popular with the residents of Mayfair, but the temperature had apparently kept many riders indoors, for the company was small. A single chaise rattled along Rotten Row, and they saw only a few riders near the Serpentine, and a few more in the rugged countryside beyond.

"You did not bring your dog," Miss MacCrichton said quietly.

"Nor did you bring Master Roderick."

She chuckled. "I do not think he even asked for his papa's permission. He knew it was no use, not when his tutor arrives each morning at ten."

"Where was this tutor when Cailean rescued the boy?"

"Off somewhere with my brother, I fear," she said. "You have met him, for he was with Chuff at Lady Sefton's ball."

"That painted puppy! Aye, I know him too well, then. He's been making sheep's eyes at my sister and, if I'm not mistaken, has even sent her posies without identifying himself as the sender."

"It is hard to imagine Mr. Coombs playing secret admirer," she said.

"Aye, perhaps. At all events, Balcardane ought to have dismissed him for his irresponsibility. I certainly would have done so."

She smiled but made no reply. A moment later, she said, "I hope your dog is none the worse for his adventures, sir."

"Not at all," he said. "I did not bring him today because I would have had to watch him in all the traffic. He did amazingly well on his own, but London streets are not safe for animals afoot. When next I call at Faircourt House, I'll bring the chaise. He enjoys riding in it, and I did promise to bring him for a visit."

"Aye, you did, and Roddy is looking forward to renewing the acquaintance."

"Do you go to Almack's tonight?" he asked. Realizing that he had spoken abruptly, he added, "My sister mentioned that MacCrichton means to attend the subscription ball there. I wondered if the whole family would attend."

"Aye, sir, we are all going, for Lady Agnes has insisted that we must."

He nodded. "Cousin Bella is much the same. I doubt that she would agree to dance, unless by some miracle the king himself were to ask her, but she is in alt at the mere thought of lending her presence to this ball."

"I expect she looks forward to watching your sister, sir. Lady Bridget is exceedingly beautiful. I daresay all the gentlemen will want to dance with her."

"Perhaps," he said.

They rode in silence for a time, and Michael found himself wishing for the first time in his life that he had a glib tongue. He knew that it was his place to lead the conversation, that a well-brought-up young lady did not chatter or talk about herself—at least, not to the extent that his sister did. He seemed to recall having more ease with such things when he was at university, but he was sadly out of practice. Doubtless that was one reason he had felt out of place at many of the events to which he had escorted Bridget and the older ladies. Perhaps it had been merely convenient to think that he missed the tranquillity of the Highlands.

He observed that she rode well—so well that she clearly

gave little thought to her horse or her seat. As they rode along the east bank of the Serpentine, she looked into the distance, paying no heed to other people or to the swans on the water.

"It is odd that they call it the Serpentine when it's got only one bend in it," he said, more to break the silence than to hear what she would reply.

She turned her head and smiled. "They say the old queen wanted it to have lots of curves, but the king refused to pay for them. Men generally have their way about such things, do they not?"

"Do they?"

"Well, don't they?"

Despite the inane topic, he felt his mood lightening. "In my household, Miss MacCrichton, men rarely get their way about anything."

"I don't believe you, sir. I cannot imagine anyone ordering you about."

"Not ordering, perhaps, but if you think I am man enough to stand against three women, two of whom have greater fortunes—" He broke off, realizing that he should not speak of such things to her. His tongue simply had taken on a life of its own, which was most unnerving. He had never known a woman who affected him the way this one did. One minute his loins burned for her and he yearned to fling prudence to the winds, the next he wanted to shelter her from the slightest chill.

Her cheeks were red, but he could not tell if it was the result of the icy breeze or if his words had embarrassed her. Then she turned her head and he saw that her eyes were twinkling.

"I am trying to imagine you in such a household," she said.

"It's a matter of widows," he told her.

"Widows?"

"Aye, widows. My aunt and her cousin are both widowed ladies who answer to no one. They are quite independent, you see, and able to do as they please without having to consider the opinions of others."

"I see how it is, sir. They do not seek your advice."

He chuckled. "Not only do they not seek it, Miss Mac-Crichton, they dismiss it when it is offered."

"And you want to be king in your castle."

"I admit that such a picture sounds agreeable," he said, "but, thanks to the disintegration of the clans, too many Highland lords—at least, insofar as being lords of their castles and all they survey—have vanished like ghosts into thin air."

A bird took wing just ahead of them, and his horse shied, momentarily requiring his full attention. When she remained silent, he glanced at her, noting at once that the color in her cheeks had deepened far too much to be accounted for by the weather. She did not look at him, nor did she speak.

"What is it?" he asked. "Have I somehow managed to offend you?"

She shook her head, still not looking at him.

Concerned now, he said as gently as he knew how, "My sister frequently accuses me of having the sensitivity of a stone, but I certainly did not mean to put you out of countenance."

"Truly, sir, it was no doing of yours." She muttered the words, her tone not so much offended as rueful.

"Pull up for a moment," he said, drawing rein. "I cannot tell if you are angry or upset, and I want to know." When she had obeyed, he said, "That's better, or it would be if you would look at me."

She nibbled her lower lip, her eyes still downcast.

"Please," he coaxed, "or has my manner put you off so much that you cannot bear to speak plainly to me?"

She looked at him then, and to his astonishment the twinkle had returned. "Faith, sir, it is nothing that you have done, and nothing in your manner. I find myself quite at a loss, however, because if I tell you what I was thinking, you will think me as daft as my brother does."

"I doubt that," he said, smiling. "You are many things, Miss MacCrichton, but I do not for one moment doubt your sanity."

"Now, I wonder what you mean by 'many things,'" she said. "You do not pay me pretty compliments, so that cannot have been one, and doubtless I'd be wiser not to inquire too closely. Indeed, I suppose I should simply be grateful that you do not—at this present moment, at all events—think me mad."

"If you are attempting to divert me, you will miss your mark. I am a stubborn man," he added, "and furthermore, I do not like seeing you so perturbed. You generally appear even-tempered to the point of placidity."

"Faith, sir, you make me sound like a contented cow."

He chuckled. "I know of no one less cowlike than you," he said. "If I were a man who finds amusement in comparing people to animals, I should more likely compare you to a friendly kitten."

"I don't know that I like that much better."

"Well, it is of no consequence, because in truth I don't think of you as cow or kitten. It is merely that I have not seen you put out of countenance before, and I find that I do not like to see it. Come, lassie, no more diversions. Tell me."

"Very well, since you insist, but I hope you will not repeat it to anyone else."

Evenly, he said, "Do I strike you as a man who indulges in gossip?"

"No, sir," she said, her eyes widening. "Nor did I mean to offend you."

"You did not offend me."

"Well, I shudder to think of what you would do if I should, then. You sounded ready to cut out my liver if I *had* dared think you a gossip."

"Not your liver, surely." He was amused, and it occurred to him that he rather liked not knowing what she would say next. Still, she had not answered his question, and he wanted an answer. He waited.

After a short silence, she sighed. "You will most certainly think me daft. Any sensible man would, and I find you eminently sensible. You see, you resemble a ghost of my acquaintance, and when you said that about vanishing into thin air—"

"A ghost?"

"Yes, sir." She eyed him uncertainly.

"Of your acquaintance."

"Aye, for some years now."

"Oh, so he is not a recent acquaintance, then."

"If you mean to mock me, sir, I think perhaps we had better return to Faircourt House."

"On the contrary," he said. "I want to hear more about this ghost."

"Perhaps we might ride on, however," she suggested. "I am growing chilly."

"Then by all means, let's warm you up. Shall we gallop?"

"Aye, since we are well beyond the Row. No one will mind, and I would like beyond anything to enjoy a good run."

He let her go first, still feeling that need to watch over her, but when he saw that she could ride like the wind, he set off in pursuit, experiencing an exhilaration unlike anything he had felt since boyhood. They rode through the woodland until they could see the gardens of Kensington Palace ahead. When next they drew rein, her cheeks were pink from the exercise and her eyes sparkled with joy.

"Shall we tie the horses to that post for a bit and walk?" he said.

"Aye, if you like."

"I would like you to tell me all about this ghost of yours."

She nodded, and he dismounted, wrapping both sets of reins around his arm while he lifted her from her saddle and set her down beside him. Then he tied the reins to the ring in the post set for the purpose and offered her his arm.

Although he had expected to have to coax the story from her, she told it willingly, explaining that she had first seen the ghost at her brother's estate as a child and had seen it several times since. She did not offer many details, but neither did he ask for them. He just liked to hear her talk, and he did not believe in ghosts. When she had finished, she raised her eyebrows, waiting for his comment.

He said, "So your ghost has a deerhound."

"Aye."

"They are rare," he said. "Had you seen one before?"

"Aye, for Lord Menzies visited Duncan once some years ago, and brought two of his. That was how I learned what breed my ghost dog was, and his lordship told us about the law that only earls and men of higher rank can own them."

"Will you save a dance for me this evening?"

Apparently not seeing the blunt request as a non sequitur, she looked into his eyes and smiled. "Aye, sir," she said quietly. "I'd like that very much."

Neither her manner nor her response startled him as much as his own feelings did. Before now, he had seen no indication that Miss MacCrichton paid him any particular heed, certainly no more than she paid other gentlemen. And he had not meant to stir any particular response. He told himself firmly that he had cultivated her acquaintance only as one means of keeping an ear to the ground, to note any progress in his effort to get MacCrichton to offer for Bridget. But there had not been any progress to note, so he was not persuasive.

Confused by what seemed to be another entity invading both his body—one that wanted to snatch her into its arms and hold her tight—and his mind, which was painting idyllic pictures of a future life with her by his side, he drew himself up short at last. What was he thinking? He had no business to think such things. Indeed, he had no business gazing at her like a moonstruck zany, doubtless leading her to expect an offer he had neither the intent nor the justification to make.

"I had best get you home," he said gruffly. "You must have a good many things to do before the ball, and they will be wondering what is keeping us so long."

CHAPTER ELEVEN

When Kintyre left Faircourt House, Pinkie walked upstairs, trying to imagine what could have happened to
change him so. One moment he had seemed interested
only in hearing about her ghost, the next he had asked if
she would save him a dance at the subscription ball. Then,
oddest of all, he had declared that they should leave, after
which they had ridden back to the house in near silence.

He had changed, she thought. No longer did he seem
as arrogant or as abrupt of manner as he had seemed
before. Even as the thought crossed her mind, however,
she realized that she had just been wondering why he had
so suddenly decided to return her to Faircourt House.
Still, there was a difference, the voice in her head insisted,
even if she could not put her finger on precisely what it
was.

To her surprise, the morning was nearly gone. Doreen
was waiting for her in her bedchamber with barely concealed impatience.

"Is it the yellow dress you'll be wantin' for the assembly tonight, miss? I must know if I'm to have all in readiness for ye betimes."

"Aye, the yellow," Pinkie said, her thoughts still on Kintyre's odd behavior.

"The man who is to do your hair will be ready for ye at four, miss. He's to do their ladyships' heads first. Will ye be goin' out at all this afternoon?"

"No," Pinkie said. "I shall want a bath, though, Doreen, before Monsieur Dupont comes to arrange my hair."

"Nay, then," Doreen protested, "ye'll no be bathing on such a chilly day."

"You can build up the fire and set screens around the bath," Pinkie said. "I smell too much of London air and horses to suit me, and it certainly will not be the first time I've bathed on a cold day."

"You'll catch your death," Doreen muttered.

Pinkie did not reply, and the afternoon sped by in a flurry of preparations and arrangements for the evening. Rothwell and Maggie dined with them, and afterward their entire party went in two coaches to the new assembly rooms in King Street.

Michael tugged at his cravat. After the icy chill outside, the interior of Almack's Assembly Rooms, crowded with people as it was, was damned hot. They had been climbing innumerable stairs from the time they had left his carriage in the too-small courtyard known as King Street, which had proven to be no more than a short, narrow alleyway that butted up against the backside of a club in St. James's Street. Thus, the street had no proper egress. More experienced coachmen than his dropped their passengers at the end of King Street. Others had to turn their vehicles in its narrow confines to get out again.

As he and the others in his party continued up the stairs, he kept one hand cupped under Bridget's elbow, knowing that she had all she could do to manage her wide hoop and long skirts, especially since she kept gaping around at the crowd and at the elaborate decor. Briefly he felt the familiar yearning for fresh air and the Highlands, but then he made up his mind to behave himself and allow Bridget and the older ladies to enjoy the evening.

Cousin Bella, chatting brightly with the Countess of Pembroke, had gone ahead, but Lady Marsali moved in their wake, making her way with greater speed than usual, clearly feeling pressure from those behind them to hurry. Hearing her voice rise lightly above the murmur of the crowd, Michael glanced back and felt a wave of relief when he recognized the Duchess of Bedford walking with her, chattering amiably. The duke, following the two, nodded a greeting, and Michael nodded back, then focused his attention ahead again.

The grand ballroom measured some forty feet by ninety in size and sported gilt columns and pilasters, not to mention glittering medallions on every wall and a host of mirrors and pier glasses that multiplied everything, making the crowd seem larger and yet somehow, at the same time, less pressing.

Bridget said confidingly, "Miss Carlisle told me that these rooms will accommodate seventeen hundred dancers. There is a tearoom, as well, where Mr. and Mrs. Almack will serve supper, and other rooms for lectures and concerts."

Lady Marsali, having parted from the duchess, said, "Don't chatter, dear. Kintyre, escort us to those spindly chairs against that wall, if you will. I do not want to stand any longer than I must, and if we do not claim our chairs at once, there may not be enough to accommodate everyone when the dancing begins."

The din was awful, and the smell none too pleasant, either. Body odors, unsuccessfully masked by heavy, cloying perfumes and laden with more acrid odors from myriad wax candles, stirred a renewed yearning for the fresher scents of the Highlands and the sea. Heather, pine, and peat moss—just the thought of open country blowing fresh with the salty tang of good sea air calmed him again.

The orchestra had already begun tuning their instruments, and soon strains of a grand march sounded above the din and trills of a flute competed with occasional bursts of feminine laughter.

As Lady Marsali took a seat, a light touch on Michael's left arm turned his attention swiftly and firmly from his reveries to the present.

An elegantly dressed young matron said to him with a smile, "Forgive me, my lord." He stared blankly at her for the few seconds it took to remember that she was Lady Molyneux, one of the lady patronesses to whom Cousin Bella had presented him some days earlier.

"Certainly, ma'am," he said, inclining his head as he took in the fact that a familiar-looking, foppish youth accompanied her. "How may I serve you?"

"I beg leave to present Mr. Terence Coombs as a desirable partner for Lady Bridget, my lord. For the grand march, at least, and perhaps for the first minuet."

Michael glanced at Bridget to see that she was blushing rosily. She curtsied to Mr. Coombs, thanked Lady Molyneux prettily, then accepted the young man's arm when he proffered it.

Watching them walk away, Lady Molyneux said with a flirtatious smile, "I thought it would be easier if I presented someone to her, my lord. You were looking thunderous enough to frighten off all but the most intrepid partners, you know."

"Was I, indeed?"

"You were," she said firmly. "You should be dancing also, you know."

"Should I?"

"Yes, indeed." Lady Molyneux gestured imperiously to a young woman who appeared to have been hiding behind her, and said, "May I take the further liberty, sir, of presenting Miss Laura Pettibone as a desirable partner for you?"

"No, thank you," Michael replied curtly. The look of shock on Lady Molyneux's face and the flushed dismay on Miss Pettibone's forced him to collect his wits sufficiently to add more politely, "I am engaged for the march and the first dance, ma'am. I thank you, however, for recalling my attention to their immediacy."

Hastily making his escape, he had the grace to hope that neither lady would note his absence from the grand march, now forming at the center of the room. Glancing back a moment later, however, he saw that Lady Molyneux stood beside his aunt's chair, her gimlet gaze still fixed upon him.

Feeling hard-pressed, he looked around and soon spied Miss MacCrichton talking with Lady Balcardane and the dowager near the wall opposite the one where his aunt sat. Without a second thought, he walked straight across to Miss MacCrichton and said, "You are not engaged for the minuet, are you?"

Turning from the other two, she blushed a little but raised her eyebrows and said, "If that is your notion of the proper way to ask a lady to dance with you, my lord, I cannot wonder why you have not yet found a partner. I take leave to tell you, sir, that your manners leave much to be desired."

"I don't want to dance. That's why I'm here."

"Dear me," Lady Agnes said, regarding him with surprise. "I cannot imagine why one would come to a ball if he does not wish to dance, my lord. I must tell you—quite confidentially, don't you know—that I should be utterly delighted to dance if anyone should be so kind as to ask me. It does seem most unfair that I should have had to wait all this time to visit London, and now, to be thought too old to want to dance—to be expected, in fact, to sit on these tiny chairs against the wall and watch young persons cavorting about— Well, it is just too utterly devastating to one who would much rather be enjoying such terpsichorean delights oneself.

"One would think that Mr. Almack would know as much, too," she went on without so much as drawing breath, "for he's as much a Scotsman as any of us, for all that he's gone and changed his name from MacCall—to please the Londoners, you know, who still think we Scots are a lesser breed of some sort. He cannot be one of those stuffy puritanical Scotsmen, either, or he would never have engaged in such puritanically forbidden pursuits as cards, dicing, and dancing in the first place. So he, of all men, ought to know what great pleasure we Scotswomen take in dancing. Why, when I was a lass, I can tell you, we found many occasions when we would dance the whole night through and think nothing at all about it. Why—"

"Mama Agnes," Mary interjected swiftly, "here is Duncan. I know you must be starving for some supper, as am I," she added in a carrying tone, clearly for her husband's benefit.

"Supper! Why, my dear Mary, we only just finished our dinner an hour ago."

"Nevertheless," the countess said firmly, "since Mr. Almack and his pleasant wife have promised that the supper room will be open from the very outset of the evening and straight on through, so as to accommodate everyone's convenience, I think we ought to take early advantage, don't you? Or we can simply walk about for a bit if you are not quite hungry now. In any event, we can safely leave

Pinkie in Kintyre's care, for I know he will restore her to us safely at the end of the first set."

With a smile at Michael, she bustled her two reluctant charges away, although not before he had encountered an enigmatic look from Balcardane. He made no effort to avoid or interpret it. Neither did he look away until the older man did. When they had gone, he said with relief, "Good, now I can talk to you."

As he guided her to a chair, Pinkie said, "What have you done with your female charges, sir?"

"Bridget is dancing, Aunt Marsali is sitting in a chair yonder, and I don't know where Cousin Bella has got to. Before you send me to find her, however, let me point out that she has been looking after herself quite well for some time."

"I expect that she has, sir, but that does not mean that she or your aunt would reject your protection amidst this crowd tonight."

A smile twitched on his lips, and suddenly he felt better than he had since entering Almack's. "If we are to exchange inquiries about family members," he said, looking into her eyes, "may I ask where your devoted brother might be?"

"He, too, is dancing," she said. "One of the lady patronesses collected him at the outset, saying that she had a desirable partner for him. No one offered to perform the same service for me, however," she added.

"That is my good fortune," he said, thinking that she had spoken sadly.

Her mobile eyebrows shot upward. "Gallantry from you, my lord? You amaze me, particularly since you asked me earlier today to save you a dance and now have announced that you do not wish to dance with me."

"Don't talk nonsense," he said gruffly. "I do want to

dance with you, but not now. First, sit down and talk with me. I must ask your advice about something."

"Now you are certainly flattering me, sir." Nonetheless she went obediently to sit in one of the little harp-backed chairs against the wall and patted the unoccupied one beside her invitingly.

Sitting, hoping the fragile-looking chair would bear his weight, he said, "I rarely offer flattery. I would not offer it to you, in any event, but I would welcome your advice. Indeed, I meant to ask you this morning, but somehow it went out of my head. You see, my sister is much enamored of your brother—"

"You are blunt, sir."

"Don't interrupt. I must be blunt. I have decided that you are one to whom I must speak only the truth, and I feared this morning that . . . Well, that is neither here nor there. You will not accept half-truths or let platitudes sway you, I know, and I doubt that you would respond well to subtle hints, either."

Her eyes crinkled at the corners. "I confess, sir, I cannot imagine you offering anyone a subtle hint. Would you even know how to phrase such a thing?"

"Now you are being impertinent. Must I remind you of my rank and stature?"

She chuckled. "What do you think I can do about your sister's infatuation with my brother, sir? I scarcely know her, and from what I have seen, I doubt that she would listen to me. Surely, you must have more influence over her."

"I do not want you to try to influence her. I am sure you could not."

"Then . . ." Her eyebrows flew upward again. "You want me to influence Chuff—Charles—that is, MacCrichton—to offer for her? I promise you, sir, I could not, and . . . and . . ." She fell silent, looking wretched.

"I think you underestimate your powers of persuasion," he said gently.

She remained silent, her usually forthright gaze avoiding his.

In the same gentle tone, he added, "This is important to me."

She looked at him then, and her tone remained even when she said, "I believe you, sir. I do not think you would ask such a thing of me if it were not prodigiously important to you, but I cannot oblige you."

People walked past, glancing curiously at them, but if she noticed them, she gave no sign. The music of the grand march had changed to that of a minuet, but Penelope paid no more heed to the dancing than she did to the passersby. Her attention was all his, but he saw nothing in her expression to encourage him.

Memory of Glenmore's letter stirred in his mind, presenting him with an image of his reputation lying at his feet like a shredded cloak. How, then, could he ever persuade the members of the House of Lords to alter the law of exclusive ownership? He could think of no credible way to prove that he had not trained Cailean to run, and the charge alone, if it became known in London, would ruin him. His supporters might pity him, but if he were named cheat and disgraced by scandal, most members would laugh or sneer. If Sir Renfrew Campbell learned—

Wrenching his thoughts back to the present, he said urgently, "You must help me. If I cannot arrange an advantageous marriage for her, I do not know what I shall do. Balcardane said that your brother is free to marry where he chooses, and he does not seem to be wholly uninterested in Bridget. Indeed, I have seen signs that he admires her. Surely good marriages have blossomed from smaller seeds than that."

"Even if he were as infatuated with her as she is with

him, sir—and I promise you, he is not—I would not press
him to marry anyone. He is too young.''

"Nonsense," Michael said. "He would be less likely to
fall into trouble if he were safely married. He has been
associating with questionable characters since he first
arrived in town, visiting clubs that he ought not to visit,
allowing himself to be influenced by fops and popinjays.
Marriage would settle him straightaway.''

"Oxford should do that, as well," she said. "His education—"

"He need not give up Oxford. Marriage wouldn't interfere with his studies. Indeed, he might concentrate better
if he had less cause to carouse with his friends. Look, I
know you don't realize how important this is, but you may
believe me when I say that it is, and that . . ." He broke
off when she began shaking her head.

"I believe that you think it of the utmost importance,
sir, but . . ."

She hesitated for a long moment, and when he did not
speak, she looked directly at him. Gathering herself visibly,
she said with a new firmness in her tone, "I do not want
Chuff to marry Bridget. I think she would make him a
dreadful wife. No," she added, putting a hand on his arm
when he would have argued more, "do not urge me to
do what I cannot, sir. I do not want to be uncivil, but I
must tell you that if you encourage her to continue making
such a cake of herself, I will do what I must to protect
him. There, I can be no plainer than that without being
unforgivably rude.''

So sure had he been that he could enlist her assistance
that her blunt refusal rendered him speechless. He felt
sick.

Her hand twitched on his arm, drawing his attention
back to her.

"Are you unwell, sir?" Her expression was anxious.

He fought to keep his voice calm. "I . . . I should not have approached you about this. It was unseemly. I hope you can forgive me." He got to his feet, pictures of ruin swirling darkly through his mind, clouding rational thought.

He did not realize that she, too, had risen until she touched his arm again.

Startled, he said, "I beg your pardon. Did you speak?"

Her lips curved, softened—not a smile, not quite—but the expression eased the darkness in his mind, making it bearable again. "I hope you do not mean to stalk off and leave me here by myself, sir. You have already created a stir by sitting here so long, talking with me."

"Oh." He looked around, aware that people continued to glance their way. He did not know most of them. Probably she did not, either, but doubtless most of them knew who he was, and she. To provide more grist for the always active rumor mills would be unkind. He offered his arm, saying, "Walk with me to the supper room. We'll find someone from your family either there or along the way."

Obediently she took his arm, and they walked silently toward the supper room. Glancing at the top of her head-dress, which was almost level with his shoulder, Michael wished that its cheerful yellow ribbons could lift his spirits.

Shifting his gaze downward, he tried to read her expression. He could not tell if she was distressed or only thoughtful. Then, suddenly, her face cleared, and he saw that her gaze had focused on some point ahead. Following it, he saw Balcardane and his lady strolling toward them.

As they met, a young man approached to ask Penelope to dance. She made her curtsy while Michael exchanged polite remarks with Lady Balcardane, but before she went off with her partner, she smiled at Michael and said firmly, "Do not forget, sir, that you promised to call upon us before noon tomorrow."

Controlling his surprise required effort, but since he could not contradict her in front of her family and her partner, he bowed with what grace he could muster and said, "It will be a pleasure, Miss MacCrichton."

Still smiling, she walked away with her partner, and he turned back to find Balcardane speaking to a plump matron and Lady Balcardane ignoring them while she favored him with a discomfiting, quizzical expression.

"Perhaps, ma'am," he said, searching for the proper words, "you think I should not call at Faircourt House before noon, since I am not a member of your family or a close friend."

Her eyes twinkled. "On the contrary, my lord. We will be happy to see you whenever you choose to call. You may bring your handsome dog if you like, too. I have scarcely heard Roddy talk of anything else since the day Cailean rescued him."

"I'll be happy to bring him, ma'am."

Recalled to duty, he looked for his sister, his aunt, and Cousin Bella. Seeing the latter two sitting where he had left his aunt earlier, chatting with a third matron, he walked over to them and said, "I am going to return to George Street, but I shall leave the carriage, of course. I know you will both keep an eye on Bridget."

Ignoring their astonishment, he walked away, noting sardonically as he left the ballroom that his sister was dancing the cotillion with young Mr. Coombs.

Returning to the house, he spent the next two hours in the drawing room, poring over his accounts, searching for some way to meet his obligations. Cailean lay at his feet, stirring only when he got up to put another log on the fire. He had found nothing helpful two hours later when the three ladies returned from Almack's.

Cousin Bella put her head into the room long enough

to bid him good night, but Lady Marsali and Bridget came right in, perhaps intending to chat for a while.

Bridget said enthusiastically, "Was not Almack's delightful, Michael?"

"You seemed to enjoy yourself," he said, gathering his papers together into a neat stack. Glancing at his aunt, he received a weary smile, enough to tell him that Bridget had done nothing after he left to upset her. "Would either of you like a glass of wine or a posset before you retire?"

"No," Bridget said, answering for both of them. "Why did you leave?"

"Too noisy by half," he said, smiling. "I fear I am not suited to town life."

"Don't tell me you want to go home," she said, appalled at the thought.

"No, no, we'll stay," he said. "How else am I going to find someone worthy of you, my lamb?"

"Well, that is a relief," she said, turning away. "Aunt, you are falling asleep where you stand."

"I confess, I am a trifle sleepy," Lady Marsali admitted.

"You must be exhausted, for a trifle sleepy is how you feel when you awaken to a new day," Bridget said with an impish grin. "Perhaps we'd better go to bed."

Chuckling, Lady Marsali followed her from the room, pausing in the doorway long enough to say good night to Michael.

He replied politely, but when they had gone, dark thoughts threatened to overwhelm him again. Looking thoughtfully at the decanter of wine on the side table, he considered certain benefits of drunken slumber only to reject them. If he sought comfort in the wine, he knew, he might not be presentable in the morning, and he did not intend to miss his appointment. Penelope's smile and the friendly look in her eyes had given him hope that she had reconsidered and would help.

* * *

The following morning at half past ten he presented himself and Cailean at Faircourt House, and the butler showed him right up to the yellow drawing room. To his astonishment, Miss MacCrichton sat there alone.

Dismayed, he said, "I beg your pardon. Your man did not ask me. . . . That is to say, he simply brought me. I did not inquire about her ladyship, although I should have thought . . ." While he was trying to collect his wits, the butler gently disengaged Cailean's leash from his hand, led the dog out, and shut the door.

"Please, sit down, my lord," Penelope said.

"But I cannot remain here alone with you. Where is your maid, at least?"

"Upstairs, where she belongs."

"But she should be here. Good God, Lady Balcardane should be here, or Lady Agnes. Where have your wits gone begging? Where is Balcardane?" He had visions of the earl storming the drawing room to pitch him out into South Street.

"I have not lost my wits, sir. Peasley will take Cailean to visit Roddy. Mary is in her sitting room, and Lady Agnes has gone out to visit a friend. I told them that I wanted to speak to you alone, and they know that I am quite safe with you."

"I doubt that Balcardane or your brother would agree with them."

"Perhaps they would not, but they need not concern us, for neither of them is presently in the house. Duncan is attending a meeting of the tobacco lords at Rothwell House, and Chuff has gone riding with friends."

He made an impatient gesture, saying, "Miss MacCrichton, perhaps you still do not understand London ways.

Your reputation could suffer untold harm if it became known that you had received me in this manner.''

"Do you intend to tell anyone?"

"No, of course I do not, but the servants—''

"You may trust the servants, sir. They are too afraid of their master's temper to risk speaking of things they should not mention. Moreover, they like me and would not willingly do me harm.''

"Even so . . .'' He fell silent when she gestured again to a nearby chair.

"Do sit down,'' she said quietly. "You have helped us. At all events, Cailean has, and therefore I feel an obligation to you. I could not help observing your profound distress last evening when I refused to help you arrange a marriage between your sister and my brother.''

"Then you *will* help!'' Continuing in a rush while he drew up the chair she had indicated and sat down, he said, "You can have no notion how much that means to me, Miss MacCrichton.''

"I can see that it would mean a great deal,'' she said gently, "but I do not want to mislead you. My sentiments regarding such a marriage have not altered.''

"Then, what can you do?'' he asked blankly.

"First, please explain to me why your failure to enlist my help has plunged you into bleak despair. Why is Lady Bridget's marriage of such moment to you? She is quite amazingly beautiful, but she is only sixteen. She can risk three more Seasons before anyone will consider her to be on the shelf, you know.''

"I shall be ruined long before then,'' he said.

"Ruined!''

"Aye, ruined.'' He left it at that, glaring at his shoes, but when she did not encourage him to speak, as most women would have, he looked up again.

She still said nothing, but her expression remained sympathetic, and somehow the silence accomplished what no amount of urging would have. Words began to spill from his tongue.

"It's Cailean, you see, or rather a letter I received from his new owner that fell like the last feather on the horse's back. The man means to sue me. He had not yet received my letter to him, but he believes I trained Cailean to run away. He suggests that he ran home so that I could keep both the money and the dog. Learning that Cailean followed me to London will only make the matter worse."

"How offensive of him," she said. "You would never do such a thing."

"Well, I don't know how you can know that about me, but I would not."

"Can you not set things right with him?"

He sighed. "Doubtless, given time and a chance to speak with him, I could, but that is not all. I sold Cailean to Glenmore to secure money to bring Bridget to London. I had hoped that her marriage to your brother would save my groats, you see. It shames me to admit that now, but you deserve to hear the truth."

"How would Bridget's marrying Chuff save your groats?"

"I owe a debt to Sir Renfrew Campbell that I cannot otherwise pay."

"That horrid man? I have danced with him, and I cannot think you chose your lender well, sir. The way he ogled me made me want to scratch his eyes out."

"I did not choose him," Michael said, his sudden urge to murder Sir Renfrew at odds with an equal urge to smile at the thought of Penelope with feline claws. Maintaining his even tone, he said, "My father, finding himself in urgent need, mortgaged our estates to borrow the money. He expected to repay it long before it came due. Instead, he died, and the only way I can imagine to repay the debt in time is with an advantageous marriage for my sister. Now you know the worst."

"When must you pay him?"

"Before the first of June."

"So soon!"

"Aye." He looked down at his hands, wondering what had possessed him to tell her so much.

She remained silent for a moment before she said, "You know, sir, your sister is not the only member of your family who could marry to advantage."

He looked up again, frowning. "I can think of no one else."

Color tinged her cheeks as she said quietly, "There is yourself."

"Don't be absurd. Who would accept such an offer from a penniless man?"

"You would not remain penniless if you married well," she pointed out. "Moreover, you hold an ancient and honorable title."

"Are you suggesting that I sell myself and my title to the highest bidder?"

"It sounds rather horrid when you put it that way, I suppose, but are you not willing to sell your sister? In any event," she added hastily, "I am sure you need not put it quite that way when you make your offer."

"And do you think the young woman I select will not have men in authority over her who will demand to know what fortune I possess?"

"I expect they will want to know that, but your estates would be clear then, and you *are* an earl, my lord. That must count for a great deal."

"Any sensible guardian would reject such a suit out of hand."

"Not necessarily."

"You don't know what you are talking about," he

retorted harshly. "No competent guardian would allow me instantly to plunder his ward's dowry to pay off my debt. Nor can I imagine any female who would agree to marry me in such circumstances, let alone one with sufficient fortune to be of any use to me."

"I can."

"Can you, indeed? And just who would it be?"

"Any number of females would agree to marry you, I think. I would, myself."

Abruptly he stood and glared down at her. "You are mad, Miss MacCrichton. I have no intention of embarrassing myself by offering for anyone, but if I did, I would certainly not offer for you." Striving to collect what remained of his dignity, he added stiffly, "I thank you for your concern, for I believe it was well meant, and I bid you good day."

He was shaking with anger, but by the time he had stormed out of the house and walked halfway to George Street, he was beginning to wonder if it was she who was mad or he. He did not know the extent of her fortune, or even if she had one.

Realizing the route his thoughts were taking, and feeling utter disgust with himself, he managed to regain sufficient wit to realize something else.

Ruefully, he turned back to collect his chaise and his dog.

Get 4 FREE Books!

We created our convenient Home Subscription Service so you'll be sure to have the hottest new romances delivered each month right to your doorstep—usually before they are available in book stores. Just to show you how convenient the Zebra Home Subscription Service is, we would like to send you 4 FREE Kensington Choice Historical Romances. The books are worth up to $24.96, but you only pay $1.99 for shipping and handling. There's no obligation to buy additional books—ever!

Save Up To 30% With Home Delivery!

Accept your FREE books and each month we'll deliver 4 brand new titles as soon as they are published. They'll be yours to examine FREE for 10 days. Then if you decide to keep the books, you'll pay the preferred subscriber's price (up to 30% off the cover price!), plus shipping and handling. Remember, you are under no obligation to buy any of these books at any time! If you are not delighted with them, simply return them and owe nothing. But if you enjoy Kensington Choice Historical Romances as much as we think you will, pay the special preferred subscriber rate and save over $8.00 off the cover price!

We have 4 FREE BOOKS for you as your introduction to
KENSINGTON CHOICE!

To get your FREE BOOKS, worth up to $24.96, mail the card below or call TOLL-FREE 1-800-770-1963. Visit our website at www.kensingtonbooks.com.

Get 4 FREE Kensington Choice Historical Romances!

♥ **YES!** Please send me my 4 FREE KENSINGTON CHOICE HISTORICAL ROMANCES (without obligation to purchase other books). I only pay $1.99 for shipping and handling. Unless you hear from me after I receive my 4 FREE BOOKS, you may send me 4 new novels—as soon as they are published—to preview each month FREE for 10 days. If I am not satisfied, I may return them and owe nothing. Otherwise, I will pay the money-saving preferred subscriber's price (over $8.00 off the cover price), plus shipping and handling. I may return any shipment within 10 days and owe nothing, and I may cancel any time I wish. In any case the 4 FREE books will be mine to keep.

Name _____

Address _____ Apt. _____

City _____ State _____ Zip _____

Telephone (____) _____

Signature _____

(If under 18, parent or guardian must sign)

Offer limited to one per household and not to current subscribers. Terms, offer and prices subject to change. Orders subject to acceptance by Kensington Choice Book Club.

Offer Valid in the U.S. only.

KN034A

‖‖.‖..‖‖...‖‖.‖.‖.‖.‖.‖..‖‖.‖.‖.‖..‖‖.‖..‖‖..‖

KENSINGTON CHOICE

Zebra Home Subscription Service, Inc.

P.O. Box 5214

Clifton NJ 07015-5214

PLACE
STAMP
HERE

CHAPTER TWELVE

As soon as Kintyre had gone, Pinkie went up to her bedchamber, grateful to meet no one else on the way. She was also thankful that Kintyre had not looked at her while he vented his anger, had not seemed to notice how his fury had dismayed her. He had not seen how her hands shook or known how weak her knees felt.

She had not intended to make such a declaration to him. The words had just tumbled from her lips without thought for consequence. Indeed, she realized, she had not thought at all before speaking.

Her intention had been merely to learn, if she could, why her refusal to persuade Chuff to offer for Bridget had cast Kintyre into black despair. The answer to that question was none of her business,.of course, and in retrospect, she knew it had been improper to pursue it. At the time, however, she had only wanted to help.

Several hours later, when Doreen came to her room, expecting to set out what she would wear for dinner and the evening ahead, Pinkie sent her away, saying that her head ached and she did not want any dinner.

Mary came up next. "Doreen said she fears you are ill, love."

"My head just aches," Pinkie said, avoiding her anxious gaze and hoping Mary would not see that she had been crying. "If you do not mind, I think I would like to stay at home tonight."

"I do not mind in the least," Mary said. "We have all been going at such a pace that an early night will do us good. I do not think Mama Agnes will mind either. She has invited Sir Horace Walpole to dine tomorrow, which I know we shall all enjoy, but if you like, we can stay home afterward, rather than going out. I do hope you are not coming down with anything serious though, my love."

"I am just tired, ma'am. A couple of early nights and I will be my old self again, I'm sure."

Pinkie kept to her room the next day, resting and finishing Sir Horace's novel. By the time she read the last page, she had had a surfeit of supernatural occurrences, none of which seemed at all like one of Mary's episodes of second sight or her own experience with ghosts. Nonetheless, she was able to tell Sir Horace that she enjoyed his story very much.

Their little dinner was a success, and her spirits began to recover, but she was glad that Mary had decided they would not go out afterward. Saturday afternoon, however, when she said that she still did not feel well enough to go out, Mary said, "We can miss Lady Pembroke's musical soiree if you do not feel up to it, but unless you truly feel unable to do so, my love, I believe we must attend Elizabeth Campbell's drum. She has been kind to us, and I think Duncan will expect you to go, for you look quite healthy again. Moreover, I have promised the children we can all drive to Richmond Park tomorrow after kirk, and I am counting on you to go with us. Is there aught amiss that perhaps we should talk about?''

"Nothing of consequence," Pinkie said, assuring her that she would attend the drum, if not the soiree. She realized that she could not avoid the Season's festivities forever. In any case, she doubted that either Kintyre or his sister would attend the drum, which would be a relatively small affair. Lady Pembroke's soiree would appeal more to Bridget's taste, she was sure, because there would be dancing for those who wanted to dance, other musical entertainments for those who did not, and a card room, as well. Pinkie felt certain they would be there, and while she might be ready to face life again, she was not yet ready to face Kintyre.

Sir Renfrew Campbell looked forward to attending Lady Pembroke's musical soiree. He had just learned that Lady Bridget would be a guest, and he intended to meet her in order to pass on some interesting information of which he believed she was unaware.

On the whole, he had been enjoying his stay in London. It was a fine city, full of opportunity for a man of sense and intelligence, and business was good. He had managed to secure a number of new and quite profitable customers for his various enterprises. In time, he would be sending Dunbeither bricks to England, along with the gravel from his pits for paving roads, and pig iron from his bloomeries for the English to refine into steel, wrought iron, or ingot iron. His ships carried other products, as well, some of which—like tobacco—produced income even as they made their way from Arisaig and Glasgow to Bristol or London.

But for two small stumbling blocks, Sir Renfrew would have called himself a happy man. The first of these was his failure to receive an invitation to purchase tickets of admission to the new assembly rooms. He would have liked to do so, if only for the pleasure of watching Lady Bridget dance, and perhaps to secure for himself a few delightful moments of her time. He resented the snub, although he knew it stemmed from simple snobbery and nothing more.

The greater block to his happiness was Bridget herself. That she consistently swore she would have none of him only made the chase more exhilarating, however, and ensured that his victory—certainly inevitable now, with so little time remaining for Kintyre to pay off his debt—would be the sweeter. It was all just a matter of time, however, and he could be patient if he had to be.

He had no intention of confiding his plan for the evening to anyone else, not even to the faithful henchman who sat across the desk from him in the sitting room of the lodgings he had hired since coming to town. Sir Renfrew was unhappily aware that this temporary abode did not suit his stature, but the cost of hiring houses in London during the Season was outrageous, and he was not a man to waste his gelt unnecessarily. So he and Mac-Kellar sat in the dingy room to discuss Kintyre.

Smugly, Sir Renfrew said, "There canna be any way for that lad to repay the old earl's debt, with but a fortnight left till the first of June."

"Nay, then, laird, but I'd no be countin' it done till it is done," MacKellar said thoughtfully. "That man's got powerful acquaintances, I'm thinkin'."

"Who? If ye're talking about Menzies or any o' them other lords he's been talking to, I ken for a fact that he's no been talking anything wi' them but dogs. And if ye're thinking Balcardane might lend him the gelt, ye dinna ken the man. Black Duncan is gey ruthless, he is, and he'll no be giving his own gelt away on a whim."

"But the lass likes young MacCrichton o' Shian."

"Aye, she does, perhaps, but ye can forget about him, for I've a plan to put an end to that."

MacKellar nodded, accepting the existence of the plan and its inevitable success—as well he should, Sir Renfrew thought complacently.

"Now then," he said, "if Kintyre had my intelligence, he wouldna be in the suds he's in. With all that fine forest land, he had only to set up his own bloomery. There is work enough for a hundred furnaces, but he canna bring himself to burn the wood, and in the end that will be his undoing. Nor does he look about him, as I do, and see where his fortune lies. When I control Mingary, MacKellar, things will be different. I will take bounty from the land, from the sea, and from the sky if I can find a way, for I am a man of great vision."

"Aye, laird, there be none tae compare wi' ye."

"Ye're right about that, and when I've taken Lady Bridget for my next wife, there will be none who can stop me. I shall become a man of even greater fortune than what I am now, and when that day comes I'll walk amongst the most powerful men in Britain. I'll even grant them favors occasionally when they please me."

"Aye, laird, they'll be as wax in yer hands, they will."

"They will, indeed," Sir Renfrew agreed, rubbing his hands together.

Sir Renfrew no sooner arrived at Lady Pembroke's soiree that evening than he went in search of Lady Bridget Mingary. He saw Kintyre before he saw any ladies of his family, however, and one look at the earl's forbidding countenance was sufficient to persuade Sir Renfrew to avoid him.

MacCrichton was present with the exquisite Mr. Coombs, but although Sir Renfrew searched for other inhabitants of Faircourt House, he saw none. All to the good, he decided. He did not need Black Duncan in the same room with Kintyre. The presence of either might cast a gloom over Sir Renfrew's little plan.

He bided his time, practicing his charm with several older ladies who seemed to find him amusing. One asked if he would not care to slip away before the dancing and the other musical activities began, to take a hand at whist in the card room, but Sir Renfrew declined. Having another game altogether in mind, he soon took leave of his would-be card partner.

He spied Lady Bridget a quarter hour later, flirting disingenuously with MacCrichton, and the knave appeared to be encouraging her.

"Damn his impudence," Sir Renfrew muttered.

A lady standing near him said brightly, "Did you speak to me, sir? I vow, I have grown prodigiously hard of hearing."

"'Tis the din, ma'am, that makes ye think your ears ha' forsaken ye." Fearing she would demand his escort to a quieter spot, he quickly excused himself and went to see what he could do to separate Lady Bridget from her admirers.

He accomplished this goal with little more than a word in a matron's ear, because a small group of musicians had begun to play for those who wished to dance, and moments afterward, when the matron presented him to Lady Bridget as a desirable partner, the young lady could scarcely refuse him. To have done so would have been the height of bad manners; and since, for the moment at least, Kintyre had taken himself off to sulk or whatever it was he did when he disappeared from the scene at such events, Sir Renfrew had the field to himself.

No more than half a dozen couples had elected to dance, so Bridget kept her voice down when she muttered, "I do not know why you persist in pursuing me, sir. I find it prodigiously annoying, and I wish you would stop."

"Do ye ken how your eyes sparkle when ye're fussed, lassie?"

"I don't care. I wish you would find someone else to admire."

"Ah, but 'tis yourself, lass, who ha' stolen my heart. I could never be contented wi' another in your place."

"You care not a whit for me, sir. You want me only to annoy my brother. If you loved me, you would forgive the debt he owes you in order to secure me, but you do not love me. And although you believe he will give me to you in the end, he will not. Moreover, I intend to marry Lord MacCrichton."

"Ah, but does Lord MacCrichton intend to wed ye, lass? That's the question that I've asked m'self, and the answer I hear each time I ask is, 'I think not.' "

"Lud, sir, how you do go on! You must have seen me enjoying conversation with him a while ago, and so it occurs nearly every time we meet."

"Aye, and I dinna blame the lad, for to be seen wi' such a lovely lassie must put a feather in any man's bonnet. Still, I've heard no word o' betrothals, have I?"

"Well, you will hear word of them, and if not with Mac-Crichton, then with someone even better. There are others, you know, who send me posies and presents, even two who write wonderful letters telling me how much they love me. Any one of them—even those two, though they do not yet reveal their names to me—would please me more than you do, sir. So, I beg you, cast your attentions elsewhere!"

He smiled. "Lassie, I want ye, and I mean to ha' ye."

"I don't want to dance anymore," she snapped. "Take me to my aunt, sir."

"Aye, I'll do that very thing, just as soon as we have a little talk. But we need not dance if ye dinna wish it, lass. We'll slip away before our turn comes to go down the line." True to his word, he whisked her out of the set, not caring in the least that their departure upset the numbers required for the pattern.

When he urged her toward a doorway, however, she dug in her heels. "I want to go back to my aunt, sir. Pray, do not cause me to make a scene."

"I ha' no doubt ye'd make a fine scene, lass, but I want a wee word with ye first. That room yonder looks unoccupied, and we can leave the door ajar if ye're nervous of being alone with me."

"I am not afraid of you," she said haughtily.

He did not reply, waiting until he was certain they had the small parlor to themselves before he said, "I wonder, lass, what ye ken of young MacCrichton."

"Only that I mean to marry him, and that my brother agrees that I shall."

"Ah, but ha' ye no asked yourself why it is your brother thinks MacCrichton would be willing?"

Bridget stiffened. "I should think you, of all people, would know that, Sir Renfrew. It is not as if I have nothing to offer a man. There are others, too, who—"

"Nay then, lass, I never meant that. Ye've your beauty and all, not to mention a fair amount of land if the thing can be pulled off and your brother's debt paid before the date."

"That debt is a nonsense," Bridget snapped. "A man worthy of me would see that in a trice. It was my father's debt. It should have died with him."

"Ah, lassie, and that is why God in His wisdom saw fit to mak' ye a female. Men ha' a broader understanding o' such things. Nonetheless, I wasna speaking of your beauty or portion when I asked if ye kent why MacCrichton might be willing."

"What, then?"

He could see that despite her childlike insistence that

she did not like him, he had succeeded in arousing her curiosity. "It is MacCrichton's weakness that your brother seeks to exploit, lass. Did he no tell ye that?"

She frowned. "What weakness?"

Bluntly, knowing that it would serve no purpose to delay, he said, "His father were daft, that's what."

She laughed. "You are the one who must be daft, sir. Lord MacCrichton is quite a wealthy man, so his father cannot have been daft."

"They called him Daft Geordie," Sir Renfrew said quietly, knowing that calm assurance would gain him more than urgent insistence would.

She looked less sure of herself. "I do not believe you."

" 'Tis true, nonetheless. His mam were known as Red Mag, and as common as dirt, she were. But Daft Geordie married her, with a preacher and all, so there is no question about MacCrichton. He inherited his title and wealth from his uncle, lass, but . . . D' ye ken aught o' how such traits make their way fra' father to son?"

"What do you mean?"

" 'Tis simple enough. A daft man is more like to ha' a daft son than a sane man is, that's all."

"But MacCrichton is not daft."

"Not yet, perhaps," Sir Renfrew said, shaking his head. "O' course, the lad's young yet, so there's no tellin', and even if the daftness passes him by, it might touch his sons and daughters. I'm told it commonly occurs so, in such cases."

"Michael cannot know of this—if it's true and not just your nonsense."

"Aye, sure, 'tis true, and your Michael knows it, right enough. Why d' ye think he lighted on young MacCrichton for ye to wed?"

"Because he is wealthy and his family is powerful enough

to help us," Bridget said instantly. "And because I swore I would never marry you."

"Aye, that all entered in, but I dare swear 'twas the fact that MacCrichton had something to gain as well—alliance with a noble name and property, and also wi' a healthy young woman who has nary a hint o' daftness in her family."

"Michael would not want to add any either, sir. Think of that!"

"Aye, sure, that's true, but he would not be adding it to *his* family, lass, only to MacCrichton's. And they've already got the taint, after all."

Bridget stared at him in dismay, then wrenched away from him and ran from the room. He wondered if she would be foolish enough to broadcast what he had told her to the world at large. It would not matter much to him if she did, but he thought she had more sense—if not common sense, then at least a strong sense of social survival.

Michael was in a bad mood. He had come to Pembroke House only because he felt obliged to escort his little family to the soiree. But at the first opportunity, he slipped away from the festivities to stroll through the nearly empty state rooms, and he had been pacing them now for a good hour.

Not only had having to return to Faircourt House after his scene with Miss MacCrichton—to fetch Cailean and reclaim his chaise—humiliated him even further, but he had been unable since then to think of anything he could do to improve his disastrous position. That she could have made such an offer to him made him want one moment to shake her for her foolishness and the next to shake himself for utter ingratitude. How much more generous could any woman be?

The least he ought to have done was thank her for her kindness, however misspent it was, but he was just as glad that he had not seen her since. If Balcardane ever learned what she had done, heaven knew what the consequences might be, and even MacCrichton could prove a deadly enemy if he thought Michael had tried to take advantage of Penelope.

How dared she, though, he wondered. Such effrontery, such forwardness—had the girl no self-respect? Had she no sense of self-preservation? What could she have been thinking, to offer herself as recompense to him for his "service" to the family? Any service, as she herself had pointed out, had been Cailean's. The thought that the dog might more honorably accept her offer than the master stirred sardonic amusement, then another wave of self-disgust.

"I am truly a villain," he muttered, more depressed than he had thought it possible to be.

"Michael, I have been looking for you everywhere!"

He turned at the sound of Bridget's angry voice, and suddenly his anger more than matched hers. "What the devil do you want?"

Her eyes widened, and she stopped abruptly some feet away from him, her skirts swaying. "I . . . I want to go home."

Whatever she had been going to say to him, he knew that wasn't it, but it suited his mood well enough. "Certainly," he said. "Where are the others?"

"Cousin Bella is playing cards, and Aunt Marsali is discussing literature with Sir Horace Walpole and Lady Ophelia Balterley."

"Do you require my escort to collect them, or shall I order the carriage?"

"The carriage, by all means," she said instantly. "I'll fetch them at once, and we will meet you downstairs in the hall."

She walked away, and he went down to deal with footmen and linkboys, hoping that Bridget would keep to herself whatever temper tantrum she had just aborted. The way he was feeling, if she dared to rip up at him, he might well slap her, something he had never done before in his life.

In the coach, Michael listened in silence while Cousin Bella and his aunt discussed the evening. Bridget, beside him, spoke only to reply briefly when one of the older ladies directed a comment to her.

As the carriage turned into George Street, Lady Marsali said, "I think you must be exhausted, my dears. I know these late nights are turning me into a hag. Perhaps we should consider rusticating for an evening or two."

"As you like, ma'am," Bridget said listlessly.

Cousin Bella exclaimed, "Why, bless my soul, we cannot rest now! Next week is filled with activities. Tuesday is Lady Helen Bray's drum, and Friday we are to attend Lady Molyneux's ball, and then after that—"

"Hush, Bella," Lady Marsali said, chuckling sleepily. "We can talk about all that later. Here we are," she added when the carriage drew to a halt.

Inside the dreary little hall, Bridget said firmly, "Michael, I want to talk to you. It's important."

He nodded. "Come up to the drawing room, then, unless you ladies . . ."

When he paused, Cousin Bella said, "I am for bed, my dears. The rest of you may stay up talking as long as you like."

Lady Marsali only nodded, it apparently requiring her

remaining strength to make her way up the stairs to her bedchamber.

Bidding them good night at the landing, Bridget looked at Michael and said, "I wonder how our aunt manages to keep going out night after night when it seems to be all she can do merely to stay awake."

"She enjoys it," Michael said bluntly, opening the door for her. Candles still burned in several sconces, and he removed one to light others, giving them more light. "What is it that's so important?"

She looked wary, and when she spoke, she did not answer his question, saying instead, "Do you really think she likes town life?"

"Aye, she thrives on it. You must know that by now. Her sleepy ways are merely habit, that's all. Now, out with it. What's amiss?"

She nibbled her lower lip, and he could feel his temper stirring again. Then, in a rush, she said, "Do you know aught of MacCrichton's parents, Michael?"

So that was it. He nodded. "I know enough. What have you heard?"

"That his father was mad and his mother as common as dirt." She paused, but her breast began to heave, and believing she would say more, he kept silent. "Well," she snapped, "is it true? Did you intend me to wed a madman, then to produce mad children? What were you thinking, Michael?"

"First of all, his father was not mad," Michael said, forcing calm into his voice. "Men say that he was slow and a little off, but no one doubted his sanity. He fought for the prince and died in his cause. If he loved a common woman, he is scarcely the first to do so, nor will he be the last. Do you dislike MacCrichton?"

"You know that I like him very much, but I do not know

how you could want me to marry into a tainted family. You
would never do such a thing yourself.''

Realizing he was by no means certain of that, at least
insofar as the MacCrichtons were concerned, he said, ''I
tell you, Bridget, that line is not tainted. I own, one reason
I thought Balcardane—and, indeed, MacCrichton himself—might welcome the arrangement was that others will
react as you have to his parentage.''

''I understand now,'' she said grimly. ''You want me to
marry well, so that you can pay Sir Renfrew Campbell,
and that is all you care about. They called his father Daft
Geordie, Michael! But since my children will never bear
the name of Mingary, you don't care if they are daft, too.
How could you!''

Suddenly feeling perfectly calm, he said, ''I do care,
Bridget, and I truly do not believe the MacCrichton line
is tainted. In fact, if it should produce daft children, they
are more likely, at this moment, to be mine than yours.''

''What?''

''You were right, weeks ago, when you said that it made
more sense for me to marry well than to depend on your
doing so. Indeed, over time, I have come to see that I was
wrong ever to let you consider such a thing. The fact is
that I did not think anyone would accept my suit, but Miss
MacCrichton has said that she will.'' He did not know at
just what moment he had made up his mind, but he felt
certain of his course now. ''I mean to talk to Balcardane
tomorrow, and if he agrees, I will purchase a special license
and marry her at once.''

''You asked her to marry you?'' Bridget's face had turned
white.

He did not reply.

''I see what it is,'' she said. ''Her family knows that no
one else would be willing to overlook her parentage, and
since your affairs are in such a mess—''

"That will do," Michael snapped.

"But you cannot marry her! Her father was crazy!"

"I tell you—"

"No, I'll tell you, Michael. I won't let her have you. I'll tell the whole world about her parents before you can marry her, and then there won't be any point!"

Cold fury washed through him. "By heaven, Bridget," he said, "if you say any such thing to anyone, I swear I will lock you up at Mingary till you are an old woman. Indeed, if you say another word tonight, I will slap you. Go to bed."

Paling at his tone, she obeyed with uncustomary speed. Taking time only to snuff all the candles in the room, he followed her upstairs.

Both Cailean and Chalmers awaited him in his bedchamber. He dismissed the man as quickly as was practical, patted the dog and ordered it to its place on the hearth rug, then went to bed. He doubted that he would sleep much, but after twenty minutes of restless tossing, exhaustion claimed him.

Thick mist closed around him, but he knew the castle he sought must be near. If he did not get lost in these cursed woods, he would come upon it soon. He must. The wonder was that he had not yet stumbled into a tree or fallen into a hole or a pond, for he could see nothing, and the heavy mist deadened all sound.

On the thought, a dark shape loomed before him, halting him in his tracks. It wavered, then grew steadier, more solid, revealing itself as the shape of a young woman. She was dressed in white, but her gown clung to her slender body, lacking fashionable hoops or panniers. He took a step forward, trying to see her face, but all he saw was a tumble of golden curls before the mist swallowed her again.

He strode forward, determined to find her, believing

that nothing could be more important to his happiness, but the faster he moved, the more leaden his legs became. If he remained trapped in the mist, all would be lost. He knew that, but the mist made it impossible even to see where he was putting each foot, let alone what direction he was going or what lay ahead.

Sudden cold touched the arch of his foot, and Michael sat bolt upright in bed, disoriented. It took several moments to realize that it was Cailean's cold, wet nose that had wakened him, that the dog had crawled under the covers from the foot of the bed again. He lay back against the pillows, for once saying nothing to the miscreant, hoping only that the dog had not picked up fleas in his wanderings.

Memory of the dream was rapidly fading. All he remembered was the mist and his fear, and the knowledge that someone else had been in the dream with him, a female in a long white dress, who had slipped away because he had hesitated to follow her. Memory flickered, and it came back to him that he had been searching for the castle but had not found it.

His intention to visit Faircourt House at once suffered a setback when he went down to breakfast, for his aunt and Cousin Bella reminded him that it was Sunday and clearly expected his escort to kirk. Bridget went with them, of course, and her silent, sullen presence irritated him, but it also strengthened his resolve.

It occurred to him then that he had no reason to believe Miss MacCrichton would still be of the same mind as she had been when she had made her generous offer. Despite his desperation, his pride had taken over then, and he had flung that offer back in her face. He had not seen her since their parting on Thursday morning, but he retained a clear memory of her dismay when he had snapped his rejection. If she refused him now, it would be no more than he deserved. The memory was not encouraging, especially now that he realized that her offer meant more to him than just the chance to save his land. Indeed, he still did not know that it would lead to any such thing. He did know, however, that he wanted more than anything on earth to make things right with her.

Accordingly he went to Faircourt House as soon as he thought the day advanced enough for the household to have returned from kirk, but when he asked to see the earl, Peasley informed him that the family had gone to Richmond Park for the day.

Returning Monday morning, he learned that Balcardane expected to be meeting with tobacco lords most of the day, but the earl had left word that he would be happy to receive Kintyre at half past ten o'clock on Tuesday morning. Forced to contain his soul in patience till then, Michael turned his attention back to deerhounds, leaving his sister to his aunt's care and hoping for the best.

CHAPTER THIRTEEN

Pinkie had not slept well for several nights, and Monday night was no different, despite having spent a good portion of it at a concert of ancient music that on any other occasion would have proved soporific. Thus, when sunlight flooded her room late Tuesday morning, she pulled a pillow over her head, muttering, "Go away till I ring, Doreen, and close those curtains."

"Nay, then, miss, I canna do that, for it's nigh onto eleven, and the mistress said to tell ye if ye want yer breakfast before she begins to receive morning callers, ye'd best be getting up. Mr. Coombs and Master Chuff—Lord Mac-Crichton, as I *should* say—took Master Roddy to ride in the park, and Himself be in the bookroom, so if ye want to wear just a simple morning frock, ye can for now."

"No, I'll dress," Pinkie said with a sigh. "If I don't, I shall just have to come back upstairs and do so after I eat."

A rattling at the door interrupted them, and it swung

open to reveal the countess carrying a tray of food. Doreen rushed to take it from her.

"My lady, you should not be carrying such things, and not up them stairs!"

"Hush, Doreen," Mary said with a smile. "I have carried many a tray in my life, and one more will not harm me. Pinkie, dear, you must get up at once."

"I am," Pinkie said, getting out of bed and turning to slip her arms into the soft pink robe that Doreen snatched up to hold for her. "Doreen just woke me."

"I know, for I sent her up myself, and I would not rush you now, love, except that Duncan sent me word that you have a caller."

"A caller? Me?"

"Aye, and since I had told Doreen you could come downstairs in anything you chose, I thought I should come up and warn you to put on something that is becoming to you. Fetch out the pale blue silk, Doreen. Eat your toast, love," she added when the maid hurried to obey.

Selecting a slice of toast, Pinkie said, "Who is the caller?"

"I do not know. Duncan was most mysterious. He told Dugald to say only that someone had called. I did ask Dugald to tell me, but he said he could not, so Duncan must mean to surprise you. Perhaps it is a young man seeking permission to court you, darling. If so, I wonder who it can be, for I have not observed anyone treating you with particular distinction. Can you think who it might be?"

"No one," Pinkie said. The only person she could think of who might possibly even have considered such a thing had stormed off angrily several days before, so it could not be he.

With Mary and Doreen helping, she dressed in record time and hurried back down to the drawing room with the countess in her wake. They entered to find the room empty, but a moment later, Duncan came in, frowning heavily.

When he looked sternly at Pinkie, she felt a shiver of fear and wondered what she had done to vex him. Then his brow cleared, and she began to relax.

"Something has occurred that concerns you," he said quietly, "and I am not certain exactly what I ought to do about it."

She said nothing, and silence reigned for several moments before Mary said, "Pray do not keep us in suspense, sir. What has happened?"

"Kintyre has offered for Pinkie's hand. He says it was her idea."

Pinkie felt heat flood her cheeks, and she could think of nothing rational to say. Both of them were staring at her. Mary looked astonished, Duncan stern and still a little dangerous. She swallowed.

Duncan said evenly, "Is what he says true, lass?"

"I do not know exactly what he told you, sir, but 'tis true enough. I did suggest something of the sort to him."

"Something of the sort?"

"Marriage, then—to me, if he liked."

"Pinkie," Mary exclaimed. "My love, what were you thinking? A young lady must never suggest such a thing!"

Pinkie's gaze was still locked with Duncan's, and she did not respond.

He said, "Kintyre told me some time ago of a debt that he cannot repay."

"So he does not make this offer merely because he feels obliged to spare our Pinkie embarrassment after her improper proposal," Mary said. "I know that he thinks we restored his dog to him, so I could perhaps understand his wish to protect her against her own folly, but . . ." She let her words trail to silence.

"It has nothing to do with the dog," Duncan said. The

harshness of his expression eased, and he flicked Mary a smile before turning back to Pinkie. "He says he told you about that debt, and that in return, you offered yourself in marriage."

"He said it like that?"

"Not precisely," Duncan admitted. "Why did you do it, lass?"

It did not occur to Pinkie to lie to him. She never had. "He said no one would want him when he's in such a fix," she said. "He would like Chuff to offer for his sister, but I knew that would never do, and I told him that I'd not aid him in such an endeavor. I suggested that he might have better luck seeking a wealthy heiress for himself. When he said no one would have him with such a burdensome debt hanging over him, I said that I thought any number would—that I would, myself."

She heard a gurgle of laughter from Mary, but still she did not look away from Duncan.

His dark eyes narrowed. "Did you mean what you said to him, lassie?"

"Aye, sir, I did."

"Do you think you love him, then?"

Pinkie hesitated. "I do not know, sir. He is kind, and I think . . ."

When she paused, trying to find words to express thoughts that were less than half formed, Mary said, "I thought you said he was arrogant, Pinkie."

"He is a nobleman," Pinkie murmured, for once avoiding Duncan's gaze. Then, realizing how that might sound, she added hastily, "That is, he is merely—"

Mary cut her off with a chuckle. "I acquit you of wanting him for his rank, love, so I must assume you see his nobility as reason for his arrogance." Still chuckling, she looked at her husband.

Duncan said, "I don't know, Pinkie. I think it is not a good notion."

"Is Kintyre still here, sir? What did you tell him?"

"I said I would allow him to speak to you," Duncan said. "I made him swear that he will ask you himself if you meant what you told him, and I said he had better not mistake your sentiments. You had better not mistake them, either, lass."

"No, sir."

He went on, "I'll say to you as I've said to Chuff, that you may marry where you choose. I would never force you into a marriage you do not want, but neither will I stand by and watch someone else do that. Be sure of him, lass."

"Aye, sir, I will."

Bustling into the room, Lady Agnes exclaimed, "I have been looking all over the house for you, Mary, and for you, too, Pinkie, my dear, because surely we shall have callers soon, and I could not imagine where you both had disappeared to. This is our day to be at home, after all, and so I think we should be prepared for an onslaught, for we have been out and about these several days past, have we not? Do you like this gown?" she added, turning her wide hoops with sufficient energy to endanger a nearby side table and the oil lamp that sat on it.

"It is a lovely gown, Mama Agnes," Mary said hastily before the older lady could catch her breath and continue to speak. "I believe that you have caught your lace on something, however, for there is a ruffle hanging at the back. Do come with me, ma'am, and let me pin it up for you. Unless, of course," she added with a glance at her husband, "you desire me to remain here with Pinkie, sir."

"There is no need," Duncan said. "I agreed to let him speak to her alone."

Lady Agnes's eyebrows shot upward. "Him? Alone! What

is this? Have I interrupted at an untimely moment? Is some gentleman offering for our Pinkie?"

"Aye, ma'am," Duncan said, "or so it would appear."

"But who? Oh, tell me at once, for I dare swear I've had no notion that such a thing could be in the wind. Not our Mr. Coombs, I should hope. For I must tell you that although I have seen how he looks at you, my dear, I do not think he is the gentleman you should marry. Too full of himself by half, is Mr. Coombs, but I cannot think who else it could be, for no one has shown you a particularity, and—"

"So I thought, myself," Mary interjected, taking the older woman firmly by one arm and urging her toward the door through which she had entered. "Come, ma'am, and I shall tell you everything that I know of the matter. Come to me when he leaves, love," she added, looking back over her shoulder at Pinkie.

Lady Agnes exclaimed, "When he leaves! Bless me, do you mean to say he is in the house even as we speak? Oh, my dear, you simply *must* tell me who—"

The door shut firmly behind them, stemming the rapid flow of words.

Duncan looked ruefully at Pinkie. "Mary will manage her," he said, "and I will arrange matters so that you and Kintyre are not interrupted, but Dugald will remain outside that door whilst he is in here with you. If you need him . . ."

"I won't," Pinkie said firmly. "Are you vexed with me, sir?"

"Not vexed, lass, just concerned and a trifle bewildered. I have no objection to Kintyre as a husband for you, although I do think you know too little of him to be certain of your heart or your good sense. I just hope he is worthy of you."

"He is an earl, sir."

"Aye, and that counts for something. He has land, too, if he can but secure it from his debtor. I've asked around, and it seems that once the land is debt free, he ought to be able to make a go of things easily enough, for he is not a gambler like his father was. Indeed, if he can overturn the law of exclusive proprietorship, his deerhounds may well make his fortune for him. However, his estates are isolated, Pinkie, in the western Highlands north of Mull, on a peninsula called Ardnamurchan. 'Twould be a lonely place to live, I fear."

"I do not require vast companies of people to remain happy, sir, and I do not think you and Mary, or Chuff, will abandon me. Surely, you'd visit occasionally."

"Very well, then, but know that the matter is not yet settled."

He left her alone, and although she felt no fear, she was nervous. Her skin seemed to prickle. When last she had seen Kintyre, he had been furious with her for just suggesting that he might consider marrying her. What had changed his mind?

He came in a moment later. She had not sat down, and as she watched him stride into the room, she felt as if her knees might fail her. He looked larger than life, and he had taken pains with his appearance. His demeanor was enigmatic.

"Miss MacCrichton," he said quietly, "Balcardane has told me that you are still willing to receive my . . . that is, that you are . . ." He paused, watching her, then suddenly blurted, "You must be mad to do this!" His cheeks reddened, and he added hastily, harshly, "I should not have said that. Forgive me. I am an ungrateful wretch, and I hope that you can believe me when I say that I am sorry for it."

"There is nothing to forgive," she said. "Do let us sit down, sir, and talk like sensible people."

He drew a chair up for her near the fire, then another for himself.

She wished that he had worn his buckskins and boots. When he dressed like a London beau and wore powder, she did not feel the same sense of ease with him. He seemed to sense her discomfort, for he shifted his chair farther back.

She waited.

He grimaced ruefully, then said, "I confess, I never could have imagined myself in this position."

Surprised, she said, "You never expected to offer for a lady's hand, sir?"

Amusement lit his eyes, and she realized that she ought not to have mentioned his intention before he did. Such delicate niceties seemed silly under the circumstances, however.

He said, "I did expect to make someone an offer eventually. That's the point. No, don't speak," he added when she opened her mouth. "Before we discuss marriage, I have something else I must say. Thursday morning I was unforgivably rude to you. You meant only kindness, I know, and I behaved like a brute."

"Aye, you did," she agreed, drawing another smile from him. She liked it when he smiled. He did not seem so much like a stranger. "I cannot blame you for your vexation, sir. I know I stepped over the line, saying what I did."

"Perhaps," he said, showing that remorse had not softened his blunt nature. "In any event, I do apologize for behaving as I did, when you meant only kindness. Pray, say that you can forgive me, Miss MacCrichton."

"Willingly, sir," she said.

"Then, if you are still inclined to accept my hand in marriage, you will make me the happiest of men."

He looked earnest, even sincere; and, failing to stifle an involuntary chuckle, she said ruefully, "Now I must apologize, sir. A lady ought never to laugh when a gentleman makes her an offer of marriage. Still, when you speak of being the happiest of men, I cannot help but recall how outraged you looked on Thursday."

"Well, in truth, I can make you no promises of happiness," he said. "I did promise Balcardane that I would make certain you had not changed your mind, however, and I hope that you have not, but we must leave the rest to Fate. I can promise that if you accept me, I will do my best not to disappoint you."

"No woman should ask for more, sir, and I can be content with that. Have you discussed settlements with Himself yet?"

"With Balcardane?" Again laughter sprang to his eyes.

"Aye. I know I am being indelicate again to mention them. They seem to fall within that arcane realm known as men's affairs, but since your need is pressing, perhaps you should not delay. You did tell him about your debt already, I know."

"Aye, and we have discussed the settlements," he said. "I promised to settle as much land in your name as I shall settle on my sister, so in time each of you will own one third of Mingary's forest lands. In return, Balcardane disclosed to me that your fortune is a good deal larger than I had any right to suppose."

"I expect it will become more yours than mine, sir. I know how financial matters generally work between husband and wife."

"So does your guardian, lass. You will retain control over a sufficient amount so as never to be entirely dependent upon your husband. Balcardane insisted upon that, and I quite easily agreed with him."

She was surprised. "I shall have money all my own?"

"You will."

"And you will still have enough to repay Sir Renfrew Campbell?"

"Aye, although a portion of that will come from Balcardane and your brother, if he's willing, and I will repay them in due time."

"Would it not be better to use more of mine and repay the whole at once?"

"Nay, lass. I've my dignity to consider as well as yours, and I've no wish to be so heavily beholden to you or to take more from you than I should. Balcardane is willing to advance me the additional sum I require, and since Sir Renfrew Campbell is here in London, I need only draw on Balcardane's London accounts and hand the money to Campbell. I had wondered how I could manage to get it to him in the allotted time," he added, "since both my banker and his are in Edinburgh."

She smiled. "I think your sister does not count Sir Renfrew's presence here in London an advantage, sir."

"I dared not intervene too aggressively whilst I remained indebted to him. Now, however, I will insist that his unwanted attentions to her must cease."

Silence fell between them, and Pinkie could think of nothing more to say. She wanted to ask questions—about Bridget, about his home in Scotland, about his hopes and plans for a family—but she felt that she should not do so, not yet.

When he stirred as if to take his leave, however, she blurted, "When must we wed, sir?"

"Must?" He frowned. "I thought you were willing."

"I am, sir, wholly willing. I meant only—in view of the debt, you know—that you cannot afford to delay long before the ceremony."

"Not long, no, particularly since none of the money comes to me until after we are wed. If you agree, however, I shall purchase a special license this afternoon and arrange the ceremony for Saturday. That will give you time to make whatever arrangements you want to make, and still allow me a week to repay Campbell.''

She swallowed. Even recognizing his haste, she had not thought the wedding would be so soon, but all she said was, "Where?"

"I thought you would like to be married from this house," he said.

"Oh, yes, I would. I know it has become the fashion here to marry in church, and we have attended Sunday services each week, of course, but I would much rather have the ceremony here at the house."

"Then so it shall be. As to my future plans, other than to repay Campbell as soon as may be convenient to everyone involved, I have made none. My cousin's house is small, but I believe that we can all live comfortably with her until we return to Scotland, which my aunt hopes to do sometime in mid-June. I must warn you, though, that I cannot offer you a bedchamber of your own in George Street unless my sister will agree to share one with my aunt or with Cousin Bella."

Everything had happened so quickly that she had not thought about moving out of Faircourt House. It was on the tip of her tongue to suggest that he could as easily move in there as remove her to his cousin's house, but she dismissed the thought as soon as it formed. He still retained full responsibility for his sister, and a duty to look after his aunt and cousin, as well. She knew that wives frequently slept with their husbands, but it had not occurred to her that she would sleep with Kintyre. It occurred to her now with full force.

"I . . . I do not think you should ask your sister to move, sir," she said, trying to sound matter-of-fact when she felt anything but. The notion of marriage—to Kintyre—was taking on a new light. Lest he again think her forward, she added hastily, "Lady Bridget has not been particularly friendly to me, nor is there reason that she should be. I do not wish to cause her distress if I can avoid doing so."

"Bridget will do as she is bid," Kintyre said evenly.

"I have no doubt that she will obey you, sir. I fear I was thinking only of myself. I will feel far more comfortable if Lady Bridget has no cause for upset."

"You are praying for a miracle, then, but it shall be as you wish," he said. Standing, he extended a hand to her. "Shall we go now and tell the others?"

"Aye." She put her hand in his, and warmth stirred deep within her when his closed snugly around it.

He drew her gently to her feet, and they went to find Balcardane and Mary.

For the next three days, time seemed inconsequential to Pinkie. She went where others told her to go, stood where they told her to stand, and dressed as they told her to dress. Had she been asked a week later what social events had enjoyed her presence during that time, she could not have answered with certainty. Only two events stood out in her mind. One was dancing with Kintyre on Friday night at Lady Molyneux's ball, and the other was that first evening at dinner when Chuff learned of her intention to marry.

"Ye've gone mad," he said angrily, his childhood accent surfacing as it generally did on those rare occasions when his temper stirred. "I ken what it is, though. In your mind, ye're no marrying Kintyre. Ye're marrying your damned ghost. Ye canna see that the pair of them are two separate entities."

Mary and Duncan were present, and Lady Agnes and

Roddy, as well, since the exchange took place at the table. The silence that followed Chuff's outburst was at first the simple silence of surprise, but when it lengthened, Pinkie sensed perilous moments ahead. She avoided Duncan's gaze, and felt grateful when Roddy was the first to speak.

"I dinna think ye should be vexed with her, Chuff. It's a fine thing, for I like Kintyre, and just think! We shall be able to visit Cailean whenever we like."

Thus reminded of the others' presence, Chuff shot Pinkie a rueful glance. The damage was already done, however.

Duncan said gently, "What is this about a ghost?" When no one replied, he added with a familiar, dangerous edge to his voice, "I am waiting."

Pinkie said quietly, "I told Chuff that Kintyre bears a resemblance to a ghost I have seen at Shian Towers."

"When was this?"

"I told him a few days ago."

"And when did you see this ghost?"

"I saw him several times, sir, beginning when I was but a bairn."

To her surprise, he did not instantly declare that she must be daft to imagine she had seen a ghost. Instead, he glanced at Mary, who looked amused.

Duncan sighed. "How clearly did you see this ghost of yours, lassie, and what was he doing when you saw him?"

"I saw him quite clearly, sir, and he was doing different things," she said. "When I saw him outside the castle, he was walking on the hillside near the woods with a big black deerhound that looks . . . looked . . . like Cailean."

"That's not the whole of it, though," Chuff said. "Tell him the rest, lass."

Pinkie shook her head. She could not speak of those earlier times, not with Roddy and Lady Agnes at the table.

Chuff grimaced. "Then I'll tell it," he said. "I shall spare you the details, sir, but Pinkie recalls at least one time, long ago, before we left Shian, when her ghost protected her from harm. She was but a wee bairn at the time, before Mary took us away from our uncle."

"Aye, I remember," Duncan said.

"You see, sir, I fear that she has seen enough of a resemblance between her ghost and Kintyre that she has endowed him with the same attributes that she believes her ghost to possess, and thus she thinks she's in love with him."

Duncan looked at Pinkie. "Is that true, lassie?"

"I don't think so," she said. "I cannot be sure, of course, but I do not think I am in love with him, or obsessed with my ghost."

"The ghost sounds real enough," Mary said thoughtfully. "There is an old legend about Shian Towers being haunted. I do not recall the details, but the ghost was supposed to be a young man in search of his true love. By the time he found her, she had married another and died in childbirth; and he died of a broken heart. I don't recall a dog, but how odd that Kintyre owns one like the one you saw."

"Especially since the deerhound is a rare breed," Duncan said. "You are certain the dogs are the same?"

"Aye, sir."

"Ghosts," Lady Agnes said, shaking her head. "One hears of them, of course, but Balcardane Castle never, thank heaven, boasted such a creature. I do not think Balcardane—your father, that is, Duncan, not you—would have countenanced one in his home. So unnerving, you know, to walk round a corner in the night and bump bang into it."

Chuff laughed. "I do not think one bumps into ghosts, ma'am."

"No, of course not," she said. "But how unsettling to think that one is about to do so and then to walk through the creature instead. You cannot deny, young man, that such an event would put one off one's supper more times than not."

"No, ma'am, I won't deny that," he agreed.

"It would be almost as unnerving as one of our dearest Mary's episodes of second sight," she added.

Duncan and Mary were looking at each other again.

He said, "What do you think of this, sweetheart?"

"Are you expecting me to peer into the future, sir? You know I cannot."

"Nothing of the sort," he said. "I wondered if Pinkie's intention to marry Kintyre has stirred you to experience any distress, that's all."

She shook her head. "None at all. I like him."

"Then she shall do as she wishes," Duncan said, turning his stern eye on Chuff, "and none of us will plague her to do otherwise."

Chuff smiled. "You know I wish you well, Pinkie. I won't be at hand to plague you in any event after Friday week, for I aim to drive down to Oxford and get settled into lodgings before the term begins. Duncan has agreed to go with me."

"Aye," Roddy said, grinning mischievously. "He promised to find you a strict tutor, Chuff. Faith, though, I'd happily give you Terence, and welcome."

"Mr. Coombs," Duncan said with emphasis and a gimlet eye directed at his heir, "is a Cambridge man. He will be returning for the new term shortly himself."

"Aye, and good riddance," Roddy said, unabashed. "I dinna like the man. He's too fond of himself to pay heed to anything that amuses me, and although he kens London right well, he'd rather explore it with Chuff than with me. Has he no promised from the first to tak' me to Mrs.

Salmon's Waxworks? Aye, he has, but have I seen them?
Nay, then, I have not!''

Duncan's jaw tensed, and Mary swiftly changed the subject to certain lists and preparations necessary for the wedding. By the time they rose from the table, she had made
it clear to everyone that there was much to be done before
Saturday if Pinkie was to be properly married.

The wedding went off without a hitch. The parson was
a kindly gentleman whose bald pate rose from a halo of
soft white hair. He kept pushing his wire-rimmed spectacles
back in place with one index finger or the other whenever
they slipped down his nose, and as he read the service,
Pinkie found herself watching to see how far they would
slip before he would push them up again. The words of
the service floated in the air around her, seeming strange
and disconnected from reality. She was far more conscious
of Kintyre's tall, strong body beside her.

Energy from the man seemed to encircle her, almost to
shelter her from the others in the drawing room, for it
was there that Mary and Lady Agnes had decided to hold
the ceremony. Kintyre's shield was not impenetrable, however. Standing beside him, hearing the steady murmur
of the parson's voice, Pinkie was distinctly conscious of
Bridget's presence behind them.

The guests were numerous, for Balcardane and his lady
had made many friends in London. Rothwell and Maggie
were there, of course, as well as Lady Marsali, Mrs.
Thatcher, and a number of the latter's friends. As the
service progressed, Pinkie felt little awareness of those others, except for the occasional sneeze or cough. Bridget's
presence, however, seemed to fill the room.

Although the girl made not the slightest sound, Pinkie
could feel her eyes boring into their backs as they gave

their responses. When Kintyre slipped a gold ring on Pinkie's finger, she could feel Bridget's fury, and when the parson presented them to the company as man and wife and Kintyre kissed her, she could feel the younger girl's outrage as if it enflamed the very air between them.

CHAPTER FOURTEEN

The wedding dinner, following the ceremony, began at three, and by five—thanks to free-flowing wine and whiskey—the guests were feeling far merrier than the bridal couple. Pinkie was pleased that Kintyre had stayed at her side throughout the festivities. She had feared that he might, after the manner of men, leave her to her own devices once the matter of their wedding was completed, but he did not.

He looked splendid, too, she thought, in peach-colored breeches and coat, the latter lined with brocaded white silk to match his waistcoat. With this elegant rig, he wore silver knee buckles, white silk stockings, and black pumps. His hair was neatly curled, clubbed, and powdered, and atop his head he wore a cocked hat with a soft peach-colored ribbon cockade. She still felt more at ease with him when he dressed in buckskin breeches, but such attire was clearly ineligible for one's wedding, and at least he did not carry an amber cane, or delicately pinch snuff from a snuffbox.

For much of the time, despite her new sister-in-law's glowering looks, Pinkie enjoyed herself, and she laughed when Elizabeth Campbell revealed to her and a few others certain amusing details of her first wedding, to the Duke of Hamilton.

"He was quite mad for her," Sir Horace Walpole said. Smiling at Pinkie, he added, "Hamilton had formed the awkward habit of making violent love to the lovely Miss Gunning whilst he was supposedly playing faro, you see. That is to say, he saw neither the bank nor his cards, and soon lost thousands, so he had to marry her or quickly lose his fortune. I was there that night, you know, at the Mayfair Chapel. 'Twas St. Valentine's Day, but only half an hour after midnight. The duke slipped a bed-curtain ring on her finger, and a Fleet parson married them."

Elizabeth chuckled. "I was but eighteen then, you see, and only two nights before, Hamilton had sent for a proper parson, but the man refused to marry us without a license or a ring. Hamilton even threatened to send for the Archbishop, but in the end we were married in Mayfair Chapel by a clergyman who was—as Sir Horace describes him—little more than a Fleet parson. He did it for a guinea, and thanks to the bed-curtain ring, Hamilton was able to declare till his death that he had married me without wasting good money on a license or a ring."

Sir Horace and the others laughed, but although Pinkie joined their merriment, she could not help thinking how horrid such a scene must have been for Elizabeth, who had been the same age then as Pinkie was now.

Lady Ophelia Balterley, approaching, said sympathetically, "What are they saying to make you blush, my dear? You look quite overcome by virgin sensibility, which is certainly the fashion for brides—poor things—but I had not hitherto thought you the sort who would be overawed by any occasion."

"No, ma'am, I do not think I am overawed."

"Excellent," said Lady Ophelia. "I am glad to hear that, although I cannot approve of weddings. Not only is the married state not generally beneficial to women, but one cannot help thinking of Mr. Richardson's insightful line in *Sir Charles Grandison,* when he describes brides in virgin white, 'like milk-white heifers led to sacrifice.' "

Sir Horace, never able to remain silent for long, said, "Isn't *Sir Charles Grandison* the chap whose bride was so overwhelmed by virgin confusion that she refused to attend a tenants' party celebrating her marriage?"

"It is not the bride's faults that concern me, sir," Lady Ophelia said, flicking her fan open, then shutting it again with unnecessary energy.

"I have no tenants' party to contemplate yet, ma'am," Pinkie said, realizing that diversion was necessary. She glanced at her husband, who stood silently at her side, and was glad to see amusement in his eyes. "I believe Kintyre does not mean to return immediately to Mingary."

"No," Kintyre said, "and we shan't be going away by ourselves, I'm afraid, since I have my sister to look after and business at home that will require my presence. My aunt has expressed her desire to return to Edinburgh in a fortnight, and I can see no good reason that we should leave London before then."

Sir Horace said musingly, "What of the lovely Lady Bridget's wishes? Your sister does not strike one as a young woman who will readily embrace the solitude of Castle Mingary after enjoying the excitement and bustle of town life."

"My sister will do as she is bid," Kintyre said, taking deft advantage of Peasley's announcement that dinner was served to separate his bride from her well-wishers and lead her to the table.

By then, however, Lady Bridget's animosity had become nearly tactile, and before the meal was over, Pinkie began to wonder again what it would be like to live with so much anger, isolated from her friends and family, at Mingary.

One part of her wanted to confront the girl, to take her aside privately and demand to know what had stirred such wrath in her. Another part of her, however, believed that confrontation was exactly what Bridget sought, that she was spoiling for a fight and believed she would win it. Just what the prize might be, however, Pinkie did not know.

After the meal, when Maggie Rothwell hugged her, whispering that Kintyre was a splendid man, and others fondly extended their best wishes for a happy married life, Pinkie's spirits lifted again. Had it not been for Bridget, glowering at her when their gazes chanced to collide, she would have begun to look forward with pleasure to her new life with Kintyre. As it was, her spirits began to sink again as the time approached for the bridal couple to depart.

Bridget had not said a word to her, and if Kintyre had noted her behavior, he had not referred to it.

Michael had certainly noted his sister's rudeness, and had he been able to take five minutes alone with her, he would speedily have brought her to an understanding of his displeasure. However, experience had taught him that it would do no good to drop a hint in her ear or to warn her with a look. Either tactic would more likely result in an unpleasant scene than in her improved behavior, so he held his temper in check until he could speak to her properly.

After a time, he had stopped watching her, persuaded that in such company she would do nothing more overt than shoot her glares and glowers. Ignoring her proved more beneficial than he had imagined, however; for, denied reaction, she soon turned her attention to flirting with young Coombs. That he was a coxcomb did not seem to faze her. Although Michael suspected that Coombs was responsible for the anonymous string of posies and gew-gaws, and even letters, that arrived in George Street on a near daily basis, Bridget knew that he would never permit her to marry such a man, so he left her to her harmless flirting. He did not fail to notice, however, that from time to time she continued to shoot barbed glances at his bride.

The new Lady Kintyre looked particularly lovely, he thought, in a gown of white lustring with elbow-length sleeves, the whole embroidered and betasseled with silver, its petticoats elegantly festooned over pannier hoops. With her golden curls unpowdered and loose beneath a lace cap, she looked childlike, innocent, and vulnerable. As small as she was, with her tiny waist and her small, fragile-looking hands in their short white gloves, he felt like a giant beside her. Listening to her gentle voice as she repeated her vows, he had felt a need stronger than any he had experienced before to protect her and keep her safe from harm. Even now, as she stood chatting with friends and family, she looked like a sprite dressed in silvery-white moonbeams—as fascinating as any moon creature could be.

"Michael, dear." His aunt's voice sounded as if it were far away.

He blinked, then smiled at her. "Ma'am?"

"Your bride is beautiful," Lady Marsali said. "I won-dered if you had lost your senses, but she is a dear young woman and, I think, quite worthy of you."

"I just hope that I may prove as worthy of her, ma'am."

"There is naught amiss with you that settling your affairs

will not cure," Lady Marsali said. "I trust that you have arranged all with Sir Renfrew Campbell."

"I sent word to him Wednesday of my intent to repay him before next week is out," Michael said, "but I have received no reply."

"It would be exactly like that aggravating man to have journeyed out of town just when you have gained the wherewithal to repay him."

"Chalmers delivered my message directly to Campbell's lodgings, into his servant's hand," Michael said. "I should think that if he had gone out of town, the servant would have said as much."

"Aye, that's true. Do you think he means to be difficult, dear?"

"I don't know." It was precisely what he feared, but there was no point in saying so, not to her and not at a moment when it could accomplish nothing other than to spoil her pleasure in the day.

Lady Marsali regarded him speculatively for a long moment, but when she spoke, it was not to press him further about Sir Renfrew Campbell. Instead, she said, "Cousin Bella and I mean to take Bridget with us to see *Hamlet* at Covent Garden, and then to put in an appearance at Lady Coulter's cotillion ball."

Michael nodded, not really caring where his sister went, so long as he did not have to deal with her just yet.

"She has not behaved well," Lady Marsali said. "I mean to speak to her."

"If you are hoping, ma'am, that by doing so you will save me the trouble, you can spare your breath. That I have not already made my feelings on the subject plain to her is due only to the solemnity of this occasion."

"My dear, she is merely jealous, I think. She has had you all to herself for so long that it is not odd if she should resent sharing you with your bride."

"She wants beating," Michael retorted, "and if I had my way, she would certainly go nowhere tonight but to her bedchamber. Indeed, I should like to pack her right back to Mingary."

"I do not really think it would be wise to order her home to George Street just yet, however," Lady Marsali said with a worried expression.

"No, that would be unfair to Miss Mac—" He broke off, realizing that Penelope was no longer Miss MacCrichton.

Lady Marsali chuckled. "For months after our marriage, your late uncle introduced me as Lady Susan anytime he did not simply say 'my wife.' It happens to most men, my dear. You are quite right, however, not to saddle dearest Penelope with Bridget and her megrims before they have been sisters for one whole day."

"I agree, ma'am, so I thank you for keeping Bridget out of my way. She will not be pleasant company for you, I believe. She is not overfond of Shakespeare."

"Well, I overheard Mr. Coombs saying that he and Mac-Crichton mean to attend the play, so I dare swear she will agree in a trice to go with us. Perhaps we might even ask the young gentlemen to escort us."

Foreseeing that his aunt would have his sister well in hand, Michael turned his attention back to his bride, who had wandered away, chatting. As he made his way through the guests toward her, she saw him and smiled.

Moving nearer, he reached a hand toward her bare shoulder, then realized he might startle her, even embarrass her. Letting the hand fall, he bent close instead and said quietly, "It is nearly six o'clock, madam; time to take our departure."

She turned her head, and her eyes twinkled. "You are the first to call me 'madam,' sir. Sir Horace was first to call me Lady Kintyre, and I must say, it is odd to hear people calling me by another name, for I feel like the same person I was when I woke up this morning.''

"Well, it is your name now," Michael said lightly. "You had better grow accustomed to hearing it.''

"So we have been telling her," Lady Rothwell said. "Is your carriage at the door, sir? If it is, I had better fetch Mary and Balcardane.''

"Aye, ma'am, it is," Michael said. Offering his arm to Penelope, he said, "Will you come away with me now, madam wife?''

"Aye, sir, I will," she said with another warm smile.

He knew she must be nervous, for what bride was not, but she looked calm and self-possessed. She placed a hand on his arm, resting her other hand on the swell of her pannier; and he escorted her to the grand stairway and down. Much of the company had managed to precede them, for they waited below.

Penelope hugged her brother and Lady Balcardane, then the dowager, before she turned to Balcardane and held out both hands to him. He drew her into an embrace, and to Michael's astonishment there were tears in the other man's eyes.

The earl relinquished her to Michael but said grimly, "Mind, you take good care of her, lad.''

"Aye, sir, I intend to," Michael said.

The footman brought her mantle and draped it gently over her shoulders. Then her tiring woman appeared, carrying a small portmanteau; and a moment later, Michael, his bride, and her woman were in his coach, on the way to George Street. The day had seemed long, yet two hours remained before the sun would set.

They sat without speaking until the coach turned into Piccadilly. Then he said, "I did warn you that my cousin's house is small, did I not?''

"Aye, sir," she said. "Tell me about Mingary.''

He began by describing the castle, and before long, he was telling her about the people and the precious forested hills rising from the sea. She listened silently, but he could see that she was interested. "I hope you'll like it there," he said at last.

"I'm sure I will, sir. It sounds beautiful, does it not, Doreen?"

"Aye, mistress."

When the coach drew to a halt in front of the house, Michael opened the door himself and put down the step. As he was helping Penelope to the pavement, Sal opened the front door and peered out, curiosity plain in every line of her body.

"Welcome, my lord," she said as they approached, "and my lady."

"This is Sal," Michael said. "She is one of Cousin Bella's servants. This is Lady Kintyre, Sal, and her woman, Doreen, who is to share your bedchamber."

Sal grinned at Doreen. "Aye, me lord, we met when she brought some of her ladyship's clothing and such to the house. Doreen, ye'll be wanting to get your lady settled, I shouldn't wonder. Come along with me, and I'll show ye where we've put her things. Will ye be coming along up, your ladyship, or . . ." She paused tactfully.

Penelope looked at Michael.

"You may do as you like," he said. "Cousin Bella insists that you treat this house as your own."

"Then, if it please you, sir, I should like to change out of this dress into something more comfortable."

"I like that dress," he said.

She twinkled. "I hope that does not mean you want me to continue wearing it. The panniers are squashed from riding in the coach, and I've had my fill of hoops for the day. I've got a lovely *robe à l'anglaise* upstairs. Did I say that right?"

"Quite right," he said.

"Well, I am never sure of French phrases," she said. "I can read French well enough, but I've rarely had opportunity to speak with a Frenchman."

"I like the way you speak."

Her cheeks grew rosy. "Shall I go up with the maids, sir? I own, I feel a little strange invading your bedchamber."

He arched his eyebrows, quizzing her. "Would you feel less strange about it if I were to accompany you?" He heard the teasing note in his voice and wished he could unsay the words. He did not wish to embarrass her.

To his surprise, she chuckled. "I suppose I asked for that," she said. "If you do not mind, I shall go with Doreen and Sal now and hope that you left the room looking presentable. If you are anything like Chuff, and your man has not had time to tidy up after you, I shall have trouble finding my way about."

He shook his head. "Not in that room, you won't. It's scarcely big enough to swing a cat."

She wrinkled her nose at him, making him smile again.

"I believe I shall also make myself more comfortable," he said. "I'll go upstairs with you and see what arrangements Chalmers has made. I expect he will have relegated me to my dressing room, so you can have the bedchamber to yourself whilst he brushes this damned powder from my hair. I doubt that it will take as long as it will take you to change, but Sal can show you down to the drawing room. Perhaps, now that I think of it, you might like some wine, Miss Mac—"

"Yes, please," she said, her eyes filling with laughter again. "Also, I did not eat much, sir, so perhaps if someone could find some bread and butter, or . . ." She paused hopefully.

Sal said, "I'll see to that whilst ye dress, my lady."

Michael followed them upstairs, marveling as he had

before at the ease with which ladies with hoops and wide skirts managed the steps. He had been amazed at the speed with which most Londoners tripped up and down numerous flights of stairs many times a day. He was not unaccustomed to stairs himself, of course. Mingary possessed many, but one was not obliged frequently to run up and down them each day. Here in London, it seemed that whatever floor one was on, the thing one wanted was on another. He found the inconvenience annoying, but Cousin Bella seemed to think nothing of it. Clearly it did not dismay his bride, either.

He found himself looking forward to seeing how she would look in a *robe à l'anglaise*. The only time he had seen her without hoops was in her riding habit, and with its voluminous skirts, she might as well have been wearing a farthingale.

Upstairs they found Chalmers awaiting them outside the bedchamber door. "Begging your pardon, my lord," he said after Michael had introduced Penelope, "but Miss Munn and I thought that perhaps you would like to use your dressing room whilst her ladyship uses the bedchamber. We have arranged a dressing table for her. I hope that will meet with your approval."

"Yes, that will do very well," Michael said. To Penelope, he said, "My dressing room is a pea-sized closet behind that next door. Another door leads from it into the bedchamber, but I shall leave you to Miss Munn for now and meet you downstairs at your convenience."

Her lips twitched, and when he raised his eyebrows, she said, "It sounds strange to hear you call Doreen 'Miss Munn.' How her stature has increased! She will soon grow to be as high in the instep as Mary's Ailis is."

"I do not think you need worry about that," he said, opening the door for her.

* * *

Twenty minutes later, when Michael entered the drawing room, he found the curtains drawn, candles burning in every wall sconce, food and wine on a side table, and a cheerful fire crackling on the hearth. Sending silent thanks to his aunt and Cousin Bella for their tactfulness in letting him and his bride have the house to themselves for the evening, he poured himself a glass of wine from the decanter on the table, and another glass for Penelope, then carried his to the fireplace.

Poking up the fire, he stood again and looked down into it, letting his thoughts about the day catch up with him. He told himself that it was not at all unusual for a man to marry for money, that wise and noble men did it every day of the week, that a sensible man did what was necessary, that it had certainly been necessary for him, and for Mingary.

Surely marrying Penelope for her money was no worse than when he had considered giving Bridget to Sir Renfrew Campbell or wedding her to young MacCrichton. That he had accepted her refusal to marry the former, and that she had convinced herself she was in love with the latter, hardly altered the fact that he had been willing to exploit her to repay a debt. If it made him uneasy to think he had married Miss MacCrichton—Penelope—to repay his debt to Campbell, would it not have been as bad or worse to have sold his sister for the same purpose?

With these thoughts for company, it was no wonder that his mood bordered on morose by the time his bride joined him in the drawing room. Hearing the rattle of the doorknob, followed by her gentle voice dismissing Sal, he turned and set down his glass, still half full of wine, on the mantel.

In the flickering candlelight, the soft, pale-yellow robe

Penelope wore glowed like springtime sunshine spilling through a window. She paused inside the room, looking around at the jumble of furniture and gewgaws that Cousin Bella had collected. He waited for her reaction.

"My, this is quite cozy," she said. "What a lot of interesting things your cousin has."

"Would you like to see the rest of the house?"

"Not now, thank you. I've been standing a good part of the day, you know, and in truth, my shoes pinched dreadfully. They have the pointiest toes I ever saw, and though they are quite à la mode, I am glad to have them off my feet." She put one dainty foot forward, revealing a wispy sandal. "I'm very glad that we did not accept any invitations for tonight. I believe I am quite worn out."

"Come closer to the fire, then. Your feet will soon turn blue with cold." He fetched her glass of wine from the table and handed it to her, feeling himself stir when her warm fingers touched his.

Pinkie's breath caught in her throat, and she was glad he did not say anything or ask her to speak. When his fingers touched hers, it was as if a spark leapt between them, burning her—not painfully, like fire would burn, but in a different way, a nice way. She did not take the glass at once, so for moments—seemingly long moments—they held the glass together.

When she looked at him, something flickered in his expression, and she felt the warmth from his fingertips slide all through her body, making her nerves tingle and her knees feel as if they were made of soft, warm wax instead of flesh and bone and sinew.

Kintyre removed the glass from her hand and set it down on the side table again, holding her other arm lightly with his free hand while he did so.

She did not move. For a time, even breathing seemed unnecessary.

Now both his hands were on her upper arms, warm through the sleeves of the soft robe she wore. Not only was the powder gone from his hair, but the curls were gone, too, leaving it swept severely back from his brow and tied at the nape with a black ribbon. He had taken off his frock coat and wore only his white waistcoat over his shirt and breeches. In short, the London beau had disappeared; the Scotsman had returned.

She stared at his broad chest as if she were counting the silver buttons on his waistcoat. When she looked up at him, his dark gaze seemed to penetrate to her soul. He was going to kiss her again. She knew it as if he had told her so.

His lips touched hers, but it was not the tender, light kiss she had experienced after the wedding service, just before the parson had presented them to the wedding guests as man and wife. His lips felt like fire against hers, and his arms slid around her, drawing her close, so close that they might have breathed as one, if she had been aware of breathing at all.

As a child, with little experience of kisses other than the times she had come upon a pair of servants in a shadowy corner, she could remember wondering about them, about how men and women knew how to kiss. How did they fit the parts together, noses, chins, and all? How could they see well enough once they got close together, so as not to miss and kiss a corner of the mouth instead of straight on? It all had seemed complicated, not to mention messy, and rather an odd thing to do.

It did not seem odd now. It gave her a tingling feeling that swept from her lips through the rest of her body, to her toes. When his tongue touched the opening between her lips, it surprised her, but she did not resist, and the tingling increased. The tips of her breasts were afire, and when he stroked her back, she pressed against him, not sure whether she was trying to ease the fiery sensation or increase it.

Moments later, when he released her, she felt dizzy.

He smiled, but his voice sounded gruff. "Do you still want your wine?"

Warmth flashed to heat, and she was sure her cheeks must be ablaze, because the rest of her was. Shaking her head, she said, "I feel unsteady enough as it is, sir."

"Should we perhaps go back upstairs?"

"We shall do as you please, sir," she said. "A wife owes her duty to her husband, I know, although in truth, I know little about just what that means."

"Such a lack of knowledge is not unusual in a bride," he said. "I will teach you all you need to know."

"Do you know so much about it, then?"

"Aye, enough to be getting on with, at all events."

"How did you learn?"

He chuckled. "A dutiful wife does not ask such questions of her husband, at least not about things that took place before their marriage."

"Oh."

"Convenient for husbands, is it not?"

"I suppose it might be," she said, still not certain what all *it* entailed.

Putting an arm around her shoulders, he said, "You will understand better shortly. Come along now."

Sir Renfrew Campbell was not a member of the Cocoa Tree in St. James's Street, but Mr. Coombs was, and it amused Sir Renfrew to meet at the place rumor identified as erstwhile headquarters for Jacobite activity in London. Nowadays it was a private club as exclusive as any, and few members admitted any loyalty to the Stewarts. Most, in fact, bore them no more loyalty than Sir Renfrew did.

"She is going back to Scotland soon," his companion said gloomily.

Sir Renfrew had, he decided, made a useful acquaintance in young Coombs. The lad was besotted with Bridget himself, and could not seem to talk of anything else, but that suited Sir Renfrew's plans quite well—or it had suited them until now. However, Mr. Coombs had come to him straight from the wedding at Faircourt House, in a state of flat despair.

"When does she leave?" Sir Renfrew asked.

"A fortnight at most. She said her aunt intended from the outset to return to Edinburgh by mid-June, but one did think that when her family saw how popular Lady Bridget had become, they would linger. She says that they will not, however, that unless she can induce MacCrichton to offer for her, they will leave as planned."

"And *can* she induce him, d' ye think?"

"No, and I, for one, cannot think why she would want to do so. He has little interest yet in marriage—less than most, thanks to his fortune—and when we tease him about her infatuation, he just asks us not to speak unkindly. As for my own cause, I believe it is lost. She will have none of me."

Since Sir Renfrew had long since deduced that much for himself, and since Lady Bridget's patent lack of interest in Coombs was the sole reason he had encouraged the young man to continue his pursuit, he made no comment. His quick mind was turning cartwheels, however.

His hopes had so far borne no fruit. He had trusted that by undertaking the trip to London, he would be able to charm so young and inexperienced a lady into seeing how sadly she had mistaken his character. That his efforts had not budged her from her original assessment was disappointing, but he was not averse to a change of course and had decided one might prove beneficial even before Kintyre's note had arrived. This news from Coombs made his choice much clearer.

CHAPTER FIFTEEN

When they entered his bedchamber, Michael saw with amusement that Chalmers and Miss Munn had tidied up and drawn the curtains. The wood basket held a larger than usual supply of logs for the fire, and once again there was wine laid out on a side table, along with a plate of buns and sweet biscuits. The coverlet on the high bed was turned down invitingly. He glanced at Penelope and saw that she, too, was observing these signs of welcome.

When she caught her lower lip between her teeth, he thought again of what he had done in marrying her. She was a practical lass, though; that much was clear even in the little he knew of her. She was not flighty or impulsive, nor, despite her childhood belief in ghosts, was she a misty air-dreamer. He had heard it rumored that the Countess of Balcardane possessed the gift of second sight, but he had seen no indication that his bride was anything other than practical and down to earth.

"If you are wondering where Cailean is," he said, "I

told Chalmers to put him in the dressing room tonight. He usually sleeps on the hearth." He saw no point in mentioning the times Cailean had chosen the bed over the hearth. With luck, the deerhound would show restraint now that its master had taken a wife.

She turned toward him, and he saw hesitation in her expression, perhaps even alarm at what lay ahead. "You've no need to fear me, lass," he said gently.

"Had I feared you, sir, I would not have agreed to marry you," she said. "Indeed, I fear little that I can see or understand. If I seem frightened, it is only that I do not understand the sensations I'm feeling, nor do I know what I am to do."

Still believing that he would frighten her if he claimed his husbandry rights at once, he said, "It is early yet. Perhaps we ought to see about feeding you before we go any further. You said that you ate very little earlier, and I own that with all the chatter at table, I don't recall what I ate, myself."

"Everything on your plate, and more," she said, chuckling. "I did see, sir. You appeared to enjoy a most hearty appetite."

Realizing that another appetite was increasing by the moment, he moved away from her to the side table and poured wine again for both of them. Before handing her her glass, however, he put buns and some cheese on a plate, then drew the room's two armchairs up near the fire. The bedsteps served as a table between them to hold the plate and their wineglasses.

Pleased with his efforts, he stepped back and indicated one of the chairs with a gallant gesture.

"Sit down and eat, lass. You'll need sustenance."

"Will I?"

"Aye, and shut the door." He watched her turn to obey him, then move across the room, and he was conscious,

as he had been before, of the exquisite grace of her movements. The pale golden robe swirled around her feet. It
fit her slim figure snugly at the waist and was fastened
cunningly somehow at the side. He found himself trying
to imagine the clasp or the arrangement of buttons that
would release it. He did not think she wore much beneath.
His body stirred just thinking about that.

Taking a deep breath, he sat when she did, and after
she had taken a few bites of her bun, he said, "Tell me
more about your childhood, lassie. I would know more of
my bride's beginnings."

She froze, holding the remains of the bun halfway
between her mouth and the plate.

Pinkie was still chewing bread and cheese, and the food
seemed suddenly dry in her mouth. Had he learned somehow about Daft Geordie and Red Mag? Was that why he
showed such a sudden interest in her past? No one in
London had shown any interest in her parents, and in her
concern for his predicament, she had given little thought
to her own. Nevertheless, she could not lie to him.

Swallowing her food, she said cautiously, "What do you
want to know?"

"Well, I already know that your father followed the
prince and died in his cause, and that eventually you and
MacCrichton went to live with Balcardane. However, I also
know you bear no kinship to him. Are you, then, kin to
his lady?"

"No," Pinkie said, "but she took us with her when she
went to live at Balcardane Castle, and when our uncle
died—the previous Laird MacCrichton, that is—our Chuff
inherited his title and estate." There was much more to
the story than that, of course, but she hoped he would be
content with the brief outline.

"How did the countess come to have any say in the matter? Why did you not live with the laird?"

"He was a cruel man, that's why," Pinkie said. "Chuff did not like him, and I was afraid of him, and so we went away with Mary, and then Himself kept the laird from stealing us back. And when the laird died, there was no one else who wanted us, so Mary and Himself just kept us."

"There was more to it than that," Kintyre said with a chuckle.

Pinkie said, "Surely you do not want to hear about every year of my life."

"Not all at once, perhaps, but Balcardane could not have taken control over a fortune the size of MacCrichton's without legal authority to do so."

"I suppose not. I do not understand exactly how he did that."

"Nor would I expect you to understand such things. I did hear rumors about the MacCrichton fortune being lost after the rebellion, however, and then found again. Was there any truth to that?"

"Aye, they hid it before they followed the prince, and then our father died, and only he knew the secret; but we found it again. Do you want that last bun, sir?"

"I do, indeed," he said.

As he reached for it, she said curiously, "I have heard that you are trying to get a law changed in Parliament—something to do with the deerhound law—and that Lord Menzies and others are trying to help. Is it prodigiously complicated?"

Kintyre grimaced, but the diversion succeeded, for he said, "Not really. Menzies wants the law changed as much as I do, and his title is not merely Scottish, like mine, so he has influence. The problem lies in getting men who have no stake in the matter to understand the consequences of restricting ownership."

"It does seem odd that only certain people can own dogs like Cailean."

"Not just odd," he said. "It's potentially disastrous. The breed will die out. The object was to keep their value high—and their stature, as well—by allowing only men of high rank to own them; but since we no longer have a Scottish royal family, or clan chiefs with any power, and only a handful of earls, marquesses, or dukes to own or breed them, the dogs have already become exceedingly rare."

"Could you not sell puppies to English earls?"

"Aye, we could, but few in England want so large a dog. Deerhounds were bred to hunt stags, so nowadays there is little need for them here. Private herds are small and are rarely hunted for sport. Scotland still has deer in the wild, and shooting is still a favored pastime there. Englishmen go to Scotland to hunt. If I could sell dogs to men of lower rank, the breed would flourish, but many members of Parliament think the notion frivolous. They believe that we want to change the law of exclusive proprietorship simply so that we can exploit the breed for money. They talk of its noble heritage, and spout other such nonsense. When the deerhounds are extinct, it will do no good to say we told them so."

"What will you do about Cailean?"

"I must return him to Glenmore, of course, little though I want to. I sold him for the money to bring Bridget to London, as I think I told you, and I must honor my agreement. It was hard enough to part with the old fellow the first time, however. I don't know how I shall do it again."

She reached over to squeeze his hand, and he turned it over and clasped hers within it. Again, his touch sent warmth through her body, a melting glow that stirred the tingling sensation again. She wondered if he felt something similar.

He looked at her, and she saw the warmth she felt reflected in his eyes. His lips parted, and he turned in his chair so that he faced her more directly. "Finish your wine, little wife," he said, his voice low-pitched and gruffer than before. "I would know more of you."

He did not let go of her hand, but she could easily reach her glass with the other. She did not look away. She felt as if her eyes had lost the power to shift away from his. His were darker than she remembered, so deep a blue that they looked almost black. Reflected candlelight flickered in their depths.

A spark cracked in the fire, and a log shifted. She watched him over the rim of her glass as she drank the remains of her wine.

He stood then without a word and drew her to her feet. She thought he would move aside to let her pass, but he did not. Instead, he drew her into his embrace, enfolding her and effectively shutting out the rest of the world.

She could smell a light citrus scent that lingered in his hair from the powder, and a spicier scent of cloves from his clothing. She could both hear and feel his deep, steady breathing. When he touched her chin with his fingertips, she obeyed their slight pressure and tilted her face up. His lips touched hers, softly at first, tasting her, exploring her lips with the tip of his tongue, sending a wave of fresh, new sensations racing through her body.

Intrigued, she tried doing the same to him, and he tasted of cheese and mellow wine. Her hands were at his waist, and she could feel the soft silk of his waistcoat, the nubbly silver threads of its brocading.

His fingers and palms moved slowly, tantalizingly, over her body, from her shoulders to the curve of her waist and over her hip. Then one moved upward, cupping a breast, a thumb rubbing lightly over its tip, stirring feelings she had not known existed. All the while he kept kissing her, tempting her to do the things he was doing, teasing her, provoking new sensations with every movement. She ached for him, and when he held her tightly, she could feel his body stir against hers.

One of his hands groped at her waist, its movements feeling different from before. They were urgent, seeking motions. She heard him moan impatiently.

Drawing back slightly, she said, "What is it? What's wrong?"

"How the devil does this thing unfasten? I cannot find button or clasp."

A gurgle of laughter escaped, and she said, "There are hooks, tiny ones. Here, I'll show you, but should we not put out the candles? They're getting low."

"No. I want to see you, lassie."

"Aye, well, then you shall. It's your right, after all."

"And yours, lass, to see what you've saddled yourself with."

She showed him how to unhook the robe, and it fell open, revealing that she wore only her thin cambric chemise and underskirt beneath it.

"What if someone comes in?" she asked.

"They won't." He eased the robe from her shoulders, and it fell in a pool of soft, pale-yellow wool at her feet. He stood without moving, looking at her.

Michael inhaled deeply. Her white chemise was cut low to follow the fashionable low décolletage of most gowns, and he saw that what he had thought earlier was lace edging her gown was, in fact, the lace trimming of her chemise showing above the bodice edge. The soft swell of her breasts rose above the lace. The top of the garment, threaded with a white satin ribbon drawstring, tied so that it just touched the outside ends of her shoulders.

He untied the ribbon and pushed the chemise down, exposing her breasts to his touch. Her skin felt warm and soft, and it glowed golden in the candlelight. When he touched a nipple, she gasped, and he felt his blood race at the sound. He forced himself to move slowly, though, knowing she would enjoy the experience more if he did not rush her. Stroking her with one hand, he found the ribbon for the underskirt and untied it. Then skirt and chemise followed her robe to the floor.

Naked now, she shivered, and he said, "We don't want you getting cold." As he spoke, he scooped her into his arms and laid her on the bed, pulling the coverlet over her. Quickly, he took off his clothes, snuffed the now-guttering candles except for the one nearest the bed, and slipped in beside her. His body was ready for hers, throbbing with impatience. He slid one hand beneath the coverlet, sliding it over her soft belly, lower and lower to see if she was yet ready for him.

He heard her breath catch in her throat, but when he pulled back, she caught his hand with hers, holding it in place. "Don't stop now," she said.

He kissed her, and when his lips touched hers, his hunger for her threatened to overpower him. He wanted to taste every inch of her, to possess her, body and soul. Exerting himself to go slowly, he succeeded only in increasing his desire.

Where her fingertips touched him, his body burned, and when she used her mouth and her lips as he was using his, he feared he would explode from sheer, driving lust. At last, he could stand it no longer, and he took her, fighting to be as gentle as he knew how to be but fearing that it was not gentle enough. Before he was spent, the last candle guttered and went out.

He heard her moans and knew there was as much pain in them as pleasure, if not more, and he wondered if she were already regretting her decision to marry him.

He held her close, stroking her hair. "Did I hurt you?"

"A little," she said, "but only at the end."

"It won't always hurt," he said.

"Aye, it's easing now."

Her voice stirred him again, but this time it was his protective instinct that stirred. He wanted to make the last vestige of pain disappear.

The bed vibrated slightly, and fur touched the arch of his left foot, then his calf. A cold nose touched the back of his knee as Penelope said, "What on earth?"

He felt a bubble of laughter in his throat but managed to keep his voice under control as he said, "I'm afraid it's Cailean. The door to the dressing room must not have shut tightly, because I did not hear it open."

"We might not have heard it in any event," she said, and he heard laughter in her voice. "Does he often sleep with you?"

"Only when he can get away with it. He usually waits until I am asleep, then creeps up under the covers from the foot of the bed. He doesn't have fleas, I promise. Chalmers bathed him after his adventures, and assured me—"

He broke off without finishing the sentence, because his bride was laughing so hard that she couldn't possibly hear him anyway.

The following morning, when Pinkie awoke, Doreen was opening the curtains and Kintyre and Cailean were gone. She was alone in the high bed. The sun was shining outside, though, spilling paths of gold through the tall window, across the bedchamber carpet. She looked forward to the day ahead.

"Good morning, Doreen," she said, sitting up and pushing hair from her eyes. Memory of the dog's attempt to sleep with them made her want to laugh again.

Doreen returned her greeting, adding, "I kent ye wouldna want to lie abed this morning, my lady, though his lordship said not to disturb ye."

"You were right," Pinkie said, getting up and slipping her arms into the wrapping robe Doreen held ready for her. Hot water steamed in a ewer on the washstand, and when she moved toward it, Doreen skipped ahead to pour it into the basin for her. Pinkie raised her eyebrows. "Am I to do naught for myself now?"

Smiling, Doreen said, "Ye're a countess now, m'lady. It isna fitting."

"Don't be daft," Pinkie said. "Lady Balcardane does not shy from homely tasks, and neither shall I."

"Ye will an ye wish to impress Lady Bridget," Doreen said with a sniff. "Her ladyship isna pleased with the new arrangement, I'm thinkin'."

Knowing she should not encourage Doreen to talk of Bridget, Pinkie opened her mouth to say as much but instead found herself saying, "What has she done?"

"Och, it isna what she's done," Doreen said. " 'Tis only that she makes it her business to put us wrong wi' the servants here. I havena spoken up, knowing well that ye would want me to hold m' tongue, but 'tis a trial to meet wi' disapproving looks and to see people who should ken better turn away when I enter a room."

"Bless me," Pinkie said. "I wonder what she can have said about us."

"I dinna ken," Doreen said, "but the auld ladies be

kind. They said the family doesna go to kirk till after noon, but they be at table now, so I came to wake ye."

Pinkie thanked her and dressed as hurriedly as was commensurate with tidiness, then went in search of the breakfast parlor, which she found on the same floor as the drawing room, overlooking the back garden instead of the street. The sun had not yet reached the room, for it faced northwest and the small garden below its windows remained in shadow. In compensation, however, the room itself was cheerfully alive with color.

Two walls were yellow, and the other two bore lively Chinese wallpaper, depicting brilliantly colored birds perched on gilded and flowered branches of unlikely trees. The woodwork and fireplace surround were white, and the chief colors in the floral carpet were pale green, pink, yellow, and cream. An oval table near the corner where the papered walls met wore a floor-length yellow linen cloth with a wide border embroidered with birds and flowered branches, repeating the wallpaper pattern.

Mrs. Thatcher and Lady Marsali were alone in the room when Pinkie entered, and both greeted her cheerfully; however, she had no sooner taken her seat at the table with them when first Sal entered to ask what she wanted with her toast, and then Bridget entered, looking magnificent in a morning gown of sapphire blue trimmed with deep edgings of white lace.

Sal was halfway to the door when Bridget swept in, and the maid stepped aside to let her pass, saying, "Will ye want coffee, tea, or chocolate, my lady?"

Bridget did not deign to answer, saying to her with noticeable irritation instead, "Nan told me that a letter came for me in yesterday's post—when we were at the wedding—but that you would not let her take it to my bedchamber. I want to know who you think you are to interfere with my maid!"

Sal's face reddened, but she did not answer, looking instead to her mistress.

Mrs. Thatcher said calmly, "Kintyre asked to see any letters addressed to you before they were given to you, my dear. We forgot to tell him about that one, I'm afraid— well, in point of fact, we did not know until this morning, and we did not see him before he went out. He told Sal he is meeting with Sir Renfrew Campbell," she added obliquely. "In any event, you would not expect Sal to disobey him."

"Where is my letter?" Bridget demanded.

"On the sideboard," Lady Marsali said, "but really, my dear, you must wait until Kintyre returns before you read it. There is a posy, as well, so I daresay you can content yourself with that until—"

"Don't be silly," Bridget snapped, turning to the sideboard and snatching up both the letter and the little bouquet of wilting flowers that lay next to it in a dainty silver holder. A note was tucked into the holder with the flowers, and she opened it, reading swiftly and smiling as she moved to set it down again. Then she paused and looked up with a frown. "I thought you said that Michael had gone out, but the seal on this note is broken. Who opened it?"

"I did, my dear," Lady Marsali said. "We knew that Kintyre would not deny you your posy, but I did think we should know the sender's name. You know," she added thoughtfully before Bridget could speak, "I do not think it is quite the thing for a young man to send you flowers without properly identifying himself."

Bridget raised her chin defiantly. "I think it is romantic. Moreover, you can see that the letter is directed in the same hand, so you know that it came from him, as well. If I can have the posy, I can read the letter. In any event, I intend to read it; so there." She looked at each of them in turn, and when no one spoke, she turned again to Sal and said, "I want chocolate. Be sure it is hot when it reaches the table."

"Yes, my lady." Sal fled.

Bridget glowered at Pinkie. "You are sitting where I like to sit."

Lady Marsali said, "Bridget, dear, you are being prodigiously rude again, and are putting us all to the blush. You must apologize to Penelope at once."

"Must I, indeed?" Bridget said, her tone more haughty than ever. Glaring at Pinkie, she said, "I dare swear you will agree with her. Perhaps you also agree that I should not read my own letters without permission from my brother to do so."

Having purposely remained silent, but realizing that Bridget had no intention of allowing her to do so any longer, Pinkie said quietly, "I know only that I would not defy my brother if he gave such an order."

"Your brother is not a tyrant," Bridget said. "He would never issue such an order. Nor," she added with a knowing smile, "would he want anyone to prevent me from reading letters from my secret admirer."

"Well, I do not know how you can know that," Pinkie said. Thoughtfully, she added, "I cannot say for certain, of course, that he ever would give an order like that to me, but then, I have never given him cause to do so."

"Do you think I have?" Bridget sounded outraged.

Looking her straight in the eye, Pinkie said coolly, "I do not think you have given my brother cause to do any such thing, or that you ever will."

Mrs. Thatcher, audibly choking back laughter, looked down at her plate.

Bridget shot her a look, but it was to Pinkie that she said, "I expect you think that you are clever, but you are no such thing. I know exactly what you are."

"And, pray, what is that?" Pinkie asked with an edge to her voice.

Bridget tossed her head. "You know, and I know, but you need not worry that I shall give your secrets away. I have better cause, I believe, to conceal them." She held up her letter. "I am going to read this in private."

Sal returned with a tray bearing two small, round pots and a rack of toast, but as she passed Bridget, the latter said, "I have changed my mind, Sal. You may serve my chocolate in the drawing room." With that, she swept out of the room in the same haughty manner as she had entered it.

"Dear me," Lady Marsali said, shaking her head. "Kintyre will be sorely vexed, I fear."

"As sure as eggs is eggs," Mrs. Thatcher agreed. Turning to Pinkie, she added, "Bridget seems to have taken you in dislike, my dear Penelope. I vow, I did not know where to look when she spoke so disrespectfully to you."

"Odious girl," Lady Marsali said, reaching for a piece of warm toast from the rack. "Pay her no heed, my dear. Kintyre will soon sort her out."

"I assure you, ma'am, I do not want to cause strife between Kintyre and his sister," Pinkie said. "I think perhaps I should talk to her before he returns."

"If you think you can accomplish anything by talking, pray do so," Lady Marsali said. "For my part, I wish someone would give her a good skelping."

Pinkie smiled. "I know you are too kindhearted to mean that, ma'am."

"Well, it would require more effort than I am willing to expend, so if that counts as kindhearted, then perhaps I am," Lady Marsali said complacently.

"Finish your tea before you talk to Bridget," Mrs.

Thatcher recommended. Gently, she pushed the silver salver toward Pinkie, adding, "And perhaps you would like to read some of the invitations we received this morning. You are included in all of them, of course, and indeed, several are directed to you."

"Thank you, ma'am, but I shall wait until I can discover from his lordship which of them he would like to accept."

"Dear me, child, he won't care," Lady Marsali said with a dismissive gesture. "Kintyre goes wherever we choose to go, because social functions are much of a muchness to him. He'd rather tramp along a Highland track than enjoy a country dance or a rout."

Pinkie smiled. "One cannot blame him for that, ma'am. Country life is far more peaceful, don't you agree?"

Mrs. Thatcher exclaimed, "Pray, do not tell me that you are cut from the same bolt, child! One has one's social obligations, after all, and it is a wife's duty to see that her husband does not shirk his. Why, when Mr. Thatcher was alive, it was up to me to see that he went where it did him the most good to be seen; for, allowed his own road, he would never have set foot in any drawing room but ours."

"I know that one must do one's duty, ma'am, but surely you can understand why I prefer to wait and discuss our invitations with Kintyre before deciding which to accept and which to decline. Now then, if you will excuse me, I mean to see if I cannot make peace with Lady Bridget."

Neither woman expressed confidence that she would succeed; but undaunted, Pinkie went to the drawing room, where she found Bridget drinking her chocolate in solitary splendor.

"I want to talk with you," Pinkie said, carefully shutting the door.

"Well, I don't want to talk to you," Bridget snapped. "I want to read my letter in peace."

"I daresay you do," Pinkie said evenly, "but we must talk, Bridget."

"You should call me Lady Bridget."

"Don't be daft. We are sisters now, whether you like it or not, and my rank is superior to yours. You would not happily call me Lady Kintyre, would you?"

Bridget scowled. "I don't want you for my sister."

"Faith, but you amaze me. I thought that was exactly what you wanted. Or have I been mistaken in thinking that you want to marry my brother."

Bridget's eyes shifted. "I am not altogether certain that I do want to marry him. Indeed, I had nearly decided that I do not, but I will if I decide that I want to."

"I doubt that," Pinkie said. "Still, I had hoped that since you seem to hold a tenderness for him, you would extend at least common courtesy to me. Do you dislike me so much that you cannot even be civil?"

Still avoiding her eyes, Bridget said, "You are wrong, you know."

"I frequently have been wrong, about many things; but if you mean that I have mistaken Chuff's sentiments toward you, I can assure you that I have not. I do not mean to cause you pain, but he does not want to marry anyone just yet."

Bridget looked at her then. "Yes, he does," she said firmly. "You will see, just like everyone else will." She smoothed her letter. "I know he does."

"Faith, can you possibly think that Chuff wrote that letter to you and did not have the grace to sign it?"

"You should not call him by so childish a name," Bridget said, hunching a shoulder. "His proper name is Charles. A chuff is a miser, and he is no such thing."

"I have called him Chuff since I was a bairn," Pinkie said. "The name means nothing more than that I could not pronounce Charles when I was small, but I doubt that

I shall ever call him anything else. In any event, he did not write that letter."

"You do not know as much as you think you do," Bridget said. "What's more, I'll have you know, he is not my only admirer."

"Well, everyone knows that Sir Renfrew Campbell is mad for you, if that's what you mean; and our Roddy says that Terence Coombs likes you, too."

"You would take the word of a child? I think Mr. Coombs is a coxcomb."

Although Pinkie agreed wholeheartedly with Bridget's description of Coombs, she had no desire to discuss the younger girl's admirers with her—supposed or real—so she said only, "We must learn to get along, Bridget. We will be living in the same house, after all."

"Not for long," Bridget said. "I'll soon prove you don't know everything."

"Since your brother will certainly insist that you live with us, I cannot imagine how you can think you will not."

Bridget patted the letter. "I mean that my admirer has asked me to meet him privately, and I mean to do so. When I do, he will ask me to marry him. So there!"

Appalled, Pinkie exclaimed, "Bridget, you cannot mean to do such a foolhardy thing! You do not even know who your admirer is. He could be anyone. To agree to meet him alone would be utter madness!"

"Don't tell me what to do! You have absolutely no authority over me."

"I am not telling you what to do," Pinkie said, controlling her temper with difficulty. "I merely offered advice that I think you would be wise to take. I can hardly force you—"

"You certainly cannot! Just you try, and see where it gets you. I don't know what Michael saw in you, to offer for you, but if we are to talk of madness, he must have been mad to marry you. For that matter, you are bound to introduce—"

"Bridget, hold your tongue," Kintyre commanded harshly from the doorway.

CHAPTER SIXTEEN

Neither Pinkie nor Bridget had noticed the door opening, and both looked toward Kintyre, Pinkie in dismay and Bridget with visible chagrin.

Noting Bridget's distress, and hoping to divert him, Pinkie said, "I am glad you have returned, sir. Bridget and I have been getting to know each other."

The last thing she wanted was for him to scold his sister in front of her. She had no doubt that Bridget would blame her for Kintyre's displeasure, and unless she could persuade the girl that she had nothing to fear from her new sister-in-law, life at Mingary would be intolerable.

The look Kintyre shot at Bridget showed that he knew they had not merely been getting acquainted, but Pinkie took hope when he turned to her and said evenly, "I hope you slept well, my dear."

"I did," she said. "You cannot have made a sound when you left me."

"I'm glad I did not disturb you. Cailean woke me at

dawn, scratching to go out, so I went out with him, hoping you could get a little more sleep. Perhaps now, though, you will not mind if I take a few moments to speak privately with Bridget. No, don't leave," he added swiftly when Pinkie turned toward the door. "Bridget can come with me. Now," he added with a grim look at his sister.

"Please, sir," Pinkie said, "may I have a moment alone with you first?"

"No," Bridget said, getting hastily to her feet and tucking her letter into her sash. "I do not need you to intercede for me."

"That will do, Bridget," Kintyre said. "Your behavior shames us both."

"How dare you take *her* side without—!"

"Please, sir," Pinkie interjected, "may I have just a brief word with you?"

She knew Bridget was afraid that she would tell Kintyre how rude she had been, and perhaps even that she had read her anonymous admirer's letter without permission, and hoped to meet him. The girl did not know her well enough, after all, to realize that she would never do such a thing. Pinkie wanted only to dissuade Kintyre from ripping up at her and making matters worse.

Bridget said urgently, "I tell you, you needn't—"

"Silence," Kintyre roared. "Go to your bedchamber and wait for me, and do not *dare* to speak another word unless you want to feel the full extent of my anger."

Turning pale, Bridget fled.

"Now," he said, turning to Pinkie, "tell me just how shameful she has been."

"Please, sir, I have no wish to cause trouble for Lady Bridget."

"She has caused her own trouble. She deserves whatever I choose to do."

"Well, I hope you will not do anything horrid," Pinkie

said sincerely. "She will blame me for it, you know, not you."

"Then she is a fool. She should blame herself."

"She is merely young, sir, and fearful that I shall somehow usurp her place with you. I know I cannot do that any more than Chuff's wife—when he has one—will usurp my place in his heart, but I think Bridget does not understand that."

"I do not think Bridget's relationship with me is much like yours with your brother," he said gently.

"Perhaps not, sir, but still . . ." She hesitated, thinking how she could say what she wanted to say without betraying Bridget. Finally, she said, "I am afraid that she still harbors a belief that Chuff means to offer for her."

He frowned, then said, "I have reason to think she no longer wants that."

"Do you? You mentioned once that she had received letters and posies from an unknown source, and . . . well, your aunt said that you had forbidden Bridget to read her letters until you had seen them, so I collect that she is still receiving them."

"She is, indeed. As to my reading her letters before she does, that is a duty I have neglected of late," he added calmly. "You need not choose your words with such care, lass. I have learned already that she took the letter."

"I still hope you will not scold her too severely, sir. She may well do something truly foolish—even foolhardy—if she grows too angry with you or with me. Indeed, I was going to say that I believe she thinks my brother wrote those dreadful letters to her, and she is pleased. I can assure you, he would never—"

"You need not tell me that," he said. "I acquitted him long since of even contemplating such a breach of civility."

"I am glad of that. Chuff would be appalled to think that anyone could believe that of him."

"He is not such a jackanapes. I suspect Coombs, and if I ever prove it, I'll take a horsewhip to him for his insolence. Have you anything more that you wish to say to me before I go upstairs?"

"Only to ask if you were successful in making your arrangements with Sir Renfrew. Your aunt told us you had arranged to meet with him."

"I made no arrangement," he said. "I simply went to his lodgings, hoping to find him at home. He was not there, however. His man said he had already gone out and professed not to know when to expect his return. I left another note for him."

"It begins to seem that he does not wish to see you."

"Aye," he said, "but I'll run him to earth one way or another. Now, if you will excuse me . . ."

"I do wish you would think carefully before being harsh with her," Pinkie said. "Your sister seems to—"

"I think you had better leave Bridget to me," he said curtly. "You have a far more gentle nature than I do, my dear, and I can understand that you hesitate to demand her head on a platter for the way she has behaved to you. I am not so amiable, however. I can promise that she will never speak so rudely to you again."

Pinkie would have liked to tell him what she thought of such high-handed behavior, but she did not yet know him well enough to speak her mind. Instead, she gritted her teeth and said nothing, hoping only that he would not reprimand his sister so brutally that Bridget refused to speak to her again.

For the next few days, however, it seemed that she had been wrong in her assessment of how the girl would react, for Bridget was as pleasant and obliging as anyone could wish. She acquiesced in whatever plan her aunt or hostess put forth, and generally exerted herself to be pleasing.

There were social functions to fill every day and evening,

for it seemed as if every hostess in London wanted the bridal couple to grace her party or ball. By the end of the week, if the number of invitations had diminished, Pinkie was too caught up in Chuff's imminent departure for Oxford to care. He intended to leave Friday morning, so she spent as much of the interim as she could at Faircourt House.

Her husband made no objection. He was still trying to run Sir Renfrew Campbell to earth, and rapidly was becoming exasperated with that gentleman's elusiveness. According to his man, Sir Renfrew had gone out of town but would return Friday morning.

Since Saturday was the first of June, Pinkie assumed that there would be no difficulty about the transaction, particularly since Kintyre had made it plain to Sir Renfrew that he was ready to repay the full amount. Nonetheless, Friday arrived too soon to please her. She kept her feelings to herself but made a point of riding early in Hyde Park with Chuff, so as to be at hand to bid him and Duncan farewell when they drove off in a laden chaise at half past nine.

Returning to George Street afterward with the groom Kintyre had hired to accompany her, she learned that her husband had gone to meet with Lord Menzies to discuss a new strategy, and then intended to see Sir Renfrew Campbell. Mrs. Thatcher and Lady Marsali had gone to visit the shops.

"Did Lady Bridget go with them, Sal?"

"No, ma'am. She went out alone directly afterward, though—to meet a friend, she said. She left this note for his lordship."

Alarmed, Pinkie said, "Do you know where he was to meet Lord Menzies?"

"No, and nor does Chalmers, ma'am, for I took the

liberty of asking him, and he don't know where his lordship meant to meet with Sir Renfrew, neither.''

Realizing that Kintyre's arrangements to repay the debt might take much of the day, Pinkie held out a hand, saying decisively, "I'll read that note, then, Sal."

Sal hesitated but a moment, then handed it to her.

With increasing apprehension, Pinkie unfolded the single sheet.

Dear Michael,

I am going away, and there is no use following me. My dearest love does not want his life determined by others, and nor do I. Because of England's foolish laws, we must be married over the anvil, but I shall not care about that. Indeed, Michael, I am sorry for flinging what I heard about Penelope's parents in your teeth. Your marrying her means I can follow my heart and not count the cost. Moreover, when we are safely married, if you should learn that you are mistaken in the size of her fortune and cannot pay Sir Renfrew all that he thinks he is owed, tell him I shall arrange for the rest. He is not to take your precious land. Do not worry about me, for I know exactly what I am doing, although certain persons will doubtless insist that I am a fool.

In great haste,
Bridget

Dismayed to think that Bridget, of all people, had learned the details of her parentage and passed them on to Kintyre, Pinkie found that her hands were shaking. She knew that she ought to have told him everything when he asked about her past on their wedding night. Indeed, she should have told him about Daft Geordie and Red Mag when he offered for her. Then, however, she had been thinking only about him and how he could resolve his troubles, but that was no excuse for having let it come to such a pass. Still, it was out, and there was nothing she could do about that. All she could do now was try to prevent Bridget from making things worse.

Thinking swiftly, she said, "Fetch Nan for me, will you, Sal?"

"She went out with Miss Munn soon after ye left the house, ma'am. Miss Munn said ye had given her errands to run, and she invited Nan to go along."

Hoping that Bridget's failure to take Nan with her meant that the maid knew nothing of her mistress's intention to leave, Pinkie said only, "Did Rankin drive Lady Marsali and Mrs. Thatcher to the shops?"

"Aye, he did, ma'am."

Balked of help from anyone in the George Street house, she said, "Do you know of a boy near at hand who could take a message to Faircourt House for me?"

"Aye, the kitchen boy can take it, my lady, if ye but tell him where to go."

"Excellent. I am going to write two messages, Sal, and then I shall want a coach of some sort. Have you any notion where I can come by one quickly?"

"Aye, ma'am. The mistress does hire a coachman to drive her when she goes out of town. Mr. Conlan has rooms just over in the Strand, and if he is not at home, his missus will know another who can serve ye. They are good, worthy people, my lady. Do ye mean to go after her young ladyship, then?"

Hesitating, reluctant to take a servant she barely knew into her confidence but realizing that she had little choice, Pinkie said, "You must have guessed at least the gist of Lady Bridget's note, Sal, so you will know that you must say nothing about this to anyone. His lordship would be most displeased if word of her foolishness should spread to others."

"I'd never," Sal said, turning pale.

Suppressing her own fear of his lordship's displeasure and what it would mean to their fragile relationship, Pinkie said, "You see, then, that I must go after her. I cannot waste time waiting for his lordship when he might not return before dinner, and I know of no one else whom I can ask to assist me."

"What of your brother, my lady, or Lord Balcardane?"

"They have driven to Oxford," Pinkie said. "If only I were a man, I could just get back on my horse and ride after Lady Bridget, but—"

"Ye mustn't, ma'am! 'Twouldn't be seemly."

"No, I know," Pinkie said. "Still, I must follow her, so I am going to send a message to Faircourt House, and leave another for Lord Kintyre, to let them know where I have gone. I suspect that Lady Bridget thinks she is meeting one young gentleman when in fact she is meeting another. When she discovers her error, she may simply turn around and come home; however, even in that event, she will want someone with her to lend countenance to her return. If we can put a good face on it, no one outside this house other than Lady Balcardane need know anything about it."

"Do ye know whither she be bound, my lady?"

"If she thinks they are going to be married over the anvil, they will be heading for Scotland."

"Scotland! But that be more than a day's journey. Surely she don't want to be with any gentleman overnight before she is properly married. She cannot have thought, ma'am. She will be ruined!"

"Not if I can prevent it," Pinkie said. "I do not think she thought about how long it would take. Indeed, I do not think she gave thought to anything except defying good advice that she did not want to hear." Knowing she had said far more than she ought to have said to anyone, let alone to Mrs. Thatcher's servant, Pinkie dismissed Sal and went in search of pen and paper.

Writing the first note swiftly, she explained the problem she faced and asked Mary to send a courier posthaste after Duncan and Chuff, asking them to follow her on the Great North Road. She assured Mary that she would leave word at every posting house she passed so they could find her easily.

The next note was much harder to write. It was no use to waste time trying to explain that she had never meant to deceive him, so she apologized instead for the circumstances that led him to hear the news from his sister, adding, *"I hope you can find it in your heart to forgive me, sir. That she sees it as justification for her deceit makes me all the more determined to bring her safely back to you."*

Signing simply, *"Penelope,"* she tried not to think about what his reaction would be. He would probably disapprove of her following Bridget as much as he would dislike his sister's running off with her anonymous lover. She could not think about that now, however. It was far more important to prevent Bridget's ruin.

At the last minute, when the coach was at the door, Sal said, "What if she's gone by a different road, my lady?"

"Gretna Green is the closest Scottish town, I believe, and she would take the Great North Road just to get to Scotland," Pinkie said. "It is the road we traveled to come here to London, after all."

"Did you travel through Gretna Green, then?"

"No," Pinkie said, "but I should think that anyone going from London to Scotland must begin on the Great North Road."

"There be dunnamany roads in England, my lady."

"So there are, but Lady Bridget will travel north, and I should think that she is beautiful enough to draw attention wherever she goes. I shall inquire about her at the posting houses along the way—''

"Ye'll never! Ye cannot go into a common posting house and be asking about her ladyship, ma'am. Only think what a fuss that would stir!"

"I won't go in myself," Pinkie said patiently. "I shall allow the coachman to make my inquiries. Or perhaps there is a better way," she added, thinking aloud. "If I remember correctly, Kintyre said that Cailean can follow a scent on the wind."

"The dog?"

"Aye. Where is he?"

"Generally somewhere near the kitchen if his lordship ain't on the premises," Sal said with a grin. "Shall I fetch him?"

"Aye, and the kitchen boy, as well. I must give him my message for Faircourt House, and explain how to get there. Whilst you do that, I'll run up and fetch something of Lady Bridget's for Cailean to take his scent from once we are out of town. Kintyre said he could not discern one scent amongst the many there are in London, but that on the road, he can."

A few minutes later she returned to find Sal, Cailean, and the kitchen boy awaiting her in the hall. To the latter, she handed her message for Mary, explaining carefully how he was to find Faircourt House. "I'd go myself," she said, "but for the fact that we must take the Great North Road through Highgate, and it is much quicker to reach it from here by taking Chancery Lane to High Holborn."

The boy was carefully tucking her note into his jacket, but he looked up, puzzled. "I thought Sal said ye was going after her ladyship."

Casting a disapproving look at Sal, Pinkie said, "It is not your business to discuss such things, laddie."

"Well, but if ye are going after her, ye'll not be going to Highgate, then."

She frowned. "Do you know aught of Lady Bridget's whereabouts?"

"I seen her, didn't I, getting into yon coach?"

Astonished, Pinkie said, "Who was with her?"

"Ain't nobody with her, just only the coachman. She arst where the gentleman was, and the coachman said he were going to meet her in Kilburn Wells, which it ain't on the Great North Road, Kilburn Wells ain't."

Turning to Sal, Pinkie said, "Do you know of this place?"

Sal shook her head. "I ain't never been outside Lunnon."

The kitchen boy said, "My auntie lives in Gutterhedge, she does, and when we visit her, we takes the Edgeware Road through Kilburn and Kilburn Wells. The Edgeware Road starts at Tyburn turnpike, at the end of Tyburn Lane, which is how I know where this Faircourt House must be, now that ye tells me."

"We'll ask the coachman," Pinkie said, hoping Sal was right about the man's knowledge and dependability.

If the middle-aged coachman was dismayed to see the great dog clearly prepared to climb into his coach, he did not say so. Instead, he simply asked Pinkie where they were bound.

"As to that," she said, "I think we are headed for Gretna Green, but—"

"Gretna Green! Faith, your ladyship, I cannot undertake such a great journey as that without preparation. Moreover, it would cost ye a fortune!"

"I have money," Pinkie said calmly, having taken the precaution of putting into her reticule the generous sum Duncan had given her on her wedding day. "If it costs more than I have with me, I can promise you that Lord Kintyre will make up the difference. In any event, I doubt that we shall have to travel more than a few hours at most before we will catch up with them." She had not intended to tell him exactly what her mission was, but since she had already mentioned Gretna, she was not surprised to see his eyebrows shoot upward.

"Like that, is it?" he said, nodding sagely.

"I am afraid so," she said. "I hope I can rely on your discretion, Mr. . . ." She paused expectantly.

"Oh, aye, I'll tell no one," he said. "And Conlan's the name, ma'am, Will Conlan. Have yer lad help ye in, then, and we'll be off."

"One moment," Pinkie said. "It has been brought to my attention that she might not be taking the Great North Road."

"She could, right enough," the coachman said, "but if she's bound for Gretna, they'll be more likely to head for Chester."

"Would that perhaps be by way of Kilburn Wells?"

"Aye, it could be. They can make for St. Albans from Kilburn, which would be your Great North Road, or they could make for Chester."

"We'll begin at Kilburn Wells, then," Pinkie said as the boy opened the coach door and pulled down the step. "Will you follow Tyburn Lane by Hyde Park?"

"Aye," said the coachman, eyeing Cailean with a jaundiced eye as the dog jumped into the coach. "We must pass through the Tyburn turnpike."

"Then we'll take the lad with us and let him off at Faircourt House." Entering the coach and gesturing for the kitchen boy to get in as well, she said to him, "I will go on with the coach, and you will deliver my message at Faircourt House. If Lady Balcardane is not at home, give the message to Fergus Owen, who is his lordship's steward, and tell him to get word to his lordship as quickly as he can. I have no pen to write more, but tell Fergus or her ladyship about Kilburn Wells, and tell Fergus I said to pay for you to take a hackney home. You must return to George Street as quick as you can, because you must tell his lordship the same thing that you tell Fergus. Can you remember all that I have said to you?''

"Aye, your ladyship,'' the boy said, swelled with the importance of his mission and the knowledge that he would ride in a hackney coach. His attention was soon claimed by activity in the streets through which they passed, and he sat with his nose pressed against the glass.

Pinkie settled back, smiling at the deerhound, lounging quite at its ease on the opposite seat. "You look as if you travel like this every day, Cailean,'' she said.

Cailean's ears twitched.

It seemed to take hours to reach Faircourt House—where they paused just long enough to set down the kitchen boy—and nearly as long after that to reach Kilburn Wells, which proved to be only a mile or two outside the city.

The coachman pulled his team to a halt in the yard of a small inn, and Pinkie descended from the coach with Cailean.

Looking up at the coachman, she said, "Would you kindly ask the ostlers if they have seen a very beautiful dark-haired young lady riding alone in a coach today, perhaps meeting a gentleman here?''

"Aye, ma'am, I'll ask.'' He jumped down from his box and strode into the taproom. A few moments later, he returned. "She were here, ma'am, not an hour since. They said her coach drove on soon afterward, but they cannot say for sure which way it went. One thought it headed back toward London, another that it went toward Kilburn, which would make a deal more sense, I'm thinking.''

"What about the gentleman?''

"Said there were one earlier, telling them they was to

tell her ladyship he'd meet her on the road, that her coachman knew the way.''

Pinkie frowned. "I don't like this at all. I must leave word for the others here. I'll be just a moment.'' Inside, she asked for a pen, paper, and wafers. Then, scrawling a hasty note, she gave it to the innkeeper, requesting that he give it to Balcardane or Kintyre, whoever was first to arrive.

Then, hurrying back out to the coach, she held Bridget's favorite wrapping gown for the dog to sniff, then said firmly, "Cailean, find Bridget."

Saying the words, she felt foolish and took care not to look at the coachman. Never before in her life had she given a dog such an order, and she had no idea what to expect. Perhaps there was a special command or tone she should use, and Cailean would not understand her.

But the dog sniffed obediently, looked at her as if to confirm the command, and when Pinkie repeated it, turned and loped off down the road.

"Follow him," she called to the coachman as she climbed back into the coach. "Don't let him out of your sight."

"Aye, my lady; looks like he's headed toward Kilburn, like I said." He whipped up his horses, but ten minutes later, he pulled up again and shouted, "He's turning, ma'am. Must be the Chester Road they're bound for." But a few minutes later, when a group of cottages came into view, the coachman reined his horses in again and shouted, "He's going wrong now, ma'am!"

Pinkie had put her head out the window, and was trying to watch Cailean running ahead of the coach, but with generally little success. She shouted back, "What do you mean, he's gone wrong?"

Leaning down from his box to look at her, the coachman said, "Ye said we was bound for Scotland, ma'am, but he's turned right off the road we should follow. Ye'd best call him back."

"What road is he taking?"

"I'm not sure of it myself. I'm not even certain where we are, but there's a chap yonder by that first cottage. I'll ask him."

The coach moved forward slowly, and when the coachman posed his question, the pedestrian said helpfully, "This is Willesden, and that road yonder goes to Wembley or to Hazelsden."

Pinkie frowned thoughtfully. "Are either of those towns north of here?"

The pedestrian chuckled. "Not as ye'd notice, ma'am. Wembley be to the west, and Hazelsden to the south. If it's north ye want, go straight on till ye come to Watford or to Great Stanmore. Then ye can cut over to the St. Albans Road."

The coachman said, "The dog's waiting for us, ma'am. Best ye call him back, and we'll get onto the right road."

Pinkie opened her mouth to call Cailean, but she shut it again and said to the pedestrian, "Have you seen another coach today, sir, perhaps with a beautiful dark-haired young lady inside?"

The man shook his head. "Seen two or three coaches, ma'am. Didn't notice who was inside them."

Nevertheless, Pinkie had made up her mind. "We'll follow the dog, Mr. Conlan. If they had wanted the St. Albans road, they would have kept straight on at Kilburn. I do not know why they came this way, but I am sure that they did. Cailean would not otherwise have led us here."

"I never heard of a dog as could follow someone in a coach," Conlan said doubtfully.

"I never had, either," she admitted. "But he followed his master all the way from Scotland with no more than a scent on the wind. We won't get lost, will we?"

"No, ma'am. Anywhere I can drive to, I can get home from. Never you worry your head about that."

For the next several hours, however, it did seem as if they were chasing wild geese, for the dog led them along sundry roads and lanes, sometimes heading west, sometimes south, through the villages of Sudbury, Norholt, and Hillingdon. As time passed, Pinkie found it more and more difficult not to think about Kintyre. She did not fear his anger nearly as much as she feared the likelihood that he would think she had purposely deceived him, and that he ought never to have married her. She had no regrets about their marriage, but if he resented her heritage, if everyone in London came to know of it now ... those thoughts alone made her feel sick.

When they entered the town of Uxbridge, the coachman drew up at the King's Arms to rest his horses and purchase a mug of ale for himself and a glass of lemonade for his passenger. Handing it to her, he said, "They'll be heading north now, ma'am, through Buckingham to Chester. I'd wager my best hat on it."

He admitted that no one at the King's Arms had noticed a coach with a young lady answering Bridget's description, but pointed out that it was not the only inn in Uxbridge. Sure enough, several inns later, at the White Horse, one of the ostlers said he had seen her half an hour before. The young lady had been expecting to meet a gentleman, he said, but the gentleman had left her a message, to drive on.

"How far have we come?" Pinkie asked Conlan.

The coachman looked thoughtfully at the sky. "I'd say we've come no more than twenty miles from London, ma'am, for all we've been driving nigh onto four hours since we left the city. We'll go faster on this here post road, and from what that chap said, we've gained distance on them."

Cailean had taken the opportunity to drink deep from each inn's horse trough, drawing fascinated attention from the ostlers. Uxbridge was larger than any village they had passed through before now, and Pinkie worried that the deerhound might lose Bridget's scent. The road passed straight through the town, however, and whether the dog had lost the scent or not, it seemed to catch it again when they passed the last cottage. Even so, the coachman's good cheer soon failed, for at the first crossroads, without hesitation, Cailean turned south again.

"Do we follow him, my lady?"

"Aye," Pinkie called.

"So much for my best hat." Fifteen minutes later he slowed his horses and shouted, "Faith, ma'am, I know where we are! That wall marks Stoke Place. My missus has a cousin in service there. We're not but a mile from the Bath Road!"

"Bath? Why would she go to Bath?" Pinkie asked the question aloud, but the coachman had whipped up his horses again, and he did not reply.

Five minutes later they reached the village of Slough, and the coachman drove into the yard at the White Hart and climbed down from his perch. It took only a moment to get the information they sought.

"Ten minutes ahead now," he told Pinkie. "She finally met her gentleman, right here, and apparently she was none too pleased to see him, as who can wonder after leading her such a merry chase. He would have done better to bring her by the quickest route without all that round-aboutation."

"Did anyone chance to overhear where they are bound?"

"No, and I did ask, ma'am, but it seems plain as a pikestaff, I should think."

"Why would she go to Bath?"

"Not Bath, ma'am. My guess would be Bristol or Milford Haven if you're still thinking they'll be bound for Scotland."

"Bristol! Faith, but that means—He owns ships! He's taking her by sea!"

CHAPTER SEVENTEEN

The whole truth washed over Pinkie in that instant. Knowing that Bridget believed her anonymous admirer to be Chuff, and believing along with Kintyre that it was far more likely to be Mr. Coombs, she had not given much thought to the identity of the gentleman leading them in circles, or to his reason for doing so. She had been interested only in catching up with them to save Bridget's reputation. But Bridget's admirer was not Mr. Coombs. Unless she was mistaken, Bridget had been as astonished to learn his identity as Pinkie was, for her secret admirer could be none other than Sir Renfrew Campbell.

Mr. Coombs might have been capable of taking her to Gretna. He was foolish enough and young enough to view such an act as both heroic and romantic. Still, Pinkie would not have credited him with sufficient courage to risk infuriating both Kintyre and Balcardane by running away with Bridget. She saw now that she ought to have given that detail much more consideration, for had she done so, she might have realized sooner that Sir Renfrew certainly would take such a risk. It was no great wonder that she had not thought of him earlier, however, since she had believed that Kintyre himself was meeting with Sir Renfrew that morning.

"We must catch them, Mr. Conlan, and quickly!"

"I'll do my best, ma'am. That dog's sure all atwitch to be off."

Though Conlan was willing, they soon came to a steep hill, which slowed them considerably, and by the time they arrived at Maidenhead and drove into the yard of the Saracen's Head, his team was flagging badly.

"We must hire fresh horses," Pinkie said firmly. "Have the ostlers choose what you like, Mr. Conlan, but tell them to hurry."

The inn's ostlers were more experienced than the others they had met, and made the change with more speed than Pinkie had expected. In the process, Mr. Conlan managed to glean some information, both welcome and unwelcome. "They've been this way, ma'am," he said before climbing back onto his box. "They left their coach but took the coachman along, and they've hired a chaise and four."

"Then they'll leave us in the dust," Pinkie exclaimed. "Perhaps I should also hire a chaise."

"If ye do, I shall have to return to London, and I don't mind telling ye I'd be loath to do that if you'll be going on by yourself. I don't think they'll travel a deal faster than we shall, for they'll encounter traffic, you see, and they'll want their dinner soon, too. We ought to catch up with them then if we don't before."

Recognizing the common sense of his words, and realizing that she had no wish to catch up with Sir Renfrew and Bridget without someone large and masculine to support her, Pinkie agreed to continue as they were. Realizing now that Sir Renfrew had taken such a roundabout course to throw off pursuit, and certain that he could have no notion they were following him, she called Cailean into the coach but left the window down, hoping that if the chaise ahead altered course, the dog would be able to sense it and give them warning.

Having expected to catch up with Bridget quickly, she could not help feeling depressed. When they learned in Reading that the chaise had gained distance and was again thirty minutes ahead, she had to fight a renewed urge to hire her own chaise in place of the lumbering coach. Conlan thoughtfully purchased a bun and some sliced beef for her, however, and although she shared it with Cailean as they drove on, the food soon lifted her spirits.

It was nearly seven o'clock when the coach turned into the yard at the Globe in Newbury, having paused at nearly every inn since Reading so its driver could ask questions. They learned only that Sir Renfrew had twice changed horses, but at the Globe, Conlan quickly discovered that a gentleman traveling post with a very young lady had hired a private parlor to dine.

"They be here, ma'am," he said.

"Thank heaven," Pinkie said with feeling. "I think I should confront them first alone, Mr. Conlan, since my sister will not thank me for introducing a stranger to such a scene. Perhaps you will be good enough to await me here with Cailean. I will either bring her out in a few minutes or send you word to join me inside."

"If you're sure, ma'am."

"I am," Pinkie said, gathering confidence. After all, she had met Sir Renfrew more than once, and he had always been perfectly polite to her. Nor did she expect trouble from Bridget. Having learned that her secret admirer was Sir Renfrew Campbell would undoubtedly make the younger girl perfectly willing to return to London, even if it meant facing Kintyre's wrath.

Descending to the yard, Pinkie shook out her skirts, took a deep breath, and walked into the inn. The innkeeper met her in the hall, and when she explained her wish to speak with the couple who had hired his private parlor, he escorted her upstairs, where he rapped sharply on one of the doors along a narrow corridor.

Receiving a command to enter, the innkeeper pushed the door open, saying, "I've brung ye a visitor, sir."

Pinkie walked past him into the room, to find Bridget and Sir Renfrew seated opposite each other at a small round table before the fireplace, where a fire crackled and shot sparks up the flue.

Bridget gasped and started to rise, but Sir Renfrew reached across the table, grabbed her wrist, and said firmly, "Sit down, lass. I'll deal with this. Leave us," he added curtly to the innkeeper, who left at once, shutting the door behind him.

Pinkie did not object to his leaving. This was no business to conduct before strangers. "I daresay you are surprised to see me," she said, moving nearer the table.

"Where is Michael?" Bridget demanded, looking past her as if she expected to see her brother stride into the room. The girl looked pale, and her voice had less animation than usual. Her eyes shifted back to Sir Renfrew.

He remained silent, watching Pinkie.

"I do not know where he is at this moment," Pinkie replied honestly. "I left word for him to follow me, however, so he could be along very soon."

Sir Renfrew said, "How did ye follow us, lassie? I vow, I'm right interested to hear that, for I'd have said that no man could do it."

Pinkie nearly told him, then decided that it was none of his business. Instead, she said, "I mean to take Lady Bridget back to London with me, Sir Renfrew. She had no business running away in such a slapdash manner and at such risk to her good name. My coach is waiting in the yard." Turning to Bridget, she said, "Fetch your cloak if you have one, please."

Bridget did not move. She seemed spiritless, unlike her normal self.

"She will stay with me," Sir Renfrew said calmly. "I have no objection, however, if ye wish to come with us, madam. No doubt the lass will welcome the company of another female."

Pinkie shook her head. "You cannot mean that," she said. "It is bad enough that you have abducted her. Surely you do not think you can simply abduct me, too. I told you, sir, I have a coach waiting, and the coachman is a quite large and burly man. I have only to call him—"

"Ye'll no be callin' anyone. MacKellar!"

At her left, a door that she had not previously noticed opened and another man entered the room. He was taller than Sir Renfrew, younger and more muscular, and clearly was his servant or henchman.

"Aye, sir," he said, looking curiously at Pinkie.

"Lady Kintyre has managed to follow us here," Sir Renfrew said, "and she tells me she's got a coach and a driver waiting in the yard. I'll attend to them, but ye'll need to keep an eye on these two lassies whilst I do."

"Aye, sir," MacKellar said, pulling a pistol from his coat pocket as casually as if he had reached for a handkerchief.

Pinkie stiffened. "What on earth do you think you are doing?"

Sir Renfrew said, "I told ye, lass, I'm taking Lady Bridget to be my wife. If ye're concerned about Kintyre's debt, ye need not be. I've told him I'll accept the lass in lieu of half the debt, and I'm a man o' my word. He need pay only the other half, and I'll give him what time he needs, seeing as he can scarcely pay me when I've left England without settling the arrangements with him. 'Tis hardly fair, that, and I'm a gey fair man, I am."

"How dare—"

"Now, madam, dinna be wroth with me. I'm a man in love, is what I am. Bide ye now with MacKellar, and dinna be thinking he will not shoot. He's a faithful lad, is MacKellar, and he kens well that if he murders ye, I'll see him safe out of England before ever anyone else discovers his crime."

Glancing at MacKellar, Pinkie doubted that he would shoot two innocent females in cold blood, but when she raised her chin, the big man raised his pistol.

"Sit down," he growled.

"Ye'd best do as he says, lass," Sir Renfrew said amiably. Rising and picking up one of the wineglasses from the table, he strolled over to stand beside and just a step behind her, as if he would bar her way to the corridor.

Pinkie rapidly considered her options. She still did not think MacKellar would shoot either of them, but if she screamed, neither could she depend upon the innkeeper to take her side in the matter. Even Mr. Conlan would be reluctant to take on a man of Sir Renfrew's standing, and she knew she could not depend upon Sir Renfrew to speak the truth to her coachman. He was much more likely to lie.

He was watching her, and he smiled, saying, "Ye've a verra expressive face, lass. Ye'd ha' done better to bide a wee and hope Kintyre were right behind ye."

Before Pinkie realized what he intended, he snapped his free arm around her neck, forcing her chin up. The moment she opened her mouth to object, he tipped the contents of the wineglass down her throat, and she swallowed reflexively, gasping and choking, sickened by the horrid taste.

"I prepared that dose for my Bridget," Sir Renfrew said,

"but I'll just pour another for her if she requires it. If she behaves sensibly, she need not have more than she's already had. I fear, though, that ye willna be such a complacent prisoner, Lady Kintyre, and I havena come this far only to be done in by a wee lass like yourself. Ye'd best sit down now, before ye fall down."

Still coughing violently, Pinkie strove to catch her breath, but it was several moments before she could speak. "Wh . . . what was in that wine?"

"Nobbut a wee dose of laudanum; enough so that ye'll soon sleep soundly and give us no trouble."

Pinkie opened her mouth to scream, but he clapped his hand over it and dragged her to the chair he had been sitting on. "Fetch the curtain cord, MacKellar."

Putting the pistol back in his pocket, the henchman drew a *skein dhu* from his boot and cut the cord, handing it to Sir Renfrew, who swiftly used it to bind Pinkie to the chair. Then, turning to Bridget, he said gently, "I'm just doing this so she'll stay quiet, lass."

Bridget said, "Did you really only give her laudanum?"

"Aye," he said, binding a handkerchief over Pinkie's mouth and knotting it at the back of her head. "It's nobbut what I gave ye earlier, in the coach, so ye ken she'll recover her senses in time."

"That stuff gave me a headache," Bridget complained.

"I dinna doubt it; however, if ye'll sit doucely here whilst I deal with yon coachman, ye needna have more o' the stuff. I give ye my word on it."

Feeling dizzy and nauseous, and knowing the dose would likely act swiftly since she had eaten little that day, Pinkie concentrated on inhaling deeply and keeping her eyes open, hoping to delay its effects. If Mr. Conlan should come looking for her, she could at least moan or make some sound, so that Sir Renfrew would not get away with simply telling the man he had not seen her.

Sir Renfrew left them alone with MacKellar, and although he was gone for some time, no one else came to the parlor. Bridget seemed to have more interest in her plate than in her predicament. She kept glancing at Pinkie while she pushed food around with her fork, but she made no effort to speak to her.

Long before Sir Renfrew returned, Pinkie was fighting to keep her eyes open. Her body felt like a limp rag. She was dimly aware of his return, but his voice came to her as if through a heavy fog.

"Yon coachman will give us no trouble," he said. "I paid his fee back to London and told him her ladyship had decided to remain here overnight and return with the lass in the morning."

Bridget said, "Did you tell him that you are the man who tricked me?"

"Nay, then, lassie, why would I tell him such a daft thing as that? I told him I was your uncle, that I'd guessed what ye meant to do, and that I'd got here afore ye and sent the vile lad who abducted ye off wi' a flea in his ear. He congratulated me heartily on my good sense, and said he was glad . . ."

Pinkie heard no more.

Michael had enjoyed more success in his meeting with Menzies than at any other thing he had done that day. Since persuading the Lords to overturn the law had so far proved unsuccessful, they had decided to work toward amending it instead. Satisfied that Menzies would present a strong argument, he had gone in search of Sir Renfrew Campbell, hoping to settle his debt at last.

He arrived at Sir Renfrew's lodgings only to learn from the landlord that the man had gone.

"It is important that I find him," Michael explained.

"Did he chance to say where he was bound or when he will return?"

"Not so as I could be clear about it, sir. He said he were visiting friends in Buckinghamshire and would return in a few days, but he did not leave a scrap behind, nor his servant neither. Nor did he give me so much as a penny on account, so I'll not be holding the rooms for him. I've another gentleman moving in today."

Michael's temper stirred at the likelihood that Campbell had left London on purpose. As it stood now, there was no way to give him his money before June 1, and he wondered if the man hoped to claim the land by making it impossible to settle the debt. He did not know the law well enough to be certain such a plot would fail, but he doubted that any magistrate would agree that Campbell could declare default by avoiding payment when it was clearly at hand. Still, if the man went back to Scotland, he could make matters difficult.

Hoping he could learn more about Campbell's destination from one of the urchins on the street, he wasted another half hour making unsuccessful inquiries before he returned to George Street to find the household in an uproar.

After silencing the two with the most right to speak their minds and decreeing that he would hear, in turn, each person who had something to say, he managed to curb the older ladies' flights of fancy and glean what little the servants knew. Although it was no mean feat to sort fact from opinion, and the whole business took more time than it should have, he finally did manage to ascertain, first, that his sister had run away, and second, that his bride had run after her. Only then did Sal think to hand him Bridget's note. As he read it, he wished fervently that his sister were at hand so that he could vent his temper on her.

"You should read Penelope's note, too, dear," Lady Marsali said.

"Do you mean to say that there's another one?"

"Well, you certainly do not imagine that she would have gone off like she did without telling you where she was going, do you?" Lady Marsali handed it to him.

"Ma'am, at this moment, I do not know whether I am on my head or on my heels," he said, breaking the seal. "Here is my sister, writing that she is running away to Gretna Green with her lover, and I do not know who he is, nor does she bother to enlighten me. Has my wife rectified that omission, I wonder?"

"If you mean, did she name the man, she certainly did not tell Sal, and she sealed her note to you, so we could not read it," Cousin Bella said in a tone of deep resentment. "If she knows who he is, I think it prodigiously unconscionable of her if she has kept the information from you."

"From us, you mean," Lady Marsali said with a twinkle. "Did she tell you who it is, dear? You look as if her note has made you angrier than Bridget's did."

Michael stared at the words Penelope had written, trying to make sense of them. Looking again at Bridget's note, he realized what his bride had thought, and what she must be feeling. The knowledge made him want to strangle his sister.

"Do not fret, Michael, dear," Lady Marsali said soothingly. "You will find them. I am sure that Penelope will leave word wherever she can. Sal said that she intended to take the Great North Road to Scotland, but the kitchen boy tells us they were heading for Kilburn Wells, which argues the Chester Road, Bella tells me. You will need this, in any case," she added, handing him a thick wad of banknotes.

Sincerely thanking her for her foresight, and hoping that she was right in her expectation that Penelope would leave a clear trail, he sent for the kitchen boy, to hear that young man's message for himself. Learning that the lad had taken another message to Faircourt House, Michael sent for Chalmers and told him to pack a bag with clothing for at least two days. Not waiting for a reply, he next told the kitchen boy to run to the nearest public stable and have them send round a post chaise.

Chalmers said, "I took the liberty of packing a bag for you, my lord, and there is a chaise awaiting your pleasure in the mews."

"Good man," Michael said.

"I have packed a bag for myself, as well," Chalmers added.

"That won't be necessary," Michael told him. "If I have to chase them all the way to Scotland, I shall want you here to escort Lady Marsali back to Edinburgh. I'll get word to you one way or another."

He waited only for the chaise and four to come round to the front, then ordered the postilions to take him to Faircourt House, where he found the Countess of Balcardane and her mama-in-law in the drawing room.

Both ladies greeted him with undisguised relief, and Mary said, "Oh, sir, we are so very glad to see you. Have you had any word from Pinkie?"

"No, ma'am, only the messages she left for me. I was hoping that you might have learned more."

"Nothing," she said. "I sent Dugald, our footman, after Duncan and Chuff posthaste, to tell them what happened. I collect from what her young messenger let slip that you do not know the identity of Bridget's . . ." She paused tactfully.

"I have a strong suspicion," Michael said, reluctant to share it with her.

"I, too, have formed a suspicion, sir, but whom do you suspect?"

Lady Agnes exclaimed, "Aye, who could it be? The lassie is as pretty as she can stare, but I vow, sir, she has a manner that is not conciliating, and I have seen no one in particular making up to her. We have seen a great deal of her since you arrived in London, too. Why, I dare swear you have attended nearly every event that we have attended. Indeed, it seems that we were always seeing you, but perhaps that is explained by your falling tail over top for our Pinkie, is it not? Oh, I do hope she does nothing foolish."

"She has already done something foolish," Michael said gruffly. "She had no business to go haring off after my idiotish sister."

Mary smiled at him. "Now, sir, you know you do not mean that. From what Pinkie wrote to me, she believed there was nothing else she could do. She had no one at hand from whom she could seek advice and did not know where to find you."

"She could have discussed the matter with you, ma'am."

"Yes, she might have done that, and I might have sent Dugald with her, and sent someone else after Duncan and Chuff. However, I cannot think you would rather have her haring after your sister with a footman at her side to see and hear all, and I doubt that she would have allowed Dugald to accompany her, in any event."

"You might have commanded it," Michael said, but there was no strength in his voice, and he added hastily, "I should not have said that, ma'am. I know that she thought she was doing the right thing, and that she was thinking only of protecting Bridget's good name. When I get my hands on my sister . . ."

"Yes, I can see that you would like to wring her neck for this," Mary said, "and in all candor, I do think she needs a stronger hand to guide her."

"Well, it's not just *her* neck I'll wring," Michael said

grimly. "The young scoundrel who seduced her deserves whipping."

"*Young* scoundrel? But I thought—Pray, sir, won't you tell us whom you suspect? Indeed, we may be able to assist you if only we know who it is."

Grimacing, Michael said, "I hoped to have proof first, ma'am, and in truth, I do not like telling you, for the simple reason that he has strong ties to this house."

"Not Chuff! No, you cannot suspect him, so—Mr. Coombs? Oh, my dear."

Michael spread his hands. "You can see why I did not like to speak."

"Oh, yes, but it cannot be Mr. Coombs."

"No, indeed," Lady Agnes said. "Mr. Coombs is soon to return to Cambridge, after all, and besides, he cannot have gone off with Lady Bridget, my dear Kintyre. It would have been utterly impossible, for he is only one man."

Michael waited for her to continue, but for once in her life she did not. She merely returned his steady gaze with a brightly expectant one of her own, as if she were waiting for him to choose someone else. He looked to Mary for enlightenment.

She smiled, and he was suddenly aware of how serene her smile was. He felt himself relaxing, even though he knew she was about to give him news that would further complicate matters.

"Mr. Coombs was here this morning," she said, "after Pinkie's message arrived. He is not here presently, or I would allow you to speak to him yourself, so you could be perfectly satisfied. He has taken our Roddy to visit Mrs. Salmon's Waxworks. They will return shortly, but I daresay you do not want to wait."

"No," Michael said, "but if it was not Coombs . . ."

The countess tilted her head a little to one side, and

suddenly he knew that he ought to have seen the truth much sooner.

"Sir Renfrew Campbell."

"Yes, I should think so," Mary said. "You will perhaps think I ought not to know about your business with him, but Duncan confided a little to me about your situation when you offered for Pinkie. I love her dearly, you see, and I did not want to see her make a mistake. We thought . . . No, I should not speak of that. I do think Sir Renfrew is capable of making off with your sister, do not you?"

"Aye, I do, and what's more, if he did, he'll not be heading for Gretna."

"Bristol or Holyhead?"

"Bristol, I should think. He has at least one ship berthed there, if not more. I won't wait, my lady, not for Coombs or for Balcardane. I've a chaise waiting outside, and if I cannot make Bristol by morning, I shall be surprised."

"Yes, you had better go straightaway," she agreed. "Duncan will not come here first, in any case, for he, too, will recognize the likelihood that Sir Renfrew will make for the coast."

"How could he? He scarcely knows the man."

"Well," she said, looking self-conscious, "I'm afraid I suggested it to him in the message I sent with Dugald. It seemed so very likely, you see, once I gave it some thought."

Pinkie's first thought was that she was going to be sick. The rocking of the coach made her feel dizzy and nauseated. She opened her eyes and saw that the sun was peeking over a hill not far behind them. A shaft of sunlight touched her face and was doubtless what had wakened her from her opiate slumber. She was hunched in the corner of a coach, facing Sir Renfrew, who was snoring on the forward-facing seat beside Bridget. The girl reclined in the corner of the coach most distant from Pinkie. Her eyes were shut.

Pinkie moved, intending to sit straighter, and could not repress a moan.

Bridget's eyes opened, and in a low voice, she muttered, "Did that awful stuff give you a headache, too?"

"Now that you mention it," Pinkie murmured, grimacing. "I hadn't noticed before, because my whole body aches from sitting so long in the same position." Gingerly, using the strap to steady herself, she managed to pull herself upright.

She would have liked to let down the window and breathe fresh air, but she did not want to waken Sir Renfrew. Instead, she pressed her forehead against the glass, closing her eyes again and savoring the sensation of its coolness against her aching brow. After a moment, she opened her eyes again, then stiffened at the sight that met her gaze.

Cailean, faithful Cailean, was loping along behind the coach.

"What is it?" Bridget asked. "What do you see?"

"Aye, Lady Kintyre, tell us what you see that surprises you so," Sir Renfrew said, sitting up. "It canna be Kintyre, for we must be nearing Bristol by now, and the only way he can have followed us is if he stopped at every inn and posting house, seeking word from you. Had he done that, though, he'd be a full day behind us, so what is it that you see?"

"Nothing," Pinkie lied. "Nothing at all."

"Aye, sure, I can see that for myself." Leaning forward, he let down the window and put his head out. "Well, damme, so that's how ye managed it!"

"What is it?" Bridget demanded. "Why does no one tell me anything?"

"It's that great hound of Kintyre's," Sir Renfrew said.

"Cailean?"

"He'll not harm you, sir," Pinkie said hastily. "Let me call him."

Sir Renfrew chuckled. "What, and invite him into this coach with us? Nay then, lass; I dinna mind having to give up our chaise to accommodate ye, but I won't travel with yon great brute, and we canna have him following us through the streets of Bristol like a mute in a funeral procession either. He'll draw the eye of everyone we pass. I'll soon be rid of him, however." Putting his head out again, he shouted at MacKellar to stop the chaise.

"Give me your pistol, man," Sir Renfrew said, opening the door and getting out of the coach.

Pinkie heard his words, but at first they made no sense to her. Then, with a rush of horror, she knew what he meant to do.

Forgetting her aches, and even her own safety, she scrambled out of the coach in his wake, shrieking at the top of her lungs, "Cailean, no! Go back, run! Oh, go!"

The big deerhound paused and looked confused.

Sir Renfrew took aim.

Pinkie and Bridget screamed as one, "Cailean, run!"

A deafening shot echoed through the morning air, and the gallant deerhound dropped in his tracks.

CHAPTER EIGHTEEN

When Michael's chaise rattled through the Walcot turn-pike on the outskirts of Bath, he knew that he had traveled one hundred and six miles from London, for the milestone sat at the side of the road just before the gate. The time was ten minutes before nine o'clock. He had not stopped along the way other than to change teams and postilions, for he was as certain as he could be that Sir Renfrew would head straight for his ship at Bristol harbor. If he did not—if they had gone by another route or to another destination—he would not find them in time, in any event.

Upon setting out, he had half expected to meet Penelope and Bridget on the road, on their way back to London, for he believed his bride to be a woman who accomplished what she set out to accomplish. Once darkness fell, however, he realized that if she had succeeded, they might pass each other in the night without knowing, and it would serve no good purpose to worry about that. He had made up his mind to go to Bristol, and to Bristol he would go.

If he dithered over other possibilities, or took time to stop each oncoming coach, assuming they *would* stop, Sir Renfrew would easily succeed in carrying off his sister.

When the chaise entered the city of Bath, the road forked ahead of it. The chaise kept to the right and, according to a sign painted high on the first building, passed along a road called—most oddly, in Michael's opinion—the Paragon Vineyard. Straight ahead he saw the huge sign atop the York House Inn.

Although he had spent all of the money he had carried on his person upon returning to George Street and a good deal of that which Lady Marsali had given him, it did not occur to him to alter his means of travel. Traveling post at nine pence per mile—plus added inducements to make the lads travel faster than the legally ordained five miles per hour—was ruinously expensive. However, the present boys had assured him that their Bath replacements would take him right down to the harbor in Bristol. Any other vehicle, he knew, would waste a great deal of his time. A driver hiring out himself and his coach would be less willing than the postilions were to spring his horses, and it would take time just to find a reliable man who knew his way around Bristol. Michael had never been there.

The change at the York House was quick, but he took a few minutes longer to eat a bun and drink some coffee that a servant brought out to the chaise, and then they were off again. The new postilions maintained a pace similar to that of the others, but now that he was nearing his destination, the twelve miles to Bristol seemed to take forever. In reality, they took less than two hours.

The chaise wended its way downhill through narrow, twisting streets, then alongside the River Avon, which Michael recognized because the road from Bath frequently had run beside it. They drew to a halt at last in an enormous square in what appeared to be the lower end of the oldest part of town.

As Michael emerged from the chaise, he thanked the postilions but expressed his surprise that he had not yet caught sight or smell of the sea. "I expected you to deliver me to the harbor," he said.

The older postilion chuckled. "The harbor be all around us here, my lord. Queen's Square be the very point o' land where the River Frome joins the River Avon. Them lads we changed with said ye'd be wanting the Customs House."

"Aye, that's true, but where is the sea?"

"The sea be a good distance from Bristol, my lord. It be nine or ten miles yet before the Avon flows into the Bristol Channel, and nigh onto a hundred after that before any ship reaches open sea. Don't fret yourself, though. We've got plenty o' ships here to serve ye. Ye'll find one to take ye wherever ye wants to go."

"I see," Michael said. "Where shall I find the Customs House, then?"

"Just there in front of ye, m' lord," the man said, pointing to a large building that formed the central block on what Michael judged to be the north side of the square. "Ye'll find the quay and most berths for larger boats and barges on the Frome side, yonder beyond those buildings." He pointed to his left. "Smaller ones be on the Back, the Avon side, where we turned in." He gestured to his right.

Queen's Square was enormous, larger than any square Michael had seen in London, and very handsomely built. Walks and rows of trees occupied its center, along with a fine equestrian statue. Shops flanked the Customs House, and he saw a tavern and a coffeehouse.

Dismissing the chaise, he walked to the Customs House, and as he went up the steps, he noticed a small crowd of people gathered near the northwest corner of the square, on what the postilion had called the Frome side, but he paid it little mind. Inside, he learned that Sir Renfrew did indeed have a ship berthed on the quay, and that it was called the *Lass of Arisaig*.

The customs agent said, "I believe that ship departs for France this morning, my lord, if it has not already done so. Its captain claimed his drawback yesterday, after our agents had supervised the transfer of Sir Renfrew's export goods from our bonded warehouse to the cargo hold, where they remain under our seal."

The news sent a cold chill through him, but he did not think Sir Renfrew had any intention of sailing to France. "What does he export?"

"Numerous things, I'll warrant, but it's the tobacco that he offloaded to our warehouse and then loaded again last night."

"I must hurry if I am to have any chance of catching up with him," Michael said, seeing no point in delaying further by telling the agent that if Sir Renfrew was dealing in tobacco, that tobacco was doubtless destined for English shores rather than French. He took time only to get directions to the *Lass of Arisaig*.

Hurrying outside and turning toward the quay, he saw that the small crowd still lingered at the corner. In his hurry, he would have walked on had he not heard the familiar whine of an injured animal. Though he knew it likely was only a stray hit by a speeding coach or chaise, he could not pass without making certain that someone was looking after it properly, if it had a chance to survive, or would put it out of its misery if it did not. Forcing a path through the gawkers, he said, "Let me have a look. I know a good deal about helping injured animals."

Willingly, they made way for him, and when he saw what lay at the center, he gasped in shock. "Cailean!"

Michael knew that Penelope had taken the great dog with her, and he had been glad, for he knew that Cailean would protect her. But he had also assumed that the dog would stay with her in the coach, and that it was with her still. That it was not, and that it had been injured, stirred a host of unwelcome suspicions.

He quickly knelt at Cailean's side.

"He's dead," an urchin said. "Just look at all that blood!"

"No, he's not dead," Michael said after a swift examination. "He's been shot, though, and he's worn to the bone. He must have—"

"Kintyre! The devil, sir, is that you there?"

Looking up, he saw the harsh face of the Earl of Balcardane peering over the shoulders of nearby onlookers. MacCrichton, looking worried, stood beside him. Michael had never been so glad to see any two men in all his life.

MacCrichton said, "I say, isn't that Cailean?"

"It is," Michael replied grimly.

"Then you have not yet found Lady Bridget," Balcardane said.

"No, I have not, and matters have altered now considerably, sir."

"In what way?"

"Because if Cailean is here, like this, it can only mean that Campbell has now got Penelope as well."

MacCrichton exclaimed, "Pinkie?"

"Aye, lad, and according to the customs agent, his ship is departing for France this morning."

"What ship?"

"The *Lass of Arisaig,* berthed on the quay."

"Look after the dog," Chuff snapped. "I'll see that the ship stays where it is." He left at once, breaking into a run, his long strides soon taking him beyond sight. He returned, however, just a few minutes later, as Michael was laying Cailean gently on the seat in Duncan's chaise.

"He's already gone, and he's got both women with him," Chuff announced angrily. "The harbormaster tells me he saw them himself, and they sailed over an hour ago. What's more, we cannot follow till tomorrow unless the wind shifts."

"How can that be?" Duncan demanded.

"Something to do with winds and the tides, and the proximity of the mouth of the Avon to that of the Severn," Chuff explained. "I did not try to understand it all, for once the man told me that Campbell had gone and that the tide had turned so no more ships can leave until nearly seven tomorrow morning, I ran back to tell you. We must find a ship bound for France and book passage for ourselves."

"He's not going to France," Michael said. "He's bound for Scotland."

"But they say he's got tobacco aboard which must go to France."

Michael exchanged a look with Duncan, and the older man said, "Do you think he might be one of our smugglers?"

"I do, sir, for I've never heard him speak of exporting goods to France."

"You'll be taking a big chance, going north when the evidence points south."

"I don't care about the evidence. I know Campbell." Michael paused as another thought occurred to him. "Do you know how much it costs to take a ship to Scotland? I'll be cleaned out soon."

"Don't worry about the cost," Duncan said. "Amongst the three of us, we'll find enough to get you there."

"I'm going, too," Chuff said.

Duncan nodded. "Aye, you should, but we cannot all go. One of us must return to London to tell the others what we've learned, and to look after them."

Michael nodded. "If you would be so kind as to see that my aunt and our servants get safely back to Edinburgh, sir, I'll be much obliged to you."

"I'll do that," Duncan promised. "You just find Pinkie and your sister."

"Aye, I will, but I warn you, when I do, no one is going to be happy."

Duncan nodded. "I know you must be wroth with your sister, lad."

"My sister is a disobedient chit who defied my orders and must suffer the consequences," Michael said grimly. "But she is not alone in this, sir. My wife displayed a foolhardiness I'd not have expected in her, and whether you or MacCrichton agree with that assessment, she will soon learn what I think of it, and then she will wish that she had thought twice before haring off after Bridget as she did. As for Sir Renfrew Campbell," he added, his tone hardening, "when I catch that bastard, I'm most likely going to kill him."

The *Lass of Arisaig* took two and a half days to reach Poll Beither Bay, because, for the first ten hours or so, the wind blew steadily from the north, and soon after it shifted to the west, the ship dropped anchor for a couple of hours. Why or where it stopped, Pinkie had no way of knowing, for she and Bridget were locked in a small, stuffy cabin belowdecks, where they had to make do with a single cot and an odd sort of slops basin boxed into a corner for their personal needs.

For some time after Sir Renfrew shot Cailean, both young women had sat in a near state of shock, and it had taken no more than a threat to force more laudanum down their throats to make them board quietly. Even so, when Pinkie saw the harbormaster watching from the quay, she would have cried out to him had Sir Renfrew not put his hand over her mouth and scooped her up in his arms.

To a curious sailor, he muttered, "Lass fainted, poor thing. I'll just take her below and see she's made comfortable."

She was not comfortable. What food they received consisted of bread and tea, except for bowls of some sort of stew that MacKellar brought them the first evening. The second evening the water was rough, so they had only bread and some water from a jug. Thus, when MacKellar came to tell them they had arrived, both of them were more pleased to hear it than one might have expected.

On deck, Bridget looked around and said, "Well, at least I know where we are. That's Dunbeither House on the hillside there, so this is Poll Beither Bay."

Pinkie said, "How far are we from Balcardane?"

"I don't know, but we are only about eleven miles from Kilmory by sea, and Kilmory is but six miles across the peninsula from Mingary. From Mingary, Michael told me that he went to Balcardane in a day by riding through Glen Tarbert to Loch Linnhe, then sailing across and hiring a horse at Kentallen Inn."

"We'll be going ashore straightaway," Sir Renfrew said from behind them.

Wondering how much he had overheard, Pinkie made no reply. Twenty minutes later, they entered Dunbeither House. Like a tour guide, Sir Renfrew told them that he had had the huge, sprawling house built himself when he realized that the house on his mother's estate near Arisaig was too small and too far north to let him keep close watch over his property.

When he began to tell them how he had imported the marble for the hall floor from Italy, Bridget interrupted him. "We don't care about your stupid house, sir. We are tired, hungry, and filthy, and we want to go home."

"Ye are home now, lassie," he said. "This is your home. I'll take ye upstairs to your bedchamber m'self, and Mac-Iver there can get some lads to draw ye a bath. Ye'll want to be clean and sweet-smelling for your wedding night."

"I am *not* going to marry you," Bridget snapped without glancing at the man near the stairway to whom Sir Renfrew had pointed.

"Aye, but ye are. I've sent MacKellar for the parson, and we canna waste him, after all. Would ye like me to carry ye upstairs, lass?"

"Beggin' yer pardon, sir," MacIver said hesitantly.

"What the devil do ye want?"

"It's Gabhan MacGilp, sir, and his cow—the one ye ordered Mr. MacPhun to put yer brand on."

"What about him?"

"MacGilp still hasna got the gelt to pay his shot, but he's been stirring up trouble over the wee cow. . . ."

Pinkie took advantage of the diversion to say in an undertone to Bridget, "You had better do as he says, I think, for now."

Bridget shot her an angry look, but she did not argue.

". . . and Mr. MacPhun says—"

"I'll talk to MacPhun," Sir Renfrew growled, "and I'll put a flea in MacGilp's ear, as well." Dismissing MacIver, he turned back to the women. "Come along now, the pair o' ye. I'm in no mood for more of your nonsense."

They followed him upstairs to find that the bedchamber he had prepared for his bride was spacious, and since it faced west, the setting sun filled it with light. When they entered, a plump, middle-aged woman turned from smoothing the bedcovers to greet them.

"This is Mrs. MacIver," Sir Renfrew said as the woman made her curtsy. "She'll see to your needs and help ye bathe if ye'd like her to do so."

Keeping her tone firm but quiet, Pinkie said, "I shall help Lady Bridget."

"Do as ye like," he said with a shrug. "I should ha' thought maiding the lass would be beneath ye now ye're a countess and all, but I willna stop ye. This is Lady Kintyre, Mrs. MacIver. She will be our guest yet a while."

"Aye, sure, and welcome, m'lady," Mrs. MacIver said, smiling and bobbing another curtsy.

"Just what am I supposed to wear after I've bathed?" Bridget demanded. "No one has brought up my portmanteau, so I do not even have a wrapping gown."

"Someone will bring your box along, but ye dinna need it, lassie. My lads will bring ye a trunk wi' clothes aplenty, for I took the liberty o' purchasing a few things in London for my bride, ye see. I even had a wedding dress made up for ye."

"I won't wear it," Bridget said. "It probably won't fit anyway if your idiot seamstress tried to make it without so much as a single fitting on me."

"Ye'll wear it if I have to put it on ye m'self," he said with a grim look. He said no more but left the room, whereupon Bridget dissolved in tears.

"How could Michael have let this happen?" she wailed.

"Stop that or I swear I will box your ears," Pinkie said sharply. "This is not Michael's fault. It is no one's fault but your own. Mrs. MacIver, unless you have other chores to see to here, you may leave us. I trust that bellpull by the fireplace will bring you back when I ring."

"Aye, my lady." Without another word, the woman left the room.

"Now, you may listen to me," Pinkie said to the still sniffling Bridget. "You have behaved just about as badly as anyone could, and I don't intend to listen to you snivel about it now. I did not say anything before, because I had no notion what we were in for and I could not imagine that berating you would accomplish any good. Now, however, it appears that this horrid man intends to marry you and to keep us both prisoner. I do not think any parson will agree to perform the ceremony, but just in case he has got one who will, we need to form a plan. So you can just stop feeling sorry for yourself and try to think sensibly instead."

"But what can we do?"

"I don't know, but we cannot have much time. If he has sent for the parson, he must mean to marry you quickly, although I should think he will wait until morning, at least, so as not to cast a bad light on his marriage. But that only gives us the one night, so we must both think as hard as ever we have. Here come the men with your bathwater now, I think," she added, hearing noises outside the door.

Two men brought in a large tin bathtub, and two others carried a heavy trunk behind them. Setting these things down on the floor, all four left, only to return minutes later carrying buckets of hot water, with which they filled the tub. While they were working, Pinkie and Bridget opened the trunk.

"Faith," Pinkie exclaimed, "he's bought you a fortune in gowns!"

"Brussels lace," Bridget said, fingering the bodice on top.

"Would you like to change your mind?" Pinkie asked dryly.

"Don't be stupid. I want to go home."

"Well, let's bathe first. We can plan while we get rid of some of this filth, and then, if you don't mind, perhaps I could also find something in that trunk to wear. It never occurred to me that I'd not run you to earth in an hour or so, and I have only the clothes I'm wearing."

"Take whatever you want," Bridget said. "Those things are as likely to fit you as they are to fit me, for all that you're smaller than I am. Is there a screen for that tub? I don't want that horrid man walking in on us."

As she helped Bridget bathe, Pinkie found herself wishing that Michael really were her ghost, and could appear out of the thin air to help them. She knew that he would try to follow them, but even if he had somehow managed to do so, she knew he must be far behind. She had left messages for him and for Duncan wherever she and Mr. Conlan had stopped, but she knew that if the others stopped at every likely place along the road in hopes of finding such a message, their journey would take them twice as long as hers had.

"We still do not have any plan," Bridget said a half hour later as she tied the sash of a wrapping gown around her waist. They had changed places, but she did not offer to help Pinkie bathe, moving instead to the dressing table, where she found a brush and began brushing her hair. "What are we going to do?"

"I don't know," Pinkie said, scrubbing and enjoying the warm water despite their predicament. "I've thought and thought, and I cannot think of a thing except that we've got to find a way out of here before that parson arrives."

"But even if we could get out of the house, there are people all over the place. How could we get away?"

"I saw small boats in the harbor," Pinkie said. "I can sail one if I have to, if you know where we can go."

"That's easy. We'll go to Mingary."

"Do you have men-at-arms there? Can they protect us when he follows us?"

Bridget frowned. "Not many—not anymore—and

they're not men-at-arms exactly, only tenants, herds, and servants. Do you really think he would follow us?"

"Certainly he would, and he'd have an army with him. You saw how many men there were outside when we arrived, and most were wearing swords."

Bridget sighed. "Then where can we go?"

"The first problem is how to get out of this house." As she was emerging from the bath a few minutes later, a rap on the door announced Mrs. MacIver's return. "I told you to wait until I rang for you," Pinkie said.

"Aye, my lady, but the master said I were to come up and help the young lady dress, and I hope ye'll no refuse to put on the wedding gown, miss—that'd be the blue one, he said—because he said he'll be up himself in twenty minutes."

Bridget exchanged a look with Pinkie but made no further complaint, and it was just as well, because it was nearer fifteen minutes than twenty when Sir Renfrew returned. By then, however, both young women were decently clad.

Pinkie wore a simple shell-pink silk bodice and skirt she had found in the trunk. By draping the skirt over her own demi-hoop, then rolling it at the waist and having Mrs. MacIver lace the vee-shaped stomacher bodice tightly, she believed she presented a respectable appearance.

Bridget wore Sir Renfrew's exquisite wedding gown of aquamarine silk, trimmed with white Brussels lace over pannier hoops that swayed enticingly when she walked. If the bodice was tight across the low-cut bosom and a little loose in the waist, neither defect reduced the gown's beauty, or hers.

Sir Renfrew nodded with approval. "Aye, sure, but ye're a lovely lass," he said. "Go now, Mrs. MacIver, and tell the parson we'll be along shortly."

"He's here?" Bridget and Pinkie spoke as one.

"Aye, sure, he is. Ye'll be a bride within the hour, my love, but first we are going to enjoy a wee chat."

Pinkie said, "You cannot have found a parson willing to perform a ceremony with an unwilling bride, sir."

"Have I not, then? The matter willna arise, in any event, because the lassie will be willing enough when the time comes to say her lines."

"I won't do it!"

"Then ye'll be verra sorry, Bridget, for I mean to take ye as my wife before the night is done, with or without a parson saying the words. In the end, by good Scottish law, our joining will be as legal either way."

Indignantly, Bridget said, "That is rape, sir!"

"Aye, sure, and I'd prefer a willing bride, as I've told ye, but willing or no, ye'll be mine. Moreover, I'll no have ye shaming me before the parson. I should dislike having to be harsh with ye, but I shall punish ye severely if ye give me cause. I mean to have my way, lass."

"The parson will take me away from here if I tell him I don't want to stay."

"Nay, lass, he will not, for he kens well how many armed men I have, and he is but one man alone. We'll do him no harm, but my lads will escort him home again, and it will be his word against mine and all of theirs as to what passed here. Ye might also give a thought to your brother, when all is said and done."

"What about him?" Pinkie asked anxiously.

"I'm thinking he might come here to find you," Sir Renfrew said, looking thoughtfully at the ceiling. "It would be a pity and all if some accident were to befall him, especially since he has not yet repaid his debt to me. Not only would all his lands come to me, but unless Lady Kintyre here is already with child, you would inherit a portion of the castle, and thus it would come to me, as well."

Remembering how easily Sir Renfrew had raised his pistol to kill Cailean, Pinkie shivered at the thought that he might do the same to Michael.

Bridget said angrily, "If you hurt Michael, I would never speak to you again, and, I promise you, you will have to force me every time you want to couple!"

"I see ye are beginning to accept the inevitable, lass. Nothing will happen to Kintyre so long as ye go through the ceremony peaceably—and that goes for you, too, my lady. I believe my lass should have a woman to stand up with her, and folks would wonder why ye did not do so, since ye are here. Ye can do so willingly, or I can lock ye up till it's done. If ye agree, I'll expect ye to keep your word."

Pinkie nodded, seeing nothing to be gained by pointing out that his word was not exactly dependable. Still, she could accomplish nothing if she were locked up somewhere, unable even to know what was happening. "I give you my word, sir."

"That's a good lass."

He gave them no more time to think, let alone to talk privately, hustling the pair of them back along the corridor—lighted now by candles in wall sconces—then downstairs to the hall and into a room with a large fireplace, in which a fire roared. More candles lighted the room, an elegant French floral carpet covered much of its floor, and the furnishings made it clear that he used the room for many purposes. A dining table stood at the far end, and a desk at the near end. Chairs and sofas rested against the walls, ready to be drawn forward when needed.

MacKellar was there with an older man, who smiled at their entrance.

"This lovely creature must be your intended bride, Sir Renfrew."

"Aye, Parson, and she is lovely, is she not? Shall we get on with it?"

"Have you not invited other guests, sir, perhaps her family?"

"This is her sister-in-law," Sir Renfrew said smoothly. "She will stand up with the lass."

"And what is the bride's name?"

Sir Renfrew hesitated for the first time. "Bridget," he said at last.

"I am Lady Bridget Mingary," Bridget said, raising her chin.

"He requires only your given name, lass," Sir Renfrew said.

Pinkie saw his hand tighten on Bridget's arm, and held her breath when she saw the girl stiffen.

Bridget remained silent.

The parson said, "Lady Bridget Mingary? Then you must be Kintyre's sister. This seems very strange to me. Surely there were settlement papers to sign, so I do not understand why your brother has not honored the occasion with his presence."

His hand still grasping Bridget's arm, Sir Renfrew said in a false, easy tone, "Kintyre don't approve of the union, Parson, and that's plain fact, but it need not concern us tonight. Lady Bridget loves me and I love her, and we are going to be wed." An edge crept into his voice that made the parson turn pale. "If ye canna remember the marriage lines, I will find me another parson."

The parson looked narrowly at Bridget. "Art thou truly willing, lass?"

Pinkie stared hard at her, terrified that Bridget would continue to think of no one but herself. Marriage to Sir Renfrew might be a terrible fate, but women often married men they hated, and had done so throughout history.

Besides, the ceremony was no more than that. There might still be time to save Bridget from the worst of its consequences. But if she spoke now and Sir Renfrew got rid of the parson—perhaps even murdered him—Michael would be next, and maybe Pinkie herself.

CHAPTER NINETEEN

Bridget flicked Pinkie a glance, then said quietly, "I am willing."

Pinkie reached toward the desk to steady herself, and the parson glanced at her curiously. "Is aught amiss with ye, my lady?"

"Nay, sir," she said. "We have not eaten since this morning. I daresay I am but a trifle hungry."

Clearing his throat, Sir Renfrew said, "There will be supper aplenty when the ceremony is done. Get on with it, Parson."

"She is quite young, sir, and learning that her brother does not support this marriage must give second thoughts to any man o' the cloth. I'll no refuse to perform the ceremony," he added hastily, "but I would feel better about it if I knew you had made arrangements to protect the young lady in the event of your death. Surely you have drawn up proper settlement papers."

"Nay, then, I have not," Sir Renfrew snapped, "but your

point is a good one, Parson. I'll willingly do that little thing." When the parson smiled and waited expectantly, Sir Renfrew grimaced and said, "Verra well; I'll attend to it at once." Striding to the desk, he sat down, yanked a sheet of paper from a drawer, and dipped a pen into the inkwell, beginning to write without even testing the nib. He dashed off two or three lines, scrawled his signature, sprinkled silver sand over the whole, then got up and handed it to the parson, growling, "Will that do ye, sir?"

Reading swiftly, the parson looked up and said with surprise, "This be quite generous, Sir Renfrew."

"Aye, well, I've no intention o' dying yet a while, and I mean to get a few stout sons on her afore then, but it will do for now. Get on with the ceremony."

Fifteen minutes later, declaring Sir Renfrew and Lady Bridget husband and wife, the parson frowned a little when Bridget visibly resisted her husband's kiss, but did not speak of it.

Straightening, Sir Renfrew said dismissively, "I'd invite ye to stay to dine with us, Parson, but 'tis nearly dark, and there'll no be a moon yet a while, so I ken ye'll be wanting to get home. Here's a bit toward a new kirk roof," he added, handing him a small purse. "MacKellar, see that Parson gets home safe, but first tell MacIver to serve our dinner. Then he's to dismiss the servants and take himself and his wife off away for the night. I want to be alone with my bride."

"Aye," MacKellar said. "Then I'll no see ye again till the morning, m'self."

"Tell the lads to keep a sharp eye on the bay for visitors though, especially any coming from Mingary way," Sir Renfrew added. "They'll come by water if they come, for they've no had time to come by land." When MacKellar had gone, he turned to Pinkie and said, "Mrs. MacIver can show ye to your bedchamber, madam. We ha' no need for more o' your company this night.''

"I want her to dine with us," Bridget declared boldly.

"Do ye, then, lass, and what will ye give me an I grant your request?"

Bridget glowered but made no move to stop him when he took her chin in one hand and tilted her face up. He kissed her lips again, taking his time, clearly savoring the fact that although she did not respond, neither did she dare resist. At last he released her, then turned again to Pinkie, saying with a courtly bow, "We'd be honored an ye would join us at table, madam."

Despite Bridget's frequent and rather frenetic attempts to stir conversation, dinner was a somber affair, and although she clearly hoped to prolong the meal, Sir Renfrew seemed as eager to bring it to an end. He had commanded the servants to set all the dishes on the table at once—along with two bottles of wine—and then leave; so they served themselves, and the meal took less time than usual.

"I'll bank down the fire," he said, drinking off what remained in his wineglass before getting to his feet and walking unsteadily to the fireplace.

Having encouraged Bridget to drink two glasses of wine, he had drunk much more of it himself, so Pinkie was not surprised to see him look a bit tipsy.

He took the poker that hung on a hook beside the huge fireplace, nudged the logs apart with it, and poked them toward the back. Then, after three unsuccessful attempts, he put the poker back on its hook and turned back to his bride.

"We'll go upstairs now, my love."

Bridget stayed where she was.

"Lass, dinna mak' me fetch ye. I've the night and all to

tame ye, and I doubt that ye'd want her ladyship to witness your submission to me here and now.''

Visibly swallowing, her face draining of color, Bridget rose from her chair and moved toward him. Her hands shook, and she hid them in the folds of her skirt.

"Ye'll come upstairs with us, madam," he said to Pinkie. "The servants ha' gone, but I'll show ye where ye're to sleep.''

He reached for Bridget, and when she shrank from him, he grabbed her and put an arm around her shoulders, urging her toward the doorway into the hall. When he glanced over his shoulder, Pinkie stood as if to follow obediently. Satisfied, he returned his attention to Bridget.

Hoping he would not look again, Pinkie caught up her skirt and sped silently across the carpet to the fireplace. Snatching the poker from its hook, she concealed it in the folds of her skirt just as Sir Renfrew glanced back. She smiled, saying, "I do not mean to dawdle, sir. This skirt is long for me and a trifle awkward.''

"Then snatch it up, lass, and hurry along. I grow impatient to enjoy my lovely bride.''

She would have liked to run up behind him and hit him with the poker as he crossed the hall with Bridget, but she knew that on the marble floor he would hear her heels. On the stairway, his head was too far above hers, and in any case, she risked hitting Bridget if her aim were not true, for he continued to cling to the girl.

Upstairs, he paused, pointing to a door just along the corridor from Bridget's room, and said, "That be your room there. I'd meant to ha' the lads put ye in a less pleasant one, and lock ye in, but I've better things to do than take ye there myself.''

"I am grateful for your kindness, sir," Pinkie said quietly.

"Aye, I'm a charitable man. Take yourself off now, and dinna be thinking that because there's no lock ye can escape in the night. When my lads catch ye, and they will, I'll use my riding whip to school ye no to do it again. Then I'll give my lass a whipping, too, for being so foolish as to invite ye to dine with us."

"Good night, sir," Pinkie said, keeping her dignity with difficulty as she passed them, and carefully shifting the poker from behind her skirt to the front.

Glancing back to find his stern gaze still upon her, she went into her room and shut the door. Then, pressing an ear to the oak, she listened until she heard a squeak from Bridget, followed by the solid clunk of the other bedchamber door closing. Slipping off her shoes, and moving as slowly as she dared to prevent making any sound Sir Renfrew might hear, she carefully opened her door again and stepped out into the corridor.

Her impulse was to go straight to Bridget's room, but she knew that would be foolhardy. First, she had to be sure no servant had stayed in the house to clear away the dinner mess. Carrying the poker in one hand and holding up her skirts with the other, she ran silently along the corridor to the stairs, and looked down into the hall.

No one was in sight, and several candles were guttering in their holders. Surely, if any servants had remained in the house, they would have checked to be sure their master had light enough to find his way upstairs. And if they knew he had gone up, they would have cleared the table before leaving. She stood listening for several moments, but the only sound she heard was a crack of sparks from the room where they had dined. She had left the door open when they left.

Hurrying back to Bridget's door, she put her ear to it and listened. She could hear the girl's voice, but the door was thick and she could not make out her words.

Still listening, striving to remember where furniture stood inside, she silently set down the poker and kirtled

her skirts under her bodice. Then, picking up the poker
again, she grasped the doorknob and began ever so slowly
to turn it.

At that moment, Michael, Chuff, and Cailean were somewhere northwest of the Isle of Man in the Irish Sea. Although the men had managed to find a ship leaving on
the first tide from Bristol, and the shift of winds to the
west had given them speed for their first day's sailing, they
did not enjoy the luxury of a private vessel. The ship they
boarded in Bristol was bound for Glasgow, with ports of
call at Holyhead and Douglas.

The only thing that reconciled the two men to booking
passage with its captain was the latter's assurance that he
would help them find a vessel at Holyhead bound for Fort
William, which lay at the head of Loch Linnhe; and he
had been as good as his word. Their present ship had
sailed within an hour of their arrival at Holyhead, heading
into the North Channel. It would stop only at Oban, at
the south end of Loch Linnhe, before proceeding to Fort
William.

Michael had no intention of going so far, however. He
had friends in Oban and knew he would easily find a boat
there to carry him through the Sound of Mull to Mingary.
There he could gather armed men to accompany him to
Dunbeither. In the meantime, he had to contain his soul
in patience.

The winds continued to blow steadily from the west, and
although he would rather have had one strong and steady
wind from the south to give them the greatest speed, he
knew the westerly winds would not slow them unduly, and
they were far more favorable to their progress than more
winds from the north would be.

Chuff had had the forethought to bring a pack of cards,

and the two men passed many hours playing piquet. The first night, Michael had slept fitfully, and endured yet another recurrence of his dream. There was a difference this time, however, a stronger sense of urgency than he remembered feeling before. If he knew its exact cause, the knowledge eluded him, for he seemed able only to think of making speed. He knew that she was at the castle, and if he did not get there in time, she would die and his future would die with her.

Then, as he was thrashing his way through a forest overgrown with bracken and shrubbery, and filled with strange and horrible, howling beasts, where the ground beneath his feet was likely to open up and swallow him if he put a foot wrong, suddenly the darkness vanished. Sunlight streamed through two tall windows, and he was alone in his bed with Penelope warm and snug beside him.

He reached for her, felt the soft, smooth skin of her bare shoulder beneath his fingertips and felt himself grow hard in anticipation of possessing her. Gently, he pulled her toward him, and she turned with a happy little humming sound. Her eyes opened, and she smiled. Filled with love, he moved over her, bent to kiss her, and awoke to find himself on his stomach clutching the narrow wood frame of the too-short, too-narrow cot attached to the bulkhead in his cabin. It was pitch dark, but he knew he was no longer dreaming, for he could hear Chuff's even breathing in the bunk above his, and Cailean's snuffles from the floor beside him.

Fear that he had been refusing to acknowledge swept over him. His stomach clenched, and his throat felt raw. After all she had done for him, he had failed to protect her when it mattered most. Even if he succeeded in finding her, would she—could she—forgive him? How, after reading Bridget's note, would she believe he had never thought of her as tainted by her parents? How would he convince

her that he had had to fight against falling in love with
her from the moment she had stepped out of the sedan
chair and smiled at him, or that he had long since stopped
fighting.

If Sir Renfrew dared to harm her, he would do worse
than kill the man. As for his sister, who had gotten them
all into this with her peevish, spoiled ways ... But he
pushed that thought away, just as he had since leaving
London, whenever it had stirred in his mind. It was not
Bridget's fault alone that she was what she was.

Still, Michael thought, if Sir Renfrew succeeded in marrying the wicked brat, he wished him joy of her for the
short time he would stay alive to appreciate it.

The doorknob squeaked, and Pinkie froze, her ear still
hard against the wood. Sir Renfrew was talking now. From
the tone of his voice, he was issuing commands. She could
discern no hesitation, no pause to indicate that he noticed
the doorknob's movement or heard the squeak.

Inhaling deeply to steady her nerves, she turned the
knob till it would turn no more. Knowing that this door,
unlike the one on her bedchamber, might possess a lock
or bolt, although she did not recall one, she pushed gently.

"... and ye'll no get your way here by giving way to
tantrums, lass. I am more likely to put ye across my knee
and skelp ye till ye do as you're bid."

"You're a horrid, horrid man!"

"Aye, sure, but I am your husband nonetheless, and I'll
have your obedience. Now, take off that gown unless ye
want me to rip it from ye."

Pinkie could hear their voices clearly, and she thought
Sir Renfrew sounded as if he hoped Bridget would force
him to rip off her gown. He also sounded nearer the door

than Bridget, which was as Pinkie had hoped, since it meant he would be facing away from the opening door.

Trusting that Bridget would have presence enough of mind, despite her predicament, to hold her tongue if she saw the door move, Pinkie pushed it until the opening was wide enough for her to see one of Sir Renfrew's shoulders a few feet away. The bed was against the wall to her left, and Bridget stood near its foot, her frightened gaze fixed on Sir Renfrew. If her eyes flicked toward the door, Pinkie could not tell, which meant Sir Renfrew was even more unlikely to have noticed. She pushed the door wider and clutched the poker tightly.

The thought of what she was about to do, and its potential consequences, nearly stopped her where she stood. She might kill him. She knew that if she did, Kintyre and Duncan between them could protect her in any Scottish court, but she was not certain they could protect her from the British Government. This was no time to think such thoughts, however. She pushed the door wider, and this time, she saw Bridget stiffen, then look at her.

Panic rising, Pinkie shook her head in warning.

Instantly Bridget recovered, and her gaze darted to another corner of the room, as if she sought escape where there was none. She said too loudly, "I am not accustomed to undressing before a man, sir, nor am I accustomed to undressing without my maid to help me."

"I'll be happy to maid ye, lassie." He stepped nearer.

Bridget shrank away from him.

Without giving consequences another thought, Pinkie darted forward, raising the poker and bringing it down on the back of his head as hard as she could.

He dropped without a sound in an ungainly heap at her feet.

Bridget's hand flew to her mouth. "Faith, what have you done?"

"Don't stand there asking stupid questions," Pinkie snapped. "We've got to get out of here as quickly as we can."

"But where will we go?"

"We'll worry about that when we get free of the house."

"How can we? He'll only come after us as soon as he wakes."

"Hush; let me think." Looking swiftly around the room, she said, "Fetch the sash from your wrapping gown. I'll see what else I can find. We must tie him up."

Resorting at last to tearing strips from the bedsheet, they soon had Sir Renfrew bound and gagged. Pinkie did not know whether to be glad or sorry when he regained consciousness as they were leaving the room. His glare was murderous.

"Oh, hurry," Bridget implored her. "If he gets free—"

"He won't," Pinkie said, "and if we are lucky, no one will dare put a head in this room till quite late tomorrow. But we cannot run out the front door in these clothes. They will spot us in a trice. Let's see what else we can find."

They hurried downstairs, but as Pinkie turned toward the nether regions, Bridget ran across the hall to the room where they had dined. Pinkie began to follow, but Bridget returned almost at once, tucking a paper into her bodice. "The settlement papers," she said. "I don't want him to tear them up, or lose them."

Shaking her head, Pinkie pushed her toward the kitchen. Their search ate up more precious time, but she decided it was worth it when they found breeches and shirts hanging to dry near the kitchen fire, quilted jackets and several pairs of boots near the scullery door, and knitted caps on a rack above them. The clothes bagged on them, and when they had changed, they looked at each other and laughed.

Bridget said, "If I look as dreadful as you do . . ."

"Never mind," Pinkie said, bundling their dresses, chemises, and shoes together and tying the bundle with laces from the remaining boots. "At least we no longer look like women. Take care now, and follow me."

"I don't know about this, Penelope. . . ."

"Call me Pinkie; it won't sound so feminine if someone overhears you."

"And you'll call me Bridge, I suppose. It won't matter, though, in the end. That horrid man is my husband. Can he not simply order Michael to send me back?"

"If I'm not mistaken," Pinkie said, tying the last knot and shouldering the bundle, "he will not remain your husband for long, since he did not consummate the union. I know a little about such things, because I've heard Duncan and Mary discuss them. I think you can easily obtain an annulment under these circumstances. Then it will be as if that ceremony never took place."

"If that's true, I take back every wicked thought I ever had about you, and every wicked deed," Bridget declared.

"What deeds?"

Bridget looked at the floor.

"Would they have aught to do with the way Mrs. Thatcher's servants treated me and Nan, or the information you flung in your brother's teeth? I read your note."

Bridget winced. "Aye. I was angry then, about your parents. I know I ought not to have—"

Pinkie sighed. "Who else did you tell, Bridget?"

"No one, I swear, and I am most dreadfully sorry now, but—"

"This is no time for excuses or recriminations," Pinkie said. "I should have told your brother myself. It was wicked of me to marry him without telling him."

"But—"

"Not now, Bridget. Let's just get out of here."

The moon had not yet risen, and the temperature had

dropped considerably, bringing a chill to the wind that blew across the kitchen yard, but the sky was clear and filled with stars. By their light, the two young women hurried toward a nearby thicket, expecting at any moment to hear voices shouting them back. They made the cover of the trees, then had to pick their way carefully.

"Which way?" Bridget whispered.

"Keep moving away from the house," Pinkie said. "Recall that he told his men to watch the sea. They won't watch this side so carefully."

"But we must get to Mingary."

"No, it's the first place he will search. We need protection, men-at-arms. We'll make for Balcardane instead."

"Faith, do you know the way?"

"No, but if we head for that ridge we saw behind the house, we can follow it until we find someone to ask."

"They'll tell!"

"Not if we only ask the way to Loch Linnhe," Pinkie said patiently.

They pushed their way through shrubbery and followed trails that Pinkie knew must have been made by deer or other woodland creatures. An hour later, for what seemed like the hundredth time, Bridget said, "I don't like this; I'm cold."

"Hush," Pinkie muttered, as she had every time before, turning her head to be sure Bridget heard her. As she turned back, she bumped into what was unmistakably a burly human body. Large, strong hands clamped down on her shoulders, and the only reason she did not scream was that the scream got caught in her throat.

"Now, where d' ye think ye're going, me lads, sneaking aboot like thieves?"

For once Bridget kept silent, while Pinkie tried to think of something sensible to say. They were too close to Dunbeither House for him to be other than one of Sir Renfrew's men.

From nearby came a pony's whicker and sounds of a hoof pawing the ground. Pinkie felt her captor jump. "Who are you?" she demanded.

"Never mind that," he said hastily.

Somewhat reassured by this odd exchange, she said, "We need help. Sir Renfrew Campbell brought us to Dunbeither House against our will. We escaped, but we need to get farther away, and quickly. Can you help us?"

"Where is himself?"

"I do not think we should tell you that. I have risked much already in telling you what I have."

"Bless ye, I've no love for himself. I just want tae ken he's no hot on yer heels the noo."

"He is not, nor will he be before tomorrow—hopefully, late tomorrow."

Before she realized his intent, the man snatched the cap from her head and pawed at her hair. "Bless me, ye're no lad; ye're a lass. Be that un a lassie, too?"

"Aye," Pinkie said, "and if you will help us, we will see you well rewarded. Our families are powerful and will be grateful to you."

"Ye're the twa lassies himself brought home off his ship the day."

"Aye, we are. Please, will you help us?"

There was just enough light to discern his shrug. "I've no call tae love him, but I've kinfolk hereabouts. Still, ye can come along as far as I'm going the nicht."

'Where?"

"Ah, now, that would be telling; but come along this way."

They followed him, and soon came upon a pony laden with bundles.

"What is it carrying?" Pinkie asked, feeling one of the bundles. "It feels like a bag of bricks."

"Aye, then, and so it is, for I've kinsmen who will pay for them. The master willna miss them, I'm thinking, and I've sharp need for the gelt."

"We want to reach Loch Linnhe," Pinkie said. "Do you travel that way? We must know, you see, because if you go another way, you cannot help us."

"Aye, then, I'll tell ye. 'Tis over Shielfoot way to Loch Sunart I go, and into Glen Tarbert. Gin ye follow the glen, she'll tak' ye straight on to Linnhe."

"Faith, but that's perfect," Pinkie said.

"What is your name?" Bridget asked.

"Gabhan MacGilp," the man said. "What's yours, then?"

It took Sir Renfrew a good part of the night to free himself, but he lost no time after that. Shouting for his men, he sent one group riding toward Fort William in search of the runaways, and another with MacKellar to ride the rough shore track to Mingary, while he ordered still others into boats to sail to Kilmory with him.

Waking the innkeeper there, he demanded horses for his men, and an hour and a half later, arriving at Castle Mingary, he demanded admission.

When MacKellar's group arrived hours later without having caught sight or sign of the two young ladies, Sir Renfrew joined his forces and led them through Glen Tarbert to Loch Linnhe, intending to make for Balcardane Castle.

The wind blew steadily through the night, but the gentle, wooded slopes of Glen Tarbert sheltered the travelers from the brunt, so the rolling, white-capped gray waves that greeted them when they reached the western shore of Loch Linnhe early the next morning came as a shock. Clouds that had hidden the starlight long before they had reached Shielfoot had lingered into the morning, and darker ones billowed ominously in the northwest.

"How on earth will we cross?" Bridget demanded wearily as she slid down from the pony she had been riding.

Pinkie glanced at their companion, a young cousin of their friend MacGilp. Long before they met up with his kinsmen, Pinkie realized that Bridget's stamina was flagging and the girl would not make it all the way to Loch Linnhe if she had to walk. MacGilp agreed, so he had offered her his pony, as well as a young cousin to guide them through the glen. "I've only tae say I lent him the beast," he said. "There be none that'll quibble wi' that. They'll just think I wanted tae move the poor thing oot o' the master's sight, lest he set his own brand tae it, like he did tae me cow."

Though their intent had been to take turns riding, Pinkie let Bridget keep the pony, deciding that the girl needed it more than she did.

Young Geordie MacGilp was only fourteen or so, but by Highland standards, he was full grown. Receiving Bridget's demand with a long, thoughtful look at water and sky, he said, "We've boats here on the bay."

Pinkie said, "Can you get us across, then?"

"Aye, I can do that, right enow, but where be ye bound, ma'am?"

"Into Loch Leven, if you can get us there, and then to Balcardane Castle."

"Nay, then, I canna do that wi' the wind blowin' straight down the loch as it is. We'd be blown about like a teacup in a storm. I might could get ye tae Kentallen, but I'm thinking that would take a couple o' hours. I'd ha' tae tack back and forth, ye ken, agin the winds."

Pinkie shivered with cold and fear. She had felt compara-
tively safe in the darkness, but with the gray light of dawn
had come recurring fear that Sir Renfrew had freed himself
long since and was hot on their heels. Even if he had
ridden to Mingary first, once he caught their trail, he would
ride faster than they had, because he would have light.
That he could not know for certain where they were bound
was all they had to protect them, and they did not know
how great a force he could muster to follow, or how many
parties he had sent out and about to search for them. If
anyone saw them on the loch and realized who they were,
Sir Renfrew or his men would catch up with them long
before they could reach Balcardane.

She said impulsively, "What of Loch Creran?"

"Aye, that'd be gey easier," he said. "We'd ha' the wind
behind us."

"Then that is where we will go," she said.

"Where is that?" Bridget asked. "Why would we want
to go there?"

"It's just beyond the south end of Loch Linnhe, where
it meets the Lynn of Lorne," Pinkie said. "More to the
point, Sir Renfrew is unlikely to think of riding that way,
and both Balcardane's Dunraven and my brother's castle
are there."

Bridget looked at the darkening sky. "There's a big
storm brewing, Pinkie."

"Aye, I can see that, so the sooner we get across, the
better. Where is your boat, young Geordie?"

"Yonder." Gathering the pony's reins, he led them to
a sheltered area where several boats had been pulled onto
the shingle above the tide line. Tying the pony to a bush
higher on the shore, he pointed to one of the boats.

With effort, the three of them were able to launch it,
and Geordie swiftly put up the sail. After that, skimming
before the wind, it took but twenty minutes to cross the

loch and reach the entrance to Loch Creran. Entering on the incoming tide posed no difficulty for their helmsman, and once off the larger loch and past the Oban-to-Appin ferry crossing, the wind diminished. Rain began to fall, but another twenty minutes brought them to the dock near the water gate at Shian Towers.

Pinkie scanned the top of the high wall until she spied a lookout. Knowing the man would not recognize her in her male clothing, she pulled off her cap to free her hair despite the rain, and waved at him.

"Where are we?" Bridget asked when the man waved back.

"Shian Towers."

"Why here? If Dunraven belongs to Balcardane, won't there be more men and arms there?"

"Aye, but we're safer here, I think," Pinkie said, jumping out of the boat with the bundle she had carried from Dunbeither House. Then, turning to help Bridget, she said to Geordie, "Our thanks is not nearly sufficient payment for your help, lad, but I promise to tell his lordship all you did for us. Will you at least come inside to dry off and have something hot to drink before you return?"

"Nay, then, for I left the wee beast tied on the shore, and I must fetch him home before some thievin' reiver steals him." He waved, and before Pinkie and Bridget had passed through the water gate, his boat skimmed around a bend in the loch and out of sight.

"Safe at last," Bridget said with a sigh as they walked toward the main entrance and the servant shut the water gate behind them. "Is there a fire where we can dry ourselves, and perhaps some food?"

"Aye, there will be," Pinkie said, looking around the damp courtyard. Seeing one of the cook's two children watching them curiously from a doorway, she called him over to her.

He was about the same age, she realized, that Chuff had been when he and she had lived briefly at Shian Towers. The boy looked her up and down before he said, "Miss Pinkie, be that you?"

Bridget said sternly, "You must call her—"

"Hush," Pinkie said. "There is no need to stand on ceremony now. Yes, Tam, it's me, and this is Lady Bridget. Tell your mam that we shall want breakfast—porridge, at least, and some toast. Come along, Bridget," she added as the boy ran off. "Let us find a place to change our clothes before we scandalize all these men."

"I don't want to put that horrid dress on again," Bridget said.

"Then I will, and you can wear the other one," Pinkie said. "I do not have any clothes here. When we come, we generally stay across the loch at Dunraven."

"Then why did we come to Shian?"

Not wanting to admit that she felt safer at Shian because of her ghost, Pinkie said only, "Because if Sir Renfrew should chance to follow us to Loch Creran, he is more likely to go to Dunraven than to come to Shian, that's why. The point of this exercise, you will recall, is to keep you out of his hands until your brother can find us and take you under his protection. If he can obtain an annulment, it will be as if you never married Sir Renfrew."

"Then I wish Michael would find us," Bridget said. "Are you sure that Sir Renfrew will not find us first?"

"He should not do so before we can get word of our whereabouts to Balcardane Castle and Dunraven. Our men will not tell Sir Renfrew where we are, of course, but their knowing will help Kintyre find us before he does."

She was soon to learn how mistaken she was. She and Bridget were still sitting at the dining table, and the cook's little daughter had just brought more hot water for their tea when one of the men ran in, yelling, "There be boats coming to the dock, Miss Pinkie, three of them!"

Jumping to her feet, she said, "Is it Himself or Lord MacCrichton?"

"Neither, miss. Two of the boats be filled with armed men, and we dinna ken their leader. He's a big man, and squinty-eyed, with his wig abristle in the wind."

CHAPTER TWENTY

Thanks to the gathering storm and gusting winds, it was late morning before Michael and Chuff landed at Oban, several hours behind schedule. Cailean had grown stronger and seemed more his usual self, but Michael knew the dog would not be fully recovered for some time.

When they disembarked, before Michael had even begun looking for a boat to take them to Mingary, he heard a familiar voice shouting his name.

"That's Connal," he exclaimed. "What can have brought him to Oban this morning from Mingary?"

"He's your man?"

"Aye, and he's no business to be here unless . . ." He left the rest of the sentence unspoken as he hurried to meet his henchman. "What is it, Connal?" he demanded. "Have you had word from Lady Bridget?"

"Nay, laird," Connal said. "Not to say word *from* her, but dawn visitors brought us word, as ye might say, *of* her ladyship." He looked curiously at Chuff.

"That's Lord MacCrichton," Michael said curtly, adding in an even harsher tone, "What visitors, man? Come, speak up."

Chuff said calmly, "Stop snarling at the poor man, Michael. You'll scare the liver and lights out of him."

Connal grinned, "Nay, then, he willna do that, m'lord. I'll no deny he's looking gey fierce, but I've known his lordship since we were lads together, and I've known Lady Bridget from her cradle."

"Where is she, Connal? Sir Renfrew Campbell abducted her from London."

"So I thought, laird, since it were Sir Renfrew himself that banged on the gate at dawn this morning, looking for his wife, he said."

"The devil you say!"

"Aye, and there's another thing." Connal shot a quizzical look at his master. "He were looking for Lady Kintyre, as well. Said she were with Lady Campbell, as he called our Lady Bridget."

"Did he happen to explain when his marriage took place, or how he happened to misplace his bride and Lady Kintyre?" Michael asked grimly.

"Said he married her at sundown yesterday. He didna say how he chanced to lose the pair o' them. Is it true then, that the other lass is Lady Kintyre, laird?"

"It is. She is my wife, Connal, and if you have any notion where she is bound, I want to know. We've got to find them before Campbell does."

"They'll make for Balcardane if Pinkie has her way," Chuff said, "and knowing them both, I'd guess she will make the decisions."

"I don't know," Michael said. "Bridget is . . ."

"We all know what she is," Chuff said when he hesitated, "but you and I also know Pinkie. Since they did not go straight to Mingary, she is calling the tune."

Michael nodded and turned back to Connal. "You have a boat, do you not? We'll take it and make for Balcardane at once."

Connal shook his head. "The wind be fierce, laird, and blowing straight from the north. There's a storm brewing, too," he added, gesturing toward a sky growing darker by the minute. "I'm thinking we'd better borrow horses, or hire them."

"How far is it to Balcardane from here?" Michael asked Chuff.

"Twenty-five miles or so, but it is a fair enough road."

"It won't remain fair for long in a driving rain," Michael said when raindrops spattered his face. Feeling increasing urgency, he made up his mind and said, "Hire or borrow them, Connal, but find good horses. I want to be off within the hour."

"Aye, laird," Connal said. "I ken just who will lend them. Mayhap they'll lend us a hand, too, in case we hear word o' the lasses before we reach Balcardane."

Michael agreed, and his man soon returned with three stout-looking geldings, several men who had agreed to ride with them, and packets of food one of their wives had sent along. Transferring what baggage they had brought to saddlebags, Michael, Chuff, and their henchmen were soon off, heading right into the storm.

The urgency Michael felt increased more as they rode until Chuff said, "We can take the track up Glen Creran through the hill pass. Not only is it shorter, but on the way we can collect men from Dunraven to ride with us."

Michael's thoughts had shifted to another track, and mention of Dunraven stirred them anew. "What is Dunraven like?" he asked. "Does it have high walls with round towers at each end, and a sort of tower-house keep?"

"Dunraven's more like a manor house," Chuff said. "It had a curtain wall long ago, but the side facing the loch has come down and most of the wall is in ruins. The place hasn't been attacked in nearly fifteen years, after all.''

"Balcardane was not the one, either," Michael muttered. When Chuff glanced at him curiously, he said self-consciously, "Is there a castle hereabouts like the one I just described?"

"It sounded more like Shian Towers than any other I know," Chuff said.

"Your place?"

"Aye."

"You will think me mad, but does Shian by chance possess a bottle dungeon beneath the great-hall floor?"

Clearly astonished, Chuff said, "Aye, it does. Have you been to Shian?"

"No. Are there thick woods on a hillside behind the castle, standing off away from it in a sort of a semicircle?"

"There are. What the devil is this, Michael? How can you know so much?"

"Very thick woods, and there is a burn flowing through them that comes down a nearby glen, with a pass at its head?"

"Exactly so. That is the River Creran, but how can you know all this if you have never visited the place?"

"I dreamed it," Michael said. "There are three entrances to the courtyard—the main entrance, a postern gate, and a water gate. From the postern, one crosses diagonally to the keep, which forms the southwest corner of the curtain wall."

"Aye, that's it, for a fact. What else do you know?"

Closing his eyes, Michael said, "Wood steps lead to the entry, with an iron yett behind an ironbound, wooden door that opens onto a spiral stone stairway. At the first level lies the hall, where a trapdoor opens into the dungeon. At least one man died there some years ago."

Chuff's eyes were wide. "Faith, do you know how he died?"

"I believe that a child was there, perhaps two. One of them—"

"Faith, sir, say no more! You are raising the hairs on the back of my neck."

"My own, too, but I think we head for Shian now, not Balcardane."

"I know that Pinkie would head for Balcardane," Chuff insisted. "There are few men-at-arms at Shian, and they would provide her small protection."

"To get to Balcardane, she would have had to take a boat, would she not?"

"Aye, but we've kinsmen in Moidart and Morar who might have helped her."

"I'm thinking, even if they did, unless she headed north from Dunbeither, through Glen Finnan to Fort William— a great distance—she would have had to sail into the wind. Under the circumstances, she would be more likely, I think, to make for Loch Creran, especially with two havens on the loch from which to choose."

"Then she would make for Dunraven. Duncan keeps a full contingent there."

"If we go to Dunraven and she is at Shian, how long will it take us to get to her? Are there boats? Can we sail across the loch quickly? How long to ride round the loch if need be?"

Chuff frowned. "There are boats aplenty, but again we would be fighting the wind. There are boats at Shian, too, and we could get to Dunraven quickly. To ride from one to the other around the loch would take about half an hour."

"Then it's settled. We'll send some of these men to Dunraven, in case they are needed there, but we'll make for Shian ourselves. I know she is there, Chuff."

"You are not talking about Bridget now, are you?"

"Nay, lad, I mean my wife, and she's in danger, mortal danger. Let's ride!"

Spurring after him, Chuff said, "Did Pinkie tell you about her ghost?"

"Aye, she did."

"Did you tell her about these dreams of yours?"

"I did not."

"Well, I think perhaps you should."

Michael grimaced at the understatement. "First I must find her," he said. He could feel his heart pounding in his chest, and his stomach tightened at the thought that they might be too late. He would not let that happen.

The men at Shian put up no fight against the visitors, who came heavily armed. Chuff's men, having had little cause over the years to maintain full preparation for war, were ill-prepared to deal with them. Rather than see anyone killed, Pinkie had ordered them to admit the intruders.

Sir Renfrew entered the hall with an arrogant stride. "I dare swear you two lassies didna expect to see me so soon."

"We hoped not to see you at all," Bridget snapped.

Seeing him glower, and the cook's little daughter, Flora, backing out of his way in fright, Pinkie said quickly, "How did you find us so fast, sir?"

"Met your helmsman when he returned to the mouth of Glen Tarbert," Sir Renfrew said. "My men persuaded him to tell us exactly where he had taken you."

"You didn't murder the poor lad, I hope," Pinkie exclaimed. "He is scarcely more than a child and was only doing us a kindness."

"I do not harm bairns," Sir Renfrew said with a sniff. "It took no more than a wee hint that we would burn down his family's cottage if he did not tell us what we wanted to know. And now, madam, I must ask you to leave us. I have unfinished business with my wife that will wait no longer."

"What business?" Bridget demanded suspiciously.

He leered. "Ye ken well what business, lass. I'd meant our first coupling to be private, as such times between man and wife should be, but given present circumstances, and the fact that ye might dare to demand annulment on grounds that we never consummated our marriage, I mean to ha' witnesses now when we do."

Bridget gave a shriek of dismay. "How dare you even think such a thing!"

"I am your rightful husband, lass. That is how I dare. You will recall that I promised you a whipping, too," he added, grabbing her by an arm when she tried to step away. "Take that wee bairn with you," he said to Pinkie, pointing to the cook's little Flora, who stared wide-eyed at him from where she stood by the fireplace, still holding her kettle. "This be no sight for the likes of her."

"Put the kettle on the hob, Flora," Pinkie said. "Then come with me."

"You go along, too," Sir Renfrew ordered one of his men. "See that her ladyship is locked up in a room upstairs, where she canna get free. I dinna want her creeping up behind me again. Thanks to her, I've a knot on my head the size of an apple. Set men on guard throughout the castle, too," he added. "I dinna want anyone leaving till I say they can go."

Pinkie pushed the little girl ahead of her into the stairwell. Then, hurrying up the steps so the henchman would not be near enough to hear, she murmured, "Flora, you

must tell your mam we need help. Tell her to send someone
to Dunraven as quickly as they can go, and tell them to
send as many men to us as they can.''

"That man said no one can leave," the child whispered
back.

"I know, but your mam must find someone willing to
take the risk. Our very lives may depend on it. Now, hurry
ahead, lassie; then go down the service stair from the next
level. Sir Renfrew gave no orders about you, and I do not
think that man behind us will bother to look for you.''

Obediently, the child ran on, and since the spiral stairway had hidden her from the man behind them from the
start, Pinkie hoped he would not remember that the child
had been with her. At the first landing, she paused.

He said gruffly, "Be this the top level?"

"No, there is another.''

"Go up, then, lass. We must be sure ye canna jump out
a window.'' He chuckled at what he clearly thought was a
joke—and, indeed, since any window at that level was thirty
feet above the ground, it was a joke to think she might
jump.

Pretending a meekness that she did not feel, Pinkie went
to the tower bedchamber at the top of the stairs and pushed
open the door, pulling the key from the lock as she did
so and hoping he would think it was kept elsewhere.

"I heard that, lass. Give me the key now.''

Wanting to cry for her clumsiness, she gave it to him,
then listened with a deepening depression while he locked
her in the room. Fighting tears, she went to the nearest
window to stare out at the storm. Since that window over-
looked the courtyard, she could not see the loch, but the
room lay at the southeast corner of the castle and a narrow
archway led into a small round tower room. From there,
she could see rain beating down on the loch. The sky to
the west looked lighter than it had been, and she could

see the opposite shore, so the storm would soon blow itself out. In the meantime, though, if the cook managed to persuade someone to go for help, perhaps the rain would provide them some cover.

It was a spark of hope in the midst of overwhelming gloom. She had failed Bridget, but worse than that, she had failed Michael and probably ruined any chance they might have had at a happy marriage, now that he knew about Daft Geordie and Red Mag. She was sorry that she had not told him, sorrier still that Bridget had; but Bridget was being punished now far more severely than any misdeed warranted.

Fearing that Michael might even believe that she had purposely kept their existence secret in order to trap him into marriage, Pinkie felt as if her cup of woe would overflow. Much of his reason for marrying her, she knew, had been his determination to protect Bridget from Sir Renfrew, and now she was Sir Renfrew's wife in name and soon would be his in body, too, if he had not already taken her.

Tears of frustration and failure spilled down Pinkie's cheeks. Turning from the window, she moved to the bed, realizing that she had grown very cold. A fire lay ready to light in the fireplace between the door and the tower room, but she could find no tinderbox. Shivering, she climbed onto the high, curtained bed, sat back against its pile of pillows, and pulled the coverlets over her.

Shutting her eyes, she concentrated on relaxing and getting warm. Her hair was still damp, which did not help, but there was nothing she could do about it.

She did not think she had fallen asleep, but a noise in the room startled her, and she opened her eyes. Her heart leapt, and she sat bolt upright.

"Michael!"

The figure in the archway between the bedchamber and

the tower room turned, and she saw instantly that it was not Michael. He wore the ancient plaid, and the dog standing beside him was not Cailean. Indeed, she had not seen the dog at first, not until she thought about it. Then, there it stood, like a dark shadow at his side.

CHAPTER TWENTY-ONE

The figure gestured commandingly toward the tower-room window and stepped out of the archway toward the fireplace. Its demeanor was such that Pinkie felt a rush of fear that something dreadful had happened. Slipping from the bed, she hurried toward the little round room. The figure nodded encouragingly, then stepped farther away, gesturing with more urgency than before.

Inside the tower room, she looked out and saw at once what the ghost meant her to see. The wind had shifted again to blow straight down the loch, where a small sailboat pitched and tossed on the roiling waters. She saw two children struggling to manage sail and rudder, their efforts as nothing against the force of nature, and with a surge of horror she recognized Tam and wee Flora.

Whirling from the window, she saw that she was alone again. Just when she needed him most, her ghost had vanished.

He certainly was not Michael or anything like him, she

told herself, for Michael would never have been so cruel as to show her the children's plight when she could do nothing about it.

Neither Sir Renfrew nor his men would heed her screams, and even if she did manage to draw someone's attention and persuade him to free her, it would be too late. As these frustrating thoughts flitted through her mind, she was nevertheless hurrying to the door, her fists raised to beat the solid oak to splinters if necessary.

To her amazement, when she approached, the door moved as if stirred by a draft, as if Sir Renfrew's man had never shut it or turned the key in its lock.

Without pause for question or disbelief, she jerked the door wide and flew down the uneven stone steps, screaming for help as she ran. It did not occur to her to fear Sir Renfrew now. Her only thought was to reach the children before it was too late. Had she considered him, she would have dismissed him as a threat, certain that her ghost would somehow keep him at bay. Thus, it was with profound shock that she found him on the landing outside the great hall, barring her way.

"Just where do ye think ye're going in such a rush, lass?"

"Stand aside, sir, and let me pass in the name of mercy," Pinkie begged urgently. "Tam and Flora, the cook's children, are in a boat, and the wind has caught them. The storm will sweep them away if we can't reach them first."

He caught her arm, holding her. "What the devil are they doing on the loch?"

"That's not important. We must get to them!"

When she pushed him aside and passed him, he made no effort to stop her. Behind him, in the doorway, she saw Bridget, clutching the tattered remnants of her gown around herself. The girl's eyes were red-rimmed, her cheeks tearstained. She muttered something, but Pinkie did not hear her and could not wait in any case.

Holding her skirts nearly to her waist, she ran down to the main door. The yett was in place, but she knew the trick of it and had it open in a trice. The iron bar across the door seemed light when she lifted it and set it aside, though she knew it was not light at all. In moments, she was down the rain-drenched wood steps, running across the sodden courtyard toward the water gate.

Men gaped at her, and several of Sir Renfrew's men moved to stop her.

"The children," she shrieked at them. "On the loch! Their boat will sink!"

The men approaching stopped, watching mutely as she wrenched open the heavy water gate.

"Hold there, miss!" One of Sir Renfrew's henchmen, recovering more swiftly than the others, caught her by one shoulder, his grip bruisingly tight. Without letting go of the gate or looking at him, she struggled to get free.

"Release her," Sir Renfrew snapped, striding up behind and pushing past them both, through the gateway. "There they are, may God save them!"

Following, Pinkie had all she could do to maintain her balance against the heavy wind. Her gaze swept the churning water, and fear threatened to paralyze her when she could not see the little boat. Then, following Sir Renfrew's pointing finger, she saw its slender mast pitching wildly to and fro in the harsh winds gusting across the water. So fierce was the gale now that raindrops seemed to fly sideways.

Having spied the mast, she found the boat easily when it rose to the crest of a wave, then lost sight of it when the turbulent water seemed to swallow it. Waves and wind tossed the small vessel about like a toy.

In a lull, she heard Flora scream Tam's name, and the little girl's terror sent chills racing up Pinkie's spine. Though she was certain that the children had meant to sail across the narrow part of the loch at its northeast end, the north wind had caught them and swept them into the longer, much wider part. It threatened now to blast them right up the loch's center to the Lynn of Lorne if they did not end in Kingdom Come long before that.

"Man the other boats," she shouted to the men, now crowding onto the dock behind her. "Go and help them!"

No one moved.

"Hurry!" Grabbing one burly man by a rain-soaked arm, she tugged, trying to push him toward the nearest boat. He didn't budge. Turning a fierce eye on Sir Renfrew through the rain, she snapped, "Are your louts all cowards, then, as well?"

"They canna swim, lass. Of course they're affrighted in this tempest. They were afraid, crossing the big loch earlier, but the wind was not so great. These boats are no bigger than that pea-pod one the bairns are in. My men live by the sea. What boats they ken best are larger than these. Even so . . ."

But Pinkie was no longer listening. Running to the nearest boat bouncing and banging against the dock, she untied it. Holding on to the painter with one hand and her flying wet skirts with the other, she tried to get in.

"Hold, lass," Sir Renfrew shouted, grabbing her shoulder. "Even if ye could manage that sail or those oars on your own, ye canna reach them in time."

"Maybe not," she shouted back, "but at least I'll have tried!" Tears of frustration and rage mixed with raindrops streaming down her cheeks. "Stand aside, and let me go!"

"I'll go," a man said, his deep voice carrying above the screaming wind. Turning, Pinkie recognized the huge MacKellar and realized from his voice that he was the one who had grabbed her shoulder earlier. To Sir Renfrew, MacKellar said, "I canna swim, laird, but I can manage a sail and row verra well, as ye ken. The brave wee lass will never manage on her own."

"Ye're a good man, MacKellar," Sir Renfrew bellowed, clapping him on the back. "Damme if I willna go with ye. There, lass, it's done. Ye can stay here now, safe and sound, and we'll see if we canna get to them before it's too late."

"Oh, stop gibbering and go," Pinkie cried. "I cannot see them any longer. They may already be over!"

Sir Renfrew and MacKellar got into the boat, and as they fought to raise the small sail, she jumped into the boat, and would have fallen into the water but for MacKellar's quick hand to steady her. Awkwardly, she flopped down in the stern.

Holding on to the mast but giving up his attempt to raise the sail, Sir Renfrew snapped, "Damnation, lass, ye must stay on the dock. Ye'll only slow us down."

"Too late," MacKellar shouted, leaping for the rudder. "We're awa'."

Wind and current had caught the boat and whisked it away toward the bend in the loch.

"Nothing could have made you much slower," Pinkie yelled over the wind's roar when Sir Renfrew, struggling with the oars, scowled at her. Taking care to keep out of MacKellar's way, she said, "Must I help you with those oars?"

She knew the question was unfair. Even expert oarsmen would have had difficulty under such conditions, but her demand seemed to invigorate Sir Renfrew. He got the oars seated properly at last and began to row. MacKellar had been doing all he could to keep the boat steady, but now he nodded to Pinkie to take the rudder, and moved up beside Sir Renfrew to take one of the oars. When both men began rowing together, their strokes became more efficient, digging deep and true.

Pinkie shouted directions. With rain and her own hair

blowing around her face, she could barely see the foundering mast, its sail ripped to shreds, but their boat moved
steadily nearer. With wind and water pushing them, the
pace seemed unnaturally fast, but even so, by the time they
were close enough to see the other boat, it looked as if
Sir Renfrew had been right and they would be too late.

"They've swamped," Pinkie cried. "They're going
under!"

The men put more muscle into their strokes, and both
rain and wind eased, letting waves settle, so she could see
the children holding fast to the foundering boat. The mast
crashed to the waves, and the children saw them, as well.

"Hurry, she's keeling," Tam shouted, his voice high-
pitched, his terror plain.

"Hold fast, lad," Sir Renfrew shouted over his shoulder,
picking up the stroke. "We're coming! How far yet, lassie?"

"Ten yards," Pinkie said, fighting to hold the rudder
steady. "Straight on! We'll come up on their starboard
side." The wind picked up again, so that her words seemed
to blow away, and she could barely hear Sir Renfrew's
reply.

"Good lass," he said. "Ease up when we're halfway,
MacKellar. We dinna want to shoot past the bairns."

The wind blew as fiercely now as before, but the rain
was not pelting as hard, and Pinkie could still see the other
boat clearly. "Ease up," she cried. "It's breaking apart.
Oh, careful now, careful!"

As they drew alongside, Sir Renfrew pulled the oar nearest the foundering sailboat from its oarlock and held it
out over the water toward Flora. "Catch hold, lassie," he
cried, leaning farther and steadying himself on the gun-
wale.

The child lurched toward the oar just as a rolling wave
struck the rowboat. She missed her mark, and when the

boat lurched, Sir Renfrew lost his grip on the oar. A wave snatched it and carried it quickly beyond reach.

"Damn and blast," he swore.

"She's going under," Pinkie cried, rising in horror to her feet. "Flora!"

The little girl disappeared beneath the waves, and without a thought for her own safety, Pinkie dove after her. As the chilly waters of the loch closed over her, she wondered what madness had possessed her. Then she felt cloth at her fingertips, and opening her eyes, she recognized Flora's shadowy figure. Clutching the child's body with one arm, Pinkie kicked and stroked with the other one to regain the surface. Her heavy skirts tangled dangerously around her feet when she tried to kick, threatening to drag her to the bottom of the loch. Just when she thought she could hold her breath no longer, her head broke the surface.

Gasping for air, she inhaled a mouthful of water instead when a wave hit her full on. Struggling to keep her head above water, she managed to take a deep breath at last, and heard with relief the child gasping and choking beside her.

"Kick, Flora!" she shrieked. "I can keep us both afloat if you help, but don't try to climb up me. Wherever is the boat?"

"There," Flora gasped, waving a shaking hand toward a spot behind Pinkie.

Glancing over her shoulder, Pinkie saw with dismay that the boat was drifting away. She could see MacKellar rowing as hard as he could, but rowing against both wind and waves was impossible. They were too strong for one man alone to overcome, and MacKellar was alone in the boat.

Hearing a shout nearer at hand, she saw Sir Renfrew some ways ahead of them holding Tam with one hand and what looked like a plank from the children's broken boat with the other. Pinkie knew that she and Flora could not catch up with them, nor would the small piece of timber the others held be enough to support all four of them. Eventually, she knew, they all might make shore somewhere, but she did not think that she or Flora would last long enough to find out where.

The storm had slowed Michael's party considerably, although the full force of the wind had not struck them until the horse ferry had deposited those who had crossed with him to the other side of the narrows, where Loch Creran emptied into the Lynn of Lorne. Hunched in their saddles, the men leaned into the wind, pressing on, urging their mounts to dangerous speed on the rocky track. Chuff led, followed by Michael and the deerhound, which miraculously managed to keep pace beside him.

Nearly overwhelmed by the urgency driving him, Michael would have ridden ahead had he known the road as well as Chuff did. He did not know it at all, however, and in the punishing wind and rain, he knew it would be easy to lose sight of the narrow, mostly unmarked, track they followed.

They had hesitated only once, at the narrows, to divide their group and discuss their route after the ferry men told them they had seen three boats enter the loch earlier, carrying armed men.

"You lads send reinforcements from Dunraven," Chuff said to the two men leaving them to follow the Dunraven road. "We've enough men there for an army."

Once across, however, he said with a worried look, "Maybe we should have gone with them, Michael. We've only got your dream to tell us that Pinkie made for Shian, but if she's at Dunraven instead, and Sir Renfrew followed her there—"

"Then she is quite safe," Michael interjected, "unless you think Balcardane's men would hand her or Bridget over to him. No, lad, we go on to the tower house."

They might have debated longer, but the deerhound lifted its head just then, its long muzzle pointed into the wind. Without so much as a glance at its master, it loped off toward Shian. Silently, they followed—Chuff leading, Michael behind him, with the three remaining men to bring up the rear.

The dog still felt its injury, and its pace was too slow for Michael. As the tension within him grew, he pressed forward, shouting to Chuff, "Can you not go faster? Something is terribly wrong. I can feel it."

Chuff glanced back, his mouth open to protest, but he did not speak. Instead, he faced forward again at once and spurred his horse to a canter.

It was a dangerous pace. Even the agile Highland-bred ponies had trouble maintaining their footing on the treacherous path. Though the rain had let up a bit, the wind drove it into their faces, stinging their cheeks and blinding them.

Head down, murmuring silent prayers, Michael tried to put his faith in Chuff and the ponies. He thought only of reaching Shian Towers with as much speed as possible. What compulsion made him look up a quarter hour later he would never know, or why he looked out at the loch. Perhaps he'd heard a growl from the great dog struggling to keep pace with them, perhaps a faint cry borne on the wind. What it was did not matter, not then or ever.

First he saw the masted rowboat with its single, straining oarsman. The man was rowing hard against the windblown waves, making no progress in the direction he rowed, being driven steadily toward shore instead.

Although Michael could see the rower's face, he was certain the man had not seen them. He kept looking back over one shoulder, toward the center of the loch, straining at his oars, grimacing at the effort each stroke cost him; but his movements were sluggish nonetheless, his exhaustion clear.

"Chuff," Michael yelled when his gaze lighted on something else, in the water beyond the rower. "Look yonder on the loch!"

Chuff's attention was fixed on the narrow track ahead, but at Michael's shout he looked at the loch. At the same moment, clearly, Michael saw figures some yards beyond the rowboat, struggling in the water.

"My God," he cried, "there are people out there, an overturned boat!"

Chuff roared to the man in the rowboat, "This way, man! To us!" Along with Connal and the others, he reined in his mount, then urged it toward the shore.

The rower, energized by seeing help near at hand, whipped the little boat around with a few deft strokes and gratefully let the current carry him to them.

Michael could not wait. Assessing the situation swiftly, he shouted, "You and Connal take the boat, Chuff. I'd only weigh it down. I'm riding on!"

Chuff frowned, and Michael knew that the younger man thought he was abandoning them to ride to Shian. His first impulse was to ignore the look, but instantly he decided against it.

"She's out there in the water! I'm sure of it. If you and Connal each take an oar, you may reach her in time, but you'll still need help. With the current behind me, I can swim to her nearly as fast as that boat will take you there."

Without waiting to see if Chuff had understood, he pressed his heels to the pony's flanks and gave it its head.

"Go on, fellow," he muttered, "as fast as you dare." His impatience communicated itself, for the pony thrust itself forward. Balancing himself on the saddle without effort,

Michael kept his gaze on the figures in the water. At first he saw only two heads, but then he saw four, and a jumble of flotsam that looked like parts of a boat. He was upcurrent from them now, but not yet far enough. A rocky point jutted into the water some fifty feet ahead. He reached it in minutes and leapt from the saddle, pulling off his leather jacket and belt as he hit the ground. His boots were next, and he had to sit to shed them, but he knew the time was well spent. He could see the rowboat, and Chuff and Connal amidships, each manning an oar. Even so, it looked like heavy going.

Boots off, Michael flung himself into the water. He hit it flat, arms churning in long, powerful strokes. The waves carried him swiftly, and he saw, as he had expected, that he would reach the struggling figures before the rowboat did.

He realized that his view had grown clearer. The rain had stopped. Till then, he had been swimming with his head up, to see where he was going, but the urgency that had driven him all day grew stronger yet, and he put his head down, knowing he would swim faster.

The next time he looked up, the rowboat had made progress but still had some distance to go. He was closer, nearly there, but to his horror he saw only one head bobbing.

Pinkie fought to keep her head and Flora's above water. She knew they were drifting, and wished they had something to hold on to, like Tam and Sir Renfrew did. She had lost sight of them in the rolling, foam-crested waves. When she shouted, no one answered; or, if they did, the wind blew their words away.

She could see the shore now. The rain had stopped, and either the wind had shifted, or the shore had moved, for it seemed closer. She blinked. Her thoughts tangled themselves in perplexity. Perhaps she was losing her senses.

Flora sputtered, and Pinkie tried to hoist the child higher but succeeded only in submerging herself. Fighting her way to the surface, she felt dizzy. She was exhausted and numb with cold. She had tried to swim at an angle with the current, but her skirts and the clinging child soon made that impossible. Logic told her they were going to drown. She knew they could not last much longer.

"Where's Tam?" Flora cried when she could catch her breath. "I dinna see him or that man!"

"I don't know where they are," Pinkie gasped, "but we cannot think about them now. Try to float, love. Keep your face up. That's it."

The wind's howling took on a new note, and when the next wave lifted them, Pinkie saw a dark, shadowy shape on a rocky point to the north and a little behind them. It looked like Cailean, but Cailean was dead, so the shape could belong to only one animal. Her ghost must be nearby. He would see them to safety.

The thought warmed her, and she shut her eyes for a moment, but her legs kept tangling in her skirt. She had managed to untie her petticoat strings, and the garment now lay somewhere at the bottom of the loch, but the skirt of Bridget's wedding dress still impeded every movement of her legs. The shore looked no nearer. The wind still howled, and the water rolled and tumbled around them. Where was he? She could hold on no longer. Her strength was gone. She had done all she could. When the blackness came, she greeted it with near relief.

CHAPTER TWENTY-TWO

Frantically, Michael scanned the surface. He saw the boat nearing the lone figure, saw Chuff hold out his oar, saw the little boy grab it. Then, right in front of him, another child's head broke the surface.

"Oh, help me!" Reaching one small hand toward him, she gasped, "I've got hold of her dress, but she just closed her eyes and sank!"

Shouting to Chuff and Connal, Michael caught hold of the child. Chuff was hauling the boy into the boat while Connal held it as steady as he could with the oars. At Michael's shout, Chuff heaved the boy in, and Connal began rowing, bringing the boat alongside Michael in a twinkling.

Reaching down, Michael had found the child's other hand and the material to which it clung. "I've got her now, lassie," he said. "Into the boat with you."

Fearing Penelope's gown would tear if he yanked on it, he dove and grabbed her arms, then hauled her to the surface, praying that she was not already dead. The boat was but a few feet away, Chuff still pulling the little girl aboard.

"Here," Michael yelled. "I've got her! She can only have been down a moment or two, or she'd have dragged the bairn down with her. Aye—God be thanked she's coughing!"

"Bless the lass and the Lord above," Connal bellowed as he shipped oars and, taking care not to swamp their boat, helped Chuff lift Pinkie inside.

"Put her on her side or facedown," Michael ordered. "She must have taken in gallons of water."

"The lad says Sir Renfrew was with him," Chuff said, seating his oar again.

"Aye, he were," the boy said. "He said the wee board would hold one of us, but it wouldna tak' two, and he let go. He swam some, and then a big wave came and I didna seen him the more."

All three men searched the water. "I see no sign of the man," Connal said, "and the waves are settling. We'd see him or hear him if he were afloat."

"Well, don't spare any more time looking for him," Michael growled. "You must get Penelope and the children ashore."

"Aye, but what about you, laird?" Connal said. "You can hang on if you like, but I dinna believe the wee boat will take us all."

"I'll swim," Michael said. "Don't fret about me. I can make it easily now that I know my lassie will be safe."

Chuff glanced worriedly at his sister, lying in a heap at his feet. Then, giving the handle end of his oar to Connal to hold, he shrugged off his wet overcoat. "She cannot get any wetter, but perhaps this will help keep the chill off," he said.

Bending to the oars, the two men rowed at an angle

with the current to the shore, beaching not far from where they had begun.

Michael pulled himself out of the water nearby, realizing only then how tired he was. But the urgency had left him. He was still worried but content.

While Chuff rubbed Penelope's hands, Connal clasped Michael's shoulder. "I'll send a man to fetch your horse, laird."

"No need," Michael said, gesturing.

Over the rise trotted Cailean, head high, tail wagging, with the horse's reins in his mouth. The horse trotted obediently behind.

Pinkie opened her eyes to see her husband's face close to hers. At first, the rocking motion made her think they were in a boat, but she quickly realized they were on a horse. They were also both soaking wet.

"It *was* you," she said. "I'm glad you came for me."

"Aye, and when you're better, I'm going to beat you soundly, sweetheart, for giving me such a fright. What madness overcame you to try to swim the loch on such a heathenish day?"

Hugging the endearment to her heart, she said, "The children?"

"Safe now, both of them. Two of my men took them on ahead to Shian."

She nodded. "I was not trying to swim the loch. You know that."

"Aye, I do. Tam told us what happened. You're a brave lass, sweetheart, but I'm still going to skelp you till you screech."

"They needed me," she said simply. "I knew you would come, though."

"I'm not your damned ghost, you know," he said, as if

the thought had just struck him that she might think he was.

"I know, Michael," she murmured, resting her head contentedly against his shoulder. A moment later, she roused enough to say, "Where *did* you spring from?"

"From Oban, thanks to Connal and Sir Bloody Renfrew Campbell," he replied. "Connal met us there this morning when we arrived, and he told us that Sir Renfrew had visited Mingary, searching for you and Bridget."

Remembering how she had left Bridget, and how disappointed he would be at her failure to protect the girl, she stiffened at hearing her name but said only, "How did you know where to find us?"

He hesitated, then said dryly, "I had a dream."

"A dream?"

"Aye, I've had it, or similar ones, since I was a lad, about searching for a castle and something or someone else, and when I described the castle to Chuff and he said it sounded like Shian Towers, I made him come here after you."

"But we might never have come here. We could have hidden for a time, you know, and then made our way to Mingary after Sir Renfrew had been and gone. That's where Bridget wanted to go, after all. You could have missed us easily."

"Aye, I've no doubt that I might have, but I knew that Bridget would not be making the decisions. I trusted you to know that Mingary would be the first place Sir Renfrew would search, and to head right away from there."

"Well, I did think we would be safe here, but he questioned the lad who sailed us across Loch Linnhe until he learned where we had gone. I had thought of making for Balcardane, of course. It is much more easily defended than Shian, or even Dunraven, for that matter."

"Why did you come to Shian then, lass?"

He did not sound displeased, merely curious, but she

would not have thought him a man to follow a dream, so she was not sure she could trust her perception.

"I . . . I'm not sure," she admitted. "We had to cross Loch Linnhe, and the wind blew too hard to make Loch Leven, but I knew we could walk or find someone to lend us horses. Then I realized we could reach Dunraven easily. I knew Duncan's men would be there, but something . . . You'll call me foolish, I expect, but the truth is that I thought of my ghost, and suddenly Shian seemed safer. Where's Chuff?" she asked to divert him, not wanting to hear, despite his dreams, what he might have to say about her ghost. "I tried to get word to him and Duncan at Oxford, so you'd not have to come after us alone."

"Aye, and we met at Bristol, the three of us," he said. "Duncan thought he'd best go back to London and look after the others, but Chuff came with me. I had the devil's own time persuading him to come to Shian, but he came, right enough."

"I expect that Bridget was glad to see the pair of you."

His smile was grim. "I haven't seen the wicked lass yet, so I cannot say if she will be glad or no. My guess is that when I tell her what I think of her behavior she will wish me to the devil."

Pinkie sighed. "I expect that Duncan will be angry with me, too. He warned me not to put myself in danger again, or I'd know his wrath."

"As to his anger, I cannot say, lassie, but it is no longer his business to deal with you. It's mine, and whether you believe I'll beat you or no, I *will* have some few things to say when you are better. You should not have gone after Bridget by yourself. For now, though, I'm just glad to have you safe again. Bridget is another matter, though. It is my business, and no other man's, to deal with her."

Pinkie took a moment to decide how much to tell him,

then decided that nothing less than the whole truth would do. "She is married," she said quietly.

"Aye, I know. Connal told us Sir Renfrew was seeking his wife at Mingary."

"He forced her, Michael. He had a tame parson waiting, and he forced her."

In a tone far more gentle than she had expected, he said, "Did he bed her as well, or did all this ruckus prevent that?"

Believing that he hoped he could still get the marriage annulled, she hesitated to reply. He was already angry, both with her and with Bridget, and could get much angrier. She could not blame him if he did. Nothing, however, could alter the facts.

"There can be no annulment," she said. "He made certain of that."

"Witnesses?"

"Aye, or so he threatened, and so it looked to me when last I saw Bridget."

To her surprise, he nodded with evident satisfaction.

Bewildered, she said, "I thought you would be furious to find your sister wedded to that awful man."

"If I do not mistake the matter, my sister is now a widow," Michael said. " 'Tis better, under the circumstances, that he did marry her, I'm thinking."

"A widow? Is Sir Renfrew dead?"

"So it appears. Chuff and Connal are searching, but Tam said Sir Renfrew went under, so it's a fair guess they'll find him dead if they find him at all."

"Bridget will be a wealthy widow if that's so," Pinkie said.

"Not necessarily," Michael said, "but that does not matter. I am concerned about her reputation. A widow is much more respectable than a runaway brat."

"She is wealthy, nonetheless," Pinkie said. She explained about the parson's conditions and the settlement paper. "She inherits all that is not entailed, sir, which means all but the title and Sir Renfrew's mother's house near Arisaig. Everything else is hers to do with as she pleases unless she should have a child by him."

Michael was silent for a long moment, but when Pinkie shivered, he noticed at once and urged his mount to a faster pace.

The sky had lightened, and clouds overhead were parting. When a shaft of sunlight struck the hilltop ahead, Pinkie saw the shadowy figure waiting there.

"Cailean! It *is* Cailean, is it not?"

"Aye, lassie, it is."

"I thought it was the ghost's dog when I saw him before. Oh, I'm so glad he's not dead, after all!"

"I expect he is pleased about that himself," Michael said with a smile.

Sir Renfrew's men joined the searchers as soon as they learned that he was missing. Less than an hour later, two of them carried his body into the hall on a plank and set it up on supports well away from the fire. By then, Michael and Pinkie had changed into dry clothes, and had warned Bridget that she had likely become a widow. Neither the warning nor the reality appeared to distress her in the least.

Without comment, Chuff, Connal, and the other searchers retired to change their clothes, and Michael stirred up the fire. The hall was chilly.

Having looked to be sure that Sir Renfrew truly had departed this life, Bridget returned to warm her hands at the fire, saying, "Now that I am a widow like Aunt Marsali and Cousin Bella, you must not scold me anymore,

Michael. You no longer have that right, so I can do as I please."

"I am still your brother, Bridget. That alone gives me the right to speak as I will to you. Do you honestly think your widowhood would prevent that?"

She looked annoyed, but when she spoke, it was in a smaller voice. "I think I shall prefer to live in London or in Edinburgh."

"You may certainly do so if you choose," he said, "but before we can make that decision or any others, there will be many things to discuss and to arrange."

Pinkie, noting a newcomer peeping in from the stairwell, exclaimed, "Mrs. Conochie, do come in. How are the children getting on?"

The plump cook bustled in, tears streaming down her cheeks, her hands held out, saying, "Och, miss, 'tis splendid they be, praise be to God and to ye and them others. When I heard my bairns had taken the wee boat onto the loch, I feared the worst. I dinna ken whether to hug them or skelp them, I tell ye."

"They were very brave," Pinkie said, taking both outstretched hands in hers and giving them a squeeze. "They were going to seek help, you know."

"Aye, so they tell me. I told them 'twas too dangerous for the men to try to steal away, and so they slipped out the postern gate themselves, believing no one would stop them." As she talked, she kept glancing curiously at Michael.

"This is my husband, Lord Kintyre, Mrs. Conochie. Lady Campbell is his sister. Sir, Mrs. Conochie is the cook here at Shian. Tam and Flora are hers."

"So I had collected," Michael said, smiling and nodding politely when the cook turned from Pinkie and bobbed a curtsy.

"They told me what you did, sir, and I'm most grateful

to ye." She went on at length in this vein, repeating her thanks to Pinkie, expressing amazement that Sir Renfrew had died saving young Tam, and giving thanks to God for sending aid to the children in time. "And that great, elegant creature yonder," she added abruptly, eyeing Cailean with the same curiosity she had shown toward Michael. "I am sure 'tis the largest dog I have ever seen, sir. Is it friendly, and all?"

"Quite friendly," Michael assured her.

"But rather tired at the moment," Pinkie added. "Cailean helped bring our rescuers to us, all the way from Oban."

"Did he, now? What a clever fellow!"

Cailean, recognizing a friend, thumped his tail but remained curled up in front of the fire.

Mrs. Conochie glanced doubtfully at Bridget's set face and said to Pinkie, "I will not intrude on you any longer, my lady. I did just want to say my thanks and to see if there is aught you will need for supper."

"We'll not be staying, Mrs. Conochie," Chuff said from the doorway. "There will be men arriving from Dunraven soon, and we will go back there with them when they leave. You would find it hard to feed so many with what we keep here, but Dunraven is always prepared to accommodate Balcardane and any number of guests. We'll leave Sir Renfrew's body to be prepared for burial, however, if you will be kind enough to supervise that task."

"Aye, I will, and gladly, but will his lady not wish to help, my lord?"

"She will not," Bridget said evenly before anyone else could speak.

Mrs. Conochie said no more about the corpse, but she lingered to express her deep appreciation to Chuff for his part in the rescue, repeating herself to Connal when he returned. Then, with a final curtsy, she returned to her kitchen.

Without waiting for her footsteps to fade, Bridget said, "I never knew such a one for encouraging familiarity in servants, Pinkie. How you did let her go on!"

"I have known her since I was a child," Pinkie said quietly. "She was a scullery maid at Balcardane when Chuff and I first went there to live."

"Hardly a recommendation for friendship," Bridget said with a sniff. "We were talking about more important matters, anyway, were we not, Michael?"

"Not so important that it excuses your rudeness, Bridget. I merely said there were matters we must discuss."

"That's exactly what I mean, for goodness' sake." When he frowned, her lips tightened. "I know that to live in Edinburgh I must have a proper house," she said, "but when Aunt Marsali returns, I can stay with her until we find a suitable one. I shall need clothing, too. People will expect me to mourn him for a year, I suppose, but although I shall purchase all the proper attire, I shan't mourn him for anything like that long. He was horrid, and I'm glad he is dead, although it *was* thoughtful of him to die whilst rescuing the children, was it not?" Her spirits visibly lifting, she added, "Why, people might even call him a hero."

"That will make it easier for you to mourn him," Michael said dryly. "However, I was not speaking of your living arrangements or costume requirements. I referred to arrangements we must make before you can get your hands on any of his money. There is also the small matter of my debt to him."

"But surely—" Breaking off, she looked at him in astonishment. "Do you mean to say that you now owe all that lovely money to me?"

"Of course I do. Our father owed it to Campbell, and I inherited the debt just as you will inherit his estate. Since

I now owe that money to the estate, in due time it will be yours. Before then, however, if you are not to make a mull of things—"

When her chin rose sharply, he said hastily, "Don't fly into the boughs. What I mean to say is that you cannot begin running up debts in the expectation that the estate will settle them. Since you do not know the extent of his fortune, that would be madness. For the present, I think you'd be wise to let me continue to frank you. You can keep a reckoning if you like," he added shrewdly, "and repay me later."

Her expression altered ludicrously. "A reckoning?"

Pinkie looked at Chuff and saw his lips twitch.

Meeting her look, he donned a more serious expression and said quietly, "I know you do not wish to hang on your brother's sleeve now that you are a widow, ma'am. Indeed, I believe you will find it quite unnecessary to do so."

Bridget looked more favorably at him. "How do you know?"

"Thanks to Duncan's insistence that I understand my own fortune from the start, I have experience in such matters. You must learn as quickly as you can who manages Sir Renfrew's affairs, then inform that person of your altered status. Once he knows, you can begin to receive an allowance from the estate. I should think it will take no longer than a sennight to put the matter in train."

She looked at him gratefully. "I certainly would prefer that, sir."

"I, too," Michael assured her. "Nonetheless, even with an allowance, I think you must return to Dunbeither House for a time, at least. Penelope and I can go with you, if you like, to bear you company and to learn how matters stand there. You will not want to be thought uncaring, my dear, especially if you want your late husband to be remembered for his heroic deed. Indeed, you must not go into company for at least six months."

Bridget began to look stormy again. "I will *not* stay at Dunbeither House for six months, Michael, and you need not think that I will. By then it will be the depths of winter, and even if it proves a mild one, I should be stuck there till March or April. I mean to spend the winter in Edinburgh."

"We can discuss that later," he said, clearly hoping to fend off another tantrum. "Doubtless we can arrange something more to your taste, but in the meantime, there are other important matters—"

"I cannot imagine what could be more important," she snapped.

Chuff said evenly, "Perhaps you should decide what you intend to do with the corpse, ma'am."

She looked at him in astonishment. "Corpse? Goodness me, I don't know what to do with it. Mrs. Conochie said she would look after it."

"She can prepare it for burial, and one of the men here can make a coffin for it, but what then?"

"What do you mean, 'what then'? Can you not just bury him here?"

"No, I most certainly cannot," he said. "Of all the shatter-brained notions!"

"Well, I don't know what to do with it. Someone must tell me. Michael?"

"I think we must make every effort to return his body to Dunbeither," he said. "It is still cool enough, I think, for it to make the journey without suffering too much deterioration."

"I hope you don't mean for me to travel with it," Bridget said. "I couldn't!"

"You know," Chuff said to her, "you are the most outrageous female. You were perfectly willing to run off with him—"

"I didn't run off with him," she snapped. "I thought he was someone else altogether. In fact, I ..." Clearly realizing where this line of conversation was leading, she fell silent, flushing deeply. When the others remained expectantly silent, she muttered, "I don't want to talk to you at all. You are mean and stupid."

Pinkie could not resist looking at her brother to see if he realized what Bridget had thought.

Chuff seemed oblivious.

Michael said, "You still thought he was your secret admirer, didn't you?"

"Me," Chuff exclaimed. "Nay then, I'd never make such a cake of myself, not over any lass, and certainly not over such a shrew!"

"A shrew, am I?" Bridget's voice was shrill.

"That's enough," Michael snapped. Turning back to Chuff, he said more calmly, "How soon can Balcardane's people be ready to receive us at Dunraven?"

"They are always ready, so we can leave as soon as the others arrive. We must rest the horses we rode from Oban, and make arrangements to return them, but there are others here, of course, and boats for them who prefer them. The wind has died enough to make the crossing safe."

"Is it a long walk?"

"It won't take more than an hour," Chuff said. "One crosses at narrows a mile or so north of here."

Michael looked thoughtfully at Pinkie. "Have you walked it, lass?"

"Aye, sir, many times."

"Good." Turning back to Chuff, he said, "I think I'd enjoy the walk, and since she seems fully recovered from her ordeal, I'll take my lass along with me."

Pinkie said, "Will you, indeed, sir?"

"I will. I want to talk to you," he said. His expression was stern.

Bridget said sourly, "You'll get used to his imperious ways in time, Pinkie. He never asks anyone else what they want to do. He just assumes that they want what he wants, and if they don't, he runs roughshod right over them."

Frowning, Michael turned toward her, but before he could speak, Chuff said, "I warrant you have a good deal to say to Pinkie, sir, and she deserves to hear every word, so I'll see to everything here and meet you at Dunraven." To Pinkie, he said, "Find a shawl or a cloak, lass. You still must be chilled from your swim."

CHAPTER
TWENTY-THREE

By the time Pinkie returned with the shawl she had borrowed from one of the servants, she found Michael alone in the hall except for Mrs. Conochie and another woman, who had begun to prepare Sir Renfrew for his coffin.

Warily, Pinkie smiled at her husband. "Have you murdered your sister, sir?"

"No, Chuff spared me the effort. He offered to show her the highlights of Shian, including the bottle dungeon. When I suggested that she might like to experience it overnight, she bore him off, saying she would be delighted to see every stone in the castle if it would keep her from having to look at me."

"He cannot have taken her to see the dungeon," Pinkie protested. "The door to it is under that rug yonder by the entry from the stairwell. You cannot get into it any other way."

"Then maybe he means to drop her into the well," he suggested.

"That's not funny, sir. Chuff's people drink from that well."

"Well, I don't want to talk about Bridget. Shall we walk, my lady? We'll take Cailean with us."

"When must you return him to Glenmore?"

"I don't intend to return him," Michael said. "Menzies and I have failed so far to get the law of exclusive proprietorship changed, but as a result of our efforts, more English noblemen have expressed interest in owning deerhounds. Therefore, I mean to offer Glenmore two pups in place of Cailean, and give him his choice from my next two litters. He's said before that he'd like to breed deerhounds if there were only a market, and I mean to help him do it, so we can build up the breed again."

Pointedly, he offered his arm, and still wary of his uncertain temper, she placed her hand on it. It felt reassuringly warm. He said nothing more until they were beyond the walls of Shian, walking up the hill toward the woodland with Cailean following behind. The dog's gait was not as exuberant as usual, but it seemed to be recovering swiftly from its injury.

"What *were* you thinking?"

"That I am glad Cailean will get better."

"That's not what I meant. In London, what fiend possessed you to go after her as you did?"

She sighed. "I thought only of Bridget, I'm afraid, and of you—how you would suffer if she succeeded in eloping with her admirer. I did not realize it was Sir Renfrew until I caught up with them. I had thought until then that I should have no one but Bridget and some callow youth to deal with. It was foolish, I know."

"Well, I didn't realize that he was her admirer either, so I won't hold you accountable for that. You should have waited for me to return, however."

"But I did not know how to find you, and I was afraid if I waited, it would be too late to catch them! I did leave word wherever I could, and Mary sent a courier posthaste with a message for Duncan and Chuff, so they could find us, too. I told you all that in the note I left you."

He was silent for so long that she looked at him to see if she could read his temper from his expression. When she could not, she said bluntly, "Are you truly angry with me, Michael?"

"No, sweetheart. I was just thinking of what else you wrote in your note—about your parents and thinking I knew nothing about them till Bridget told me."

Astonished, she said, "Did you know, then?"

"Aye. It was one reason I thought Balcardane and your brother might agree to an arranged marriage with our family."

Trying again to read his expression, she said, "But if you thought that, why did you agree to . . . that is, why did you offer to marry me?"

He grinned appreciatively at her careful choice of words. "I thought they might be willing because I knew many people would disapprove of your parents, perhaps even fear to form the connection, but I think I knew the minute I clapped eyes on Balcardane Castle that most families would overlook any scruples they had about a man called Daft Geordie to ally themselves with Balcardane's power."

Her heart sank. "Is that what you did?"

"Nay, sweetheart, although after reading Bridget's fool letter, I cannot blame you for asking. I lost my heart when you put your hand in mine and stepped out of that sedan chair in the hall at Faircourt House."

"Truly?"

"Aye, though I did not know it then. I was too concerned about debts, and thinking too much about my troubles to recognize love when it clouted me on the head. I never cared a whit about who your parents were or what names they had. It might have been different if your father had been mad, because madness does seem to haunt families once it begins, but I knew he was nothing of the sort. In his own way he was clever. It was he, after all, who saved the family's groats, was it not?"

"Aye, it was." She smiled. "I'm glad you are not angry with me."

"You frightened me witless, but I know you did what you thought best," he said. "I own, I've spent the last few days in a rage, but my anger was aimed mostly at Bridget for drawing you into danger. I want to know everything that happened. Can we walk in the woods for a while before we cross to the other side?"

She agreed, and while he admired the woodland, she told him everything that had happened to her since leaving London. Midway through her discourse, he found a small clearing with a fallen log at one side of it large enough and, thanks to a thick canopy overhead, dry enough to sit upon. He drew her down beside him, and by the time she had finished her tale, she was leaning comfortably against him, warm and contented, enjoying the tranquillity of the woods.

"Michael, where are you?" Bridget's voice, raised in a strident shout, shattered the woodland peace.

With a near growl, he turned his head and shouted back, "Here!"

A moment later, she emerged into the clearing with Chuff at her heels.

Chuff said, "Sorry to intrude, Michael, but she would

come after you, and I did not think she should wander about out here alone."

"She shouldn't wander about at all," Michael said grimly.

"If you are going to be mean, I won't tell you what I came to say," she said crossly, "and then you'll be sorry."

She looked sulky rather than angry, so Pinkie wasn't surprised when Michael said more gently, "What is it then, lass?"

"Well, I have decided to forgive your debt, that's what."

"What?" He stared at her. "I cannot let you do that."

"Yes, you can. Indeed, you must, for I won't take it. It's not right to take your money. It should be as much my duty as yours to repay Papa's debts. Indeed, if you were to die without issue, all your lands would come to me, would they not?"

"Not now that I—"

"Oh, hush, and let me have my say. You think you know everything, but if you died, and I were your sole heir, I would inherit the debt, would I not?"

"Since you put it that way, aye, I suppose you would at that."

"Then I should have to pay myself. It's absurd, Michael, but if that is truly the case, then surely I can forgive the debt now. Indeed, you must allow me to forgive it, because I mean to tell everyone that you've paid it in full, so there!" And with that, she turned on her heel and walked back the way she had come.

"I'd better go after her before she gets lost," Chuff said. "She nearly did before. When we didn't see you cross to the other side, she insisted on coming out to find you, and she just charged into the woods. It's a wonder she didn't surprise a wildcat or a poacher. And in case you're wondering how she came to . . ."

"I am," Michael said firmly. "I cannot let her do it, you know."

"Well, I think you should," Chuff said. "The reason she's doing it is that I told her Sir Renfrew was most likely smuggling tobacco. Duncan told me that if it seemed useful, I should warn Sir Renfrew that the tobacco board can exact a heavy fine for his activities. I saw no reason not to warn Bridget that they can exact such a fine from the estate if they learn what he did, and that the fine could be more than you owe. She said surely Duncan was powerful enough to stop such an action if he chose, and I said he could, but that from what he had seen of her selfish ways . . ."

"Say no more," Michael said when Chuff paused, clearly pleased with himself. "Whatever I decide to do, I shall find it easier with her in such a mood. You have my thanks for that, and you may convey them to Balcardane, as well."

Grinning, Chuff turned and loped after Bridget.

Pulling Pinkie close again, Michael kissed her. The kiss deepened, and his hands began to move over her body in a way that stirred all her senses.

After a somewhat lengthy but enjoyable interlude, she drew back and smiled at him. "Do you mean to claim your husbandly rights here and now, sir?"

"Don't tempt me, lassie. If the ground were not damp . . ."

She chuckled, leaning against him again and closing her eyes, letting herself bask in the peace of the moment. A short time later, he drew her to her feet, and they walked companionably toward the crossing. When they emerged from the woods, she paused to enjoy the view.

Michael stood beside her, his arm comfortably around her shoulders.

Looking toward the castle, she said, "It's a lovely view, is it not? I hope Chuff got Bridget safely back again."

Feeling Michael stiffen, she looked up at him, saw that

he was staring toward the woods, and turned to see what had drawn his attention.

The two figures strolling together a short distance away at the very edge of the woods were not Chuff and Bridget. Neither paid heed to the thick-growing trees or dense shrubbery, and as always, both man and dog seemed unaware of watchers. Neither made a sound, though they passed so near to shrubs that would have snagged ordinary folk that they seemed to pass through them. The ground beneath their feet was damp from the rain and covered with a thick carpet of leaf mold, which might account for their silence, but still it was eerie and unnatural.

Cailean lifted his head, cocked his ears, and murmured low in his throat.

"That's a Mingary plaid," Michael said quietly.

"You really can see them."

"Aye, lass, I can, and I think Cailean does, as well. The dog looks like pictures I've got at home of Aeolus, the sire of his line."

"The man looks like you," she said.

"Aye, perhaps," he agreed. "I think your ghost and my dream are part and parcel of a whole tale."

"Mary told me that he came in search of his true love but arrived just after she had died in childbirth, and that he died of a broken heart soon afterward."

"There is a tale at Mingary that long ago a young heir disappeared whilst seeking his fortune. Rarely have Mingary's heirs been lucky in love since that day."

"Perhaps their luck has changed," she said, smiling at him.

Holding her tight, he said, "It has, sweetheart. It has, indeed."

The two shadowy figures on the hillside paused and turned toward them. The man lifted a hand in farewell.

Their arms still tight around each other, Michael and Pinkie waved back.

"Perhaps they, too, have found what they sought," she said.

"Aye, perhaps they have," Michael agreed.

They watched as the two figures turned again and vanished. Then, arm in arm, they crossed over the loch and walked on to Dunraven.

Dear Reader,

I hope you have enjoyed *Highland Spirits*. For those of you who ask where the author gets her ideas, I can tell you that the seed for this story was a Highland legend. A woman told her son and anyone else who would listen of a house about which she often dreamed. She was familiar with every corner of it, and years later, visiting Ballachulish House, she was astonished to find it the house of her dreams. So familiar was it that she was able to tell the owner about a staircase that had once been a feature of the place but had been bricked up and was out of sight. The visitor herself was even more amazed, however, when the owner told her that *she* was the spitting image of a little lady who had haunted Ballachulish House for years.

The next seed sprouted when I was watching the Westminster Dog Show on TV and a commentator said that at one time only earls could own Scottish deerhounds. I learned about the law of exclusive proprietorship and how it nearly put an end to the breed. Lord Menzies and others fought for years to get it changed but did not succeed until the early nineteenth century. Fortunately it was not too late, and the breed survived.

Tobacco smuggling posed a problem only until the American Revolution freed Americans to sell their tobacco anywhere in the world, and the profitable British tobacco trade collapsed. Much of the capital that had supported it went into building up the new cotton industry, which in its turn superseded linen and dominated the Scottish economy for the next hundred years.

The English discovered huge resources of Highland timber after the '15 Rising, when General Wade drove his roads into previously inaccessible areas. English laws against the smelting of iron with wood had to be obeyed, but the English and Scots alike disregarded the Scottish forest protection laws. At the time of maximum production, over a hundred bloomeries were operating in Scotland. The plantations of conifers we now see covering many hillsides are brave attempts by some great landholders to replace the timber, but the alien trees are no substitute for the old-growth oaks and Caledonian pines which were lost. There are still a few ancient forests remaining, however; one of the best of which is Lettermore Wood; near Ballachulish, where Colin Glenure was murdered in 1750.

If *Highland Spirits* entertained you and you want to know more about the Highlands, Chuff, Pinkie, Mary, and Black Duncan, you might enjoy *Highland Treasure, Highland Secrets,* and *Highland Fling.*

Sincerely,

Amanda Scott

BOOK YOUR PLACE ON OUR WEBSITE AND MAKE THE READING CONNECTION!

We've created a customized website just for our very special readers, where you can get the inside scoop on everything that's going on with Zebra, Pinnacle and Kensington books.

When you come online, you'll have the exciting opportunity to:

- View covers of upcoming books
- Read sample chapters
- Learn about our future publishing schedule (listed by publication month *and author*)
- Find out when your favorite authors will be visiting a city near you
- Search for and order backlist books from our online catalog
- Check out author bios and background information
- Send e-mail to your favorite authors
- Meet the Kensington staff online
- Join us in weekly chats with authors, readers and other guests
- Get writing guidelines
- AND MUCH MORE!

**Visit our website at
http://www.zebrabooks.com**